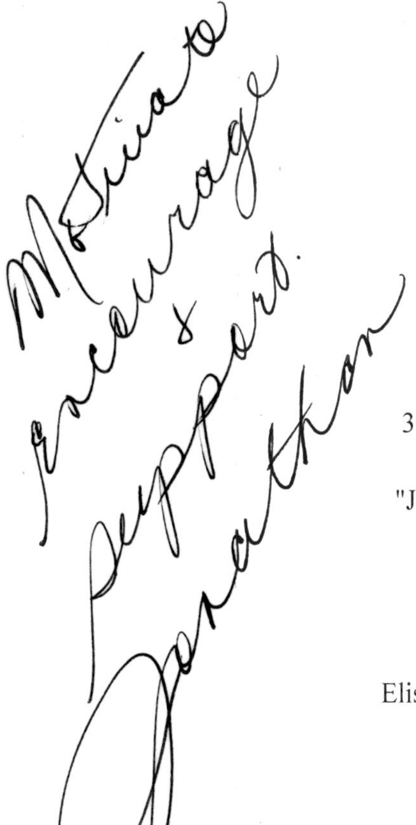

30,000 Secrets
A
"J" Team Novel

For

Elise Pelfini Laina

30,000 Secrets is a work of fiction. Characters are the author's creation. Names are either fictional or used with the permission of the owner.

30,000 Secrets and the "J" Team series portray women struggling with violence. The characters share their successes, failures, overcoming fears and apprehensions through emotionally griping dialog and defensive tactics. The agents' physical and emotional responses to antagonists draw the readers to the protagonists' techniques and style used to overcome adversity. Jessica, Rebecca and Elisabeth encourage readers; to leave abusive situations, to change their environment and to accomplish their goals and dreams. Jackson and Jason exemplify supportive colleagues, comfortable with their sexuality/masculinity, exemplifying male behavior appreciated by many women.

Praise
For

Wyoming Secrets a "J" Team Novel

"What a treat for me to receive your book! ... Thank you so much for sending it and remembering me ... Made my heart feel very very good. I had no idea you were as 'dangerous' as you are ...Heh!" Dr. Barrie Bennett University of Toronto

5.0 out of 5 stars *Wyoming Secrets*, March 4, 2012 by
Colleen
This review is from: *Wyoming Secrets A "J" Team Novel*: "J"
Team Series (Paperback)

"The beginning of the book was like a Robert Ludlum book, but once the characters are introduced, it gets very intense. I could not put the book down, and disappointed that the next book wasn't sitting waiting for me to read. I would highly recommend this book to readers."

University of Alaska

"Former University of Alaska Student Publishes First Novel. Some of you may remember Jonathan McCormick, who took graduate courses in Diagnostic and Prescriptive Teaching, while working in Hoonah before transferring to U of Portland. He has just published his first novel: *Wyoming Secrets: A "J" Team Novel*, which was released on Amazon.com recently, available in paperback and Kindle version.

Take a look on Amazon to read the synopsis, and check out his author website at www.jonathanmccormick.com, on Facebook and Twitter @lazeejjs."

"If you like to read, try this book, a very good read and hard to put down." Curtis Leithead Corrections Officer

30,000 Secrets

Jonathan McCormick

Prologue

Len Thiessen was blasting east out of StoneHead, Wyoming trying to maintain the speed limit, but anxious to put time and distance between him and StoneHead Ranch where he had wrangled for the last five years, albeit more as a mole for the Christians for a Better America, CFBA, than working cows.

He had a good thing going for a very long time; better than average wages, a spacious bunkhouse with meals prepared by a renowned chef, his own ranch gilding...a good future, but not as good as what he had been promised by Harold Richards. Thiessen just had to report anything out of the ordinary at the president's ranch on the throwaway cell Richards had given him, in exchange for monthly cash deposits in a storage locker in a nearby town.

Over the past few months, he had connected with Richards almost daily due to the increased activity at the ranch, beginning with the arrival of two Secret Service agents who seemed to be all over the property at any given time. He had run into agent Jason Spencer while bringing injured cows down to the main compound. Thiessen was shocked, to say the least, when the man he saw had no resemblance to his preconceived notion of a Secret Service Agent; long dark brown dreads, dark complexion, six-foot or so, 190 pounds, baggy jeans and a short-sleeve, bright yellow Tommy Bahama Academy shirt hanging out over his pants. The way the guy carried himself, it was obvious to Thiessen that this was no run of the mill agent; this guy was in shape and operated as though he was ready to do battle in a Nano second. He did not believe the guy was an agent at first meeting and had his hand on his .44 while the guy reached for and showed him his identification.

Then the guy started jive talking as though rapping with homeboys, not protecting the president of the United States. It was a very uncanny experience that didn't sit well with Thiessen. It was as though Spencer knew Thiessen was not what he purported to be and that could be dangerous not knowing if at any time his message passing side-line would get him fired...or worse.

5

Thiessen had no idea who or what Richards was or that he, Thiessen, was on the edge of a looming catastrophe that would put him on the run for the rest of his life.

On several occasions, Thiessen found he was calling Richards several times daily, after he spotted Spencer taking measurements and photographs around the chain link fence which ran as a perimeter encompassing the main ranch house and the adjacent ranch bungalows, creating a tight secure compound.

Thiessen thought of photographing the agent and maybe con a bonus from Richards but reconsidered given the huge closed-circuit television system integrated throughout the 3,000 acres. He knew he could be on camera at any time and didn't want to have to explain himself to the military security detail or ranch managers.

Thiessen had no idea that the ranch managers would soon be fired for hiring him or the intense efforts the agents would expend to find the mole...him. To the managers' credit, Thiessen's resume was totally legitimate; it wasn't until much later that he threw away a lifetime opportunity and jumped into bed with President Bakus' enemies.

Thiessen had finished his evening chores the previous night, had dinner and settled into the television room for a few hours of sitcoms and maybe Tom Selleck in *Blue Bloods* when his burner cell vibrated in his Levi's back pocket. He excused himself from the other wranglers and headed to the restroom and read the text. It was from Richards. Very short. Not encrypted. "Get out now and hide."

This was unusual behavior for Richards, often a man of many words, mostly superfluous and droning, so Thiessen accepted the warning; not having a clue as to the why, or where he would go. He headed back to the bunkhouse, packed a quick duffle, jammed in a couple of handguns and took off in his beater pick-up. It was still early enough that the gate guards didn't question his comment that he had to head to town for colt medication before the feed store closed.

Now Thiessen was burning pavement, furtively scanning the side mirrors every few seconds looking for any sign of a state trooper. With every mile, his heart rate slowed and his shoulder muscles began to relax, knowing that the Secret Service wouldn't be coming after him even if they knew he was the mole.

Chapter One

Captain Michelle “Bam-Bam” Nicholodian, her co-pilot Lieutenant Keely O’Reilly and shooter Second Lieutenant Billy Rae Boyanton were chowing in the ready-room, keeping their blood pressure and heart rates low while they woofed today’s special of Mongolian BBQ Stir Fry. Because they were on duty in their flight suits with helmet and gloves at the ready and required to be visual on their Cougar, their food was brought to them by officers’ mess stewards who had set the round table beforehand with cutlery, cloth napkins and glasses of ice water... milk or milk products were not consumed while on duty as the crew might develop phlegm during a flight causing difficulty with their face masks and air supply flow.

Conversations were limited or non-existent during these times per protocol and experience…this might be the last meal they have for some time if the horn blasts. Speed and anxiety aside, they did have numerous discussion topics in common. This base being in Great Falls, Montana they had become skiers, not accomplished, although Bam-Bam considered herself a black run flier, but days off fun kinda boarders. They were all getting four off at the end of this duty round so today the conversation hovered around the weather and if the clear Montana skies would continue into their leave days.

Billy Rae had just taken a bite of his Mongolian, the spicy sauce dripping down his chin when the adrenalin gong show blasted from the four mega speakers above their heads…"Gonnnnnnng! Gonnnnnnng!.."

The crew ran napkins over their faces, chugged a mouth of ice water, grabbed their helmets, gloves, and ran for their Cougar, plugged in within twenty yards of the exit door. Bam-Bam was through the chopper’s door first and scrambled to her command seat while Keely jumped into the side bench and Billy Rae pounced into his ordinance control center, each with a personalized Beretta Submachine clipped to the fuselage next to them. Bam-Bam had the five-blade, fifty-three-inch diameter composite main rotor in motion within seconds of her butt hitting the energy absorbing body seat as the deck hand simultaneously unplugged the battery charger and gave her a two handed over the head whirling motion with both arms.

After lighting his control panel, Billy Rae bounced over to the starboard 7.62 mm FN MAG-60/30 machine gun and swung it outward, chambered a round and sat. He breathed consciously and slowed his heart rate to 60 while Bam-Bam lifted fifteen thousand pounds of metal grace one foot off the tarmac and throttled to maximum, paralleling the tarmac south bound.

Keely meanwhile was processing their orders received through the onboard computer system and relaying the coordinates to Bam-Bam with Billy Rae following the conversation through his own headset, knowing action was moments away...target unknown.

"Target is a '92 Chevy pick-up, light blue, no canopy, heading presumably east out of StoneHead. No plate number yet. Intel from The Ranch and Secret Service supervisor Fukishura is the driver is a Len Thiessen, a ranch hand believed to be a mole for the Christians for a Better America, which Fukishura and her team just took down. Fukishura is confident Thiessen will not head west into the national forest, as there are no side-roads onto which he can escape. She is sure he is heading east," said Keely quietly into her com system.

Bam-Bam was scanning the skies doing a VFR, visual flight rules, for any small aircraft, which might not have noticed Malmstrom's traffic controller's flight advisory. "Copy that Lieutenant Keely. On your toes Lieutenant Billy Rae as we are only going to be able to take one pass at this guy when we find him…we will be maxed on fuel by the time we spot him given his lead."

"Copy that Bam-Bam, I'm on it", replied Billy Rae, the craft's 7.62 moving back and forth rhythmically with his head braced against the scope.

Bam-Bam moved her control stick slightly to bring the Cougar up to five hundred feet and maxed out the two Turboméca Makila 2A1 Turbo shaft engines to 201 mph while Keely followed the computer chatter from Malmstrom Air Force Base as their air traffic controllers provided approved altitude and cleared the airways for their pursuit. Malmstrom had recently made international headlines with the revelation that many of the Air Force's nuclear arsenal personnel had cheated on a proficiency exam. Thirty-four officers responsible for the launching configuration of the missiles were suspended and eleven more were investigated for illegal drugs.

30,000

"You must be deadly serious in training…your opponent must always be present in your mind, whether you sit or stand or walk or raise your arms."

Gichin Funakoshi's
First Rule for the Study of Karate-Do

From:

The Martial Way by Forrest E. Morgan, Major United States Air Force.

Chapter Two

Thiessen found his shoulders relax, his steering wheel grip soften, and the white knuckles disappear as the confidence of his escape overcame his previous hysteria.

They would send the state troopers, since Wyoming's highway system was trooper jurisdiction, and he was sure he had gotten enough of a head start to be in the wind. He even laughed a few times at his success, of the months and years of spying for Richards and the stash he had accumulated.

After he had left StoneHead Ranch last night he had driven a short distance then pulled off the road into the tumbleweed and out of sight of the highway. Throwing his shoulder into the battered driver's door he scrambled out, pulled a smoke from his breast pocket, zippoed, then sauntered over to a rock pile and plopped his tired butt and tried to think what he was going to do, where he could start over and how much trouble, if any, he was in.

He felt so sure of his success that he became pensive, reflecting on how it all began. He had always been viewed by other cowhands as somewhat of an oddball, given his buzz cut, neat appearance and somewhat correct use of the English language compared to the other often scruffy, unshaven, slept in their clothes cowhands.

Thiessen could have been mistaken for a schoolteacher with his clean-cut 6' 2" slender frame, rather than an on-again-off rodeo player, never making enough to cover his expenses and always bumming rides for himself and saddle. Wrangling was all he'd ever wanted in life from as far back as he could remember, sitting on the fence rails watching locals get their asses kicked by breeding bulls made to buck with a strap around their genitals.

He began, as all ranch kids do, with mutton riding...riding a large bovid and holding on to the neck fur. He'd learned quickly that his 8 seconds of riding was more fun than sitting in the dirt and having the rodeo clown pick him up by the shirt collar. Oh, the embarrassment.... he learned to hold on tight. In junior high, he skipped so many weeks of school to rodeo that he failed his entire eighth grade. With academic failure as his town label, he shucked school to hit the rodeo circuit, lying on his application when the entry form had a minimum age of nineteen.

By the time he was in his early 20's, the younger ropers and buckers were getting better times than he ever achieved and he found himself losing more than winning. He accepted the reality that he was a has-been rodeo bum and that if he wanted to stay out of the hospital and have any kind of life he'd better wrangle for Wyoming and Montana ranchers.

It never occurred to him that it was his appearance and low-level career achievement that was the attraction for subversives.

They saw a way to dangle money and a promise of a solid future by just keeping them informed. He never knew why Richards wanted the information and Richards never offered an explanation. Thiessen knew Richards was a local businessman and figured he wanted the Intel to know when Mr. Bakus was in town to plan for a customer influx. His refusal to acknowledge that the exorbitant money being paid to him was far more than any local businessperson could afford would come back to bite Thiessen in the ass...big time.

Thiessen had been enjoying a few beers with other cowhands at the Parrot, a local watering hole, when Richards had spoken to him in the restroom, usually the last place men engaged in conversation, particularly with strangers. Thiessen was naturally skeptical, expecting the older man to hit on him. It never happened and yet Thiessen never picked up on an ulterior motive, never wondered why a total stranger would engage him in a conversation in a men's room.

Richards offered to buy him a beer and started a casual relationship over lunches and Friday nights at the Parrot that grew over the following months, culminating in the job offer. Thiessen made more money in three months with Richards than he did in an entire year at StoneHead Ranch. Now he had quite a stash in a storage locker in Casper, about 3 hours east of StoneHead. He had no solid idea as to why Richards had phoned, but the stressed tone of his demand screamed, *Cops.*

He figured he could grab his future and then ponder where he would get a fresh start, knowing he had burned all his bridges in StoneHead. He returned his thoughts to his battered ride and continued to Casper and the bright future tied to the thousands waiting for him.

30,000

The Air Force gun ship found the pick-up maxing out the speed limit between StoneHead and Casper, heading southeast, not east, as Agent Fukishura suspected. Spotting it was quick and with little fan-fare given the openness of Wyoming highways and the almost non-existent vehicle traffic. Bam-Bam passed the Chevy on its west side, swung out over the Mountain mahogany scrub grasses and dropped down in front of the driver, fully expecting the vehicle to stop immediately.

Bam-Bam and Keely were giving the driver slashing motions with their hands across their necks to indicate he was to stop. The driver slammed on the brakes, pulled to the side of the road but then unexpectedly returned to the highway and accelerated.

Chapter Three

Feeling somewhat normal from his rest, Thiessen had been back on the road for a time and had become mesmerized by the monotony. He had just scanned the rear-view mirror when he was jolted from his tedium by the appearance of a gigantic object dropping over the front of his pick-up...black with huge wing-like protrusions extending from each side, making not a sound. So quickly had it appeared that his senses refused to kick in…other than instinct…to evade a collision.

He slammed on the brakes trying to avoid a crash and create a gap between the object and him...then quickly recognized the shape as that of a massive helicopter which had now swung around to face him, the silhouettes of two figures with bulbous heads evident in the cockpit giving him slashing motions with their hands.

"What the fuck?" he shouted as he cranked the steering wheel sharply to the right to avoid a hit. His front wheels hit the dirt shoulder causing the truck to start to tip to his right. He cranked the wheel back to his left, righting the vehicle and putting it back on the pavement, directly in line with the black chopper...which he could now see was equipped with dual machine guns extending from each side of the fuselage. The pilots were repeating their slashing motion...the action more violent now.

He slammed his foot to the floor, accelerating quickly, hoping to create a crash scenario the chopper would have to avoid. As he regained control of the truck and sped down the highway, the chopper pulled up to avoid the crash. "Yes!" he yelled to himself, adrenaline rushing through every cell squeezing his cognitive functions, proud he had outsmarted the arrogant cops who thought they could pull him over with a cheap threat like that. Hours later, he would wonder where he got the idea he could ever outrun a military gunship, but for now all he could do was try and contain the uncontrolled hormones that were on a crash course with him staying alive.

30,000

"Okay gang, this stupid mother fucker wants to play with Bam-Bam, let's give it to him. Billy Rae, we are fuel short and have no time to screw around here. Keely and I will make one more pass at him and you take out the pick-up. Show this piss ant why I'm called Bam-Bam."

"Copy that," said Billy Rae and Keely simultaneously, both smiling to themselves, recalling how the Captain got her handle; the hundreds of missions where Bam-Bam took out adversaries over Iraq and Afghanistan with a success rate far superior than any other flier of her generation. It began as a tease, fellow pilots, male and female alike harassing her because Bam-Bam would be hyper after each mission prancing the officers' mess two hands out front mimicking a FN MAG-60/30, shouting "Bam, Bam Brrrthdddr". She put on such a show that Billy Rae finally joined her, then Keely and the three would buzz the tables before sitting down to applause.

Bam-Bam swung the massive Cougar in a whirling 180 while forcing the Maklias to torque out ahead of the Chevy, then pivoted a thousand yards ahead of the speeding truck as Billy Rae began his barrage of 1,100 rounds per minute assault on the vehicle's front end.

Bam-Bam's Mantra

"If you know the enemy and know yourself, you need not fear the result of a hundred battles. If you know yourself but not the enemy, for every victory gained you will also suffer a defeat. If you know neither the enemy nor yourself, you will succumb in every battle."

Sun Tzu, The Art of War

Chapter Four

Thiessen's mind jumped to wondering how they could have found him so quickly and who *They* were. It had been hours since his departure and the ranch staff wouldn't have known he was gone until this morning...hours ago, the cops should be looking around town and out at the Christians for a Better America compound, not here several hundred miles from StoneHead. His body had adjusted to the rush, now his brain was coming to grips with reality…and fear set in. He could deal with the state guys, had all his life going back to his early teen years of theft and break and entering, but he knew they didn't have helicopters like this…3D, dynamic, rotating, twisting laterally and vertically as though computer generated with one objective…stop me.

His mind was still abuzz, questioning his escape maneuver and wondering what he had done wrong in the simple procedure of getting the hell out of StoneHead when he heard country singer Kenny Chesney's *Boats* coming from his waist.

"Fuck, Fuck, Fuck!" he yelled as he pounded his fist on the steering wheel, immediately knowing he had inadvertently left the ranch's cell phone clipped to his belt. Damn, he thought. How could I have been so stupid and not left it on the bunk or hidden it under the mattress. He didn't take time to read the text but if he had, he'd find it was from the chopper co-pilot telling him to stop or be fired upon.

Ignoring the repeated lyrics, he shook his head trying to rid himself of the angst rising in his throat, the sickening stomach, the fear squeezing his heart, all created by the fact that he had been traced by the GPS chip in the phone, when instantly the chopper appeared in front, this time swinging far out to his right over the vacant parched flatland sending dust clouds fifty feet in all directions, almost obliterating his vision field, then arching abruptly in front of him about hundreds of yards ahead.

Before he could react to the immediate threat, the front end of the pick-up was hit by a barrage of bullets from the gunship's 7.62-mm machine gun, taking out the radiator, both tires and splitting the steering tie rod, causing the vehicle to flip front end over end, bouncing high in the air. Its propulsion took huge chunks of pavement in the process, the black missiles jettisoning in a wide arc, the truck landing in a cloud of dust…flying truck parts thirty yards off the pavement, the truck on its roof, wheels spinning and engine spewing oil and gas, puddling quickly around the crushed vehicle carcass.

Gyrating like a rebellious Ferris wheel, the truck's tires were a blur as the massive, flat-black titan landed in the sand off to the truck's right and two swarthy clad figures, their identities obliterated with balaclavas, ran toward their success with Beretta Submachine guns strapped across their chests.

One of the attackers pulled the driver's door open and a second reached in, cut the seat belt with one swift slice of her tactical knife, yanked the driver out and dragged his body across the sand and dumped it next to the hovering chopper...just as a gigantic explosion erupted from the truck...the gas tank having ignited by sparks and heated metal from the truck’s trajectory across the pavement.

30,000

Billy Rae had the driver strapped into a gurney and was administering first aid to numerous head and arm lacerations, applying a tourniquet to Thiessen’s bicep, inserting a catheter into a vein and starting a saline drip. Billy Rae splinted the compound femur fracture as Bam-Bam raised the Cougar from the blistering sand and engaged a heading of north-west while Keely keyed in a coded operation response message for StoneHead Ranch advising of their secured passenger, the location of the fiery vehicle and asking for instructions.

Chapter Five

Swishhh, swishhh, swishhh, reverberated through the canyon as the FBI Sikorsky UH-60 Black Hawk helicopter swept out of the darkness, its twin General Electric T700-GE-701C turboshaft muffled engines created minimum resonation as the quintet rotary blades dropped altitude dramatically, the ten SWAT members braced themselves for the decent, the chopper's forty-five degree bank and drop into the parking area in front of the Yellowstone Outfitter's compound. The Sikorsky's undercarriage high intensity lighting, a blinding illumination, was muted by the team's amber facemasks as they exited the chopper, spread out, took the building with aggression.

Two agents skirted the main structure, flipping up the darkened bug-eye covers revealing compact night goggles, rushed the rear door while two more waited by the front entry. Lead agent Carson counted down, "3, 2, Now," into his throat mike. On *Now*, all four SWAT members broke through doors, silenced H&K MP5SD fitted with under barrel tactical high intensity lights, hugged tight to their shoulders and swept each room.

Carson's front entry teammate had just cleared the bathroom when he heard glass shattering and the sound of broken pieces being cleared. "Fuck", he yelled into his mike as his body slammed against the bathroom door, sending the knob through the wall. Training and instinct told him to check the last room even as he heard a suspect was running, having escaped through a smashed window. A quick room scan then Jones ran quickly on the balls of his feet bouncing out the torn back door to see a shadow disappear around the corner of a barn. He took off in pursuit. As Jones hit the barn corner, he dropped to his knees, did a quick peek around with his night goggles, and spotted his quarry scrambling up a grade, making his way to the bush. Jones was on his feet dashing after the Scrambler within seconds. Just as Scrambler was about to reach for an over-hanging bush to pull himself to freedom, Jones let off a short burst of twenty rounds above Scrambler, shredding the bush, sending Scrambler tumbling backwards down the embankment. Jones flipped his night goggles up and had Scrambler lighted with his tactical beam as he landed hard on his butt at the bottom of his decent. Scrambler didn't move…his dirt covered face fearful of the dark clad silhouette hovering, dominating Scrambler's space.

Jones pointed his H&K at Scrambler and indicated he was to get on the ground. Once the suspect was on his stomach, Jones whipped out plastic zip cuffs from his cargo pants, dropped his left knee into his suspect's back, swung his H&K over his shoulder onto his back then forcefully brought Scrambler's hands together, hands back to back, slipped the plastic cord around his wrists and pulled tight. Jones then grabbed the guy's head back, stuffed a black bandana in his mouth, and then slipped a black balaclava, like his own but without eye holes, over his head. Jones backed up, kicked his suspect in the ribs, and then pulled him erect, prodding him with his rifle, a silent command for him to move ahead of him.

When Jones got his captive back to the idling Black Hawk, he pushed him forward until his head hit the fuselage. Before Scrambler could react, he was grabbed by another agent, hauled aboard, and chained to a seat beside two others similarly clad. Jones spotted Carson and the other agents standing guard by the main building's porch and jogged over, disconnected his mike and spoke with the team leader.

"We've swept the place clean and these are all we could find. No sign that anyone took off on our approach. Only two places set for dinner in the bunkhouse. Inside was a pigpen. Don't know how these guys can live like that. Too much time around animals and they turn into them," said Jones.

"I didn't get the barns done, wanted to bring my guy back and secure him first. I'll head back there with Peterson, Toteronie and MacLean and secure them."

"Leave me MacLean and Peterson and take the rest," said Carson, "We have no idea what these country boys have here and make sure you check each entry for explosives."

"Right!" replied Jones as he made a spinning motion with his left hand, gathered the agents, turned on his mike, and headed out.

Chapter Six

Carson and his team were part of a squad of FBI SWAT agents which recently attacked the Christians for a Better America compound outside StoneHead, Wyoming where Democratic
President James Bakus maintained his family's sprawling cattle ranch. Attack was probably a misnomer considering the role they played was clean-up after Secret Service agent Jessica Fukishura's "J" Team had taken out every male member of the CFBA except for Richards, their leader. He had escaped into the night as Jessica and Secret Service agents Rebecca Simpson, Elisabeth Peltowski, Jackson Pennington and Jason Spencer swept the area, dropping CFBA anarchists with rifle butts, and silenced H&K MP5SD automatic rifle rounds.

The incident was the culmination of weeks of Secret Service undercover work. Fukishura, a supervising agent with a law degree from U.C. Berkeley and a Black Belt in Combat Martial Arts, gleaned her "J" Team from various world assignments.

Rebecca Simpson had been sequestered by the FBI and had been using her Montana bred tracking skills to trace suspected Al Qaeda members training Native Americans on southwestern reservations. Her one hundred and fifty-pound, 6-foot frame was intimidating to the all-male FBI crew and she spent more time defending her skill level than executing it.

Elisabeth Peltowski was playing secretary to Britain's MI6 operatives after taking the national secret service to task, in writing, regarding the country's lax airport security procedures. She was primed to return stateside for the presidential detail, but was hesitant to work with a female supervisor.

Jason Spencer had been identifying Al Qaeda and Taliban trainees in North Africa for CIA contractors to eliminate. His three-year desert experience keyed him for battle against America's domestic terrorists.

Jackson Pennington was on an Idaho mountain top scouting a Christians for a Better America compound for evidence of an explosives depot. His photos of the compound and the adjoining barn's contents were uploaded to an FBI assault team nearby. Jackson had just descended the pinnacle as the FBI attack helicopters dropped into the group's marshaling area disgorging twenty SWAT agents when he received orders to return to Seattle and fly immediately to the Secret Service Training Center in Rowley, Maryland.

While waiting her team's arrival to Rowley, Fukishura headed to Toronto for a few days of R&R with her parents; Glenn, an education department head at the University of Toronto and Shelia, an executive assistant to a Canadian Member of Parliament.

In route on a ninety-minute Air Canada flight she met Karen Winthrop, a Royal Canadian Mounted Police Air Marshal, or as she liked to call herself, Sheriff Winthrop. The cops hit it off and spent time together at the Toronto Police Academy sharing defensive tactics techniques, dinning with the Fukishuras at the famed Calgary Steak House hosted by Karen's University of Ottawa classmate, restaurateur Craig Stevenson, aka Soul Train, infamous at internationally renowned Whistler Ski Resort in British Columbia for his impersonation of drink aficionado Tom Cruise's character in the movie, *Cocktail.*

Jessica surprised herself in enjoying the company of another person, particularly another woman, given her long and ingrained misanthropic demeanor. She had dated little at Berkeley and socialized even less, couldn’t stand being around girls who seemed to waltz through life without purpose, had no interest in politics or the well-being of other women. Classmates always spouted the college liberalism, but when it came time for action, few had the fortitude for social activism. She understood her anger toward society stemmed from her mother’s experience with the shooting massacre at the Ecole Polytechnique in Montreal where her mom was a student. Marc Lepine killed 14 women, separating them from the men before opening fire and not one male stepped in to stop the slaughter. Fukishura had sufficient introspection to know David Posen accurately described her in his *Always Change a Losing Game* when he wrote, “If folks are getting on your nerves, if you are irritable or short-tempered...”

That depicted her personality perfectly.

But when she gave her character perspective, she wondered why her Dad Glenn’s male example wasn’t sufficient to override the negative. She always thought she would want a partner like him, but gave up on comparing in her early twenties, realizing they were wasted emotions. She had dated lawyers, who to a man, considered her a traitor for not practicing law, cops whose background paralleled Jamie Reagan on *Blue Bloods*-Harvard degree and dead-ended in a patrol job with no ambition, hockey players with whom she thought she would have something in common, but found they were intimidated by her job. She never tried a doctor, dentist, baker or candle stick maker because she had given up in her mid-twenties. There wasn't a male colleague in any law enforcement service who wanted anything to do with her given she kicked everyone's ass in training and projected a pissed-off condescending attitude. But on the positive side, she had to admit that the "J" Team conscripts could have refused their assignment with her, so maybe things were looking up, maybe she wasn't hated by every agent after all.

But this chance meeting with Winthrop could be more than just destiny, possibly a chance to make a change. She knew, or thought she was cognizant, that her attraction to Karen was that they shared an intense formal education, similar law enforcement careers, love of extreme training, exceptional cuisine and of course questionable interest in men. But, as she mentioned to Shelia on her recent visit to Toronto, she didn't know if she was gay, straight or bi and with her biological clock ticking she knew more attention to her gender identification had to be primed.

30,000

"J" Team had regained their tactical edge at Rowley with defensive tactics training from Fukishura; gym fitness, running, defensive tactics and weapons reaffirmation. They were then disbursed cross country with Spencer and Fukishura arriving at StoneHead by SUV, taking up a routine Secret Service position of Ranch security while Pennington made a circuitous route from Maryland, to Seattle, Idaho and eventually arriving in StoneHead as a history substitute teacher recently graduated from Northern Michigan University.

Peltowski flew to Nebraska and drove the rest of the way to StoneHead arriving as a junior high computer technology substitute.

Rebecca flew to Missoula, Montana where she met Derrick, a former colleague with the Flathead County Sheriff's department. Her cover in StoneHead, Wyoming was as a horse trainer working for him. He provided a pick-up with his business logo blazoned across both door panels and would field any phone enquiries regarding her employment.

Chapter Seven

Bam-Bam had just cleared the scene and was leveling off when Keely read the encrypted computer message from Agent Fukishura at StoneHead Ranch, “Drop suspect off at the West StoneHead Hospital Latitude: 44.52, Longitude: 109.07 degrees. I will have a team waiting to take him into custody. Doctors and staff on stand-by.”

“Reply to that Keely and tell her we copy and give her our ETA. Plug the coordinates into the Fli-Map (altimetry system*)*; I want to refresh our memories on the terrain around the hospital and the approach. I’d rather not have our asses hung up on hydro wires or land in a patch of Wyoming cow shit.”

“Copy that Bam-Bam,” said Keely with one hand on the chopper’s controls and the other punching out Bam-Bam’s orders on the computer.

West StoneHead Hospital had been upgraded with an entire new wing in preparation for the president’s needs with a sophisticated security system designed by StoneHead Ranch’s resident cyber specialist. The exterior walls were recreated with a second concrete wall reinforced with steel, backed with Kevlar and all windows upgraded to blast-resistant. The ceiling was solid concrete as well making the wing impregnable except for a direct artillery attack.

The addition created an invincible facility with security developed in layers. The hospital was vulnerable only to missiles, which would have to be a shoulder projectile deployed within close range such as an AT-4 shoulder-mounted rocket launcher, which can theoretically shoot a missile nearly 1,000 feet, through buildings and tanks. After 9/11, the White House took nothing for granted and the structure was created first in a testing compound and withstood not only AT-4s but tank rounds as well. Nothing could enter StoneHead air space given Rapier, an anti-aircraft detection system, deployed 24/7. These surface-to-air-missiles encircle StoneHead in the foothills and could intercept any incoming missile or undetected aircraft.

The system was very similar to Israel’s Iron Dome system successfully employed in the Gaza–Israel 2011/2012 and 2014 conflicts.

In addition, the municipality and all surrounding roads were monitored with CCTVs, closed circuit televisions, which were wireless and satellite controlled/monitored from StoneHead Ranch's communications center. The town council and residents bought into the big brother concept without much opposition given the White House's largess. It is questionable whether the community gave the cameras much thought since so much of the country was now under 24/7 surveillance.

As the camera system expanded nation-wide, Homeland Security had braced for an avalanche of protest that never came. Officials assumed correctly that citizens had accepted the diminishment of their privacy as the price for security. Since the nationwide acceptance of these cameras, the public has acknowledged reality…they haven't any privacy in public.

The public had no idea of the massive NSA, National Security Agency, surveillance of emails, texts, and phone calls that had been in place for years with data housed in the ever-expanding Utah facility, code-named *Bumblehive*, in Bluffdale. Every computer stroke, text and phone call made in the world is recorded and stored in a system with yottabytes. A yottabyte is a septillion- bytes. Google's former CEO, Eric Schmidt, estimated that the total of all human knowledge created, "From the dawn of man to the present, if digitalized, would total five exabytes". One exabyte equals, 1,000,000,000,000,000,000 bytes with one word using ten bytes whereas a yottabyte equals 1,000,000,000,000,000,000,000,000 bytes.

The world was unaware the extent to which Washington had gone to know everything about everybody until Edward Snowden, the 30-year-old CIA computer technician, leaked documents from his covert Russian abode. Germany's chancellor and France's president and other world leaders were infuriated to discover America had been spying on them for years while StoneHead residents rubbed their hands together enjoying the fruits of the government's largess, while ignoring the evaporation of their constitutional rights.

30,000

The hospital's board of directors was loath to accept the president in medical emergency, fearful terrorists would target their facility…until the Whitehouse made them an offer they couldn't refuse, starting with a full body MRI Scanner for 5.5 million, an open Siemen's MRI for 1.5 million, and an X-ray unit for 8.8 million.

To sweeten the offer, the federal government added a complete physiotherapy unit which, not counting the addition, was 24 million and then a complete mammography system added 6.6 million and the list went on and on until the Wyoming Senator, who won the vacated seat left by President Bakus, capped it at 50 million and pressured the board to accept the offer in the best interest of the community.

Many board members were ranchers and knew Washington could break them financially by ending farm subsidies, so they chose wisely and were rewarded with state of the art equipment and affirmation of the continuation of farm subsidies for Bakus' tenure. The sweet spot of the entire financial package was the hospital kept their annual 12 million profits.

Chapter Eight

Jones gathered his six agents and spoke to them as a group through his throat mike heading toward the massive barns situated between the now secure administration buildings and the mouth of the canyon where Jones had snagged Scrambler. Leaving the chopper's high intensity lights, they were immersed in total darkness, the moon having long departed behind the pine sentries.

Flipping down their night goggles, the four agents moved to their left while Jones and the others hugged the barn's high exterior walls, moving silently toward the first human door located directly beside doors that swung out for vehicles.

There were no doors on the other side of the barn so the other agents jumped the paddock rails, their human presence creating a screaming furry of horse and mule fear, some crashing into the rails attempting to escape the unknown predators. The urban bred agents realized their mistake and quickly exited the corrals and continued down the barn's backside, hearing the mules' terror screams subsiding in their wake.

Jones found the smaller door unlocked, opened, and slid through the slot in a crouch, his automatic rifle hugging his shoulder pointing straight and his finger on the trigger guard. The other agents followed immediately behind separating themselves two for two in each direction. They swept the barn quickly finding no additional rooms or questionable equipment, save for harnesses, hay hooks and a series of empty stalls. Two agents ascended the hayloft ladder and returned shaking their heads. They knew the numerous tons of hay would have to be moved later to verify the lack of insidious materials, but for now they would classify the loft as clear. They exited the barn verifying with the other team that they too were clear.

Both teams resumed their scrutiny, approaching the next barn with identical tactics as their last. This time Jones waited for the second team to completely circle around. All seven entered the second barn in mass, assuming this barn had to conceal whatever the Secret Service agent had found...referring to Agent Rebecca Simpson and her covert operation previously where she had travelled overland through brush country and entered these same buildings, culminating in apprehending a ranch hand who had attacked Simpson during her covert barn inspection. After a one-sided fight, she hooded him, then brought him back to StoneHead Ranch where he was interrogated by Agent Jason Spencer. They spread out securing each end of the barn, scanning every nook and crevice with under barrel high intensity lights.

At the barn's end that lead out into the canyon they found what they were after.

30,000

After the firefight and the capturing of several of the Christian's for a Better America StoneHead cell members some nights previously, agents Elisabeth Peltowski and Jackson Pennington had joined Jessica, Rebecca, and Jason at President Bakas' StoneHead Ranch for a debriefing.

They were seated in the massive living room where one wall was devoted to a bay window and another to a massive stone fireplace. The view was of pine railed fenced paddocks where horses exercised during the day and were housed at night in a massive weathered, gambrel roofed red barn- a symmetrical two-sided roof with two slopes on each side-seen in the far background. This barn style is often seen in urbanized rural communities where deep-pocketed owners have refurbished old structures making them an architectural delight. The StoneHead facility was not of this design, having survived decades of weather and wear, absorbing tales of delight and joy…but more recently, that of sorrow and grief with the passing of Bakus' wife after unsuccessfully battling cancer for years.

The stone fireplace with a fourteen-foot hearth, mantel, and a fire pit large enough to roast a side of beef, was blazing with a recent insertion of three foot by twelve-inch split pine logs.

Creating an oval in front of the fire, were two, ten-foot couches in a supple burgundy leather and several matching oversize chairs in the same rich leather fronted by a ten-foot knotty pine coffee table with ten-inch round legs. The fire was emitting soul absorbing warmth, while flames danced their way through the massive cavity, arching and swirling, reaching for the stars at the end of the chimney's darkness.

The scene drew Jessica like a moth to flame, helped calm her soul and direct her focus on solving the problem before them.

All agents were seated in the oval with a cup of peach herbal tea offered by chef Marc Stucki, ready for the shoe to drop and not quite sure of the outcome. Jessica leaned forward, glancing at a sheaf of papers in her hand, her elbows braced against her knees.

Chapter Nine

When Secret Service supervisor Sorento (who worked directly under Director Jean Simmons, the first female leader in the service's history) had assigned the Wyoming White House to Jessica to update the ranch's security system prior to the president's first ranch visit since taking office, hosting a G-8 summit on anti-terrorism. She had consulted with numerous ranch staff on the current system and what was required to close the hundreds of acres to any intrusion/attack. Crews were scheduled to arrive in the next few days to begin the upgrading per the specifications submitted by Jessica to Washington and designed by senior security analyst/technician Bruce, Jason and Jessica.

Her previous conversation with Bruce and Jason occurred shortly after her arrival at StoneHead. "The perimeter fencing is electrified, preventing anyone scaling and trying to get over the razor wire," advised Bruce during his presentation to Jessica and Jason. "The face recognition software is on all the digital feed including the front gate. It's not one hundred percent, nothing is. If the system doesn't recognize a person's features, it will warn the monitoring operator who will challenge or reject the person at the gate. If recognized, and the person is expected, the guard opens the first gate and the vehicle enters. The guards then inspect the vehicle; interior, exterior including the undercarriage as well as the occupants and their identification. Each visitor undergoes a full body scan and complete body pat down. If the dog doesn't detect explosives and the visitor is accepted, the guard radios ahead and we send four military guards to escort the vehicle to the main ranch house. If the system recognizes the visage but the person is not expected, they are either rejected or detained at the main gate. The latter would occur if the guards had an Interpol, FBI or CIA flag on the person.

"Excuse me Bruce, and I apologize for asking a dumb question, but with the facial recognition, what if the individual has had Botox work, face lift or similar face altering surgery?"

Everyone but Bruce smiled and had a little chuckle over what they thought was Spencer's attempt at humor, albeit ill timed.

Before Bruce could answer, Jason added, “No, really, I’m not being a smart ass, I thought my question had validity because any facial alterations would not give the system an accurate reading”.

“You are absolutely right Jason, and humor aside…it is kinda funny thinking someone would alter their appearance to breach our system…the software would automatically reject any face not composed of nature chemistry and alterations destroys that natural balance. The system will also detect any alternation around the thin skin areas such as eyes and eyelids.”

Bruce moved on with his explanation, "IDs are similar in technology to the new passports that contain a chip, and all federal law enforcement personnel IDs are coupled with iris scanning. Any irregularity is reported immediately and the vehicle and occupants detained. At gunpoint, I might add. You can't get in here with just a driver's license. You guys experienced all of this when you arrived.

"What we're most concerned with is explosives at the main gate or anywhere on the perimeter, so we will install a vehicle X-ray system which will detect objects hidden within a vehicle framework. Then we’ll add explosive detecting equipment inside the corridor created by a second fence running the entire perimeter. This will be patrolled by dogs and two-person teams with sporadic scheduling and electronic check-in points. The guards will be on quads and monitored every step of the way by our existing system. Each guard will be equipped with a helmet wide-angle tactical camera, capable of night vision, identical to that being worn by many proactive police departments. The cameras will produce HD digital feed directly to our existing system.

"The perimeter cameras swing in opposite directions so the entire circumference is covered one hundred percent, leaving it unlikely explosives will be set next to the fence, but we can't make that assumption so we will install odor drones.”

“What is an odor drone?” interrupted Jessica, reading from Bruce’s printed synopsis.

Bruce laughed and said, “Yeah, it does sound funny as though it is supposed to catch cows farting, but here the Fire-X, an amalgam of Northrop Grumman’s sensors is the gist of the system and is affixed to the underbelly of the Bell 407 helicopter. We will adapt that to several small drones which will circulate and pass the outer perimeter and relay information to our nerve center here."

"How good is this detection system? I mean, can it duplicate what a well-trained sniffing dog can do?" asked Jessica.

"That was the main concern of the Fire-X from the get go but the trials and operating track record was phenomenal. The drones won't replace the dogs at the front gate but cover the perimeter", replied Bruce. "We believe the miniature drones are like those used by civilian police forces for drug detection and surveillance, will fit our needs perfectly.

"Back to the perimeter. The next level needs to be a seismic intrusion detection system between the last fence and the buildings. Geophone sensors will be placed in the earth and the software integrated into our existing system which discriminates between actual intruders and natural disturbances.

"The final layer is the interior security and guards. The installation team is expected from Washington in the next few days for implementation", finalized Bruce.

So went the security briefing approved by Jessica and Sorento in Washington. The upgrades and modifications were in the system, now he team was bracing itself for the repercussions from their actions of the past few days.

Chapter Ten

Jessica saw the anxiety on the faces of her handpicked team and knew they were all wondering if their next assignment would be in Paraguay. She felt their pain…having been the recipient of Washington's wrath on numerous occasions, but felt she could keep them together and turn the massive screw up around. The next few minutes would make it or break it. She leaned further into her bent over position, taking one more glance at the mesmerizing flames, shook her head slightly and started.

She began with the positive and presented the group with Sorento's decision to designate the "J" Team a new branch of the Presidential Detail assigned to locate and eliminate the other CFBA cells they believed were scattered across the country. No one moved or spoke…knowing bad was on the horizon.

"Sorento was not happy with any of the operation after things got sorted out. He is livid that we had no authority to be on their farm which will take years and millions of dollars in law suits to unravel. I could explain to him that the covert operation was legitimate; it was Jackson being spotted and the resulting shoot-out that created the problem. However, he also knew we couldn't leave an agent there to be shot or captured. Right now, the media is confused and plucking away at any thread they can grab, but that is about to change as the cell members return to the farm. They may choose to keep quiet, not wanting to open the Pandora's Box but chances are someone will talk. In addition, the sheriff hasn't a clue and the media is hounding him for information. He undoubtedly feels like a fool having a shoot-out in his county with no knowledge, no follow-up, no one to interview, and no investigation. I expect to have him at our gates any time.

Our job is to lay low and not become an object of the community's queries, so Jason and I will stay put here. When the sheriff arrives, I will convince him it is in his and the county's best interest to divert any queries to national security. I believe we can put a plan together that will avert any further media or citizen inquisitiveness. If Jason or I must leave it will be by chopper. Our appearance in town would cause too much of a stir and motivate folks to start asking questions, referring to the non-existence of

Asians in StoneHead or black dudes with long dreads. We move on and leave the rest to Washington."

Jessica then informed the agents that Dean, Lela, Kay, and Andy were fired because of Thiessen. "I know, I know, they were incredibly efficient and ran the ranch perfectly but Sorento insisted, in fact that was the last thing he said before I got off the phone…fire them, as they were responsible for vetting. He was most critical of himself for approving civilians being so close to the inner circle here even though Dean et al were hired with the understanding that Mr. Bakus would not be using the ranch while president. Sorento acknowledged we need ranch hands to keep the operation functioning, but to let Thiessen slip through the system was unforgiveable.

"On that same note, Shepherd, Marrington, key figures in the national Christians for a Better America terrorist consortium, their wives, and children have been released from federal custody. After their interrogation in Seattle, they were granted attorneys, who, as you can imagine, chomped on the case with glee, and in short order played the religious angle and the case evaporated. I know it is disappointing that the justice department didn't follow up on all the evidence that categorically points to their involvement in large scale bombings, but Justice refused to prosecute, allowing politicians to dictate the paradigm not to prosecute religious groups.

"Both suspects have rotating FBI tails to keep tabs on their new location. Everyone figured they would go underground but they…are you ready for this? They are back at the Idaho fortress Jackson helped take down. Can you believe it?"

Everyone shook their heads in disbelief, but all acknowledged the reality of the justice department's revolving door. Jackson was particularly peeved…but maintained his professionalism and did not vocalize his anger…given the time and effort he put into taking the group down. Jackson had scaled a brush thickened mountain during a moonless night and photographed the group's barn stored chemicals and uploaded the jpgs images via satellite to the Secret Service Seattle branch. The SWAT assault occurred while he was descending the mountain. The agents had taken the compound leaders by total surprise, rousting them, their wives and children from slumber.

Although disappointed that his efforts had been reversed, Jackson was delighted the group had returned to their compound, since he had an exceptional knowledge of their facility and surrounding terrain. He knew the "J" Team would capitalize on his knowledge by monitoring the group's behavior.

"There is a bolo out on Thiessen with a description of his ride and the Air Force has sent their top gun-ship team after him, so we should know soon," Jessica continued. "In the meantime, Rebecca, you need coordinate with Derrick to partner on the guide outfitting business so we can maintain that operation and follow-up on the drug line James had been running," referring to the pack train smuggling outfit which Rebecca had busted and now was being flipped as a source.

"Jason, we need more from James. There is no way he operated that drug and explosives pipeline between here and Idaho without knowing how to contact Richards and his crew, but I'll get to that momentarily.

"Oh, and Rebecca, that doc you hang out with…Barker?
She is still in the dark about you, right?"

"Yeah, she buys my cover and although we hang she has no idea of my activities here other than the horse training," replied Rebecca.

"What about those guys you beat up outside Cassandras, guy by the name of Jake and his redneck partner. Didn't Barker question what you did?"

"Not really boss. When we first met, we chatted about our background etc. and I mentioned my Black Belt and I think she had listened to me put those guys down in the bar and just figured I could take care of myself. If that changes, I'll let you know.

"On that note though," continued Rebecca, "I've been thinking of the deal you want me to make with Derrick with The Ranch covering the transaction etc., what about having Dr. Barker join us for a partner investment? She would certainly add to the cover and I understand she has a nest egg from a grandparent inheritance in Minot, North Dakota and might like to invest a little. That could be our way of paying her back when this is over, if Sorento could guarantee her at least an eight percent return."

Jessica looked pensive, ran a hand through her short 'do then said, "Sounds like it could be a great extension of your cover. I'll pass it by Sorento. But she cannot be involved in the day to day operation of the guide outfitters. She would have to be 100% a silent partner and you must be particularly cautious when the train gets mobilized."

Rebecca nodded her understanding and smiled at the thought of her friend being the only one making money on the guide outfitter investment and replied, "Agreed, Penelope has a very successful veterinarian practice so the lady is very busy, I doubt she will have much extra time to be hangin' at the operation. Having her on the deed will bring me into the local mainstream, since she is well liked and been here forever."

Jessica replied quickly, wanting to move on and get the others on task, "Okay, you set it up with Derrick that way and I will get Sorento's approval…but in a day or so, right now he is still chewing on Thiessen…which, by the way, we have to end quickly and silently.

"Jason, you won't be having another go at James, I will take that on but get a team to the hospital, secure it and I will advise when the Air Force has Thiessen," Jessica said, not acknowledging openly that he may already be in the wind, up one of the numerous canyons and in hiding. Jason had not heard any rumblings about his interrogation of the outfitter and was trying to figure out why he had been taken off that assignment. Jessica's system had always been to allow her agents to follow through with whatever they started and she didn't have a history of taking assignments away.

"Jackson and Elisabeth, you guys continue with your covers, we need to know the community gossip regarding our taking the CFBA down and what students know of the sect. Elisabeth, Shelly was arrested along with her mother and my guess is she will be back in your class and will bend your ear during the lunch computer tutorials you run. Her take on the night's events and the follow-up should be interesting."

Elisabeth and Jackson nodded in agreement, each reflecting on their contribution to the assignment with their undercover jobs as teachers; Jackson at StoneHead High instructing world history and Elisabeth teaching computer programing at the junior high.

The agents had hit it off with students immediately with their flair for cooperative learning rather than lecture/text book assignments. Kids gravitated to their own accelerated knowledge and comprehension and were surprised at their enjoyment of previously boring subjects. The agents built on the acceptance, attempting to also win colleague approval, which to date had failed. They were meet with annoyance, jealousy and bitterness at what the old guard felt was the new teachers' interference in a system they believe worked. It was imperative the agents find adult acceptance to facilitate a community involvement in their undercover assignment, so they persevered even to Jackson's accepting the inevitable…a date with the sister of a colleague…with his dating track record a disaster waiting to happen.

Jason had been instrumental in researching the ranch's security by travelling the perimeter, analyzing the existing paradigm, then working with Bruce and the National Security team to lock down the facility.

"Lastly, we have all experienced failures in our careers and bounced back, so let's put it behind us and let Sorento and the attorney general work their legal magic. We won't hear about it again, be called to explain or testify. Remember the Columbian fiasco, referring to a DEA, Drug Enforcement Administration, agent procuring a prostitute for a Secret Service Agent on duty at an international conference, or the Fast and Furious scandal, referring to Project Gunrunner where the ATF allowed 2,000 firearms to be purchased by illegal buyers hoping to track the guns to Mexican cartels. Border Patrol agent Brian Terry was murdered with one of the guns?

"Nothing became of either of these embarrassing and tragic incidents because the justice department preventing any investigation, which benefits us. We move on as the 'J' Team. Are we ready?"

Each agent glanced at the other to gauge their reaction to what had not been the dressing down they had anticipated. Smiles were unanimous with a resounding clink of mugs and relieved facial expressions. They were heading to their respective assignments avoiding any association with The Ranch.

Or so they thought.

This being a professional meeting, the agents didn't socialize as they left, didn't ask the other what s/he was doing on the weekend or engage in the chatter of normal colleagues, they just left. Except for Jason.

As he was leaving, Jessica said, "Jason, hang back a moment, will you?"

Jessica led the way back into the living room, now void of the previous energy and somewhat ghost-like in its lack of emotional warmth. She grabbed her mug and a tea refill and nodded to Jason to follow her down the hall. Jason quick stepped to find his tea and chased after her, not knowing what his future was or if he may be the scape goat in the recent CFBA fiasco. Jessica stopped at THE room, the furthest in the hall, turned the knob and pushed her shoulder into the heavy oak, lead lined door, holding it open as Jason scooted by her trying not to spill.

The door closed automatically, assisted electronically, and clicked into place. Jessica settled her mug on the only table, turned, positioned her forehead against the iris scanner, coded a seven-digit pass, placed her right palm vertically on a scanner and heard the system kick into place. The room was now sealed and she was cleared to log into The Ranch's security system.

The interrogation/conference room was two of the residence's bedrooms outfitted as you would expect any country sleeping area, sans windows, with a rustic deep brown leather couch, matching occasional chairs, accessory lamps and a twenty-foot heavy oak table with executive chairs in matching leather and five roller-wheeled legs. To alleviate claustrophobia during long meetings, Washington's technical staff had created a virtual bay window complete with moving scenery including clouds, pastured horses and passing birds. Dorky as it reads, agents found it made a huge difference in their concentration. The room's far end displayed a fifty-inch screen projecting a virtual fireplace. The device was multi-purpose, switching to either an encrypted conference telecast with Washington and/or a DVD player.

They sat simultaneously, Jessica at the end with Jason beside her facing the door. "Time for you to head back to university for your masters Jason," Jessica said with a sly grin.

Jason leaned back in his chair, put his head down between his spread knees and ran two hands through his dregs then threw them back and looked at Jessica, "Any particular discipline you have in mind?" he said with confusion and dismay.

"Environmental Studies would be my guess. It should lead you in the right direction" Jessica said with a dead-pan expression.

"Okay, care to clarify?"

"Sure, here is what we know to date. During Shepherd and Marrington's interrogation, the FBI deduced that both men were educated at the Colorado Fundamentalist University and based on what these suspects didn't say, we believe the school's Environmental Studies graduate program is a shroud for the CFBA's covert explosives delivery technique. We're sure the training is not on campus so we need the location. We also require knowledge of their recruitment protocol; is it from graduating seniors, those currently enrolled in ES or some other method. Your assignment is to infiltrate the group and locate the training facility and acquire as much knowledge as possible. Once we have that data, we can isolate the participants whom we feel are going to attack Congress."

"Wow, this is not at all what I had expected this conversation to encompass. But I like it…a lot. I can make this work. I also assume time is of the essence. Any idea for my cover?"

"Actually, Sorento has that prepared. Your days of skateboarding in south LA are going to pay off. He has you ecstatic about competing in the Rocky Mountain Meet in Colorado Springs. You can handle your skill development etc. and include longboarding since that would obviously be something you wouldn't get to try in Los Angeles or anywhere within driving distance. Your undercover work with LAPD and ATF, Alcohol, Tobacco and Firearms, was epic, and that experience, your ability to blend with whatever background and/or dialect, will produce quick results."

Jason couldn't stifle the joy and recollection of those months posing in Los Angeles as a Caribbean weapons dealer smuggling automatic weapons into Los Angeles and selling to the very south L.A. thugs of his childhood neighborhood whom he arrested frequently as a patrolman. Lots of anger and disdain towards him as a cop and personally considering him a traitor, an Uncle Tom, to his brothers and his culture.

Ignoring Jason's obvious reminiscence, she said, "Bruce has all your paper work with a copy of your new BA degree showing your recent UCLA graduation, application for and acceptance by CFU, but no hint as to your dissidence or discontentment with the current federal government status quo, that you can develop on sight."

"Excellent! I can get my head around this. When do I leave?"

"Tonight. Bruce also has information on an affordable vehicle with Colorado plates, driver's license, off campus apartment, student loan account with ATM card, pretty much all you should need, but if there is anything missing, you can create it yourself or text me on your encrypted Blackberry and I will arrange."

"Sounds good. I report to you of course."

"Exactly! Now, for the finale to your assignment. We are all aware of the problem the White House has with information leaks, the lack of cooperation between Congress and the president, as well as the failure to share information between agencies. That has ended." Seeing Jason's raised eyebrows, she continued with appreciation for his enthusiasm. "Cheryl Chapman is our new Super Cop.

"She is a former Chief Petty Officer and Navy SEAL, recently promoted to Commander." Jessica waited the Nano-second it took Jason to pick up on the concept and she wasn't disappointed with his response. It was classic; eyes wide, mouth open and arms spread in a mock, "What the?"

Smiling at his confusion she continued. "I met Chapman at Sorento's direction when I was in DC preparing the "J" Team roster. I was skeptical at first, but grew to accept her after a while…there is no way anyone can have those credentials carrying a personal ID from President Bakus. Her position is highly classified and would be denied by the White House if queried. She and Rebecca could be relatives by their physical resemblance. Chapman is six feet, 150 pounds of curvy muscle, *a body I have tried unsuccessfully to develop for years, short curly brunette mop,* she thought to herself. Her personality is acerbic, so much so that at first, I thought she had been isolated with Jarc too long, but I later discovered that what I saw was who she is and she gave no apologies. Of course, you know that drew me to her immediately."

Jason mused, thinking the personality comparison was that of Jessica and Chapman, not Rebecca Simpson.

"Don't say it!" Jessica smirked, "I know the comparison. Her SEAL team is part of a covert organization called Jarc, Joan of Arc. It is an all-female group, composed of many teams identical in every aspect to the male contingent, except they train in Texas at the Big Boogy National Wildlife Refuge south-west of Houston on the Gulf of Mexico coast. They access the center covertly from the Gulf of Mexico and depart on missions by chopper to Laughlin Air Force base in Texas.

"Jarc was the back-up team to SEAL Team Six which took out Osama bin Laden. The coalition forces created an interesting diversion for Jarc. The team was aboard the Canadian Destroyer *Athabaskan* patrolling the Gulf of Oman as the ship was on normal duty. The team had been choppered aboard the ship during the desert blackness, team members' faces were covered and were housed in separate quarters for the attack's duration. When one of Team Six's choppers went down, *Jarc* was mustered and airborne, heading to Islamabad for a rescue. Team Six regrouped and escaped with bin Laden's body, so Jarc returned to the ship to await their stand-down orders, which came 24 hours later.

"You may have been assisted during your North Africa stint by Jarc unknowingly since they operate in total secrecy. They do not speak with or interact with anyone other than fellow Jarc SEALs. The body movements and tactics are identical to their male counterparts so you would not be able to distinguish them apart.

Knowledge of Chapman and the Jarcs is on a need to know. You need to know because you are going to be accessing the country's first mega data base in Utah which she created. You won't be feeding it intelligence, just accessing the data base, your pertinent data will be sent to me here via Bruce who has your access codes and direct link to his security center. Questions?"

She knew there would be none but was being polite, trying to access the management skills Sorento insisted she practice. She felt no need to share with Jason the reason Jarc was formed in the first place but she recalled the conversation with Chapman; how Bakas' predecessors wanted a totally covert, black unit which was responsible to a limited overseeing group, one which didn't attract attention either through their operations or funding. Hence Jarc.

"Okay then, I just created your timetable," she said impatiently, "Malmstrom is sending a chopper for you tonight at 23:00 hrs. They will deposit you at the Denver International Airport where there is a rental waiting reserved in your name. It is the oldest piece of crap Bruce could find given your limited grad student budget," she added with a broad smile, knowing Jason would have no problem blending in to appear destitute. "Bruce has a credit card and a California driver's license for you."

With that Jason rose, picked up his mug as Jessica moved to disengage the room. "I'll be in touch boss," as he high fived her producing his $500.00 grin and headed to the kitchen to grab a snack and head up to his room to pack.

As he quick-stepped down the hallway, Jessica stuck her head out of the secure conference room and said, "Remember Jason, in all seriousness, we do not know who leads this group, female or male, so be careful you do not inadvertently hook up with an organizer or leader unknowingly."

Jason didn't skip a beat, didn't turn, just raised his hand and waved, acknowledging her comment and giving it a classic Spencer, *Duh* wave.

Chapter Eleven

Jessica secured the conference room and slowly walked back to the living room, noting Jason had already left and the horses had been moved from the pastures into the barns for their nighttime safety. The security flood lights were basking the outbuildings in an artificial sunlight which was so effective an insomniac would have trouble differentiating night and day.

She moved slowly around the leather grouping in front of the dwindling fire, reached into the wood pile next to the stone edifice and placed three, four-foot logs onto the grate. Chef Marc Stucki, knowing her routine and persona, had arranged a plate of appetizers of caramelized onion, goat cheese and herbs on French bread baguettes with a bottle of Stone Creek Winery's 2004 Cabernet Sauvignon Reserve.

She poured a large goblet of the Red, popped one of the baguettes, took several more in her hand and tumbled into the couch with a sigh. Chewing slowly, her taste-buds marveled at Marc's unique talent to create and prepare such delicacies and entrees for the president, and all from a guy who just turned thirty.

She sipped her cabernet, tasting the ripe cherries and a hint of spice, put her feet up on the massive pine coffee table and mused her last task; sending Jason into harm's way while having to take over the interrogation of Rebecca's suspect, coordinate the supervision of the mole in the hospital, interrogate him back at the Ranch while trying to be inconspicuous in this white dominated conservative community.

She didn't necessarily believe residents of this small western hamlet were bigots or racists, but her direct order from Sorento was to keep a low profile. Common sense told her that any federal agent appearing at the hospital, let alone a female Japanese American, would start tongues wagging, and not necessarily in a supportive way. She had to create an approach to hospital staff and local law enforcement to elicit information and not rejection.

That was tomorrow's rumination, for tonight, for now, this was her time, just a few moments of life's rhythm to let her mind empty of thoughts that burred into and attached to her soul, weighing her psyche and slowly creating a personality aberration.

The primary reason for her staff choice was her anonymity; they didn't know her, had no clue to her agency reputation as a ball buster, a non-team player with a personal grudge against the opposite gender. All characteristics she acknowledged, at least to herself, and all without reservations or apologies. She laid her head back against the supple burgundy, rolling her head and neck side to side relieving the stress from…what? Today, yesterday, last year, or an accumulation? Free of the neck confinement, she sipped her Sauvignon and allowed a smirk to creep across her face as she placed the glass to her nose, inhaled deeply, then sipped swishing the liquid around in her mouth, allowing the taste subtleties of tobacco to wave through her senses.

For years, she allowed her convictions to restrict her emotions, then freed them with the resulting explosion against her colleagues in training, against potential and real assailants. Not to her discredit but to her superiors' accolades, their acknowledging her exceptional physical and intellectual superiority. The down side of her success has been almost a total removal from her male colleagues. She dated at one time in her life, but every attempt was met with rejection after the first encounter, some even before, if the conversation got around to her occupation. Often the guys were so enamored with her law enforcement status they would ask to see her gun. She had exited many restaurants after these comments, only to hear through the morning after grapevine that she was, "A pompous bitch." Not once has she had a male social encounter who asked questions about her career, personal motivation or even if she had a family, the latter of which she would have gladly flaunted.

But tonight, she was letting that flow through her body, empty into the living room's vastness, swirl around the vaulted ceiling for her casual observation, then be swept through the roaring flames and into the night, to be free to infest some other soul or disappear forever into the realm of the universe.

Her cheeks were stretching their limits as her smirk broadened into a smile, the likes of which she hadn't experienced for so long, she touched her face, not sure what to expect. Another sip. Another glance at the flames dancing in rhythm to her rising enthusiasm for the turn of events; Jason leaving, forcing her into the investigative and interrogative role, the Team's redemption by Sorento with a pass on the compound attack and her rising star within the agency.

She refilled her glass, picked up the remaining morsel, scooted further back into the welcoming leather's comfort, pulled a rustic patchwork quilt around her legs and savored the baguette. She reflected on her love life, or lack thereof and wasn't sure if it was the wine or just the moment in time, but instead of the experience being cognitive she found it quite emotional, uplifting, remembering the few love-interests she had cultivated, those which held promise, the others terminating as one-night-stands.

Tipping her glass again, she glanced at the fading warmth and decided it was time to turn in. In one smooth motion, she tossed the quilt over the couch, grabbed the bottle of Sauvignon and headed down the long hallway to her suite, wine glass in hand. Keying the passcode on the security panel, she entered her *She Cave* with its inviting feminine décor; the crisp look and fresh attitude of chintz fabrics. Voluminous chintz curtains adorned the floor to ceiling windows which covered two walls of the eight hundred square foot suite. The floor was painted with a pale, glossy shade of jade-green, with the walls done in a muted, brushed rose, while the couch and two matching occasional chairs were in green and white stripes. Jessica would never have chosen a canopy bed for herself...in fact this room was an antithesis to her own apartment...but for a reason she couldn't identify, she felt amazingly comfortable here. The decorator was flown in from Las Vegas by Sorento, given carte blanche with the result being an ambience, a décor, which she should find repulsive but instead found it enveloping.

She moved past the canopy bed of flowered chintz bedspread and throw pillows and into an idyllic bath of watery green polished Venetian plaster walls blended with offset marble floor tiles in slightly darker green, creating a spa illusion with its sunken whirlpool, four-person tub and corner glassed shower with six water-heads.

Jessica put the wine glass and bottle on the tub's corner and ran the water full blast, stripped and stood in front of the full mirror, facing the shower. Not bad, she thought, as she ran both hands through her short ink black bob, then around her face and down over her small full breasts, noting they hadn't changed much over time. She did a little twirl, moving her five-foot, seven inches through a petite ballet move with her head and legs, satisfied that she still had something to offer.

As the water reached the max line, she poured a healthy drizzle of jasmine oil into the tub, stepped gingerly into the depth, sat and leaned back, allowing the quiet jets to soothe and massage while grasping for the red.

Taking a healthy gulp, she maneuvered her body toward the various jets and felt one travel across her chest, gently caressing her nipples, a somewhat aggressive action, yet one creating a feeling...the almost forgotten tingle, rise through her upper body and descend to her pelvis, then to her toes. She allowed her feet to float to the surface, wiggled her toes then submersed quickly before the room breeze change the mood. Moving again, she found a jet combination which centered on her pelvis and chest simultaneously and immediately her body tensed with the erotic fondling. Forcing herself to relax and enjoy the concupiscence, she closed her eyes and her thoughts drifted to Karen Winthrop and the sight of her showering at the Toronto Police Academy locker room. Karen's taunt, slender body came into perfect view. Karen was lathering and moving the soapy body sponge up and down her chest making circular movements around each breast, then letting her hand slide through her open legs.

Without a preamble, her body began shaking uncontrollably with the most luxurious warmth and mindless flow of energy she had ever experienced. The thrashing seemed to go on for several seconds then slowly retreating, leaving her exhausted. She moved into the jets allowing the force to increase the closer she got to the source, setting off another wave of body quivers, warmth and calmness which merged her body, mind and soul as one, an experience never before realized.

After a long moment, she felt in control again, but her hand was shaking as she reached for the Cabernet, finishing it in one short swallow. She rose from the orgasmic bath and walked unsteadily to the shower, opened the door, turned on the coordinated shower heads and leaned against the tiled wall allowing the jets' stream to rinse the luxurious lather from her exhausted body. Minutes later, she emerged, dried, walked into the bedroom, slipped under the duvet and entered a tranquil sleep, one so new to her that she slept ten uninterrupted hours.

Chapter Twelve

Rebecca Simpson left StoneHead Ranch after the meeting which, having begun with a heavy veil of possible dismissal, terminated with a solid round of support for Jessica and the "J" Team. They acknowledged that this assignment was one any agent would covet, so each put the CFBA solecism in their rear-view mirror, praying it would not come back to bite them in the ass.

Since Jessica's arrival, the Ranch had created a circuitous route leading from the guarded main gate back through the evergreen terrain to come out several miles from Bakus' property to create the allusion she was exploring/hunting/sight-seeing and not at StoneHead Ranch…which would be difficult to explain in a small town. Just a one lane fire road punched out by a ranch hand on a CAT blended with the existing bush road system. Carrying a shotgun across the back window of the pick-up for hunting grouse, a pigeon size bird, prepared locally like chicken, was a Rebecca's perfect cover. She still had to move through the perimeter fencing, guard stations etc., but they were not visible from the highway.

Rebecca headed back to her cabin to call Derrick, her former partner, a Flathead, Montana Sheriff Deputy, who had created her horse trainer cover. Derrick had provided the truck with Flathead Stables logoed on the doors and confirmed any enquiries to her authenticity while she worked as a horse trainer in StoneHead. As Flathead Deputies, Rebecca and Derrick had teamed to catch drug smugglers bringing their illicit cargo, usually cocaine and marijuana, by pack-train through Trail Creek Valley, which ran from Alberta's Waterton Lakes National Park into Montana's Glacier National Park. Rebecca and Derrick never intended to pose as recreational horseback riders, but numerous suspects made that assumption and their subsequent capture easy. The two always caught the smugglers off-guard since the deputies appeared to be a couple out for a ride. Rebecca had chased many a bad guy down on horseback. Her tactical operation was to move beside the felon, grab him with her left hand while neck reining her quarter horse to the right and leaning back in the saddle, stopping her horse. By the time the guy had cleared his head from the crash she was on him with a knee to the chest, flipping him over, cuffed, hog-tied, swung over a saddle, arms and legs tethered under the horse's belly…yes, just like in the old west Hollywood movies.

Her one hundred and fifty-pound, six foot curved, muscled frame was always overlooked by male suspects because they couldn't get beyond her fair complexion, stunning short blond hair and runway model face. She used her looks to her advantage frequently, catching the bad guy off guard just nanoseconds before she dropped him with a well-placed kick to a leg or back-fist to a face followed by a hip throw and handcuffs.

She reached Derrick as he was putting more burger patties on his Stainless Steel 32-inch 4-burner built-in propane grill with rear infrared burner, the latter of which he had no idea of its purpose other than to impress his male friends…and entertaining neighbors on their patio. His burgers were enshrined in his Montana hood with their legendary Victoria Epicure spices from Saanich, B.C. He was relaxing in a Columbia chameleon green, long sleeve Tamiami shirt hanging out over a pair of Tommy Hilfiger regal red Hounds Tooth shorts, with his 9mm tucked neatly in the small of his back, with a bottle of Flatlake Brewery's Lager, regaling his neighbors with soccer tales when his wife handed him the cordless phone.

Derrick excused himself, giving the spatula over to his teen-age son to carry on the broiling, "If you burn them son, Mom will have us both!" he said with a head toss towards his wife and a bit of a laugh so the boy would know he was kidding. "Hello."

"Hi Derrick, Rebecca Simpson, how are the bad guys faring in Flathead?"

"Hi Rebecca, puttin' them away as fast as we can," he chuckled. "I've been wondering about you. How's everything going?"

"I'm doing well, and you?"

"Still trying to keep felons behind bars and right now doin' the backyard BBQin' with lots of supervision from the kids," he snorted, beer bubbles spouting from his nose, glancing sideways at his kids hovering by the BBQ, salivating, breaking off little bits of burger and squirting them with French's.

"Do you have a few minutes?"

“Sure, I have time. What’s up?” He accepted another beer being offered from one of his neighbors and wandered off into the backyard for privacy.

“I can't go into details over the phone,” she said, glancing around the cabin as though to check on her privacy, raising her eyebrows at her absurd behavior, “but I have an offer you can't refuse,” she continued. “An extension of our current agreement. There is a guide outfitter’s operation here in StoneHead, just on the outskirts that is for sale. I need a silent partner and was wondering if you might be up to looking at the financials?"

Derrick’s quick thinking kicked into high gear, reading between Rebecca’s lines knowing she was being covert over an unsecure line. He knew whatever she had in mind the Secret Service was the money behind any agreement and all they needed from him was a signature and his support with the ruse.

“Sure Rebecca, Sue and I are always up to putting our high law enforcer’s income into an investment,” he chuckled, referring to the low salary of most Sheriff's deputies. “What do you have in mind?"

"Let me have the accountant in charge of the sale get in touch with you and we'll go from there. Will that work for you?"

"Sounds good to me, I'll let you know when I get the material. Everything else going okay?”

“Things are going great Derrick and again, I can’t thank you enough for the opportunity to run your StoneHead training operation,” referring to her undercover position of horse trainer in President Bakus’ home town.

“You are doing a terrific job from the feedback we are getting, so my thanks to you. We both might make retirement out of this expanding business. Take care Rebecca and we'll talk in a couple of weeks."

"Okay, talk to you then, say hi to Sue and the kids, and don’t burn those burgers!" she said. Rebecca’s euphemism was reference to Jessica having already been in touch with Sorento, *The Accountant.*

Derrick returned to his culinary duties and noted his son had already placed the cheese slices on each patty and was handling the responsibility with flair, leaning on the deck rail drinking a coke. Derrick acknowledged his effort with a broad grin and the guys clinked drinks, dad breaking a little off the side of a patty and popping it into his mouth.

Now Rebecca had to approach Penelope Barker, which was going to be with considerable trepidation. Rebecca had mixed feelings about including Penelope in the undercover operation. Although she cherished the relationship she had nurtured, she was first and foremost a federal agent and the job came before a personal life. This conundrum had occurred numerous times during her career but usually with men with whom she would start a relationship, work them for the required information, then disappear. But this relationship was different; she was based here for the foreseeable future and she enjoyed Penelope's company. She smiled to herself remembering the various outings they enjoyed together, the connection they seemed to have on a personal level that men couldn't grasp and Cassandras…oh, yes, there would be many more Cassandra nights, hopefully without Jake and his dumb ass partner, but lots of girls' nights at Cassandras.

She pulled herself out of the reverie and thought of a simple way to bring Penelope into the picture and settled on breakfast at the Bread Basket where they had first met regarding Rebecca's horse training prospects. She called Penelope on her cell and arranged for an early 7am waffles and eggs.

She spent the remainder of the day getting her thoughts in order and planning the next day's colt training for Tom Radke, a local rancher who had hired Flathead Stables and Rebecca to put thirty days of training on one of his colts. She'd head back to Radke's in the morning after breakfast and continue with the training while she waited for Washington to put together the Yellowstone package.

Washington would set up a dummy corporation with Derrick, Rebecca and Pen as principles of the Yellowstone Guide Outfitters, but she would be the operator for all intense and purposes. In her short stay in StoneHead she'd created quite a stir in the horse community with her training skills and expressed her desire to relocate. It was a natural progression for her to either continue with the branch of Derrick's business, start her own, or a partnership. She would have others to do the guiding while she continued to train colts for locals. Her greatest task was to find federal agents to pose as wranglers who could ride a horse and manage the trails, as there was no other way through Yellowstone National Park to the Idaho drug source.

Chapter Thirteen

William Shepherd and Ken Marrington sat in the massive living room of their Idaho compound and smiled at their tenacity and success. The massive log structure was located just below the timber line on Huckleberry Butte outside of Orofino, Idaho. Surrounding them were the trappings of a typical western five-star hotel minus guests. They were sitting in the Christians for a Better America bastion, recalling the assault several weeks previously. The buildings were swarmed by the FBI SWAT team of twenty agents so quickly and efficiently the occupants didn't have an opportunity to respond. Two massive helicopters swooped out of the night sky disgorging agents who had every man cuffed, hooded and strapped to a long bench in the choppers and air lifted back out within fifteen minutes. This was the first time either man had recounted what happened to them after the initial capture.

"What kept me going during those endless hours of light, white noise then interrogation was knowing we were executing our plan identically," Shepherd said, with a lift in his tone Marrington hadn't heard in some time.

"Me too", replied Marrington. "I had to laugh to myself many times when they thought I was about to talk, the FBI thinking they had broken me. Laughing of course, knowing you were presenting the same wall. I know we were moved from one facility to another. The first one I recall was in the country within a couple of hours flight time from here. There was a barnyard odor and the faint whisper of horses nickering. And of course, the last one was Seattle," continued Marrington, leaning back and putting his feet up on the pine coffee table, recalling the first glimpse of daylight, the ocean smell, and gulls screeching when they removed his hood.

Neither were ever concerned for their safety, their welfare or worried that the CFBA goals and objectives were in jeopardy. So many hours had been expended between the national center in Colorado, their attorneys and the movement's leaders, that the result was a foregone conclusion. What did puzzle all of them was why the feds would even attempt the move against them when they had to know no federal judge would approve a warrant. Even the idea that the FBI found a judge to issue one for the raid was mystifying.

"Pisses me off they took the nitro methane, although it was on the warrant. It would be interesting to fight their confiscation if just for the fun of sticking it to them, but the solution can be easily replaced. Our immediate need is to connect with the guide outfitter and get the products moving again," said Shepherd as he leaned forward and put his elbows on his knees and looked intently at Marrington.

"When the family returns, I'll head back to Orofino and contact the Indians and see where we stand from that end. And we should also contact Richards. He fared better than we did. He and a couple others were the only ones to make it out of the barrage at the farm. We should do something about that jackass. What the fuck was he thinking going gun for gun with the FBI and Secret Service?"

"Wasn't the FBI, on the initial assault, it was the Secret Service from Bakus' ranch in StoneHead. Nobody is talking and the local sheriff is totally pissed, said he predicted something like this would happen with Bakus coming back. I don't think the sheriff is much of a fan of the president. He may be delighted when this all comes together and the conservatives have control of all three branches. That raid is one mess our attorneys are going to be sorting out for some time. We just have to be happy the feds are looking for a conspiracy with their heads up their asses and we can keep moving forward," commented Shepherd.

Marrington took another swig from his long neck, shook his head and said, "I know, it is funny when you think about it, that they think we are so stupid as to put together bombs from Timothy McVeigh's system."

Still leaning over his knees, Shepherd reached across the coffee table with his long neck and clinked Marrington's saying, "That it is Kenneth, that it is, with the day of reckoning coming quickly from a source they will never anticipate, screen for or cope with the aftermath."

30,000

"Malmstrom Airforce do you copy? This is Airforce 1-5-65", keyed Keely while scanning the on-board computer screen for confirmation of the verbiage.

"Air Force 1-5-6-5, this is Malmstrom reading you five by five, you are cleared to land at West StoneHead Hospital landing pad coordinates 44.5 Longitude by 109.0 Latitude descending from five hundred. Do you copy?"

"Copy that Malmstrom Air Force. ETA two minutes. Out," replied Keely. "Air Force 1-5-6-5 out."

"Copy that Keely," added Bam-Bam. "Billy Rae, how is our passenger doing?" she asked, while checking her altimeter to adjust to the five-hundred-foot requirement and making her approach to the hospital.

"This guy is in pretty rough shape Bam-Bam, but fortunately he was buckled in so I think he escaped serious internal injuries. He's still out and he's consumed about a half liter of the saline drip," commented Billy Rae.

"Copy that Billy Rae, coming in for final approach so in a few minutes he will be the hospital and Secret Service's responsibility. Keely, do a visual as I kiss Ms. Cougar's butt to the tarmac," she finalized as she concentrated on dropping the massive machine five hundred feet onto the landing pad.

"Copy that Bam-Bam, you are clear 3-6-0," said Keely as she braced herself for landing, still not used to the way Bam-Bam brought the Cougar in so softly or how she was never reprimanded for her obvious sexual references on the radio. Oddly Keely thought, Bam-Bam was very quiet, almost introvert when not in her flying fortress.

The airborne beast approached the concrete with a slowness one would think impossible considering its size. Through the swirling dust and debris Ms. Cougar rested her bulk sweetly on the tarmac effortlessly.

As the Cougar settled and Bam-Bam shut down the rotors, several trauma nurses and doctors rushed the chopper pushing a gurney with a pre-hung drip line ready to switch with the intravenous line Billy Rae had inserted. The velocity of the procession appeared chaotic, yet orchestrated, as the scrubs attacked the Cougar's open bay.

Chapter Fourteen

Martha Sarkowski had the day off, the first of four in a row after four-night shifts of twelve hours each at West StoneHead hospital. She was beat, so after she had gotten her kids off to school and her husband had left for his insurance office, which he ran with his brother Joe Sarkowski, she headed back to bed to try and recoup from her exhaustion. She had found over the last few years that the hospital schedules she originally loved had become a physical burden, each rotation becoming more arduous with the tiredness almost impossible to recoup during her four off days.

She had just settled under the duvet, sliding into sleep when her iPhone vibrated on the night stand. Not being on call she hadn't set her subconscious for the hospital call and grabbed the phone without thinking…she could have ignored it and let whomever was calling send their message to voice mail.

"Hello", she mumbled after the fifth ring, rubbing her eyes with the other hand as she tried to focus on the voice.

"Hi Martha, sorry to have to call you on your first off rotation but we have instigated Pasture One and need all hands-on deck, ASAP," said the day shift supervisor.

"Yes ma'am," replied Martha automatically, knowing that code was a presidential emergency and no nurse or staff member had a choice whether to work or not. "On my way, Ma'am," Martha replied, then hung up the phone without waiting for her boss to respond, knowing further talk was superfluous.

Martha jumped out of bed with the adrenaline rush born of many such calls over her career, dressed quickly in her scrubs, grabbed her keys off the night stand and rushed to her car, stopped once to lock the door, then headed to the hospital, five minutes away, wondering what the Pasture One classification was, not having heard that President Bakus was at StoneHead Ranch.

Unknown to Martha, as she was blasting to the hospital, her brother-in-law Joe Sarkowski was speaking with Harold Richards of the Christians for a Better America on their burner phones. Richards had been the only escapee from the Secret Service/FBI raid on the CFBA farm outside of StoneHead, all the other men, women and children having been arrested and airlifted to an interrogation site in eastern Washington. Sarkowski had taken a pass on the Sunday outing claiming he had to work.

Richards and several other men had been working the CFBA farm northeast of StoneHead on a Sunday afternoon when Elisabeth Peltowski showed up as a guest of StoneHead Evangelical Church, the religious group which operated the extensive ranch and farm operation, where Shelly, one of her keyboarding students at the junior high, was a member with her family.

Chapter Fifteen

Elisabeth was rudely and suspiciously received, being the only stranger in the congregation. But her attire; a simple, plain, tangerine calf length seersucker dress with a white collar and cuffs, taupe flats, no make-up and subjugated manner, softened any immediate threat the parents, preachers and congregation felt. Her cover story of being a member of the Dumfries Fundamentalist Church in Omaha, Nebraska, a shoestring off-shoot fellowship, which several deacons confirmed, lead to the lunch invitation.

After lunch Elisabeth and Shelly went for a walk along the many connecting trails and weeded roads, having been shooed away from kitchen duty by the mothers. After passing the grazing cattle and milk cows they came across an old barn several miles from the main farm house. Shelly's insistence on looking inside, thinking the building might be an animal nursery, produced the scene that brought Agent Jackson Pennington covertly that night to gather proof of domestic terrorism…without a warrant.

Pennington had been decompressing at his rural rental about five miles from StoneHead High School, sitting on his covered porch with a beer listening to the approaching coyote pack when his encrypted cell chirped announcing his assignment.

Pennington's cupped mini-light had been spotted from the farm house as just an instant flash by a female CFBA member as she shut down the kitchen for the night. Her reporting the incident to leader Harold Richards had produced the armed response that had pinned Jackson down with no escape. An encrypted plight brought all agents to his rescue along with an FBI SWAT team, resulting in the arrest of most of the attackers, the death of some and Richards' escape through a hidden one-hundred-foot culvert running through an overgrown hill.

53

30,000

Rebecca was getting a late start to her day which was unprecedented given her predictable morning regimen of coffee and a long workout. Today she found herself waking past her built in alarm to a vivid memory of the attack on the Christians for a Better America compound; starting with the blast on her Blackberry without uuencode...a verbal message from Jessica; the race to the compound to rescue Jackson who was surrounded by heavily armed revolutionists. Her dream relived the adrenaline rush, the thrill of taking down the bad guys without concern for their civil rights or superiors' condemnations; negative experiences she had endured a life time ago as a deputy sheriff.

She quickly texted Penelope telling her she'd be fifteen late, skipped her morning routine, grabbed a quick shower, threw on her usual of ripped faded jeans, Wrangler blouse, torn Tony Lamas, grabbed her jean jacket and headed out the door running her hands through her short blonde 'do, turning to fob the house security system as she slid onto the truck's smooth leather bench seat.

Chapter Sixteen

Len Thiessen lay on the gurney in the president's secure hospital wing with two Secret Service Agents at the door; gowned, a FNP90 submachine gun slung across their chests, one hand on the stock, the other on the trigger guard. The FNP90 is the standard Belgium made firearm the Service has used since 2003 which uses a 5.7 mm specialized rifle ammunition which leaves the muzzle at 2,300 feet per second. The bullet fragments upon body entry destroying the organs and vessels. By not exiting the body bystanders are not recipients of the rounds, hence its choice in the secure emergency wing.

Thiessen hadn't regained consciousness from the Air Force assault and was sedated immediately upon entry to the protected unit. Doctors were running a battery of tests to determine the full extent of his injuries; liver, spleen, possible punctured lungs or fractured bones.

Nurse Martha Sarkowski was monitoring Thiessen's vitals, checking his blood pressure, oxygen level and IV drip. She had no knowledge of the patient's identity or why he was brought to the hospital's secure unit, but the fact that each staff member was physically searched and wanded spoke volumes, which alerted Marta to another responsibility.

At her first opportunity, she removed herself from monitoring, had a colleague cover for her and headed to the women's restroom. Locking herself in a cubicle, she stood on the toilet seat and reached up to the air vent, removed the grate and extracted an outdated cell phone.... she rotated the battery weekly so the current unit was fully charged. A quick ten second text, send, delete the text, clear cookies, data, history, and slide the phone back in the vent, return the grate. Anyone finding the old phone would think sexual, not covert, not national security.

Sarkowski flushed the toilet, opened the cubicle door and was washing her hands when another nurse joined her. "Hi Martha. Man, this is really an adrenaline rush, isn't it?", commented her young, petite, blonde colleague who had joined the hospital staff right out of nursing-school the previous fall. The colleague entered a cubicle and continued to chat.

"That it is. I wasn't ready for this given the President isn't at StoneHead Ranch. Wonder who the guy is?"

"I overheard one of the agents say he was lucky to be alive after Bam-Bam shot him," whispered Junior from behind the door conspiratorially.

"What is or who is a Bam-Bam?"

"No idea Martha," Junior continued while flushing the toilet and joining Marta at the sink, "I just overheard the Air Force guys chatting briefly as we wheeled the guy from the chopper. Those guys with the weird looking guns scare the shit out of me. I don't know how you can concentrate with them having their fingers so close to the triggers," added Junior as she did an involuntary shudder and washed and dried her hands.

"Believe it or not, it still bothers me after all these years. We haven't had too many during the president's tenure but before the renovations and security upgrades we would get emergencies with the Sheriff's deputies guarding patients behaving similarly," commented Sarkowski as she held the door open for Junior, "It certainly adds excitement to our day though."

Chapter Seventeen

The Bread Basket's parking lot was packed as Rebecca nosed Derrick's Silver Ford 2500 pick-up into a slot in the far corner of the rather large gathering area. She left the truck running while she gathered her thoughts as to how she was going to approach Penelope. She sat upright with her hands on her lap as she took numerous deep breaths through her nose, practicing the yoga technique Ujjayi. Rebecca had been mulling the conundrum over for the past few hours trying to figure out a way to get Penelope to believe she wants to participate rather than have it be Rebecca's idea.

Within a few moments her head cleared as she felt the rush of fresh oxygen---she had a plan that would work. As she turned the ignition off, grabbed her keys, jumped down, ran her fingers through her short bob and fobbed the rig she waved to several people who had noticed her drive in, "How ya'all doin' this mornin' guys?"

"Just fine Rebecca, ya'all have a great feed in there. Janis has some really good flapjacks this morning", replied several female ranchers heading to their rigs, smiling and waving at Rebecca. Her affable personality had been a magnet to the locals, particularly the females who generally rejected an outsider coming to their territory, especially a woman with Rebecca's physical attributes. But the new horse trainer had impressed everyone that she was pure professional who wanted to make StoneHead her home and had no design on any pair of pants, male or female.

Rebecca entered the Basket, holding the door open for two wranglers who smiled and took in her six-foot frame with one glance and a touch of their cowboy hats, looking over their shoulders twice before they made their way to a booth. Rebecca smiled to herself, never tiring of male behavior.

She spotted Penelope immediately in a rear booth, sitting with her back to the front of the restaurant, leaving the opposite seat for Rebecca. Penelope was easily to spot given her almost identical attire to Rebecca's sans the cowboy hat. "Hey Doc, good morning, been waiting long?" Rebecca said as she slid into the booth and high fived Penelope. Some cow folk remove their hats when entering an eatery but Rebecca never did, a habit she learned from her mom who did likewise saying the hat was more hygienic on her head than on the table. Of course, her dad never did either but his reasoning was he just didn't give a damn, an attitude that affected Rebecca's life philosophy more than she realized.

Penelope had just started to say something when Janis came over with the coffee pot and poured a generous plop of their esteemed black into both of their sixteen-ounce mugs. "Good morning girls, you have something in mind for breakfast or can I bring the menu? We have a special on today, buckwheat stack, eggs and sausages for seven dollars."
"Sounds delicious to me, I'm good for that," responded Rebecca.

"Make it two Janis and thanks," commented Penelope.

"So, whatcha been doin," asked Rebecca as an opening comment to gauge Penelope's general mood as she took a sip of the scalding coffee.

"Not a lot with me, just the usual this time of year, routine stuff, a few horse lacerations and so on, not the usual busy time like summer. How about you? You had to have heard about all the commotion out at the Evangelical farm northeast of town?"

"Not really," replied Rebecca with raised eyebrows while sipping the black. "What happened?"

"The details are really hush, hush and I don't think locals are supposed to know, but there was something big going on there the other night. I don't know if it was a break and enter or cattle rustlers or just what, but apparently, there was a lot of shooting and someone said they saw a black helicopter fly low over the foothills just outside of town around the same time. Nobody seems to know specifics or if it is connected to President Bakus. We never know if he is at the StoneHead Ranch or not. It's not like the White House sends us an email," she laughed and took a coffee sip.

"Never heard a thing. I've been breaking the colts during the day and just hitting the sheets early every night. We get so much of this cloak and dagger covert shit in Montana from the Air Force base we pretty much just ignore it. Probably not the smartest move but this could be more of the same, maybe training missions for when the president does come, or if he is here now. I did hear though that there is something going on at the hospital. An Air Force chopper dropped someone off, then took to the skies quickly. Difficult to tell what is happening since that Bakus section of the hospital is totally off limits to civilians," Rebecca added, trying to move the conversation away from the operation in which she played such a pivotal role.

She took a sip of her Black, holding her mug close to her face and glancing off toward the front door, contemplating her next move, just as a Park County Deputy Sheriff entered, taking a visual bead on her presence.

30,000

Len Thiessen was relaxing by his small, isolated deck on Santo Island, Vanuatu, off the Solomon Islands in the South Pacific. The property overlooked the ocean with the rectangle pool stretched between the Vanuatu hardwood decking and the Pacific. The home was not ostentatious given the multi-million-dollar neighboring properties and he wanted to keep his digs as simple as his ranch upbringing. His paradise was a three bedroom, two bath 1,800 square foot older house with a separate office, family room and full-length terracing overlooking the harbor. Thiessen had questioned his desire for a hidden oasis so far from the US and one prone to cyclones, but his dream had fitted cyclone shutters and security bars which gave him comfort when not in residence.

He was laying in the only visible recliner with a tall mimosa in his hand, squinting at the passing sailboats heading for the marina's evening safety. He wore a faded Air New Zealand ball cap, pulled down to shade his eyes and a pair of yellow board shorts. The luxury he felt and the overwhelming aura of comfort was mystifying since he couldn't remember how he arrived at this oasis in the sun.

He did notice though that his head was starting to throb, beginning with a distant memory of pain and slowly moving its way to the front of his head. He looked down at the mimosa to take another drink and his hand was shaking and the drink was fading in and out of his vision, when the sounds of a man and woman speaking softly wove through his sub consciousness and the tropical scene slowly evaporated. "His vitals are fluctuating drastically Phil, and his Hb/Hct is 7/21, referring to his hemoglobin/hematocrit. With the full whole blood transfusion and IV fluids he should make it", commented a female voice off in the distance of his auditory hallucinations.

He tried desperately to pull himself back to Vanuatu and his exquisite home with the white stucco walls, soft taupe furniture and local artistry decorating the interior walls. But he failed and his eyes slowly opened, the pain increased, spreading to his chest and legs as his memory of recent events slowly returned.

Thiessen was unaware that his seat belt had saved him from severe injury when Billy Rae had taken out the front end of his pick-up and it catapulted end over end, landing in the desert beside the interstate. Had he been unbelted, his injuries would have killed him, probably with an aortic dissection....an artery torn by a severe blow to the chest, such as hitting the steering wheel. His knees received meniscus tears, tearing of cartilage in the knee, as they were abruptly twisted and turned during the assault. But other than that, and a few lacerations, he was not severely injured and would make a complete recovery in time. His fear mounted as he became more aware of the past twelve hours, the escape attempt from the Air Force attack helicopter, the shooting, the terrifying aerial assault or the armed guards outside the door.

And yet the pain was so intense he had trouble concentrating, trying to bring himself back from the island paradise to fully understand what was happening. He didn't need to worry long as he could see someone inserting a syringe into a long tube and shortly he felt himself drift off, visualized his deck and once again enjoyed his delectable mimosa.

Chapter Eighteen

Jackson had slipped back into his classroom routine with little fanfare given the town's recent activities. Students were abuzz with rumors but without any confirmation...the Sheriff claimed no knowledge of any Secret Service action...they seemed satisfied that the president was either at StoneHead Ranch or on his way, hence the training sessions. Life returned to normal for the high school teens with attention centering on their own lives; the upcoming school dance, the weekend girl's hockey tournament and texting course content to each other....in total violation of school policy.

Jackson continued to work each class with cooperative learning teaching techniques, breaking classes into small groups and assigning a task to solve. Each group had a spokesperson, a recorder, a timer and a cheerleader and all participated in solving the problem or adding to a discussion on current events, world history or similar problem-solving issue. His classes had never received instruction in this manner, having reached the senior high level with instruction from stand and deliver teachers. The students learned the techniques quickly solving complex issues together with their test results confirming the acclaim of Dr. Barrie Bennett's teaching method.

On a personal note, Jackson continued his Friday night rendezvous at the Parrot, the local watering hole, where he clinked long necks with his colleagues and other StoneHead professionals Friday evenings. He hadn't any further smash and grabs with Jake and his inebriated sidekick, the same two who attacked him in the Parrot's parking lot bent on teaching him not to socialize with, *Their Women.* The same two who visited his rural rental later that same evening bent on beating him with a baseball bat, only to find Jackson sitting in the dark, on his back porch, commiserating with a pack of coyotes and his semi-automatic pistol on his lap.

Elisabeth returned to her computer technology teaching position at the StoneHead Middle School with considerable trepidation; she wasn't sure how much Shelly was aware of the incident at the church's farm the other day. Elisabeth was sure the worshipers wouldn't make a connection between Elisabeth's visit during the day and Jackson's shoot-out at night.

Elisabeth had been hired as a substitute for Ms. Panigon while Panigon was sequestered for professional development improvement for the remainder of the semester. Elisabeth had immediately captured her student's interest with her youth, infectious enthusiasm and exceptional computer skills. She was teaching both basic and advanced computer technology using gaming as her hook and every student was fascinated with her unique approach to an otherwise boring subject. Girls were particularly drawn to Elisabeth because so often their gender were ignored by science teachers.

Elisabeth had been befriended by Deb at Elisabeth's morning breakfast hang-out and that friendship spiraled to Deb's daughter Sandi and Sandi's friend Shelly gravitating to their new teacher. The girls arrived early that first Monday morning to confide in Elisabeth and share the rumors which were spinning uncontrolled in the community coffee houses.

Chapter Nineteen

Blake Harrigan embodied the outdoor Wyoming male stature, some would say *Hunk*; 170 pounds, five-foot, ten-inch, thirty years old, single, with sandy, brown, short cropped hair under a chocolate brown Resistol Panhandle felt cowboy hat, the crown emblazoned with the StoneHead Sheriff's logo. The dark hat, tan shirt, brown chinos, taupe Tony Lamas and Italian complexion, enhanced his natural handsomeness, which in any other setting would have brought female glances, but the star on his chest and .45 resting on his left hip put him in a class by himself, negating glances by either gender, albeit a few stolen ones from curious diners.

He spotted Rebecca immediately and held his stare until she glanced up and met his eyes. He nodded, and started to walk over to her table only to be intercepted by Janis and her ubiquitous coffee pot.

"Whoa, there Blake, can I offer you a spot at the counter? Looks like all the booths are taken for now?"

"That's okay Janis, just stopped by to chat a bit with your two pretty patrons over there."

"Well hold on there, Blake, these girls are just about to have my special and I don't want their appetites drained by any police business. You wait here while I check with them and see if they are receiving breakfast visitors," she said sternly, giving Blake a squinty eye.

Blake could hardly stifle his grin and didn't do a very good job at it as he replied, "Certainly Miss Janis, I'll wait right here like a Wyoming gentleman", and glanced around to see every guy in the Basket was getting a kick out of the Deputy being put in his place by Miss Janis.

He watched as Janis meandered over to Rebecca and Pen, bent over and whispered, looking over her shoulder and nodding at Blake, then returning to converse with the women. Momentarily she returned to Blake and gave him a simple nod and a word of caution to behave himself while pouring him a large white mug of black.

Blake replied with, "Yes, Miss Janis, I'll only be a few moments" and walked over, greeting those he knew by name and some he tried to forget.

"Good morning ladies, may I join you for a cuppa?" he asked, removing his Resistol, placing it in one of the numerous hat racks beside each booth and sliding in beside Rebecca, facing the front of the restaurant.

His presence was not a surprise to Rebecca who had anticipated a visit, if not here then somewhere on the road, after she saw the look of horror on the face of the couple sitting near the front with their two small children as she walked by and her jacket caught on the plant stand, revealing her .45 H&K in the shoulder holster.

Pen on the other hand was confused. Although she had known Blake for several years, had shared many a dance at Casandra's, her involvement was completely social and couldn't figure out what would prompt him to join two women for coffee.

"Sorry to interrupt your breakfast ladies but the Sheriff received a call that one of you ladies is carrying a firearm and the Sheriff wanted me to drop by for a social visit," he began. The Deputy had no real legal position enquiring about either woman carrying a firearm since Wyoming required no permit to carry concealed.

Rebecca replied without missing a beat or putting her mug down, "First off Deputy, I don't believe I've had the pleasure and I would remember a handsome and charming StoneHead male of your qualifications," she said, keeping a straight face and avoiding looking at Pen, knowing the two would crack up if she made eye contact with her friend.

Harrigan blushed immediately and wiped his face and ran his hand throw his hair trying to gather his retort. He had none and had learned in his 30 years never to try and outwit a woman, so he said, "Ya, well, yes, ma'am, I just was askin' about the firearm and everything, just doin' my job you know." He cleared his throat, slid out of the booth, grabbed his hat and headed to the front door where he immediately 180'd and returned to the booth and said, "Good Morning ladies, may I join you for a cuppa?"

Both women were so taken aback by his determination they burst out laughing and Rebecca slapped the seat beside her and said, "Sorry about that Deputy, just having a little girl fun with you at your expense, now, what can we do for you?"

"No offense taken ma'am, you just caught me by surprise talkin' about me like that, don't get that kinda talk too often around here, particularly in my job." He took a deep breath and tried to regain his composure and jettison the awe shucks demeanor. "Ladies, there is no law against carrying a concealed weapon in Wyoming as you know, but the Sheriff encourages every citizen who does carry to take the course and become licensed, not so he can track you but to have you as someone he can rely upon in an emergency."

"First of all Deputy, I'm Rebecca Simpson", she said as she extended her hand.

"Blake Harrigan," and it is a pleasure to meet you, as he shook her hand. Nice to see you again Dr. Pen."

Pen was too amazed at the conversation to say or do anything but nod.

"Blake, you don't mind me calling you Blake, do you?"

"No Ms. Simpson, Blake is fine."

"Okay, but it is Rebecca and it is I who is carrying. I have a H&K in a right shoulder holster. I'm a horse trainer for Flathead Stables out of Montana putting time on some colts here in StoneHead."

"Now that you mention it, I do recall hearing about you working for Tom. Good reputation is what I'm told."

"Thanks Blake, I appreciate that. I'm planning on settling here and have been thinking about the Yellowstone Outfitter's place that is for sale, but I don't have all the down for it and the owner of Flathead Stables can't swing it either so I'm going to be looking for a partner. You don't happen to have a few thousand stashed somewhere do you?"

Blake laughed, shook his head and said, "Not really Rebecca, StoneHead Sheriff's Deputies are not far from the poverty level to be able to put much away for investment. But I sure thank you for askin'. I see Janis is on her way with your breakfast so I will leave you to it. Please consider the Sheriff's suggestion Rebecca, we can use all the support we can get. Have a great day ladies."

And with that he slid out, grabbed his hat and headed for the door, stopping as his hand reached out to push, placed his hat on his head, took one last look at Rebecca and Pen, smiled, touched the hat brim and was gone.

"What the hell was that all about Rebecca, do you have a firearm on you?"

"Yeah, I do Pen, I hope that doesn't bother you."

"Bother me? Shit, no, I think it is great, I am a proponent of women carrying and just feel like a jerk for never getting around to taking the course."

"Well, you heard Mr. Pretty Boy there, no need for the course here in Wyoming but if you have never handled a handgun before it is wise to learn."

Pen laughed at Rebecca's reference to the Deputy and said, "Well, why don't we both take it and have some fun doing the course together?"

Rebecca knew she couldn't do that and have the Sheriff check into her background. Jessica was adamant that the Sheriff was not to be involved in Secret Service business as it would open a Pandora's Box with no chance to close the lid, so she replied.

"I'd love to train with you at the local gun club and do some shooting exercises but I've taken too many courses to do it again. Sorry."

"That's okay, so long as you can give me some pointers. Would also love to learn some of those moves you did on Jake and his pecker-head friend."

"Firearm's pointers I can give you but the defensive tactics is not tricks or a couple of moves but a mind-set that takes a while to develop."

As they were chatting Janis brought their food, refilled their coffee mugs and the women put the chat on hold to enjoy their meal.

Chapter Twenty

Thiessen was comatose, flat on his back with IVs in both arms, a condition of which he was unaware. His knowledge of his current condition was the slight pink ting of his skin as the sun slowly set behind the few sail boats making their way to the harbor.

As he sipped his mimosa, a figure slid in and out of the muted window's light and moved silently to his IV, quickly inserting a syringe of 100 units of insulin, the effects of which will kill him within a few moments. His breathing never changed as the figure slid out the door and past the two, armed Secret Service agents and disappeared in the quiet of the hospital's maze.

He was oblivious to his clammy, sweaty skin and shaking; he was enjoying the beauty of the South Pacific lair provided by Richards, feeling very grateful for the wisdom to accept the covert assignment so many months previously.

Time moved in slow waves, oscillating between visions of his social traumas as a kid, then euphorically gravitating to his limited love interests, then to an aerial setting observing him languishing over his refreshments.

Activity outside his hospital room remained stagnant save the two guards at his door who, although very intimidating given their automatic weapons and steel demeanor, had been accepted by the veteran staff as part of the job in the president's town.

As Thiessen's body plummeted toward eternal oblivion, a short, petite, brunette female moved hastily toward the guards who, although totally aware of their surroundings and on high alert, were taken aback by her bold and direct approach to their presence.

She slid past the two and pushed on Thiessen's door only to be stopped by the senior agent, "Excuse me nurse, but your colleague just checked on the patient just now, what is his need?" he asked authoritatively.

"I'm sorry agent but I am doing his routine vitals check. Please let me by that I might do my job," she retorted sarcastically, pissed that non-medical people were allowed input to her patient's care.

So, surprised were the guards by what they felt was her unwarranted attitude, they simply replied, "Certainly nurse".

Junior continued her mission, briskly swinging the door open, followed by the senior agent two steps behind.

As Junior approached Thiessen, she immediately noticed that his skin was pale. She reached out and touched his face, noticing its clammy, cool condition and shook his shoulder to wake him. Getting no response, her training kicked in automatically. Swinging her stethoscope from her neck, she slipped the oval under his gown and heard a rapid heart-beat.

Knowing his sedative was not that strong to knock him out in this manner, Junior knew immediately what was causing Thiessen's unconsciousness. She spun a 180 and pushed passed the agent who grabbed her by the arm and spun Junior back around to face the agent and demanded an explanation. "Get your hands off me you fuckin' idiot, this man is dying. Follow me if must but get the fuck out of my way!" she yelled as she twisted her arm out of the agent's grasp and ran for the door.

"Any woman who chooses to behave like a full human being should be warned that the armies of the status quo will treat her as something of a dirty joke…She will need her sisterhood."

Gloria Steinem

The guard let her go immediately and ran after her as Junior headed for a crash cart parked next to Thiessen's room, grabbed a preloaded D50 syringe and raced back to Thiessen and injected the needle into his IV drip and plunged the unit to the max, allowing the 50 ml of 50% glucose to rapidly flow into his body. She immediately ran back to the crash cart, grabbed another and rushed back to Thiessen, took his pulse, then swung her stethoscope from her neck to check his heart and breathing.

"What the hell just happened nurse", demanded the agent, who knew instinctively that shit was hitting the fan and she hadn't ducked.

"I don't know agent but the patient's blood sugar took a nose dive and I don't know why. This glucose may pull him out of it. If it doesn't work, he will lapse into a non-reversible comma and die. He should come out of it quickly or I will give him another 50 ml.......hopefully he'll make it. Go to the nurses' station and tell my supervisor to contact his doctor STAT!"

The senior agent immediately ran out the door to be replaced by the second coming into the hospital room placing himself in the far corner with his automatic rifle shoulder ready swinging back and forth between Junior and the door, finger on the trigger guard, tension dripping from his every move.

Junior stood next to Thiessen reading her watch, prepared to inject a second unit. She knew there was no way the patient's blood sugar would have dropped so violently naturally, but he was her patient and she had just checked him thirty-minutes prior and he was sleeping soundly, the effects of the evening sleeping medication effective.

After the agent notified the nursing supervisor, she radioed StoneHead requesting ear time with Fukishura, then proceeded to the secure presidential wing's access door, keyed in today's code, placed her hand in the scanner, then her eyes to the retina data bank, heard a click and entered and closed the door. A short conversation with Fukishura was all that was needed to lock down the hospital and her on a chopper to the hospital within 5 minutes.

Chapter Twenty-One

Elisabeth was sitting at the computer master console facing the classroom door when the girls arrived early in the morning of the first day back after the nocturnal farm raid and motioned them to join her at the back of the classroom.

"Good morning girls, how was your weekend?"

"Ms. Peltowski you will not believe what happened over the weekend...well last night really!" exclaimed Shelly, almost breathless in her attempt to get the news out quickly.

"Wow, it must have been one heck of a Sunday. Did something happen after I left?"

"Well, father swore me to secrecy but I just have to tell someone and Sandi doesn't believe me and I figure you would since you are a Christian evangelical like me," she burst out, coming up for air as Elisabeth thought through her response.

"Sure Shelly, I can keep a secret, what happened?"

"I don't know everything because mother and I went home in the afternoon while some mothers worked in the kitchen and the fathers did the chores. But I heard father talking on the phone late last night and he said that there was a bunch of shooting at the farm and all the men were taken away by other men in helicopters. I haven't seen any of my church friends yet but I bet if they know they were told to keep quiet too. What can I do Ms. Peltowski?"

Elisabeth knew this was her opportunity to solidify her relationship with Shelly and be welcomed back the next Sunday and possibly into the church's inner circle. Elisabeth knew there was a connection between what Jackson had found in the Idaho Mountains, the Yellowstone Outfitters and the church and she was determined to find out so she replied, "I wonder if it was an exercise for the Secret Service. If President Bakus is coming to StoneHead Ranch, then the agents may have asked the farm folks to participate in a training activity. Might that be possible?"

"Oh, Ms. Peltowski, I never thought of that. I just thought father was in trouble. That must be what happened. See Sandi, I told you I wasn't stupid."

"But I agree with your father Shelly, this needs to be kept a secret since the agents will not want everyone talking about it."

"I can do that. And thanks Ms. Peltowski for helping me, it sure makes me feel better. I really like you as a teacher you know, the stuff you put on the computers is way cool!"

"Well I'm glad you girls are enjoying it. Let's get ready for first class and I will see you later this morning."

With that the girls rushed out to their lockers as the school busses started to arrive and the halls filled with teenagers. Elisabeth smiled to herself, content that she had contained an otherwise explosive situation and moved herself closer to the church congregation, then went back to programing the master computer for today's lessons.

Chapter Twenty-Two

Rebecca and Pen were finishing up their breakfast with neither talking until now. Pen took a sip of her black and said, "So, are you going to ask him out?"

"I was just thinking the same thing as I watched his cute buns parade themselves toward the door. Has been a while since I've had anything that good between the sheets", Rebecca laughed, almost snorting her coffee at her own humor. "Plus, my vibrator is out of batteries!"

Pen couldn't contain herself and had to put her mug down and hold her napkin over her mouth to not spit coffee all over, finding Rebecca's crude humor hilarious. "How about we make it a double? There is a new teacher at the high school, Jackson Pennington. I met him at the Parrot the other night and he looks yummy too. Friday night at Cassandras?"

Rebecca almost had a coronary at hearing Jackson's name given their assignments were specifically designed so their paths wouldn't cross. But now if she backed out of Pen's suggestion, it could affect Pen joining her at Yellowstone, so she said, "Sounds good to me, why not stop by the boys' work and ask them this morning? I like doing it face to face so they don't have a chance to think?"

"Done. Six at Cassandras Friday! This will be monumental and you can spend your battery money on a beer for Blake!" she added almost falling out of the booth with her own laughter.

"Oh, I almost forgot to ask. You and Blake were talking about the Yellowstone Outfitters and your needing a partner. My grandma passed recently and left me a bunch of money to invest.
How about I become your partner?"

Rebecca managed to look surprised and shocked and replied, "Whoa, that would be excellent Pen, but do you know anything about the horse business? "

"Well no, but I could be a silent partner, just a finance person, and you would run the show. What do you think?"

Rebecca couldn't believe how easy it was and felt somewhat bad that she was misleading Pen. But on the other hand, Sorento had promised to guarantee Pen a minimum of eight percent return on her investment when the operation was done, so she was okay with it and said, "That would work. You sure you won't feel left out with my running the show?"

"Not at all, as you said, I don't know the first thing about the horse business, but I can guarantee you first rate vet services...for a reasonable fee of course!" she added with a laugh.

"Okay, that will work then. I will approach the seller that we are interested, get a price we can agree on and put the package together, then you can have your accountant and attorney check it out. I will include all of my credentials solidifying my ability to operate the business," she said and offered her hand to Pen to shake.

"Done deal. Oh, how exciting. Grandma will enjoy my using her gift this way as she was my biggest supporter of my going to vet school." She raised her mug and said, "Here's to you grandma, we will be thinking of you every day at the Yellowstone Guide and Outfitters."

"Now that we have that settled, the big question is what to wear? I have absolutely nothing; my entire wardrobe is pretty much what you see on me times about six. Suggestions?" offered Rebecca.

"I'm really much the same since neither of us dress for Cassandras. Oh, oh, I have an idea. How about a few days to Denver's Nordstrom? What do you say?" "That would be fabulous. How about a long weekend?"

"Let me see what it would cost to fly Friday, do a stay over and come back Sunday. You okay with that?"

"Sure, give it a try. Can't hurt. God knows I haven't shopped for clothes in ions," she replied as Janis came by and refilled their mugs. Rebecca took a sip, watching Pen navigate her iPhone. It always bothered her to see friends and particularly teens, using their smartphones to navigate the web knowing the NSA was observing their every move. The public has no idea the extent of the government's surveillance. Elisabeth was currently monitoring the entire community through her data base links with NSA and the counter terrorism unit in the bowels of the White House. Edward Snowden had revealed that in his work with the NSA, the agency had developed data streams which track social apps, geographical apps such as Google Maps, http linking, web mail and all the MMS data, the mobile system for sending photographs and multimedia. The data Pen was searching would be automatically placed in Elisabeth's massive hard drive and that of the NSA central processing center. The agency's budget increased from $204 million to $767 million in one year, financed no doubt by China, which itself is spying on America. Weird world in which she worked, Rebecca mused to herself.

Penelope interrupted her pensiveness with, "So, we can get a room at the downtown Four Seasons and an hour flight. $320.00 each for the flight and $250.00 for a double room...and of course whatever we drop at Nordstrom. I know it seems steep but driving will take us 16 hours round-trip and hey, what else are you going to spend your money on?" she said, taking a sip of coffee and raising her eyebrows begging a positive response.

Rebecca hadn't spent the agency's clothing allowance she was originally given that was supposed to cover an entire new wardrobe. She had made one stop in Montana on her arrival at StoneHead for some jeans, blouses and underclothes and that certainly didn't break Sorento's bank, so she smiled and said, "Sound excellent to me, a two-day shopping holiday with my best bud!' and offered a clink of mugs to seal the deal.

"Okay so we leave day after tomorrow, I best get to gettin' and do as much as I can before we head out. This is very exciting Rebecca, I don't think I have really shopped since before vet school, Yowzer!!"

With that, both women slid out of the booth, placed $20.00 each on the table which included a $10.00 tip, both women believing servers were grossly underpaid, and headed to their rigs to start their day, Rebecca wondering how she would broach the subject of Pen and Jackson with Jessica. This will take some conniving she thought, as she passed the family still in the booth, the husband giving her that *deer caught in the headlights* look.

Chapter Twenty-Three

Set off in an obscure corner of Manitoba is a little-known world secret, duplicated only one other place on the planet...in South-West Africa. Missile guidance systems are entirely dependent on this Canadian product as are global positioning satellites, GPS, industrial gauges, drilling fluid, food sterilization, surgical equipment and cancer treatment systems.

Embedded in the granite rock below the lake floor of Babine Lake is an unfathomable quantity of Lithium, tantalum and Pollucite. It is from the latter that Canada leads the world in the extraction and production of cesium.

North Dakota and Minnesota lie just south of Manitoba and their water shed topography pales by comparison with the massive Hudson Bay drainage basin; much of the water channeling into Lake Winnipeg, the Nelson River and on to the world's iconic polar bear territory in Churchill, Manitoba.

Babine Lake's surrounding topography is the Canadian Shield, a geological phenomenon that spreads east towards much of Quebec and spider-webs into large parts of northern America. The area consists of rolling hills with limited soil covering the volcanic rock base. The flatness is the result of millions of erosion years reducing the jagged peaks to their current status.

The massive mine sits on the lake's shore with the cesium being extracted from the underground mining of pollucite. The rock is ground with the cesium and the latter is separated with a chemical process.

Cesium can be further developed with a radioactive component resulting in cesium 137. This substance became the subject of controversy during the Iraq war resulting in American occupation with accusations the 137 was stolen after the facilities were bombed in 1981 by Israel and in 1991 by American forces. The fear is that the 137 could be the basis for the construction of dirty bombs.

The world's security forces concentrate heavily on 137 given its potential for catastrophic damage while ignoring the commercial use of basic cesium, which was the basis for a massive covert operation by Citizens for a Better America.

Chapter Twenty-Four

Brian Sawyer ran a huge drug operation in south Alberta in a little known forested area not far from the Canadian Pacific Rail lines which snake their way into Idaho and the Nez Perce First Nation's lands where a switching station sent cars on their way to further distribution locations spread across America. Sawyer's entrepreneurial opportunity began with an unemployment streak brought about by a drop-in oil prices and work force reduction in the Alberta oil fields, shutting down welding operations for several months. Having lived the high life and saved zip, he was caught in a cash flow dilemma until he met "Stan" an older self-starter criminal who had expanded his small personal marijuana operation to one covering scores of operators like Brian.

Brian developed his branch far from any public access road, in a heavily wooded area next to an escarpment, home to a deep cave, the entrance of which was concealed by decades of old growth. His operation was buried in the tundra below the frost line, encased as a cement bunker housing hundreds of marijuana plants. The operation was self-sustaining with a mechanized water/fertilizer supply and a diesel power system vented to the nearby cave. Standing right over the operation with the ten feet of dirt/cement buffer, an observer couldn't hear the generator. The operation had a security system which utilized lasers, motion sensors and ground vibration detection, monitored directly to his encrypted smartphone.

His crop was packaged inside the bunker, then transported with his quad to a Canadian Pacific Railroad staging area where trains wait their turn for passage south. The trains being exceptionally long, and the wait time extensive, he welded containers underneath the cars undetected. He stashed an entire growing season in multiple cars then headed to the east coast of Costa Rica for the winter months.

Nez Perce First Nations locals outside Lewiston, Idaho met the trains at night and downloaded the shipment and hauled it overland through Yellowstone National Forest to the Yellowstone Guide Outfitters near StoneHead, Wyoming. The drugs were distributed to CFBA cell members who then sold it, often at universities and other post-secondary schools, then purchased explosive chemicals and sent them overland back through the national forest to a Citizens for a Better America mountain retreat above Orofino, Idaho where they were mixed for the correct explosive combination.

It was the chemicals which agent Peltowski found and Pennington attempted to verify at the CFBA farm outside of StoneHead when the leaders found him and chaos erupted, bringing the FBI and the rest of the "J" Team. Rebecca had discovered the marijuana in the outfitter's barns and it was this operation which she was attempting to take over if she could convince the CFBA cell to accept her as a horse trainer with minimum income, wanting to expand her resources.

The Idaho compound was just one of a huge network throughout the country which had stockpiled explosives for an integrated attack on the Democratic candidates for Congressional seat in the next election.

Chapter Twenty-Five

By the time Fukishura got to the hospital and did a threat assessment, Thiessen was stabilized and although nowhere near being physically ready to be discharged, he was coherent, which gave her an opportunity to begin interviews/interrogations.

Her first task was to interview all those who had access to Thiessen since his arrival, starting with the nurse who pulled him out of his crisis, Junior. She asked the charge nurse for Junior's location and mentioned to the supervisor that she would return to ask for her input regarding the incident. The recent graduate was in the break room nursing a diet pop when Jessica popped her head in and asked her if she felt okay to talk. Junior nodded, so Jessica pulled up a chair, slid her credentials across the table and turned on her smartphone's recorder.

Immediately Junior tensed, staring down at the phone waiting for the agent to read her rights with mirandizing. Jessica smiled and told her that the recorder was simply for her own use and nothing more. Junior sat back, took a sip of her soda-pop and placed her arms across her chest, intimidated by Jessica's overbearing personality which, unknown to Junior, had been kicked up a notch with having to maximize the time with Thiessen.

"I am Special Agent Jessica Fukishura in charge of the unit at StoneHead Ranch and you are?" she said extending her hand to shake.

"Jasmin Hastings. Am I in trouble here? I don't know what I could have done wrong. My supervisor said I did everything per medical protocol. Why do you have to talk to me?" "Jasmin. Do you mind if I call you Jasmin?" Hastings nodded her approval.

"Okay Jasmin. You do know that this wing of the hospital is designated as a high security unit for President Bakus?'

Again, Hastings nodded.

"Good. So, then you can deduce that your patient is not connected directly to the president. Although his identity and the reason for being here is a matter of national security, you have a clearance category qualifying for this wing and you know that anything and everything you see or hear in this wing is top secret?"

Hastings nodded yet again and adjusted her arms across her chest, scowled and dropped her head, somewhat in submission.

"No, look, you are not in trouble. If anything, you are to be commended for saving your patient's life, from what I am told. So, kudos for your quick analysis and expertise, even though my agents were somewhat taken aback by your telling them, 'To get the fuck out of your way'," Jessica added with a huge smile which had its desired effect, as Hastings took a drink of her pop and offered a thin smile.

"Terrific. Now that we have that settled, I need to know the specifics of your patient's condition when you made your rounds, then when you found him slipping into a coma."

Hastings went through the details, stopping short of commenting on what transpired between her visits.

"The patient log doesn't show nurse Sarkowski entered his room sometime between your two visits. Do you know why she would enter between your checks and not log in?"

"No ma'am other than she might have felt a need to check on my work, I am still on my probationary period, but it would usually be my supervisor who would do that just as a matter of course. Martha isn't my supervisor so I don't know why she would feel the need to check on me."

"Do you know her very well? Are you friends outside of work?"

"No to both questions. I just met her today in the restroom. We were making small talk, chatting about the patient and how he arrived surreptitiously, delivered by an Air Force helicopter team lead by a Bam-Bam," Hastings said with a quirky smile, not knowing if the comment was germane.

"Captain Bam-Bam is the pilot of the helicopter and its crew. But getting back to my queries, you do not know her outside of work, have had no contact with her socially, have no idea if she has an agenda besides nursing? Do you have a professional opinion on why he crashed?

"No, absolutely not, I do not know her at all. You are scaring me Agent Fukishura. I was just doing my job. My patient crashed, I reacted as I was trained and I believe I saved his life regardless of what those dumb ass guards might have told you. I believe he crashed because his blood sugar dropped drastically, which is unnatural. He was fine when I last checked him, all his vitals were in recovery mode and he was slated to be released soon. If I may be frank, I believe someone injected insulin into his meds drip line," Hastings said, rather aggressively thinking she had better take the offensive before this secret service agent started to slide her onto a suspect list.

"Whoa Jasmin, relax. No one is accusing you of anything. In fact, the guards, in hindsight, thought you were gutsy to stand by your professional principles and be as assertive as you were. I appreciate your professional input and I will follow up on that idea."

"Oh, okay. Sorry about my outburst. I am very passionate about my job and my commitment and tend to get a little carried away."

"That's okay Jasmin, I understand and commend you for your ethics and principles. So, we are done here. I doubt I will have any other questions but if I do I may have to contact you at home if you are off duty. And remember, this is a national security issue and you are forbidden to discuss the matter with anyone but me. Understood?"

"Yes ma'am, I do. Do I continue as his nurse or are you going to have me reassigned?"

"Jasmin, I obviously have failed to ensure you that I am not displeased with your efforts on behalf of your patient, quite the opposite. But I have to find out why he crashed and if there was there an attempt on his life."

With that, both women got up, pushed their chairs back and, with Jessica leading the way, holding the door for Jasmin, left the break room, Hastings to return to her duties and Fukishura to interview the head nurse to discover why nurse Sarkowski would be in Thiessen's room just before he crashed.

The Nightingale Pledge: Nurses' ethics and principles. It is an oath to, "Abstain from whatever is deleterious and mischievous" and to "zealously seek to nurse those who are ill wherever they may be and whenever they are in need."

Chapter Twenty-Six

Babine Lake Mine in Manitoba had just completed their night shift with a crew topping off a shipment of cesium for delivery that day by the Mounted Courier Service from Winnipeg, Manitoba.

The soft, white pliable composition reacts with air and water creating an explosion and is extremely corrosive, necessitating storing and transporting it in a stainless steel, triple walled container, which looks oddly like an exercise training bell, albeit far heavier, with two handles.

Cesium is radioactive when combined with other elements in the development of nuclear devices such as bombs and power. Although pure cesium is stable, it emits energy along the electromagnetic spectrum, the concept used in the development of atomic clocks which control global navigational satellite systems, GPS.

The public often confuses radioactive with stable cesium. It was the former which killed many Brazilians and made many others ill, all of whom had scavenged cesium from a medical machine exposing them to radiation poisoning.

The courier crew didn't have a concern for their safety handling the stable cesium and since there is little commercial value to their cargo, Mounted Courier sent an non-armored, unguarded van with a crew of two to transport the cesium from the mine to Winnipeg's James Armstrong Richardson airport to be flown to a Vancouver research center.

The white van with the company distinctively noted on each side and door also sported artistic red whirls, twists and twirls. The distinctive vehicle arrived on time at nine in the morning and was quickly loaded by the mine crew. The one-hundred kilogram, two-hundred and twenty-pound Kettle was strapped to a wooden pallet. The entire unit slipped into the back of the van smoothly where the courier crew locked it in place to prevent any movement.

Babine Lake Mine was nestled on the southern border of the Nopiming Provincial Park with the main road leaving the mine connecting with the provincial road ten kilometers southwest of the compound's origin. The drivers quickly gained speed and settled in at the posted speed limit and were negotiating a slight curve in the road just beyond where

Eagle Lake made a pass under the highway when they spotted temporary construction signs and were stopped by a highway crew of three men wearing hard hats and reflective vests. Although three were bearded with dark sunglasses, neither employee had nefarious thoughts considering beards were in fashion country wide. The driver noted to his passenger that there didn't seem to be any highway structural damage on the way up to the mine and were commiserating on what the problem could be when one of the men approached the driver's window.

As he obediently rolled down his window, he was met with a 9-mm pistol, held by a gloved hand being shoved in his face. Before he could react, the gunman said, "Out".

The passenger was immediately frightened for his life and turned automatically to his window searching for an escape, when he too was met with a similar scene, this gunman gesturing with his weapon to get out.

The passenger was brought around to the driver's side and both men were tied with their hands behind them, soft plugs slipped into their ears, their legs bound together, heads hooded then each laid on the ground. Immediately an identical white van, sans the artistic markings, quickly approached and backed up to the courier vehicle's rear doors. The cargo was transferred from one to the other and strapped to a similar pallet, the doors closed and the two employees hoisted into their van and tied to the pallet. The barriers and road signs were loaded into the second white van. The only word the Mounted crew having heard spoken was, "Out".

The Mounted Courier van was driven onto a nearby forest road and into the bushes by one of the thieves who then joined his partners in the white van. All three exited the forestry road and headed south, with one more task to complete.

A few kilometers south of their first encounter, they pulled onto another forestry side road, unloaded the road barriers/signs and set them up in a similar fashion as before except in the northbound lane. One team member drove the vehicle just enough to make it not visible from the road, then the three set their ploy on the road and waited.

Their timing was exceptional with the second van arriving within ten minutes. They performed the exact same procedure as moments previously, this time putting the road barriers/signs in the back of the black van emblazoned with HBB and attractive red and white graphics depicting explosions in mining/forestry operations, then drove it passed their truck and into the bushes with the two employees blindfolded, tied and bound to the vehicle's inside support columns, making it impossible for them to get free.

They returned to their exit plan, not to the Winnipeg airport but to skirt the city entirely, join up with Highway One and head West to deliver their packages to their client in Alberta.

Chapter Twenty-Seven

RCMP Corporal Karen Winthrop and Toronto Police Service Tom Hortonn were finding it easy to maintain both a professional and personal relationship working with David Kopas and CSIS, Canadian Security Intelligence Service, after both were sequestered from their respected employers with Winthrop receiving a promotion to corporal and a significant pay raise. Both law enforcers were given new ID cards and shields making them officially operatives of Canada's spy organization attached to the anti-terrorism unit.

Winthrop began her segue from RCMP Sky Marshal to terrorist hunter after her first meeting with Fukishura on Jessica's flight from Washington, DC to Toronto for a brief visit with her folks. The two hit it off and enjoyed numerous Toronto delicacies, defensive tactics training and a memorable meal at the Calgary Steak House with the Honorable Cathy McGregor, Member of Parliament for the Toronto area, Shelia Fukishura's boss, and David Kopas.

When Jessica and Karen wanted to spend a day training, honing their skills, Karen reconnected with Tom Hortonn who was the Police Service liaison with the Toronto Transit Authority.

It was the Calgary's general manager, Craig Stevenson, AKA, Soul Train, who had been the topic of conversation when Winthrop and Fukishura met Hortonn at the Toronto Police Service headquarters prior to their training session. Stevenson, Hortonn and Winthrop had been students at the University of Ottawa and Soul Train, who earned his moniker in Whistler pouring Orgasms on the Beach to impressionable female drinkers laying on the bar. He was a crowd pleaser, a skill he had mastered while working part-time at the Oar House in Ottawa during his university days.

The relationship renewed, Hortonn asked Winthrop out for dinner to, where else, the Calgary. After an outstanding culinary experience, compliments of Soul Train, the duo returned to Winthrop's apartment after a brief encounter with a thief in the Calgary parking lot, in which Hortonn deferred to Winthrop as she relieved the attacker of his weapon and disable him just as law enforcement arrived.

The reuniting, exquisite dinner and tactics drama created a palpitating aphrodisiac which culminated with intense mutual sexual pleasure and for Karen, a first ever G-Spot orgasm.

The two got together during the ensuing months but regrettably, only periodically given their busy and kinked schedules...Karen having an unscheduled layover in Los Angeles due to a labor dispute between Air Canada and the flight attendants.

Tom surprised Karen during her unscheduled vacation at the Channel Road Inn, a small, intimate B & B, a block from Santa Monica Beach. She had taken the Spa Suite expecting to pass the time luxuriating in the uniquely jetted tub, strolling the beach and taking in Santa Monica boutiques, never expecting to have Tom as a tub mate. He had been waiting for her when she arrived, having beaten her arrival by about an hour by snagging a chopper ride from TPS to Pierson International Airport and a direct flight to LAX, the last one before the shut-down. Karen had arrived from Miami and was just that much behind him.

They spent the few layover days doing exactly what Karen had expected to do alone and the mini-vacation was luxury at its finest with every day having the delight of several new restaurants, strolling Santa Monica's pier, the promenade and exploring their erotic zones. The labor dispute was short lived with a call to return to duty coupled with an encrypted text from Dave Kopas asking for a meeting when she returned to Toronto.

Hortonn was already being groomed by CSIS for a sequestered position given his experience after 9/11, creating a heightened awareness and tactical preparedness for the Toronto Transit Authority. Kopas was unaware of Karen and Tom's relationship when he approached her in a Toronto coffee shop with the offer she couldn't refuse.

Since that first meeting, Winthrop and Hortonn were involved in months of training acquiring CSIS operational procedures, then the duo landed in Vancouver for an international anti-terrorism conference at the Fairmont Airport Hotel. Maintaining a certain decorum and propriety, each registered, obtaining separate rooms, albeit on the same floor with most other attendees.

The conference was not quite covert but was not open to public scrutiny or advertised and the media was out of the loop, allowing participants to come and go at their leisure without being confronted by either paparazzi or local reporters.

The German, Italian, French and Spanish delegates shared details of the un-vetted refugees throughout the EU, creating a security nightmare with no solution in sight, given the fluidity of all their borders. All the conference attendees wanted information from the Canadian delegation on how they had the foresight to investigate applicants from so many war torn countries and specifically how they eliminated single men, which are currently dominating the European landscape, free to come and go with the countries' security forces totally ignorant of each man's background; were they all simply honest villagers fleeing the bombing of their homeland or are some Al Qaeda or ISIS soldiers now part of the movement's Trojan Horse?

The American delegation was not interested in Canada's position with refugees and considered the country to be ignorant regarding national security and international affairs. This attitude raised numerous eyebrows, notably those of Winthrop and Hortonn who had learned of the costly debacles in various hot spots of the world where the CIA and Secretary of State had made decisions based on political capital rather than sound intelligence. The rest of the delegates were determined not to allow the Americans to control the direction of a collective counter terrorism agenda.

Protocol required delegates to meet during the day but also to continue the dialog during meals and breaks. Canada, as host, changed that process and was determined not to raise the radar of journalists. In today's social media climate, a photo of any one of the participants would be tweeted world-wide creating a media storm, which would negate the entire agenda, so delegates dined in pairs, which worked perfectly for Karen and Tom.

Their first day was exhausting with their flight, registration and assisting the foreign affairs team with final preparations, so around six o'clock they begged off for the night, returned to Karen's room, showered…together and ordered room service.

Although both had travelled extensively for business, particularly Karen, neither had ever had the luxury of the Fairmont Airport Hotel and certainly were not prepared for the hotel's room service menu. They started with a bottle of Burrowing Owl's Athene 2012 from British Columbia's famed Okanagan wine country, which boasted aromas of blackberry, raspberry with a hint of oak from its eight aging years. Karen opened the bottle, poured, nosed, sipped and swirled, then poured Tom a glass. Hortonn was both amused and confused by Winthrop's apparent knowledge and expertise of wines, but made the wise decision to keep his thoughts to himself.

They each chose the Albacore Tuna, a wasabi aioli drizzle side with a cucumber and red onion salad presented artistically with a miso vinaigrette. Relaxing in front of the fire with the drapes having closed off the outside world, they chatted about their previous dining enjoyments, some dating back to their childhood with chicken fingers being the extent of their collective culinary culture. A luxurious soak in the jetted soaker tub for four and they fell into bed, exhausted, but delighted for the time together the next few days.

Chapter Twenty-Eight

High Plains Air offered the best deal for a round-trip from StoneHead to Denver at $320.00 each. They snagged an incredible deal with the Four Seasons, a fabulous room with a mountain view on the sixteenth corner floor with two walls entirely glass, floor to ceiling. When Pen made the reservations, she off-handily mentioned they were out of town Nordstrom shoppers and the Four Seasons gave them a discount. Two king size beds, an oversize bathroom with both a shower and jetted tub greeted them upon entry as well as a chilled bottle of California Napa Valley Chardonnay and a cheese/fruit plate for two.

After seeing the welcoming spuntini, aparitivi, they showered, donning men's boxer shorts and oversize tank tops, then dragged the coffee table loaded with goodies and the two occasional chairs, uncorked the wine, poured two glasses…no nosing for them…kicked back in the chairs and started in on the cheese and fruit with their feet on the window sill. Pen said, "We really need to bring the Cassandra girls here the next time," marveling at the dramatic view; the mountains of the Arapaho National Forest to the West.

Rebecca turned, raised her cold goblet saying, "To be sure, but at least two bottles of this divine Napa…each!"

They spent about an hour relaxing and chatting about various teenage experiences ranging from boys to riding, snowmobiling and dog racing then, having finished the bottle of Napa, they dressed again in jeans, blouses and boots…neither of them owning a dress or skirt. They had the concierge call a cab and headed to Alto un Miglio (Mile High), one of Denver's supreme Italian restaurants recommended by Giovanni, the bell boy who brought up their luggage.

They were not disappointed and were delighted with the reception given two single women, neither having been greeted with such warmth and enthusiasm before. Once seated and the maître d' was satisfied they were happy with their table and his flirtation was getting him places, they ordered another bottle of the delicious Napa and a plate of Fritto Misto; calamari, lightly fried with scallops, rock shrimp, bitter greens and coral aioli.

Continuing their chat and gawking like true tourists, neither having been to Denver previously, they were oblivious to their server standing in the alcove watching them and responding to their empty wine glasses, replacing the empty Napa with a chilled fresh one, brushing the bread crumbs off the table and otherwise dealing with their every need…and only them, he was not serving another table.

Their entre` was Agnello di brasato, braised lamb, Colorado lamb shank braised in San Marzano tomatoes & Arneis white wine, with orange gremolata. Neither woman had a clue as to the pronunciation and asked their server, who rattled the entre` off in eloquent Italian, smiling at his accomplishment, with a little of his euphoria generated by his view of Rebecca's muscular, broad shoulders highlighting her breasts, accentuated by her fitted Lee cobalt blue blouse.

Pen got a kick out of his darting eyes; from her upper body to Rebecca's and back again, then his face turning a blazing red when he saw them laughing.

While Rebecca and Pen were enjoying their elegant meal, and playing junior high with the server, a member of the G-7 Counter-Terrorism American delegation was preparing her delivery for the next day, one that would shock the American participants and bring substance to the EUs refugee struggle and their mounting terrorist attacks.

Chapter Twenty-Nine

Jessica headed straight for the supervising nurse after leaving Hastings, the neophyte wondering if she would have a job by the end of the day.

Stone was not the stereotype nursing supervisor with her five-foot, seven-inch, slender frame, auburn bob with blonde streaks darting in and out of her bangs. Her black, semi-oval reading glasses softly framed her face, setting off her dark hair and hazel eyes. She looked up, slipping her glasses on top of her head as Fukishura approached.

"May I help you agent?"

"Hi. Yes, you may. I am supervising Secret Service Agent Jessica Fukishura assigned to the StoneHead White House Ms. Stone, reading the nurse's name tag, and I need information regarding your recent crashed patient Thiessen."

Nurse Stone extended her hand to shake and Jessica took it, acknowledging a firm, confident greeting. "Certainly. Do you prefer Agent Fukishura or Ms. Fukishura?"

"Either is fine, and your last name is?"

"Stone. And please, no hyperbole about Basic Instinct or her age, I am much younger, far more attractive and have skills that Stone could only dream of," the nurse said with a huge smile, attempting to soften the very tense situation.

Jessica laughed and wondered to what skills the nurse was referring, professional or sexual, but she kept her thoughts to herself and said, "I just interviewed nurse Hastings. Was she the only staff member to see Thiessen before he crashed?"

"According to the patient's records she was, but something tells me you do not believe that."

"The guards said a nurse Sarkowski was in the room moments before the patient crashed.

Any idea what she would have been doing there if she didn't note her presence on the chart?"

"I have no idea Ms. Fukishura. Martha has been with this hospital for years. She and her husband are solid StoneHead citizens and very active in the evangelical church. Her husband Joe has an insurance business here in town. I cannot think there would be anything nefarious about her treatment, she probably just forgot to note it on the chart."

"That is possible of course, but do you not think it a coincidence that moments after she saw Thiessen, his blood sugar plummeted? Plus, she is nowhere to be found. One of the guards checked the entire hospital and she is not around and has not signed out. Where is she?"

"I have no idea Agent and this conversation is far beyond the purview of my job description. I am not going to get involved in any conversation regarding staff. If you have further enquiries, I suggest you discuss them with the hospital's administrator."

"Fair enough Sharon. Just one more question. When can Thiessen be discharged?"

"The chief resident responsible for the president's unit must make that decision, but it appears Mr. Thiessen should be ambulatory by late this afternoon if his vitals remain stable."

"Thanks. That is all I need to know. I will arrange for him to be transferred to StoneHead Ranch."

"Whoa, wait a minute Agent. I said he was dischargeable, meaning to somewhere comfortable where he can continue his rest and recovery, not to your inquisition sight."

"Now nurse Stone, to what are you referring, that we would interrogate Mr. Thiessen?" Jessica said with somewhat of a sarcastic lilt in her voice.

"You can allay your concerns. We will see that he receives all the care and attention he deserves as an employee of the StoneHead Ranch." With that, Jessica did her infamous foot twirl, where she pivots on the ball of one foot and springs forth with the other at the end of the 180-degree, as though to execute a front leg kick, with a smug look on her face, knowing she had all the information she needed and this prick Thiessen would be under her control by the end of the day.

By the end of the day she did indeed have Thiessen unhooked from all intravenous leads and transported in an ambulance to the Ranch. She made a quick call to Sorenson to make the necessary arrangements to have nurse Hastings sequestered to the Ranch to care for Thiessen if the need arose…from his injuries…not her interrogation…she hoped.

Chapter Thirty

Jason Spencer had successfully infiltrated the Christians for a Better America university graduate program in Environment Studies. Sorenson had the CIA's documents section prepare Jason's identification and university records, then sent them to Elisabeth who hacked into the subject school and implanted the records. Jason's ID, credit cards, clunker, old clothes and a used longboard were left for him at a Denver drop-off spot.

None of the other students or professors commented on his age but they were wowed with his longboarding techniques which he demonstrated frequently on Denver's Cherry Creek trail, receiving the criticism of dog walkers. He participated in a huge longboarding exhibition on Pecos and 64th, a four-lane busy highway with a gentle running downhill slope. The contest accelerated campus chatter regarding his skills and became the topic of discussion in campus pubs.

Jason had longboarded Beverly Glen hills during his down time as an LAPD patrol officer and had missed the adrenaline rush. That nostalgia quickly dissipated when he was in North Africa where he enjoyed the accelerating hormone frequently. After the training at Rowley he had become bored and although there was a little excitement with creating StoneHead Ranch's security and the firefight, he missed being solo, creating his own agenda and being solely responsible for the outcomes.

Within months of arriving in Denver, demonstrating his academic prowess and social interaction skills, he was invited to the research facility northwest of Denver in the Rocky Mountain National Park. All the research materials had been delivered some months ago by a pilot the group kept on retainer.

At the end of the second term of the PhD. program, the team gave up their dorm rooms, stored their meagre belongings and packed a bag of their essentials and headed to the Colorado Leyden Airport, then stored their gear aboard the single engine Otter and climbed into their designated seats and prepared for pilot instructions and the next segment of their exciting grad program.

During the early morning flight Jason sat shotgun and could socialize somewhat, utilizing the headset and microphone, with the pilot, Daniel Jenewein. Jenewein said that he had made numerous flights to the lodge over the past few weeks, storing food supplies and various chemicals the research team would need for their extended residency. He got a chuckle reminiscing about hexamethylene triperoxide diamine, known as HMDT. Jenewein ran the three words together implying it was one compound when Jason knew it was three. Jason also knew that Jenewein did not transport this compound as it was highly explosive. What he probably hauled was hydrogen peroxide, hexamine and powdered citric acid since it is these three which comprise HMDT. Jenewein said he was almost crapping his pants thinking the cargo could explode mid-air.

The conversation solidified Jason's suspicions about the long-range objective of the group; to create an explosive device which could do the maximum amount of damage. Now he had to figure out the target. But in the meantime, he had to communicate this information to Jessica. The pilot brought him out of his musings.

Jenewein notified the passengers that they were approaching thirty minutes until landing and that he would circle the lodge several times so they could get their bearings as he pointed out the facility and what each building contained.

Jenewein got a kick out of these ten university students and their collective enthusiasm for research in this remote location and wondered if he would get a call in the middle of winter with one or more going crazy with cabin fever. He was not going to tell them about the kitchen door which was torn from its hinges, the long brownish hairs lodged in the upper part of the door frame or the pungent odor that was prevalent during his extensive clean-up.

He had mixed feelings about this group; somewhat envious of their paid holiday and yet appreciative of their expertise and ability to create the delivery agent for the various explosive devices.

As an Al Qaeda sleeper, he was quite comfortable with killing the president and anyone else his handlers requested he eliminate. Growing up in Harlem and home schooled by his Iranian mother, he was convinced the only true believer's role in life was to bring down those who opposed his chosen homeland and its ideology. He learned at his father's hand that life was a chosen path as was death, and that a person moved from one medium to another like a star extinguished by humanity's light.

His father graduated from Shahid Beheshti University, formerly The National University of Iran, with advanced degrees in physics and chemistry and took responsibility for Daniel's science education while his mother handled languages, religion, and philosophy. His father's meager earnings as a cab driver were far from sufficient to maintain their side-by-side apartments, the second of which was leased to an absentee international wholesaler who sent periodic FedEx packages containing more than sufficient quantities of cash to sustain the family's lifestyle. The two dwellings afforded the senior Jenewein a high-tech lab in which he taught his son chemistry elements and bomb making techniques. In hindsight, he knew his since deceased father was more an academic than a practical jihadist, for the elder's formulas were concentrated on complex methods and ingredients, which for all practical purposes were unattainable.

Jenewein began the process of circling the compound, smiling at the sounds of, "Oh, wow" and "awe" from the passengers. He knew that if they could devoid themselves of their current social life and concentrate totally on their temporary, if prolonged, task here, they could enjoy this luxurious retreat.

Jason felt the plane bank, pulling him out of his revere about the explosives and gazed out the window, admiring the many areas he could explore once he was settled. The reality of proving his cover for so many months had been and continued to be stressful and he saw his opportunity to get some exercise.

The Otter landed smoothly, then cruised slowly, docking at the wharf. Jason exited first with Jenewein crawling over the passenger seat to exit next, then opened the rear doors, allowing the students to tumble out and regain their land legs.

Jenewein left and returned with the Kubuta and trailer, then everyone pitched in, loading the gear, then walked behind Jenewein as he headed to the main facility.

The ten thousand square foot main lodge appeared utilitarian from the air, with drab, weathered wood siding and blocky uninviting windows. But as you stepped through the main doors you were greeted by twenty-foot ceilings with pine walls and taupe ceiling to floor drapes covering wall to wall triple pane windows.

A mossy rock floor to ceiling fireplace commanded the longest wall. The skillful use of antiques brought an immediate calmness to the space with social settings dominated by leather couches and occasional chairs…either black or red the prevailing color. The living room was so massive a guest might expect to be greeted by gigantic wagon wheel chandeliers. What met them instead was subdued lighting imbedded in the ceiling and walls highlighting each piece of western art, the fireplace and each social setting, leaving the rest of the space darkened. Enormous, thick Persian rugs accented each seating area, brought warmth to the room, intensified by the already dominant ambience from the ten-foot stone fireplace.

As the researchers wandered through the lodge they saw that each room expressed a distinct personality through either wall design such as bookcases, local paintings and the pressed tin ceiling in the kitchen.

In the living room, the seating arrangement of leather couches and occasional chairs in front of the fireplace were accentuated by a twelve-foot cocktail table with spiral copper legs and glass top.

Jenewein had backed the quad to the kitchen door and transferred the gear into the large commercial gallery. Jason was not surprised the door was unlocked. The likelihood of anyone being this far remote was limited and if a lost hunter were to stumble on the lodge, bush protocol required an open invitation to use what was available and either replace it or leave money, hence the unlocked doors. Once the gear was inside, Jenewein took the students to their respective rooms, finished the tour, then invited them to meet him in the massive living room in an hour for wine, cheese and a celebratory toast to their future.

Jason was the last to get his room and as he put his gear down Jenewein cleared his throat and motioned for Jason to follow him. They moved through the living room, down a hallway and into a large storage area where Jenewein stopped beside a huge steel safe, which Jason instinctively knew held firearms.

“I was told by the university that you are a competitive shooter so they have designated you to be the lodge’s security,” he said, not waiting or seemingly expecting and response from Jason.

“In here you will find numerous beauties,” he said as he manipulated the combination dial and swung the door open.

“You recognize these for sure. Here is a Winchester .30-30 lever action Trapper model with iron sights, three Winchester .338 Magnums, all with Leopold variable scopes, two Ruger .44 Magnum revolvers, 6” barrels with leather shoulder holsters and a couple of .22 caliber revolvers with 6” barrels. On the bottom shelve there is ammo for each weapon. These are your walkabout pieces which I encourage you to carry any time you are out and about the property. There is an identical safe in your room behind the closet. Just slide the rain gear to the side and it is there with the identical combination. That safe has three M-16 fully automatic rifles with twenty, thirty-round magazines with .30-06 caliber cartridges. On the bottom shelf of that safe there is a thousand rounds of .30-06.

“You understand the difference between the fire power?”

Jason nodded his head in agreement, knowing his room safe was security weaponry to protect the researchers, while the safe in front of him was personal protection for hiking trips or strolls on the trails.

“Good. I strongly urge you to accompany anyone wanting to venture out and about and carry the .338 Mag. There are a few grizzlies which make this lake their home…they den just up in the hills. As well…this may sound bizarre and I am not sharing this with the other researchers, because I do not want to scare them. When I got here on one of the supply trips, the kitchen door was smashed in, the cupboard doors were ripped off and many of the perishable supplies were scattered around. It was obviously not the work of a lost hunter and hikers do not venture to this remote region. In addition, there was a very strong pungent animal odor, like that of a bear or fox. But I discounted either of them being the culprit because of the tuffs of hair I found on the door frame…at the very top.”

It took a great deal to shock Jason, considering his days thwarting Los Angeles gun runners and fighting Al Qaeda in North Africa, but this tale might just be the one to raise his heart rate. He looked at Jenewein waiting for a punch line.

Getting none, he said, "You are serious, obviously. Was anything stolen?"

"Not that I know of. It was just the destruction and mess. I brought surveillance equipment on my last supply trip. It is behind you on that shelf. We can install the cameras and get the software up and running on the house computer system before I leave. That should give you a better perspective."

Jenewein had no illusions regarding the illusive creature roaming the hills behind the lodge, but he wasn't about to share his theory with this researcher regardless of how mature and responsible the university claimed he was. He had completed his moral responsibility, one man to another, and that was the extent of his involvement. Spencer would have to deal with the issue on his own terms.

Jenewein was also confident that Spencer would not find any sign of Edgar's dismembered body back in the bush. Edgar had been part of the graduate project whom the advisors felt had been properly vetted, but they were wrong. Once past the mandatory classroom segment of the program and the team was exploring political philosophy; what changes were necessary for America to recapture its world dominance, bring the economy back and stabilize the future. Edgar exhibited an increasing disdain for the direction the project had taken and he had to be eliminated.

Jenewein had knifed him in the plane during a supply trip which Edwin was invited to participate and peruse the facility. He dismembered his body, allowing the wolves and coyotes to scatter the parts throughout the forested area. Whatever they didn't eat would be unidentifiable after nature's decomposition.

The men made their way back to the living room and Jenewein opened four bottles of Colorado winery, Creekside's Chardonnay 2007, cases of which were stacked in the dry storage room. Creekside's 2007 had a citrusy taste with a hint of melon and pineapple and thought the researchers might enjoy. Jason familiarized himself with the walk-in fridge and prepared several plates of rustic crackers topped with cream cheese and smoked salmon, then joined Jenewein in the living room to arrange the snacks.

The researchers drifted in around the hour mark, grabbed a glass of wine and a plate of appies and sat around the various occasional chairs and couches. Jenewein jumped right into the subject of the lodge's intricacies including Jason's role regarding firearms. Neither Jason nor Jenewein expected a negative reaction from these politically far right grad students and they were not disappointed, quite the contrary, Jason received an applause.

Jenewein's delivery being short, the remainder of the social time was spent with staff wandering around the lodge, seeing what was available for their prolonged stay.

The senior researcher was a twenty-five-year old with under graduate degrees in Political Science and Master's Thesis on the Erosion of American Conservativism. He wasted no time in getting the group organized for their prolonged stay and to begin their work tomorrow. He suggested the group organize themselves in teams of two for meal preparation. Jason had already started to feel comfortable in the kitchen with the appetizer preparations so he volunteered to do dinner with the help of Sandra, a twenty-five-year old from Costa Mesa, California; the nucleus of California's conservative Orange County and its high end real estate.

Meal prep for eleven isn't much different than for one Jason felt, so they butterflied chicken breasts, thawed in the microwave, then stuffed them with a mixture of feta cheese, sun dried tomatoes, oregano, basil, pepper and served them baked with a tossed green salad and slices of warm focaccia buns.

During the preparation, Jason chatted with Sandra. He had weathered the extreme political philosophy of the group through the numerous classroom discussions and pub debates, but it was this one-on-one that both enlightening and alarming.

Sandra shared some of her family history; how she grew up in a very conservative community with political views so right wing as to make Rush Limbaugh, Glenn Beck and Ann Coulter middle of the road pundits. "I remember as a little girl overhearing my daddy and his friends talkin' on the back porch over beers during the last election campaign of George W. and my daddy saying that someone should just put a bullet in Gore and be done with it. I was really shocked and scared that my daddy and his friends, men I had known since as far back as I could remember, would want to be violent."

"Did you notice any more depth to their political philosophy as you were growing up?"

"Oh sure. I was pretty turned on by politics anyway, and all during high school and college my daddy would coach me on how to win the various debates at school. He said that the Florida decision which won Mr. George W. the presidency in 2004 was a disgrace and that many republicans were too ignorant or too lazy to vote and that had to change. He said that Mr. George would have lost the election had it been decided by popular vote since Mr. Gore received 543 thousand more votes than Mr. G. Mr. G. received 271 and Mr. G. 266 electoral votes. It was very close.

"Since then my daddy and his friends have been committed to taking back the country. They were very angry when Barack Obama won two elections. They didn't have anything nice to say about that man, calling him a traitor to America, that he wasn't even born in the United States and that he was a Muslim, not a God-fearing Christian like everybody should be."

Jason was speechless and chose to take the buns out of the oven and put the chicken breasts and salad on platters then called everyone to dinner, rather than respond. The conversation, did however, cement his resolve to stop the Citizens for a Better America in whatever manner necessary. He knew her Dad was William Shepherd, the guy whom Jackson helped take down in the Idaho mountains and Shepherd was deeply involved in whatever the plot might be.

After dinner, Jenewein and Spencer installed the outdoor, wireless security cameras in strategic locations around the compound and along the various bush trails, uploaded the software on the main computer frame, verified they were all recording, then headed for bed.

Spencer was quite taken aback by his accommodations, actually by all the bedrooms considering the lodge's remoteness, but when he stopped to acknowledge the project's massive funding, the opulence was not out of character.

His room fit the lodge's theme and was befitting the Ritz-Carlson in Aspen or the Park Hyatt in Toronto. Being on the second floor it hosted French Doors leading to a spacious balcony, overlooking the lake. The six hundred square foot room had a corner gas fireplace with stone wall inlay on either side. The walk-in closet joined a marbled bathroom with a four-person shower featuring numerous water jets and overhead rain shower heads.

Jason questioned how this facility could exist in such a remote location, then remembered Jenewein mentioning the various out-buildings which undoubtedly housed the heating and water plant and with Jenewein being here so frequently there was little chance of equipment failure.

He showered, relishing in the luxury for which CFBA was paying and that thought alone seemed to create a greater enjoyment. Rather than slipping on the terry-cloth robe which was hanging in the closet, he walked naked to the bed, pulled the sheets down and crawled in.

Normally sleep came quickly to Spencer but this night with Sandra's conversation weighing on his mind and the chemical experiments beginning tomorrow, sleep was elusive. He forced his mind to move from the present and slip back to the first months after his arrival at the university. He had been socializing with several grad students at an off-campus pub when he excused himself and headed to the restroom for much bladder relief. As he entered the Men's Room he was pushed from behind by a fellow student…Colleen.

He considered himself a strong practitioner of the Color Code of Awareness, but tonight, either the camaraderie, the beer or a combination, got the better of him and before he could respond…action being faster than reaction…she had pushed him into the men's room, removed her blouse and shoved him into a cubicle. What followed was probably the hottest and quickest sex that he could remember. He was recalling the joys of that evening as he tried to fall asleep. As a calmness enveloped him, he drifted off, no longer evaluating the stash of chemicals awaiting him in the morning, but relishing in the firmness and speed of Colleen's body.

As Jason drifted into his erotic dreamland, the lodge's exterior cameras were processing their first visions of the intruder Jenewein had mentioned, all being recorded on the computer's main frame.

"He is safe from danger who is on guard even when safe."

Publilius Syrus (85-43 BC)
Syrus is known for his Sententiae, moral maxims. He was a Syrian slave brought to Italy and eventually freed and educated by his master.

30,000

Martha Sarkowski had left the hospital calmly as she would after any other shift with no one paying attention to her withdrawal. She made her way to the staff parking lot, quietly entered her vehicle and left the grounds.

She knew it was only a matter of an hour or so before the hospital administration would be looking for her, calling her cell and home phone. How far behind these enquiries were the police she had no idea, but figured it was close, if not simultaneously. Calling her husband Joe or Harold was out of the question since tracing her calls would be the first thing the cops would do. She figured she had completed her task by killing the guy, whomever he was, as directed by the cell text and now she had to disappear.

She drove to an industrial complex on the outskirts of StoneHead to a small warehouse the church used to store seasonal equipment such as that used for Christmas plays etc. She quickly drove in, closed the garage door, wiped down the car for any prints, grabbed her handbag and left in the nondescript faded green '94 Chev pick-up hidden there if escape became necessary, then headed for the safe house in Sheridan, three hours east. The house was registered in the name of a CFBA member in Florida with no trace to the church, Joe, Harold or herself. She would be safe there with all the living supplies she would need.

As Sarkowski traveled, Fukishura had obtained a license plate number and physical description from the Wyoming Department of Motor

Vehicles and relayed that to Bruce and had him call up a Predator Drone, four of which were hangered at the Ranch. The Secret Service's Predator system included four aircraft, one ground control system housed in the Ranch House's main security complex along with a Trojan Spirit II data distribution terminal. Their Predators are 8 meters in length with a 15-meter wingspan, operating at an altitude of 8 kilometers with a range of 740 kilometers.

Sarkowski had been followed after the first ten minutes and Bruce was monitoring her progress East.

Fukishura had taken custody of Thiessen and had him transferred via ambulance to StoneHead Ranch, accompanied by two guards. Once back at the Ranch, she updated Sorento who advised her it was time to bring in the Sheriff and the StoneHead Police Chief. He reminded her of her lack of interpersonal skills and that to piss these two guys off would have catastrophic repercussions, not only for the Secret Service but President Bakus…and her.

Chapter Thirty-One

The first two days of meetings at the Fairmont Airport Hotel in Vancouver were uneventful in that each delegate put forth the crisis their country was experiencing and highlighted threats by various terrorist groups, individual ISIS or Al Qaeda operatives which were suspected of being within their borders. Each outlined what their respective country had done to stem the tide of refugees, noting that hundreds of suspected insurgents had slipped in with the legitimate displaced persons. Collectively, they needed information on the who, what, where and when of people moving from the Middle East and North Africa. Currently they were operating blind with huge camps of men; lingering, bored and becoming more agitated by the day, with no movement toward being accepted. They could not process any refugees without background information and that was what they were seeking today…how to obtain valid data.

Every delegate had been given, and taken, the opportunity to participate and deliver her/his contribution…all but one.

Cheryl Chapman was basically invisible, always wearing indistinct outfits that blended with the basic black of her male delegates. She entered the conference room after the meeting was called to order and slipped out unnoticed at each break.

Few knew her real persona, save her SEAL colleagues. Not Mr. Bakus, not former teachers, classmates or professors. Some may say she had bi-polar disorder, but they would be in the minority and certainly not in the position to offer insight. What no one knew was that unlike those who suffer from Bi-Polar with the uncontrolled mood swings from depression to mania, Chapman controlled her emotions, until she exploded with vicious physical destruction. While attending a course, in of all things, Understanding and Preventing Sexual Harassment, at the Naval Academy at Annapolis, Maryland she encountered a Second Lieutenant, who had very little interest in the course and chose to make unwanted advances, sexual innuendos and other inappropriate comments. At one point, she had left the classroom and entered a stairwell, destined for the second floor when the aggressive male midshipman rushed her from behind, pushing her up against the bulkhead (wall) and began groping her, running his hand up and down her bare leg. Expecting Chapman to respond as most women would with aggression to escape, he met a very calm female who quietly encouraged him, whispering in his ear that his touch was enjoyable. The encounter and her response was very short, ended very abruptly when she grabbed his right hand with her left, placing her thumb on the back of his hand, then swiftly reaching around with her right hand to join her left, pressured down and turned his wrist counter clockwise, while simultaneously pivoting on her left foot, swinging him over her right hip. The startled lieutenant fell backwards, his right arm controlled by Chapman who proceeded to kick him in the ribs then stomped on his groin causing severe damage to his testicles and surrounding area. Then she jammed her left soft leather, military-inspired, cap-toe Steve Madden Troopa boot, into his carotid artery and held it there until he passed out.

Not satisfied that she had inflicted sufficient damage to her assailant, she withdrew her 5" Spyderco stainless steel blade, flipped it open one handed and sliced open his right pant leg from ankle to crotch, across the zipper and down the left leg, cut off his underwear and deftly carved, *NO* on his abdomen. While replacing her knife into her waistband, she placed an anonymous call to a female reporter with the local affiliate, leaving a message of her assailant's location.

No one knew Chapman.

This afternoon she sat near the back, wearing a bright orange Akris punto ribbed silk Aline dress with a pair of stunning purple Fendi shoes matching her coat perfectly. The coat, which lay across the chair next to her, was a Fendi cape; wool-felt, bright orange with violet color-blocking. She had seen Kerry Washington in the outfit on a recent episode of Scandal, dropped into Saks in New York and bought everything immediately. The ensemble set her back over $2,000 but what else was she going to spend her money on? As a Navy Captain, she made over $10,000 a month, her apartment and utilities were paid for as were all her expenses while traveling for the president…and when was she not? She had been in New York, meeting with both the FBI and the New York Police

Commissioner, slipped out of a meeting for a quick bite and returned with a jaw dropping outfit. She was making so much money that during a recent meeting with the president, she candidly dropped a hint that she could use a financial adviser. Without skipping a beat or asking any questions, Bakus picked up his phone, asked for a private line, punched in a memorized number, waited for a moment then said, "Terry, John Bakus. I am doing well, and you? Great to hear. Terry, I have a colleague in need of your expertise. She is a highly-classified staff member whom I would like you to meet as soon as you can. Whenever you can make it. Right now, would be terrific. How about doing lunch here first, then I will leave you and Ms. Chapman alone to work out a program. Okay, see you in a few."

And that was it. The president's personal financial advisor arrived within thirty minutes and the three had another exceptional meal in his private dining room chatting about every day social activities. An hour later Mr. Bakus excused himself leaving Chapman and her new financial advisor alone to map out an investment program for her eventual retirement…which she found too frightening to even vaguely consider.

But today was now and she was the last on the agenda and quickly made her way to the podium after her name, as a delegate from the United States, was called.

Every head turned to watch her rhythmically move her six foot, one-hundred-and-fifty-pound muscled frame toward her debut. Every male and female stared, not knowing what to expect, not knowing who she was, what role she played in American security particularly in such a stunning outfit. The conference room being intimate, her journey was short. Delegates saw a thirty something female carry herself like the Naval Captain she was, running one hand through her short, curly, brunette coiffure, while carrying a folder emblazoned with the seal of the President of the United States in the other.

Chapman was a SEAL, Sea, Air and Land, the Navy's special operations force. The United States Navy did not have female SEALs. That was the rule, not policy, the rule. No women. The service offered a litany of reasons to the media; women are too weak…too sensitive. And yet Chapman was a decorated Navy SEAL along with several platoons of other accomplished, strong, insensitive female sailors who were trained secretly, thousands of miles from the male SEAL's training center in California. The Big Boogy National Wildlife Refuge, six hours southwest of Houston, Texas, is home to thousands of migratory birds; geese, ducks and brown pelicans, in a 4,500-square mile marshland that opens to the Gulf of Mexico. The refuge is closed to the public and basically closed to the U.S. Fish and Wildlife staff too because the SEAL compound is in the most isolated and remote section, which Fish and Wildlife employees were too glad to ignore.

Code named, Jarc, for Joan of Arc who led French troops into battle against the English, the SEAL teams are housed in an abandoned farm house and outbuildings just east of The Boogy where their firearms, intelligence, counterterrorism and martial arts training are conducted covertly.

Jarc was the back-up team to SEAL Team Six which took out Osama bin Laden. The coalition forces created an interesting diversion for Jarc. The team was aboard the Canadian Destroyer Athabaskan patrolling the Gulf of Oman as their normal duty. The team had been choppered aboard the ship during the desert blackness. Team members' faces were covered as they boarded the ship then were housed in separate quarters for the attack's duration.

When one of Team Six's choppers went down, Jarc was mustered and airborne immediately, heading to Islamabad for a rescue. Team Six regrouped and escaped with bin Laden's body, so Jarc returned to the ship to await their stand-down orders, which came 24 hours later.

Chapman had risen through the ranks, rejected all the Navy's attempts to promote her to management and fought fiercely to maintain her qualifications, year after year. But age and time were biting at her heels. She just couldn't outrun her gerascophobia and had to face her aging.

President Bakus had come across the code name Jarc shortly after taking office during one of his daily briefings. His quiet enquiries resulted in a visit from the Joint Chief of Staff who told Bakus the classified program was started by Ronald Reagan as a black ops organization. Jarc was basically a presidential hit squad which responded covertly to international hot spots. There wasn't a congressional overseeing committee, military involvement or White House scrutineer for the illegal activity. Mr. Reagan had tired of seeing thousands of innocents being wiped out while the world wrung their collective hands and did nothing. Many believe the United Nations has a peace keeping function while in fact its mandate is to monitor, observe and report, not police. American tax-payers pony up three billion yearly, twenty-eight percent of the total UN budget and must watch as millions of fellow humans are slaughtered while the UN does nothing. Mr. Reagan changed that.

Bakus tried to convinced Chapman that now was the time for a career change, but she had no desire to leave Jarc. His pitch convinced her when he discussed the particulars of his offer; "The need for a kick-ass, no bullshit female military officer to take control of the country's failing law enforcement bureaucracy. I want a woman for this job because females have a propensity to accomplish difficult tasks without requiring accolades and they are not motivated by egos."

What Bakus had done with considerable research and a hasty meeting with Chapman, was create a Counter Terrorism Czar who was answerable only to him through a private encrypted phone line.

Today, her assignment was to deliver President Bakus' message, perform a Q & A and leave all delegates with the knowledge that the United States is cooperating one hundred percent with all American law enforcement agencies and those from member countries.

"Thank you for the invitation to make this presentation to this Counter Terrorism symposium. I am Cheryl Chapman, a United States Navy Captain, here on direct orders from President Bakus.

"Before I begin I wish to take a moment to congratulate Canada's military for recognizing women in combat since 1989 and for promoting Colonel Jennie Carignan to General, Chief of Staff, for the Canadian Army," she nodded to the Canadian delegate with a broad smile.

"Carignan has successfully led troops in Bosnia, Afghanistan and various other Middle East conflicts. It is with sincere honor that her government acknowledges her leadership skills with this promotion.

"I am a combat Naval Officer and although the U.S. officially recognized women in combat in 2016, I have been leading platoons for years, have had many encounters, developed and executed hundreds of missions against Al Qaeda, ISIS and other insurgents throughout the world.

"The United States has been negligent in sharing intelligence between agencies for as far back as before J. Edgar Hoover. There has always been a turf war between agencies; it is often a county sheriff who won't cooperate with a state agency, another county or a local police department or one city refusing to share with another jurisdiction. On the national level, it is worse. After 9/11 and the development of the umbrella agency, Homeland Security, law enforcers were led to believe that sharing information was going to be the norm, but the exact opposite occurred. Homeland became the keeper of data and shared only when, and to whom they wanted and that created confusion and distrust with millions of federal dollars wasted.

"Washington was convinced squirreling information and spending billions on foreign aid was the answer. It has directed huge sums of money to Iraq, Afghanistan and every other Middle Eastern country trying to calm the area, guarantee oil flow and bring democracy to the region. All of this has failed. The president was given the following figures for the past year. I direct your attention to the power-point screens on each of the three forward walls," as she clicked on the first data. "Israel: $3.1 billion, Egypt: $1.5 billion, Afghanistan: $1.1 billion, Jordan: $1.0 billion and Pakistan: $933 million. Africa and the Middle East receive twenty percent each of America's foreign aid and although foreign aid is less than one percent of the four trillion- dollar budget, we are giving away borrowed money and our current national debit stands just under twenty trillion dollars.

"For its foreign aid, America has bred terrorism. Last year there were 11,800 terrorist attacks world-wide, killing 30,000 people and injuring thousands more. Refugees are fleeing persecution in North Africa, Syria, Iraq and other countries overrun by ISIS. Numerous African nations have been suffering from ethnic cleansing for decades and currently we are seeing the tragedy of the terror group Boco Haram and Al-Qaeda in Niger.

"The thousands of undocumented refugees swarming the European Union, point to the disruption of a social order in the Middle East and America has to take responsibility for much of the disorder. One year we backed rebels in one country then find they are terrorists and backed the take-over power. But our ignorant interference has left high tech weapons in the hands of rebels. We walked away from Iraq leaving millions in weaponry and transportation. We couldn't even take out Osama bin Laden quickly because of botched intelligence and Washington's incompetence."

This last statement drew raised eyebrows from most delegates wondering where this speech was headed and why she was castigating her own government.

"Mr. George W. Bush acknowledged that he was misled on the existence of Weapons of Mass Destruction. Hussein was toppled and his absence was the nucleus of the Islamic State of Iraq and al-Sham, ISIS. America backed Iraq in their war with Iran so when the time came, Iran retaliated with their nuclear arms buildup. The Iranians compensated by the West's fear and ended up with a nuclear deal which gave them billions of American dollars which jump started their oil industry.

"We have killed innocents throughout the Middle East with drone strikes and/or villagers suspected of being terrorists or sympathizers. We have joined the low life we profess as our enemy and we learned absolutely nothing from our Vietnam debacle. It is my job to create a climate in which the EU, the United States, Canada and the other Commonwealth countries share all intelligence and work at eliminating the terrorist threat without being the war criminals we purport to detest and without weighing the benefits to their country. If Canada had trusted other countries it may have shared its refugee vetting process, whereby they approved 25,000 new residents within a few months. The rest of us didn't do that and look at our current situation. It is my job to convince the Canadians and the rest of you here today that America has changed and I am the ambassador of that change.

"You know of the National Security Agency's data base in Utah. It is a massive data gathering facility which collects all communications, everywhere; every key stroke, every cell call and every internet search. Those wishing to do us harm know this too and have reverted to world war two communications systems…one on one physical interaction, making the billion-dollar facility somewhat redundant.

Superfluous or not, the facility is not readily open to all agencies. When an agency can obtain a search warrant and tap a phone, the data is often a smoke screen because the homegrown insurgents create their attack plans without electronic communications. History taught Mr. Bakus that to ask any agency to solve the problem would be in vain, so he has used his Executive Privilege, created a national data base which links Utah with every law enforcement agency in the country," she paused for effect, then said, "Automatically. Agencies no longer must be processed to utilize the system. As with any surveillance, a court order is still required but once that is obtained the rest is simply electronic. This system is far superior to anything we have had previously, including the FBI's noted N-DEx which they boast is, 'A mechanism for sharing'. All American law enforcement know that term is a euphemism for, "We share what we want."

"Canada has Integrated Information Service, IIS, which links various databases allowing queries from multiple sources. No disrespect to the RCMP but this plan is riddled with bureaucracy; many data bases leaves it prone to confusion, as in; Where is the data I want? The originator of the data can classify it as *Restricted,* which defeats the entire process and keeps Canadian investigators in the dark, basically taking them back ten years of protected turf wars.

"Canada's attempt to prosecute the Air India Bombing suspects took twenty-years at a cost of one-hundred and thirty million dollars with zero convictions. Part of that debacle was the result of the tur war, the inability to work together between CSIS and the RCMP.

"I offer kudos to the Vancouver Police Department for supporting officer Kim Rossmo who began as a civilian, became a sworn officer two years later and gained his masters, then PhD in Criminology. Rossmo's PhD dissertation was on Geographic Profiling and his software contributed in the investigation, arrest and trial of serial killer Robert Pickton in 2002.

"Unfortunately, personality conflicts between Rossmo and his colleagues/superiors prevented Pickton's investigation to be fast paced, allowing the killer time to take more lives.

"Rossmo quit and is now a Criminology Professor at Texas State University. His software program was picked up by Rigel and Professional Geographic Profiling is used by many agencies world-wide.

"Which is my point. Bureaucracy's ugliness interfering constantly.

"An attempt was made with the Five Eyes Alliance program which involves Canada, Australia, New Zealand, England and the US, but as we have seen with the various terrorist attacks in Europe, it is ineffective due to the lack of immediate access by law enforcement and immigration with subversives entering various countries unrestricted, since only a few states track them.

"That is the past. All agencies, and I mean, all, are now connected to the data base I oversee. The system was designed and developed by one firm. There wasn't a bidding process or any chance of companies to compete for the contract. Again, Mr. Bakus used his executive privilege and the system was created with the oversight of a Secret Service Agent whom the president has the utmost faith and respect. She is one of the world's leading computer experts and a quintessential hacker, and I include the Russians and Chinese in that claim. This data base can't be hacked. Don't ask how that is prevented," she said with as stern an expression as she could muster.

"I am not at liberty to reveal its location. Unlike the NSA, the president feels security is mandatory given what he feels is a national information sieve. Interpol is connected to this base so they no longer must ask, they just access. Ditto American agencies connecting with Interpol. Every EU country is connected identically. Your respective governments have been waiting for this meeting to inform you of the process. Upon your return home, all the access procedures are there for you. Right now, I want you to get a quick overview of the data base's entry page and access icons etc. so here they are," as she thumbed the wheel of the mouse attached to the laptop.

She stayed on each page to give delegates a visual of what to expect when they begin accessing the data, then continued, "I have logged in on the site. You know these names from the Paris attacks: Salah Abdeslam, Bilal Hadfi, Ahmad Almohamad, Omar Mostefai, Samy Amimour and Abdelhamid Abaaoud. For us in the west, it is often difficult to get our tongues around these names let alone try and find background information on them. Had your governments, or you personally, had these names and this data base, here is what you would have discovered."

With that she hit enter and a massive data base revealed a long history on each of the terrorists dating back almost a decade of various encounters with the governments of Syria, Iraqi, the United Arab Emirates and Oman. She now had their undivided attention.

“You can undoubtedly tell that the data is extensive, accurate and reliable. The researchers’ efforts are exhaustive, relying not only on data bases and government systems from around the world, but intelligence from agents who formerly worked for the CIA, MI6, CSIS and turned operatives from adversarial countries.

“I suspect you have a slew of questions but please, wait until you return home, access the data base, experiment, then email me with your queries and we will organize conference calls. Thank you for your time. I look forward working with each of you in preparing unified policies to move us all forward in our united fight against terrorism.”

She smiled, bowed slightly at the waist, closed the laptop, disconnected the wiring and prepared to leave the lectern when the conference room erupted in applause. She was taken aback somewhat and at a loss for words as she was swamped with delegates extending their hands wanting to express their appreciation. Coffee and rolls were served and participants gathered in small groups, with Chapman making the social rounds answering as many queries as security allowed. An hour later, she slipped out of the conference room, headed for the hotel’s airport exit, hailed a cab and directed it to the Blue Canoe on Vancouver’s waterfront for a few Jack Daniels, JDs, and their sumptuous pan seared halibut with citrus beurre blanc, a creamy sauce made with butter, onions or shallots, and vinegar or lemon juice, and parmesan.

Chapman sat in the Blue Canoe’s lounge waiting for her table, sipping a fresh Jack Daniels, enjoying the quiet ambiance of the waterfront when she faintly heard the newscast on the platinum screen across the room, overhead at the bar. Picking up her drink, she meandered toward the commotion, then stood to listen.

“We are rebroadcasting this newscast from earlier in the year because of the strangeness of the incident. The National Criminal Investigation Service, NCIS, has not found any evidence pointing to a suspect, the alleged victim refuses to discuss the attack on advice from his attorney at the Judge Advocate General’s Corps. There haven’t been any assault reports filed with local police. And although there have been several assault victims admitted to various hospitals, both male and female, none occurred at the academy. Here is the original broadcast.”

"We are here at the Naval Academy covering an assault which is not an assault, but in this reporter's opinion, retribution. The unidentified Second Lieutenant has been taken to the hospital for observation but First Responders noted that he was unconscious when they arrived, his pants and underwear were cut off and the word, *No*, was carved into his abdomen above his genitals. NCIS is on the scene but are not providing this reporter with any information, sighting the event is, *An on-going investigation."*

"It would appear from this journalist's perspective that this man is not a victim but an assailant who received an unwelcome response to his attack. More news at seven."

Chapman smiled to herself, raised her JD glass toward the screen, took a deep swallow and thought, *one down and thousands to go.*

"The first anticrime bill was called the Ten Commandments."

Irv Kupcinet (1912-2002)

'Kup' was a Chicago Sun-Times columnist, television talk-show host and radio-personality.

Chapter Thirty-Two

Rebecca and Pen felt the night closing in on them, either the witching hour was fast approaching, they enjoyed too much chardonnay or a delightful combination of both, but by ten o'clock they were beat. They paid their bill, leaving a healthy tip for their server and bus boy, gave each a hug and a cheek kiss, enjoyed their embarrassment, then headed back to the Four Seasons in the waiting cab, thanks to the generosity of the maître d'.

Entering the lavish hotel lobby and on the ride to their floor, they were giggling, laughing and swaying considerably, drawing smiles of approval from the other late arrivals. Once in their room, they stripped at the door, walked to the floor to ceiling windows in their underwear, refilled their wine glasses and stood, arm in arm, gazing at the spectacular Denver light show. The chardonnay savored, they crawled into bed, Pen in her underwear, sans bra and Rebecca naked, although it was doubtful Penelope noticed, and slept a soundness they hadn't expected nor enjoyed for some time.

Morning arrived…slow and delectable with the sun streaking across their calm demeanor, wakening them almost simultaneously. Rebecca was the first to extricate herself from the bed's coziness and strutted across the immense expanse, totally oblivious of her nakedness, Pen's presence or the wide-open spaces beyond the gaping windows. On her return from the bathroom she was wearing a white Four Season's robe and held one out for Pen who, to Rebecca's surprise and delight, jumped out of bed and stripped off her underwear and sashayed up to the robe, slipped her arms into it as Rebecca held it open, then tied the belt.

Pen continued the sexual charade over to the phone and ordered a large pot of coffee to be delivered immediately, then approached Rebecca and gave her a sensual hug, running her hands up and down her back, then moved to the windows that had brought them such delight yesterday, and stared out at the morning sun that seemed to caress Denver's five thousand-foot mountain bastion.

Rebecca joined her, slipped her arm around Pen's waist and enjoyed the lingering moment, for what seemed an eternity…until the knock at the door. Pen was first to break the spell, spinning away from Rebecca and dancing to the door and greeting the bus boy, the same fellow who had brought their bags to the room. Giovanni beamed with both embarrassment and the joy of seeing his beautiful guests in a sensual state of relaxation. He greeted them professionally, placed the tray on the vintage-inspired, geometric antique brass base coffee table with its crystal clear, tempered glass tabletop which was catching the glitter of the morning rays, then handed the bill to Penelope for her signature. She complied, adding a twenty-five percent tip, then reached up and kissed his cheek, creating a back-peddling from Giovanni until he managed to exit the room with his embarrassment somewhat under control.

"Pen, you are shameless, kissing the servers twice in less than twelve hours," Rebecca said as she offered and received a high five from Pen and laughter, a levity that seemed to be consuming them on this mini-vacation.

They sat in the matching classic, luxurious club chairs, allowing the sumptuousness of the genuine brown leather, rolled arms, and an elegant nail head trim to envelop them as they chatted about their anticipated joy for their shopping day and sipped their Kick-Ass dark roast coffee from Kicking Horse Coffee in the Canadian Rockies. They decided they each needed somewhat dressy outfits for their double date with Jackson and Blake but agreed to keep things toned down somewhat, not wanting to take the good folks of StoneHead into the twenty-first century on a roller coaster. Pen said that she had her heart set on a pair of bling jeans and red cowboy boots. Rebecca laughed and retorted that she lived in an outfit somewhat similar so she is looking for a new direction, the details of which she hoped to find at Nordstrom.

Their mood shifted slowly from fashion and shopping to social responsibility and the part women played in creating and maintaining a free flow of humanity.

Pen started the conversation swing with, "Why is it that so many men, regardless of age, have a need to save women? Why is it that they cannot welcome us as equals and develop a relationship based on each person accepting responsibility for the advancement or rejection of the relationship?

"A question for the ages Pen. I have been asking myself, my parents and counselors, since I was in junior high. I understood why teen-age boys would ogle me and the rest of the girls but they always saw us, and still do, as objects, someone to use. That pretty much is the bottom line as to why I have never married or found a significant other in the opposite gender. Every time, and I mean every time I am on a date, I can tell from the lack of interest in an intelligent conversation that the guy is biding his time until the boring dinner or movie or whatever, is over so he can make his play. That is why I cherish our Cassandra time together with the other girls. Am I gay?" she quipped, with a half-hearted giggle.

As she was getting up, creating a natural change of subjects, Pen said, "Maybe we need to find out?" Pen replied, not sure of the thought's origin. She had been so busy since leaving veterinarian school building her business that she hadn't time for dating, or at least that is what she told herself. *How then did she find time for socializing several times a week with Rebecca and the hours at Cassandras with their female nurse and educator friends,* she thought.

Rebecca swiveled in her chair, turning to watch Pen walk toward her suitcase and just as she began opening the Tumi Tegra-red packing case, Pen turned, giving Rebecca a warm, welcoming smile that tingled throughout Rebecca's tranquil being, from her ears, through her groin, to her toes.

Coffeed and anxious for the day, they headed for the shower and without giving it a thought, dropped their robes simultaneously and entered the massive shower with rain-heads. Seemingly unware of the others presence, they lathered and rinsed their hair, bodies, then luxuriated in the gentleness of the rain-heads, neither realizing each was enjoying the contours of the female form next to them.

Leaving the one hundred square foot shower, Rebecca turned to Penelope, and without a thought process, slid her hands over Pen's breasts, following the curves, across her rear end and down her legs, then asked, "Bikini or one piece. Which do you think?"

Pen, without missing a beat in the conversation replied, "How about neither?" offering Rebecca a quirky smirk in response, and consciously coming to recognize and accept her physical attraction to Rebecca.

Rebecca caught the obvious innuendo but didn't trust herself to follow through…at this moment, so suggested, clearing her throat, "Well, that too, but I meant around the pool this afternoon."

Penelope shook off her reverie, cleared her throat of its emotional tightness and said, "Oh, well, in that case, if you are showing off that body, I would suggest a black bikini, but not too brief, we do not want to create an emotional wave we cannot contain."

Penelope's passion suddenly became overwhelming. Allowing spontaneity to take over, she moved close to Rebecca, overwhelmed by her scent, she brushed her palms across Rebecca's breasts, down her side, allowing the back of her hand to glance just above her smooth pubic area, then reached up, cupped Rebecca's face in her hands and kissed her.

There was no hesitation from Rebecca who moved in to make full body contact with Pen's bare torso, returned the kiss and ran her palms across Pen's rear end, then up and down her back.

Breaking the kiss, Pen felt moisture trickle down her leg as her arousal gained momentum. Knowing she had to put the brake on, if only temporary, with her heart racing said, "Should we get dressed and ready to go?" Staring at Rebecca's breasts, she came to the realization that a man's hairy chest just didn't do anything for her, while savoring Rebecca's chest was overwhelmingly licentious.

"Sounds like a plan, unless you want to skip breakfast and continue this," Rebecca replied with a lecherous grin.

"Let's savor the newness and come back to it tonight," Pen replied, knowing that was not really what she wanted.

Rebecca gave Pen another kiss, allowing her pubic area to brush against Pen's, holding it there while running her hands through Pen's hair, then turned and walked to her Baigio leather duffle suitcase, offering Pen yet another view of her taunt rear-end and muscular legs.

Penelope, scrutinizing Rebecca's exquisite body, went to her suitcase and as the two were putting on their underwear, Rebecca withdrew a Seacamp stainless steel .380 semi-automatic pistol, then a loaded clip, slipped the clip into the pistol, racked a round into the chamber, then strapped on an elastic holster around her waist and put the loaded handgun into the front slot and finished dressing.

"That is a very sweet looking gun. Very tiny. How did you get it through security?" asked Penelope, seemingly relaxed as her hormones retreated.

"Remember I encouraged us to check our luggage rather than struggle with the overhead? On domestic flights, the checked luggage is not x-rayed, so it sailed right through. I love this little .380 because it is effective…up close, and personal."

"I have never been afraid of guns, just never had an opinion at all, but now I want to learn more about them. Will you go with me to the gun range and once I am qualified, help me find a suitable handgun?"

"I would love to!"

They continued to dress, dry and fluff their hair…neither used spray or gel…a little eyeliner, grabbed their coats and headed down to the Four Season's Edge restaurant for breakfast. Entering the Edge, they passed the lounge and bar on their right. Immediately before entering the dining area, there was an eye catching, intricate, seven-foot, woven, stainless steel art work. Admiring the piece, they entered the Edge. Having their choice of seats at 6:30 am, they chose a window banquette giving them a perfect view of Arapahoe St. for people watching. Their female server was pleasant, but she was not Janis from the Bread Basket and that was okay with Rebecca and Pen knowing city folks were more formal. They each ordered the Edge Dark Roast coffee, scrambled egg whites, heirloom tomatoes with charred onions, broccoli and fingerling potatoes, then sat back and beamed at each other, Rebecca thinking that she has not been this happy for as far back as she can remember, and hoped Pen thought the same. Reading Rebecca's expression, Penelope reached out and took Rebecca's hand and said, "I cannot believe how happy I am right now. This is all new for me and it is interesting that it doesn't scare me. It is as though this is what a relationship is supposed to be. I cannot wait to ravish your body tonight," she said quietly while circling her lips with her tongue.

Rebecca responded with a broad smile, "Me too." She was going to add her own erotic comment but was interrupted by their server bringing coffee.

They enjoyed the Black while watching and commenting on various groups waiting at the corner, then boarding the busses. The two mused about each passenger's excursion, whether they were travelling for pleasure or work and what each might do for a living. When they noted two women travelling together they commented on whether they were a couple and if they were happy.

Momentarily, their server arrived with breakfast and the morning's Denver Advocate. As the plates were set in front of them, Rebecca opened the paper to the ads and quickly found several for Nordstrom. She handed one to Pen and they scanned the sales, enjoyed their meal while scoping out what outfits they would try on.

Their shopping excitement combined with their euphoria, rushed them through the egg white combination, the last of the coffee and they were out the door and headed to the concierge desk for a cab in under an hour.

"For me, growing up, even though I think I had inklings and glimmerings that I was a lesbian, the much bigger issue for me was being a woman."

Gloria Steinem

Feminist, journalist, political and social activist

"I was not gay before I met her. I never thought about it. Nobody could have been more confused than me. I think that in love, there is just love, and that is what I feel."

Anne Heche

Actress, director and screenwriter

Chapter Thirty-Three

Winthrop and Hortonn had endured the entire conference gleaning little, if anything new...until Chapman's presentation. However, the breaks were a cornucopia of information. During the down time, they networked with members of the RCMP Integrated National Security Enforcement Team and David Kopas with CSIS, as well as agents from participating countries.

They chatted about the Charlie Hebdo killings in Paris, the Freeman of the Land movement, the group which feels they are not subject to Canadian or American laws and of course the attack on Parliament Hill and Sergeant at Arms Kevin Vickers, now Ambassador to Ireland. Everyone in the group wished he had been invited to this symposium and in his absence, raised their coffee cups to him and his heroic act of shooting the gunman before the terrorist could get to Members of Parliament. Tom suggested they repeat the honor with a beer after the convention and Hortonn received a quiet round of cheers.

There was mention of Saudi Arabia being involved in the Twin Towers tragedy of 9/11 and the home-grown terrorists who become radicalized on the internet. The self described Islamic Soldier of Orlando, Florida who took forty-nine lives and injured many others was on everyone's minds. The discussion avoided the act itself, but centered on what led to the violence and what could have been done to prevent the tragedy.

Kopas weighed in with how Canada identifies these rogue shooters, then isolates them with surveillance. "The problem in Canada, America and probably your countries too, is the huge number of these insurgents and our limited LEO-power. The RCMP has taken Members off other duties to cover this increase, but of course that leaves their former duty vulnerable.

"We have found tremendous success in the use of Stingrays, which we use to mimic cellphone towers and dupe into connecting with us, not the intended tower. Do any of your agencies use them?" Several heads nodded with a bit of a smirk indicating to Kopas that they experienced success as well. "Once connected we have the caller's location, data, texts, emails and voice conversations. I personally love the system but civil rights groups are clamoring for clarification on whom they are being used and the lack of regulations. You can imagine we are staying well away from the discussion."

Winthrop provided the RCMP position, "We have been using them for years, particularly in our major crime units and organized crime investigations. Very successfully I might add. The oversight and regulation of this data collection is handled by our Covert Intercept Unit."

After the conference delegates drifted away, each with their own interpretation of events, they were mulling over the magnitude of Chapman's information and anxious to access the data base.

Winthrop and Hortonn were finding Chapman's revelation difficult to comprehend and knew it would take some time and commiseration to put it into perspective, but that was for the morning, tonight was theirs and it was going to be spent at Araxi Restaurant and Oyster Bar in Whistler Village. As they left the conference room, Karen called the concierge requesting a taxi, "Yes sir, I know it will be expensive and that is okay."

"How much is this going to cost you?" Tom quipped, holding back a grin.

"$350" was her reply, then added, "Do you want to go Dutch?" giving him a kiss as they almost danced down the hall.

They were unaware of Whistler's reputation for weekend rowdiness or that the RCMP had additional officers sequestered from other detachments to control the out of town drinkers and stem the tide of vandalism. They were also not cognizant of a white van with three passengers and one stainless steel container in the process of transferring its cargo to another van in southern Alberta.

Chapter Thirty-Four

Fukishura had two suspects in federal custody with little proof of their involvement in the CFBA. She had no problem having them prosecuted for drug trafficking and violating their national security classification but those charges would be tertiary. What she needed was a hook, someone or something to tie these two suspects together and with the CFBA movement.

She had Sarkowski under surveillance in Sheridan by federal agents and she knew where the nurse lived and all about her husband. A property search revealed a Ms. Kathy Dasovich and her son Gerard living next to the Sarkowskis for five years. Dasovich had a Wyoming drivers' license for twenty years, had lived in Cheyenne prior to StoneHead and was unmarried and not employed. Having to obtain information on the family, their daily activities etc. she assigned a field agent to surveillance.

Sorento's admonishment fresh on her mind, she moved on to another task and googled the sheriff. She saw that he appeared to be in his early to mid-thirties, dark short hair, long slender face with a narrow chin and a nose in the middle of his face…she scoffed at her slight humor, knowing that seeing his photo gave her absolutely nothing useful and that she was procrastinating. She took a deep breath and placed the call. She was unprepared for an immediate answer from the Sheriff himself, not realizing Bruce, who commands the entire Ranch communications system, had given her a direct connection.

"Good morning Sheriff Williams, this is Jessica Fukishura, Special Agent at the StoneHead Ranch."

Before she could continue, Williams responded with, "Agent Fukishura, I was wondering when you would call. I have a ton of questions about a recent skirmish up in the hills at a nearby farm."

"Yes, Sheriff, that is what I am calling about. I have wanted to discuss the incident with you. The White House has directed me to do so now."

"Understandable. I suspected your agency was somehow involved. You wanna meet here or at the Ranch?"

"How about a neutral location? The Bread Basket? Noon?"

She instinctively knew not to trust the Sheriff's office for not being video-taped during their chat and she knew Williams felt likewise about the Secret Service and the Western White House.

"How can I pass up a free meal from the federal government? Noon today it is."

"Sounds good. See you then," Jessica replied, then placed the receiver back in its cradle and blew a huge sigh of relief. Here goes nothing, she thought. Given the direct orders from Sorento, she wished she could have sent Spencer or Elisabeth since they have more interpersonal skills than I do.

Pulling her Sig from its shoulder holster, she removed the magazine, slid the action back a fraction checking for a cartridge, then replaced the magazine. In one smooth motion, she brought the weapon to her nose, rubbed the barrel against her face, closing her eyes, taking in the aroma of the gun oil, then slid it into its holster under her right arm pit. The simple movement which she has performed hundreds of times, never fails to quiet her nerves and center her thinking.

Grabbing her burnt orange Jaipur Atelier Grand Foulard shawl, from their Los Angeles collection, she strode down the long hallway which led to the numerous bedrooms and stood in front of a full-length mirror. Her white Theory Alldrew baggy pants, basic black T and Aquatalia Yulia snake print Chelsea boots seemed to satisfy her as she did her 360, spinning on one toe. Smiling, she dawned a Eugenia Kim, plum-wool-felt, floppy fedora with braided fur and chain trim that hid all but a few tuffs of her short black coiffeur and headed for the front door.

Bruce had called the detail and had her Gecko Bug brought around to the front door. As she passed the security office, Bruce stepped out and handed her a brown leather duffle and said with a grin, "It matches your outfit," then turned back to the office. Leaving the Ranch's main entrance, she felt satisfied she was putting her best forward.

She arrived at the Bread Basket a little before noon and took a parking spot well away from the main entrance. Exiting the Bug, she did her 360, scanning for any pending altercations. Finding none, she headed in and found Williams already seated in a booth somewhat isolated in the back of the restaurant, seated facing the front.

He caught her eye with a smile as she moved gracefully forward, stopped at the booth. She slid next to him, causing him to scoot to his left and giving her a raised eyebrow.

"I don't like my back to the front any more than you do," she explained then said, "Hi!" offering her hand.

Williams laughed and extended his hand in greeting just as Janis arrived with two menus and said, "Mornin" Sheriff and Miss. We must be doin' something right at the Basket, this is twice in one week we have been graced by the company of the Sheriff's department. Blake was here annoying two of my favorite customers the other day and darn it, he didn't stay for my special."

"Always a pleasure Miss Janis and I am sure Blake was just in a rush or he wouldn't have missed out on your buckwheat special. I will have the usual if you would but my friend here may need a menu."

"Hi Janis, I'm Jessica." She extended her hand which Janis accepted. "Great to meet you. I have heard a great deal about the Basket and have been dying to try it. Having this handsome guy join me is just a little whipped cream to my meal."

The sheriff looked as though he had just walked in on a lingerie party as his face reddened, he ran his hand through his short dark hair and looked at the ceiling.

Janis could not restrain her laughter and said, "Darlin, you will fit right in here in StoneHead, even though you are a might overdressed. What can I get you?"

"I don't need the menu either Janis, I noticed some folks are having a Rueben, that looks delicious. I will have one too with fries and a side salad, oil and vinegar dressing please."

"Good choice. You two want a cuppa?" she asked as she placed two large white mugs and began pouring.

Evidently, every customer has coffee.

Fukishura knew she would be overdressed wearing her chosen outfit to a small western town eatery but the attire gave her confidence…in her almost non-existent skill at communicating with men or other law enforcers. She could hear Sorento's words in her ear, *Play nice!*

"Here is what I have to date," as Jessica began, turning to face Williams. He looked at her momentarily, preparing for the worst when his eyes darted to the front door and he burst into a huge grin.

"What?"

Fukishura turned just as two other law enforcers entered; one tall, dark hair and complexion and the other in a brown uniform with a belly and carrying an antiquated .38 revolver hanging from his hip. They strolled to their booth, extending their hands and said, "Scott, nice to see you. And Ma'am, you must be Agent Fukishura. I am Chuck Braket, StoneHead Police Chief and this here is Sheriff Jones from Nez Pearce County. May we join?"

Braket slipped into the booth first, leaving Jones to sit with one butt cheek on the bench as his stomach wouldn't allow him access to the rest of the booth.

Jessica turned to Williams and said, "Your invite?"

"Seemed only natural, you and your team have been operating in StoneHead and we suspect in Sheriff Jones as well. Jeremiah was visiting Chuck on another matter and figured they would get read in too"

"Sounds good by me. I was told to bring one of you into the loop, presuming the others would be read in secondly. Chuck, Sheriff Jones, you having lunch?"

"Yup. Having my usual with a cuppa and Jones here made it two."

"Okay, so this is what has occurred so far," and she rolled off the numerous actions of the "J" Team, her suspects and what little of the on-going operation Sorento allowed her to share.

"I am not being secretive here gentlemen. Washington is handling much of the fall-out from the situation at the farm. I have been told to keep a low profile while the operation is ramped up that we can determine the origin of the explosives, the weed that is being used to finance much of the chemicals and how deeply involved the ecumenical church is in the CFBA."

Sheriff Williams nodded, then said, "The church congregation is very conservative as are most folks around here and they are fundamentalist, but I've never considered them to be the kind to turn to violence and I have never heard them be political.

"What happened at the farm? There was never a complaint filed with either my office or Chucks, we just heard rumors, which you are now confirming."

"One of my agents got invited to a morning worship and that snowballed into an invite to lunch at the farm."

Jones interrupted saying, "Invited by whom?"

"Well, you see…," she hesitated, then carried on. "Elisabeth Peltowski is a substitute computer teacher at the junior high and works for me," she grimaced, adding one more thread to their discomfort.

None of the men spoke but Jones twirled his hand indicating to get on with the story.

"So Peltowski is at the farm and after lunch she and a student of hers, who invited her, suggested they go for a walk. Oh, by the way, the student's father is the pastor." More eyes rolling.

"The two are meandering down a path and come to a barn which appeared to be unused; grass growing in the road and branches hanging over. The girl wanted to see what was in the barn, so they checked it out and that is when Elisabeth found chemicals. A CFBA member confronted her at the barn and my agent made up a story explaining their presence and left.

We thought Elisabeth's information was worthy of a covert inspection so Pennington went to the ranch after dark and took photos of the chemicals. His hooded light was seen from the farm house. Within moments the armed men had him pinned down with Jackson laying silenced rounds, but unable to escape. His 9-1-1 comes to me and I called in the troops.

When we arrived, chaos is in full bloom so the FBI SWAT team and we scatter and drop as many CFBA members as we can without using deadly force. Unfortunately, despite our clearly marked body identification, they chose to shoot at us. The FBI arrested the survivors as well as all those still in the farm house.

The FBI took over the investigation interrogating the leaders at their Twisp, Washington facility and the women and children at Ft. Lewis. When the leaders were transferred to Seattle without giving any information, they lawyered and were eventually released. They are now back at their Orofino facility aware we are onto them. We believe they will advance their action dates."

"Okay, we are getting the big picture. Chuck and I have been chatting about the various activities that have come across our desks figuring your agency is involved. Were you at the Yellowstone Outfitters too?"

"Yes, that was one of my agents. She is working undercover as a horse trainer and…"

"Simpson? She is yours? Son-of-a-bitch!" said Williams. "I knew she was too savvy to be spending her time around horses. I sent Blake here to the Basket to talk to her about her concealed weapon, thinking I could enlist her for our emergency posse. And she is a fuckin' federal agent. Well color me dumped on and a complete ass."

Ignoring his outburst and having no intention of apologizing for Rebecca's expertise, she said, "Simpson was helping the vet, Dr. Penelope out with a couple of stallions which got into it and had several lacerations needing stitching. Simpson saw something suspicious in one of the barns and came back at night, took a sample and the materials are weed and chemicals. One of the wranglers jumped her and she brought him back to the Ranch. We have him and the mole in custody."

"So, Simpson is checking out the barns at night, gets jumped and ends up getting the better of the attack and brings the guy to the Ranch?" asked Williams.

"Yes. And while I am at it and in the faith of full disclosure, I have another agent, Jason Spencer, who has infiltrated the CFBA university in Denver. Right now, he is with a group of grad students researching the chemicals and explosive formulas they plan to use. We suspect the stash in Idaho and outside of StoneHead will be activated once the grads decide…which could be any day.

"Back to what happened here so you know where you stand. The FBI took the outfitters owner, James Watson, into custody and have charged him under the federal statutes for transporting drugs across state lines. They also convinced him to sign over the guide-outfitting business to the government in exchange for a lesser sentence. He pled guilty and has been sentenced to three years which he will serve in Rawlins

Penitentiary here in Wyoming. That was part of the deal too, his home state.

"He claims he doesn't know the overall scheme and was just making money moving the goods. We will find out as our investigation broadens whether he is telling the truth.

"Simpson, for the purposes of our deception, is the proud owner of the Yellowstone Guide Outfitter's operation and is in the process of hiring wranglers, federal agents who were born and raised on ranches. There is a huge quantity of weed which needs to be moved to its next phase. Might one of you find out through your CIs who the buyer is? Then Simpson will get the chemicals to the Idaho location.

"Sounds good. We will work together and get that information to you in the next couple of days," replied Williams.

"One other thing," added Jessica. "When Simpson contacts the CFBA operatives outside of Orofino she will convince them that she can do a better job than Watson and will not be as greedy. She is very convincing, so I am positive that arrangement will be solidified soon. We have been working in the dark but now with your involvement, we should be able to make progress quickly.

"May I chime in here Agent?" asked Jones.

"This CFBA operation extends into Idaho so we are involved whether we want to be or not. Those two on the Orofino mountain top have been on our radar for some time. We thought they were just another group like that Winston Blackmore in British Columbia with his many wives and kids. We never suspected the Orofino guys were involved in domestic terrorism.

"We had a murder a while back on the reservation. Police chief Jorge George was gunned down execution style and we have gotten nowhere with our investigation, but there are rumors that several of the locals are involved in drug smuggling. Any connection, do you think?"

"Could be Sheriff. We know it is weed that is being sold to finance the chemicals. How is the pot getting to the reservation?"

Jones replied, "We have little or no jurisdiction on the reservation as you know. Maybe you could open that up for us and we can find out the source?"

"I can do that."

"Another issue. We suspected we had a mole at the Ranch and the other day one of the ranch hands took off just before dark on the pretense of going to the feed store. The Air Force found him heading East. He wouldn't pull over for the crew so they stopped him with a few rounds, then brought him to the hospital's secure unit. He was recovering when we believe a nurse Sarkowski tried to kill him with an insulin overdose. She too took off but we tracked her to Sheridan and have her being watched by two federal agents. I have her husband Joe under surveillance too but we could use some help with the church. If you guys could see what you have or can get on any of them, particularly the pastor and deacons, I would greatly appreciate the help. I believe the church hierarchy is directly involved in the CFBA and their objectives are heating up.

"On another note, since you may run into him here in StoneHead. Sheriff Jones, do you remember a guy you spoke with at the Saloon restaurant in Lewiston, drove a hot pick-up?"

"I sure do. I thought at the time he was more than he said he was, just a guy coming back from hunting. You're not going to tell me he is one of yours?"

"Yeah, actually he is. Jackson Pennington. He orchestrated the FBI raid on the mountain top and just in case you happen to be chatting with your Coeur D'Alene colleagues, Pennington is the guy who was hassled in the ice rink parking lot and left the officer embarrassed without his weapon and handcuffed to his cruiser. He is working for me, undercover as a teacher at StoneHead High."

"Shit, you guys really get around, don't you?"

Jessica didn't react but was pleasantly surprised that with the one exception, these law enforcers have not used profanity to express themselves. Having associated with male cops for over a decade, this was quite unusual and she could not help but credit the revelation to her attire. Men have a natural inclination to treat women with respect and dignity, whether they learn it from their mothers or the example set by their dads, it seems to be inherently prevalent. It was a nice feeling. She was warming to the experience, creating a calmness which she had never experienced in her career. *Maybe she has been wrong all these years and these men were bringing a light to her character and personality,* she thought. It had yet to dawn on her that her personality change was having more to do with the cooperation than her outfit.

"Jackson was in a precarious position. He was on his way here, had stopped for the night and was coming out of a hockey game when he was approached by the officer. I have no reason to doubt Pennington and his version as the cop had no reason to hassle him. Jackson could not allow the officer to pat him down or, worse, take him in for questioning. There was just something about Jackson's truck that pissed him off. If Jackson had shown him his ID, then his cover would have been blown. We all know how fast the rumor mill travels and he couldn't take the chance."

"I was equally drawn to his vehicle. The engine and beefed suspension, in our county, spoke to drug running from the reservation. I don't know what my esteem northern colleague felt," noted Jones.

Before Jessica could respond, Janis brought over their orders. "Here we go officers and Ms. Jessica. The Rueben for the lady and cheese burgers and fries for the gentlemen…and guys, I do use that word loosely!" she said, scoffing at her own humor.

"Make sure these guys treat you properly Ms. Jessica. They tend to run afoul at the mouth, but hopefully their mammas taught them manners when around women."

With that admonition, she refilled their cuppas, left the bill on the table and headed to other customers. Jessica turned to her colleagues, raised an eyebrow and Williams said, "Janis is a pistol but one of the nicest people we know. Right boys? And of course, she is right. We can be a little raw when we are by ourselves."

Jessica smiled, placed her napkin on her lap and took a bite. The men were waiting for her to start.

No one spoke during their meal but once everyone was done and were enjoying the last of their coffee, Jessica pulled her duffle up from the floor, opened it and pulled three Blackberries out and said, "Bruce, our security officer, synced these for you. They are encrypted with each of our first names on the call list. Any questions you have, just call me, or get together to share any ideas on what we have discussed. Any questions now?"

Sheriff Williams said, "I don't, but maybe one of the others do. I am sure I will think of something once I get over the shock. Agent Fukishura, it is very difficult for us to believe you are a federal agent. We all have dealt with one agency or another and every single one were uncooperative and treated us as ignorant hicks who would only hamper their investigation. And now here you are asking for our help and treating us as equals. I think I speak for all three of us, we will do whatever we can to resolve this issue and put these domestic terrorists behind bars. We have a great network of confidential informants, CI, and we will start gathering information."

"That is tremendous Sheriff. I too appreciate the support and feel free to stop by the ranch any time, particularly around meal time. The president has an incredible chef, Marc Stucki, whom you may remember from cooking locally. He does an awesome black bean and chorizo casserole that will knock your socks off…on Uncle Sam!

"Before we go, I want to share one more item with all of you, something you may find very difficult to comprehend," she noted creating quizzical expressions from the men.

"You just mentioned how all the federal agencies have an uncooperative track record. That is history. President Bakus believes that the inability of various agencies to work together and to share investigative data has led to many of the country's criminal element expanding. He has a new assistant. I met her in Washington and am convinced she has the credentials to execute his mandate. You are familiar with the NSA's Utah facility, but to gain limited access you must jump through many hoops. No longer. In your phones is a contact number to Cheryl Chapman, a Naval Commander with warrior status, having gained her chops fighting Al Qaeda and ISIS.

Your internet connection to the federal data base now provides you direct access to everything in Utah, plus a new software system Chapman created linking you to all on-going and closed cases across the country. Every law enforcement agency from StoneHead to Los Angeles to Miami is connected to the same system. No longer will you have to wonder if your suspect has priors in another jurisdiction. Gone are the days when you believe your current case is intertwined elsewhere. It will be just like

Googling as far as the simplicity is concerned. I encourage you to familiarize yourself with the system and if you have any questions, give me a call."

Each officer shook their heads collectively, smiled and high-fived each other and Jessica, finding the entire conversation so new as to be bizarre…but believable.

Lunch over, Jessica exited first and once all the others were out, she extended her hand and thanked them for the meeting, cooperation and that they would stay in touch. She picked up the bill and headed to the cashier, which happened to be Janis. Paying the bill with cash, she left Janis a thirty-dollar tip. "Whoa, Ms. Jessica, that is way too much."

"No, it isn't Janis. I suspect you have to put up with a great deal from the likes of these three over the years so I am trying to make up for it."

Janis laughed and pocketed the three tens and said, "You are somethin' Ms. Jessica. This is the first I have seen you. You work around here?"

"I do," replied Jessica extending her hand again and continuing, "Jessica Fukishura, Special Agent in charge at the StoneHead Ranch."

"Well I'll be damned. No wonder those boys were on their best behavior and me thinking they just decided to use the manners their mammas taught them."

"I think you were right the first-time Janis. I am just a cop. Federal level, but just a cop who is having the pleasure working with these outstanding law enforcers."

Janis looked over Jessica's head to see the three men beaming and said, "It would appear they are the fortunate ones darlin'," she grinned, then added, "You all have a great Wyomin' Day," and turned to take the next customer's money.

All four law enforcers headed for the main door with every head turned to see with whom their local law enforcement were dealing.

Williams held the door open for Jessica. She thanked him and headed for the Bug. As she strode the wide sidewalk to her car a large, heavy-set man approached her. Getting in her face said, "You look like someone who doesn't belong in our town lady."

Before Jessica could respond, Jones had rushed up behind the guy and kicked him in the back of the knee, forcing him to drop to the cement. Simultaneously, Jones whipped out his handcuffs and bracketed the guy while Williams and Braket came up behind and all three pulled the guy erect.

Jones got in the guy's face and said, "Walter, you are being a drunken bigoted asshole and if you do not want to spend another week in jail you will apologize to this federal police officer and get your ass back home."

Walter was obviously a drunken bigot and very embarrassed as a crowd gathered to watch. Head lowered in shame, Walter said, "I am sorry ma'am. I tend to spout off at the mouth and say stuff I don't really mean."

"Good job Walter, now get into the Basket for a coffee from Janis and tell her to put it on my tab," said Chief Braket.

Jessica was so dumbfounded by what had just occurred, sorta like a wild west schoolmarm being saved by the handsome sheriff, all she could manage was a smile and a wave as she moved around the back of her Bug, beeped it open, got in and drove off. Heading back to the Ranch she mused about her non-reaction to Jones' behavior. Previously she would have dropped Walter without skipping a beat and been pissed at any man who felt he needed to step in and help. *Something very weird is occurring,* she thought, *and I kinda like the new me emerging.*

Chapter Thirty-Five

Jasmin Hastings had arrived with her suitcases for an extended stay at the Ranch and had been processed by security, irises scanned, finger printed and set up in an elegant room on the second floor overlooking the paddocks. Her supervisor wouldn't give her a reason for her being sequestered to the president's Ranch but there was no way she would turn the opportunity down. She was confused by the temporary transfer and was intimidated by the suddenness of the change, the military presence at the gate, and all the personal scrutinizing but she was determined to make it a positive experience and enjoy the change, knowing that the aggressive agent at the hospital was behind the move.

After getting settled, she meandered around the living room and stuck her head into the kitchen introducing herself to chef Marc Stucki.

"Hi Chef, I'm Jasmin Hastings, RN, the Ranch's new resident nurse," she said, extending her hand.

"Hi Jasmin, Marc Stucki," he replied, accepting her handshake. "I didn't know we needed a nurse. Is someone ill?"

"Not that I know of. I suspect Agent Fukishura wants my recent patient and her, um, guest, cared for. I am curious why she chose me. I just graduated."

"She will be here shortly and you can ask her. She won't mind the questioning. Agent Fukishura is very assertive, aggressive is more accurate and enjoys that in others. I suspect your meeting at the hospital impressed her. She needs someone she can trust, someone who doesn't need to be told what to do all the time. Ask her.

"In the meantime, may I interest you in some appetizers and a chilled bottle of chardonnay?"

"Really? Really!?" Jasmin said, raising her eyebrows, not comprehending a job where one is served appetizers and wine by the president's chef.

"Sure, I would love that."

"Have a seat in the living room by the fire and I will bring them right in."

With a huge smile and a calmness she hadn't expected, she slowly walked into the massive living room, gazing at the various tapestries, the heavy furniture and ceiling to floor draperies.

She flopped down into the corner of one of the couches and waited for Chef Marc to arrive or someone to pinch her. *Either way, this may just be the best day of her life,* she mused.

Chapter Thirty-Six

Riding in the taxi to the Nordstrom store Rebecca commented as she snuggled next to Pen, "I received a text from the StoneHead employment agency, they have several applicants interested in working for us, both men and women. I arranged to meet them at the Yellowstone facility when we get back."

"Sounds terrific and very exciting," replied Pen as she wiggled her arm through Rebecca's and returned the affection with a cheek kiss. "I don't think I want to get a dress, unless you want to see me in one."

"I have never seen you in a dress so I presume you do not favor them either. How about we style ourselves in what's comfortable and fits our personalities? You can tell me what you like and I will do the same."

Pen's reply was to squeeze Rebecca's arm.

Cherry Creek Shopping Center arrived quickly and they exited the cab in record speed, giving the cabby a twenty for the six-dollar fare. They hustled into the mall and headed straight for the massive, white, archway and made their way to the women's section.

First stop was Casual Wear where Rebecca found a pair of Galla Ted Baker cropped pants which Baker calls his, Whimsical Forget Me Not Print, having a floral pattern made from a soft, black, cotton-blend. She took the pants, black double-breasted cotton/poly blend jacket, black camisole and Urmi lace back t-shirt to try on.

Bought them.

While Rebecca was in the dressing room, Pen stepped into a small alcove and made a quick phone call.

Next Pen was looking for the bling jeans and red boots. The jeans were easy and she found a pair of washed, distressed denim with bling on each of the rear-pockets. Now for the boots. She had planned on the cowboy boots…until she saw the ankle boot by Blondo. Trying them on immediately, she loved the topstitched suede, the inside, hidden zipper, the stacked heel and textured sole which would give her traction on Cassandras' dance floor.

Bought the boots and bling.

Pen was on a roll. She spotted a pair of Mikado Osaka pants in a dark orange material with a muted yellow and orange pattern. The outfit came with a persimmon scoop-neck tank and orange mesh pullover sweater. She took them to the dressing room with Rebecca tagging along.

As Pen closed the door and turned, Rebecca put her arms around her kissed her passionately, then stepped back and leaned against the wall licking her lips. Pen immediately took one giant step and repeated the loving gesture, then took off all her clothes with Rebecca remarking, "We may never get out of the dressing room."

Rebecca could not control her passion and ran her hands all over Pen, stopping at her shapely rear end. Breathing hard, she said, "You must stop this aggressiveness Pen or we will be here all day," giving Pen a lustful smile.

Pen turned and gave Rebecca a little butt shimmy, then tried on the outfit. Loved it. Would have loved, loving Rebecca too but more shopping won over libido.

Bought the entire outfit.

They both wanted a summer outfit of pants and plain blouse now that they had the bling and patterned pants. They saw a pair of white lace, wide legged Alice and Olivia pants which Rebecca snagged. To make the outfit she chose a knee length light pink open front vest.

Pen found a similar pair of the lace pants with a slightly different pattern which she matched with a taupe, cotton Muslimah, long-sleeve outer blouse which came to her knees.

Bought it all.

By this time, it was after one o'clock, so they decided to break for lunch and slipped into Bazilles on the second floor. The décor was contemporary; well lighted with numerous mirrors, dark marble tables set for either four or six with matching leather chairs. It being a little past the lunch rush they were seated immediately and each ordered an iced tea. Rebecca had the Roasted Turkey and Prosciutto Baguette with baby arugula and peppercorn aioli. Pen chose the Bistro Club with sliced chicken breast, baby greens, crisp bacon, Roma tomatoes, avocado, garlic aioli on a toasted bun.

Waiting for their lunch they chatted non-stop about the outfits they had purchased (and left with the clerk) and how much fun they would have wearing them out and about. Pen asked if she was not making too many assumptions about their relationship and before she could answer, Rebecca reached across the table, took her hand and leaned in and kissed it.

"A woman without a man is like a fish without a bicycle."
Gloria Steinem

Their meal arrived quickly and they devoured the baguette and club quickly as they were both anxious to get to the shoes and swim suits. Fifteen minutes. Done. Pen paid the bill with another twenty tip.

First stop…shoes. Both stopped at the entrance and said in unison, "Oh my God!" at the massiveness of the selection.

For the first thirty minutes, they simply roamed the department, admiring most, laughing at some, particularly those with three-inch heels. Rebecca picked up bright pair of yellow heels and pretended to walk and stumble with Pen laughing so hard she had to lean against a display table.

Once through the entire section they decided to get serious and choose. Difficult.

Rebecca decided on low heels to keep her six-foot height from overpowering Penelope. Her first choice was a pair of Jambu sandals with a chunky wedge sole and a caged silhouette leather upper. Trying them on, they fit like the proverbial glove.

Bought them.

Right next to the Jambu sandals were a pair of Tony Burch 'Zoey' Wedges in Taupe. She handed them to Pen who immediately loved them until she turned them over and saw the $295 price tag. Pretending they were on fire she put them down quickly and grimaced at Rebecca. A little more exploring and she found a pair of Sole Society Freyaa' wedges in a nomad suede in her price range. Tried them.

Bought them.

Meandering through the massive selection they came across Nordstrom's Fall boot collection and figured they each needed a pair.

They saw the boots just ahead but were side-tracked by a pair of UGG Otter Adirondack winter boots with shearling lining, waterproof leather uppers and Vibram soles.

Bought twins.

Pen was the first to spot the red boots! A great deal more stylish than what she had thought she wanted. These were a soft suede, leather upper, six- inch, side zipper red boot by Top Shop of their Just Have to Have Pair collection.

Bought them.

They were exhausted but determined to find a pair of low heeled leather boots for Rebecca. Pen saw them ahead on a separate display kiosk and ran ahead grabbing one, lifting it up to show Rebecca and yelled, "We have a winner!".

It was a beautiful washed, antique, leather bootie with a pointed toe and tapered, stacked leather, two-inch heel. The inside zipper closure made the deal.

Pen was so enthralled with Rebecca's boots she picked up a pair of the ankle boots for herself. They were black, full-grain leather with a stacked mid-heel and zips up the back. She figured they would look terrific with her new bling jeans and she had plenty of blouses in her wardrobe to make several outfits.

Bought them.

One last purchase and they would be done. Swimsuits.

They almost dragged themselves to the department, dreading one more try-on but knowing they needed suits for the pool tomorrow, they trudged on. Walking through the Vacation Portal, they received an immediate adrenalin rush beginning with a dark-haired hunk right off the pages of G-Q magazine, dressed in board shorts, Hawaiian print oversize shirt and sandals, offering each of them a virgin Pina Colada in a tall, frosted glass. Assisting several customers with long cover-ups was a female clerk similarly dressed in oranges and yellows.

Rebecca glanced at Penelope and gave a little smirk, receiving one in return.

Their exhaustion was history. Neither was attracted to the guy for obvious reasons and the woman was irrelevant given their commitment to each other, but they appreciated the reality to which Nordstrom had gone to market the swim wear. The Pina colada helped. The expansive Holiday department was isolated from the rest of the store with ceiling high display walls. Tahitian music enveloped the shopper's visual senses while fragrances of vanilla musk and kiwi blossom wafted their olfactics, having the immediate affect on their shopping commitment. Bathing suits and cover-ups dominated the section with each offering a multitude of sizes and color combinations.

After several suits and some laughter, Rebecca chose an L Space 'Chloe' wrap, black classic string-bikini with twisted, wraparound straps for the top and an Estella bottom with cutaway side panels matching the top.

Pen had her eye on an L Space 'Jaime' Crisscross sorbet bikini with a bralette-style top with adjustable straps and a crisscross in the back. The bottom was styled identical to the black Rebecca bought.

Bought and Bought.

Rebecca turned to Pen and said, "I am beat. How about heading back to the Seasons and a couple of glasses of chardonnay and room service?"

"Deal"

"When you change, there is a period of adjustment as you get used to the new you—how you look, how you feel..."

Dr. David Posen MD *Always Change a Losing Game*

30,000

Williams, Jones and Braket lost no time in contacting their confidential informants and getting the word out on the street and ranches that they were seeking information regarding the StoneHead Evangelical Church and its deacons, as well as the movement of weed in the area.

Answers began trickling in within hours from town and ranch informants, like an untapped reservoir of knowledge seeking a destination.

In addition to their local informants, each officer knew several Vietnam veterans who were unable to return to civilian life. They lived as hermits back in the forest of Yellowstone National Park. If anyone knew what was moving through the national park, it would be these guys, but they shunned people, particularly the law. Once a year one officer took a supply pack train to various drop off points high in the mountains, paid for by the recipients' veteran's benefits.

It had been over forty years since the end of the Vietnam War and these former Green Berets, Special Forces, Delta Force as well as Air Force vets were in their sixties now. Scott Williams volunteered to ride up into the mountains and try and communicate with at least one of them.

Chapter Thirty-Seven

Martha Sarkowski had been terrified of being arrested before she made it to the safe house. Constantly checking her mirrors and driving just under the speed limit, she made it, but now, sitting in the open garage, she shivered, placing her head on the steering wheel as she hit the automatic garage door fob. After what seemed like an eternity, she exited the car, retrieved her meager belongings from the back seat and entered the house.

Covert behavior was all new to her. She had begun the political journey with excitement, supporting her conservative husband Joe in his quest for a major change in America's federal political leadership. She was led to believe, or she naively led herself, that her contribution was simply to help with rallies and fund raisers. She was completely ignorant to Joe's involvement in the StoneHead Evangelical Church's violent plot. Sure, she was a church member and had been since coming to StoneHead, but although the pastor exhibited extreme conservative social and political beliefs, so did every congregant. There had never been an inclination to take political activity to a violent stage. Of course, now she understood that she was never part of the inner circle; those who spent Sunday afternoons at the farm where the inner circle/conspirators discussed church business, a great deal of that being the movement of drugs and chemicals across the country and through the national park.

Reality struck early on a Saturday morning when Joe thought she was still asleep from her gruelling twelve-hour shift the night before. She had woken earlier than her normal ten hours, felt rested/refreshed, so had headed to the kitchen for coffee after a trip to the bathroom. As she walked the hallway in her bare feet, she could hear Joe speaking with Harold Richard.

"Are you positive you weren't followed here Harold?"

"Very. Listen. Don't worry about me being caught. I got away the night of the raid and I will stay under their radar. With this beard, a new driver's license and a new vehicle, no one is going to know it's me. Now let's recap so we can get back on track."

"Okay. Good to know," Joe replied, somewhat relieved. "So far we know that the packing route is blown since the FBI took James and the one remaining wrangler disappeared. We have thousands of dollars in weed stacked in the barns plus the chemicals, which both need to be moved up the chain."

Martha stood mesmerized in the hallway, too stunned to move, too shocked that her husband and his friend were involved in drugs to return to the bedroom.

"What we need is a plan to get Yellowstone moving again or at least get the merchandise out of there. Getting the stuff out of that place could be near impossible with it being guarded 24/7 by the FBI and I doubt they are going to be conned into leaving even if we set fire to the place," Richards quipped with a sort of snort.

"Why don't we just abandon that operation and chalk it up? We could contact the Indians in Idaho to arrange a different route. They could fly it here in three hours or truck it in ten but either way there are risks."

Richards snapped his fingers and said, "What about the rail line that brings the dope to the Indians? Why not reroute it to StoneHead? We could easily pick it up at night in the rail staging area, it is deserted at night and the last time I was there I only saw one-night light and that was over the entry to the shipping office."

Joe took out his smartphone and googled the Idaho and Wyoming rail lines and brought up a map which showed the merchandise could be routed from Sandpoint, Idaho to Missoula, Montana, to Laurel, Montana then down into Powel, Wyoming and finally to StoneHead. He showed Richards and said, "This is doable. Not a direct route like we have been using and it will require some fancy logistics and computer software manipulation but I think we can do it. What do you think?"

"I think it is too risky. The complexity you mentioned creates too many possible failures. If one component, say hacking the computers for three rail companies, went awry, we lose. Get the Indians to reroute their cargo to the southern trail system and we abandon the dope in the barns at Yellowstone, far too risky to try and recover."

"I can do that but what bothers me is the lawman the Indians killed. I am surprised the feds have not taken over the investigation, and if they do there is no doubt the rail route is going to be compromised and they will make the connection to Orofino and the Yellowstone pack train. I considered changing the route to come south on highway 95 from southern Alberta but that would mean our production would have to be moved and we have close to a million invested in that underground operation to abandon it and even if we wanted to, it would mean the grower would have to transport the weed by truck and with the Mounties clamping down, that is a gamble I don't think we want to take."

Joe was becoming annoyed with the absurdity of a solution that would be simple to solve. It would involve the Mexican drug cartel which he knew Richards would shoot down immediately, so he proposed, "Why not do a tunnel? Now before you say no, let me explain. The rail line is going to be busted as soon as the feds take over the killing on the Nez Perce Reservation and then we will be shit out of luck in getting a system rebooted. We cannot afford that. Our deadline is too close and we can not cut off our finances. Our drug operation in Canada is very close to the border. So close in fact, the producer could very easily transport the product by quad to a tunnel starting on the Canadian side in the bush and coming out in Idaho. The Indians could easily pick up the product, transport it back to the reservation and take the southern route here. Let me consider the feasibility, see if we can get our own people to buy the outfitting business and get this all moving again. Our time table is crucial, particularly for the chemicals."

Richards appeared pissed but Joe figured it was exhaustion with trying to figure out how to rejuvenate the life-line to the operation. Richards said, "Okay, put out the information, contact our Alberta contacts and the Indians. But this needs to be done quickly." Joe nodded, made a few notes and saw Richards off.

Martha had heard it all, was transfixed and had to force herself to quickly head back to the bedroom to avoid Joe finding out she knew more than she should.

Joe poured himself another coffee and picked up his smartphone. It had been encrypted so he was confident his quick texts would go undetected and started typing to a burner in Calgary, Alberta. He then cut/pasted the message and sent it off to Jack Johntree, telling both men they needed to communicate with each other and come up with a plan to make the tunnel a reality quickly.

Martha tip-toed back to the bedroom, closed the door, then reopened it, making considerable noise in the process. As she entered the kitchen, Joe had just completed his business and had put the phone back into his pocket.

"Hi sweetheart. You sure had a long sleep. Are you rested?"

Martha stretched, yawned and gave him a hug, a kiss, and said, "I'm not sure yet. Either this job is getting tougher, I'm getting older or a combination of both, but these twelves are killing me," then went for the coffee, acting as though this was any normal morning, all the while realizing her life was being dragged into events for which she was not prepared.

She had agreed to keep Richards informed about what goes on in the presidential wing of the StoneHead Hospital and didn't give it a second thought when she texted him of the Air Force bringing in the battered driver. But she was unprepared for the instructions she received in return. When she asked why, Richards quickly admonished her that she was part of the movement and needed to do her part. His tone was what convinced her that she had gone too far to turn back.

That overheard conversation morphed her involvement to murder, an act which violated her character to its moral fiber. Now she sat in a strange house, unable to leave for fear of being recognized. Powerless, not being able to use a phone, text or email, knowing that doing so could lead to her discovery by the NSA's eavesdropping software.

"It is only the enlightened ruler and the wise general who will use the highest intelligence in the army for the purposes of spying."

The Art of War
Sun Tzu

30,000

Joe was positive his communication went undetected. When interacting in urban areas, the CFBA used physical exchanges of information, notes left at predetermined locations which were checked regularly for left messages. No electronics. But that was impossible in rural Wyoming and Idaho given the vastness of the uninhabited areas. Joe was confident he was entirely covert. The CFBA groomed America's smartest conservative youth to attend their Colorado university and it was these technical wizards who assured the leadership the phones' communications were undetectable by NSA.

The whiz kids had not met Elisabeth Peltowski, eighth grade computer instructor at StoneHead Junior High.

Chapter Thirty-Eight

Elisabeth sat in her home computer sanctuary analysing the conversations, texts and emails to and from the StoneHead area, which had been scanned in the last twelve hours while she had been at work. The majority of citizens' behavior was passed over without a nanosecond of thought. What caught her eye immediately were those activities for which she had programmed her system to highlight.

She saved a copy of Joe Sarkowski's texts and forwarded it to Jessica via Bruce at the StoneHead Ranch. Scrolling down further she hit on a link of a phone call from Richards to Colorado. Clicking on the link opened the conversation, she became mesmerized, "We need your approval to alter our transportation system. The Alberta producer's rail transportation will be compromised soon and we need to have an alternative route for the product. We believe the solution is a tunnel under the border with the Indians picking up the goods and bringing it to the transfer location."

Harold went on to bring *Intrepid* current and to validate Harold's suspicions and time-line projections for the feds to become involved. *Intrepid* responded, "Let me get this right, there was a shoot-out and raid on the farm by the feds, both FBI and Secret Service. The chemicals and bundles are still at the farm and at the guide outfitters, Martha failed in her attempt to kill our mole and she is now at a safe house, you are wanted on a federal warrant and are still in StoneHead, the mole is in federal custody at the StoneHead Ranch as is the wrangler captured earlier and you are asking for my approval for millions of dollars to be spent on digging a tunnel?"

"Yes sir. Joe and I believe all the other alternatives are too dangerous."

"You two must be out of your fucking minds. Have you lost your perspective entirely? We have a research team about to finalize the chemical formula, we have the other ingredients stockpiled waiting to be assembled, the Democratic National Convention is weeks away and you are concentrating on this?

"Regroup Harold, and do it immediately. Forget the product at the farm and outfitters. Right now, the GOP is scrambling for votes and we have more money than God. Get out of StoneHead and to the safe house in Minneapolis, that way you may be of some help when the plane arrives with the cesium. Change your appearance and use one of the new identifications. Get Joe out of there too, but send him to Los Angeles where he can coordinate that end of the operation.

"We are too close to accomplishing our years of planning to have anything interfere now. So, from here on out, no communication with me. There shouldn't be a need as the rest should go off like clock work."

Richards started to reply but found he was speaking into a dead phone. *Intrepid* had slammed the phone down, cursing that he had ever involved the right wing religious fanatics. They were difficult to control or even manage and the current situation with their cash flow was proof of that. The CFBA were not so solvent they could afford to lose the money from the marijuana that was shipped every other day, amounting to over a half million a week. But it was far too dangerous to try and sell what was there. Taking a couple of deep breaths, he picked up the phone and dialed a 424-area code number from memory. It rang once and was picked up in Marina del Rey, California. "Yes?" *Intrepid* said one word, "Now" and hung up.

"There are many enemies. Whatever you do, you must drive the enemy together, as if tying a line of fishes, and when they are seen to be piled up, cut them down."

A Book of Five Rings
Miyamoto Musashi

Chapter Thirty-Nine

At the first opportunity, Sheriff Williams saddled up and headed into Yellowstone National Park tethered to a pack train carrying a year's supply of dried staples, vegetable seeds, a wine making kit and a case of Jack Daniels. He planned to get into the high country on the first day, then camp and signal for Troy Everson, knowing he would stop by at first light. Williams knew exactly where Troy lived, had flown over his cabin numerous times during his aerial patrol, but he also knew that to get any where near that fortress would create an immediate hostile environment. Everson had to come to him and three rifle shots into the air late in the afternoon would do just that.

The very last thing Williams wanted was to recreate the RCMP's shoot out with Albert Johnson in the Yukon in 1932. Johnson, had been a trapper who had taken liberty with the trap lines of other trappers. The outdoorsmen filed complaints with the RCMP resulting in two Mounties dropping by Johnson's cabin to investigate. Johnson responded by opening fire on the officers. The Members responded by throwing dynamite through Johnson's window, only to find him hiding in an underground cave dug out of his dirt living room floor where he opened fire on the Mounties, killing Cst. Edgar Millen. Johnson escaped, resulting in a massive man-hunt, organized to locate and arrest the murderer. After five weeks on the run, an aerial patrol spotted Johnson and after a gun battle, he was dead.

Williams had no intention of repeating the *Tale of the Mad Trapper of Rat River,* so after high-lining the animals, stringing his supplies in trees out of the reach of bears, stringing a one- wire electric perimeter fence, powered by a small twelve-volt battery, setting up his tent and campfire, he let off the three shots, then settled in for the night, confident Everson would be sitting by the fire at first light.

An uneventful night brought first light, with the predawn beams sneaking their way through the massive Lodge Pole Pine limbs, reminding all who grace its shadow that its species has been king of the region long before man's intrusion. Just before four, and as predicted, Scott's horses whinnied as his guest approached. The Sheriff let his hand slide over his

.50 calibre pistol, his hand forming a grip, trigger finger beside the guard and scooted along the tent floor to peek outside.

Everson smiled, raised his coffee cup to Scott and said, "Good Morning Sheriff. Long time no see. What crawled up your ass to bring you all the way up here?"

"Good morning to you bright eyes! Give me a minute to get some pants on," Williams said, as he grabbed his jeans from the corner of the tent and stepped out, pistol in one hand and jeans in the other.

"You still carrying that elephant gun with you Scott. I would have thought you would have carpal tunnel by now in that right wrist, but then again you don't get many bad guys in StoneHead now do you, so not much shootin'?" Troy said with a wide grin.

Everson preferred his six-shot, Ruger .44 Magnum revolver, in a left thigh holster, with 270 grain bullets for close-up and personal greetings. Either that or his assault knife with its seven-inch blade strapped to his right thigh. Either or, was Troy's mantra, a position ingrained from his time in the tunnels of Vietnam. Williams' choice ammunition was just 30 grains heavier but with a much greater kick and being a semi-automatic, it tended to jam and was useless in the -50 Celsius winters.

Williams put his pants on and slipped the pistol in the back of his waist band, then gave a Troy a bear hug and said, "Sure do miss you man."

"Me too Scott," Troy said as he ran his fingers through his shoulder length hair, then pushed it back over his head, "but we both know what would happen if I came to town. Grab a cuppa, feed your buddies as I fix us breakfast. Did you know I have chickens now?" he said rather proudly.

Troy and Scott were about six-foot, slim, both having fair complexions, but that was as far as the physical similarities compared. Troy had sandy, blonde hair to his shoulders and a full facial beard while Scott had black, close cropped hair and was clean shaven. Two men more dissimilar couldn't be better friends, albeit only seeing each other several times a year.

"That is very cool. I hope you find some exceptional ingredients on this train to compliment your culinary skills," Scott retorted with a laugh so hard, he almost pissed his pants.

"Okay, you show me what you can do with eggs and bacon, but please pass on that brown shit you call, Pinto Bean Delight, unless you have added some jalapenos."

Williams' and Everson's relationship went back to when Scott first traversed the Yellowstone forests tracking a Cheyenne, Wyoming homicide suspect who thought he could be anonymous in the bush. Very much like the Mad Trapper, not realizing anonymity is in urbanization, not rural communities. Scott had no idea of the fugitive's location and after two days covering every conceivable trail, he rounded a curve in a path and there was Everson sitting on a log, sipping on a cup of his home brew. Everson knew all about Williams, but Scott had never heard and hadn't any knowledge of the Vietnam hermit. A short introduction, three inches of home brew each and Troy seemed to sense Scott's sincerity. Everson offered to help contact the fugitive.

Troy knew the suspect's location, took him within a mile of the guy's make-shift camp, then circled around behind the camp to cut off any escape.

The guy did rabbit. Hearing someone coming down the game trail, he decided not to take any chances and ran in the opposite direction, only to run into Troy, again sitting on a fallen tree, but this time, instead of a mug of his brew, he held his Winchester .30-30 Trapper, Loop-Lever Action rifle cradled across his arm. He called it, *Baby*, named after his Browning M2 .50 Calibre machine gun he carried in Vietnam.

"In both weapons and other things, one should not be biased in favor of one thing over another. Too much is the same as too little. Do not imitate or mimic others; one must have a weapon appropriate to one's size and comfortable in one's hand."

Heiho Ni Bugu No ri O Shiru To Iu Koto
(Knowing the Advantages of Weapons in Heiho)

Miyamoto Musashi used *Heiho* to explain the path to enlightenment that can be followed by those who practice *Bushido, The*

Way of the Warrior (The Honor and Morals of the Japanese Samurai Warriors).

The Book of Five Rings
Miyamoto Musashi

30,000

Everson liked Musashi's spirit and philosophy and although the .50 was a little on the heavy side, it was a magnificent weapon, capable of destroying an enemy of hundreds. He often read the Samurai's words of wisdom and found his, "Virtues of the long sword…victorious against one, ten or a thousand," to be his mantra. In the bush though the .30-.30 Winchester was his Long Sword.

Chapter Forty

After bacon, eggs, fresh bread and two pots of black, they chatted about Scott's concerns. Williams knew he was breaking national security protocol by sharing with Troy, but if he spun a bullshit story, Everson would leave and their friendship would be in jeopardy, so he began with, "The Secret Service believes there is a domestic terrorist plot gaining momentum. They have agents in Arizona observing Navajo locals being trained by Al-Qaeda operatives, several additional agents in StoneHead found a stash of weed, fertilizer and chemicals. They believe the latter, all three, are being transported to and from an Idaho compound led by two Citizens for a Better America commanders. The FBI took down the Yellowstone Guide Outfitters owner and have him in custody. He admits to moving the products, but says he has no idea to whom he delivers, says his guys just meet Indians in the bush, they trade product and his guys come back."

"So, that is what has been happening. I figured contraband like drugs or weapons but never expected this," Everson replied, never putting the upcoming election together with the Orlando shooting or countless other violent episodes. "Their target who I think it is?"

"We believe so, yes. Chuck Braket, Sheriff Jones from Nez Perce and I were read into the intel just recently," Williams said, forgetting that Troy had his own generator and satellite system and was probably more news current than some of the media moguls.

"What have you seen Troy?"

"Pretty much just what you described. I have snooped around the Idaho compound and there is a shitload of chemicals there, must be waiting for shipment. Any idea where they are destined?"

"No, and that is what is bothersome. We know it doesn't take much to duplicate Timothy McVeigh's formula. He had one vehicle and remember what he did with that. We suspect this group has numerous delivery vehicles destined for explosion simultaneously."

Williams was not read into Spencer's side of the counter-terrorism operation, but had he been and shared with Troy, Everson may have been able to shed light on the end-product, since he was an explosive technician in Vietnam, using his skills to blow up Cong tunnels.

"Here's what I think will work if you are interested," Williams offered.

"Anything Scott. Gets pretty boring here at times and stalking grizzlies to see how close I can get unnoticed or doin' the same to moose and wolf packs gets repetitive. Whatever you have in mind, I'm in."

"The Yellowstone Guide-Outfitters business was supposed to be bought by a local horse trainer, Rebecca Simpson and the vet, Dr. Penelope. Simpson is Secret Service and Dr. Pen, is, well, Dr. Pen. However, the FBI stepped in a squashed the deal, stating they intended to sell it themselves and direct the proceeds of the illegal activity to their coffers. Dr. Barker has no knowledge of Simpson's identity and I believe they are just friends, so that isn't an issue.

Simpson is confident she can take a train through to the Idaho compound with the chemicals and convince them to let her pick up the slack and continue the deliveries. Chuck sold the weed covertly and gave the proceeds of over two hundred thousand to Simpson who will dangle it as enticement. That amount should be sufficient for Simpson to be read into their operation.

"What I would like you to do is observe the exchange, record it, then email the exchange.

I have a set of ears for you in the train. It has a range of three hundred yards. You pick the spot. It may be on the trail or back at the compound. Simpson will initiate the conversation and highlight the chemicals and how she can increase the quantity if need be. Her objective is to get Marrington and Shepherd talking about the end route. The Secret Service agent in charge, Jessica Fukishura, believes the CFBA have stashes of these chemicals across the country and are putting them together with the other ingredients for a coordinated attack."

"Makes sense. That is what we did in Nam. Sometimes I tracked the Cong for miles through the tunnels and set explosives a few hundred yards behind where I could hear them, then scooted backwards. Very long ignition time for sure," he smiled, remembering his expertise and the countless lives he saved. "Sometimes the tunnels were so long and intricate

I would just set surface explosives in a perimeter and then criss-cross with additional sets. It created a huge crater and took out hundreds of Cong fighters.

"Those were military grade explosives, some of which are no longer manufactured. McVeigh's system was bulky. If you recall, he used five thousand pounds of ammonium nitrate and nitromethane to fill the Ryder truck. If the CFBA are as smart and crafty as Fukishura suspects, could all this be a rouse? I mean, storing the chemicals in a barn on a mountain top and in a church's barn. Doesn't sound too brilliant to me."

Before Williams could respond, Troy continued, "I have studied Japanese Samurai Miyamoto Musashi, who was born in 1584, and in his *Book of Five Rings* he discusses that there are many enemies and as he explains, "...observe their attacking order, and go to meet first those who attack first…cut the enemies down as they advance… whatever you do, you must drive the enemy together…"

"Is it possible the CFBA are countering that, forcing law enforcement to spread out, thereby lessening the discovery? They have the FBI concentrating on the Idaho compound, the Secret Service, you, Chuck and Jones looking at the farm and you said the feds suspect there are chemical stashes spread across the country. What agency is tracking the weed? Can you see how they may very well be performing the mosquito effect?

"I see what you mean. We are chasing our tails, but what could they be planning that would be bigger than McVeigh that is so geographically wide-spread? We have no idea their intentions or motivation, but we may be moving forward more quickly than previously.

Fukishura is interrogating a mole at the president's ranch and the guy they captured at the guide-outfitters. She has a nurse from the hospital under surveillance in Sheridan." Seeing Troy's confusion, he added, "Wait, I'm getting ahead of myself, let me back up and give you some background.

"Fukishura was tasked with getting the StoneHead Ranch ready for the president to host the G-8 Anti-Terrorism Heads of State. The Ranch was never destined for Bakus' residency while president, so there was a great deal of upgrading necessary. Agents Fukishura and Spencer worked on the security while the other two sent under cover as school teachers to determine if there was an undercurrent of conservativism against Bakus. With the three agents working under cover, they fell into the plot, almost literally; Simpson saw the weed and chemicals at the guide outfitters when she was helping suture a couple of colts. One agent ended up in the shit when he was reconning the farm, found the chemicals and was besieged by the CFBA operatives. Their leader, Richards, escaped, but the FBI and Fukishura's team captured all the others. The down side is they were released by the powers that be…no warrant."

"Why am I not surprised? How many years did we put up with that bullshit in Vietnam and how many thousands of lives were lost? We will never learn. Sorry for the interruption. Where does the nurse come into play?"

"Fukishura received a 9-1-1 call from the hospital saying someone tried to kill the Air Force's captured mole. During her interviews, she discovered that the last person to see him was Sarkowski, who had conveniently left the hospital just before Fukishura's arrival. Jessica's quick thinking resulted in the Ranch's security chief launching a drone which would track Sarkowski from her StoneHead house to Sheridan. Federal agents have the nurse under surveillance."

"That helps. Thanks. Okay, so you want me to snoop around during Simpson's pack train exchange and get a recording of these two primaries discussing their intentions?"

"Exactly! Now I am presuming Simpson will not be taking the train by herself as it isn't a one-person job, so she will be having help. I figure she has some horse savvy agents joining her. At least that is the way I would do it. She can not have civilians. I will text you with the updates and the exact day she intends to head up here."

Troy was a local legend, with his monthly disability income covering far more than his basic needs. Back in the day, he had contacted a few Marines now living in StoneHead county and they packed building supplies, solar panels and even a wood stove, broken down into moveable pieces. Although few had seen his home in person, Williams was among the few who had perused it from the air and was impressed. Troy was a hermit, there was no denying that, but living on the edge of sanity he was not. His electronics were powered by the solar panels with back-up batteries and his direct satellite connections provided him with internet speeds which were too costly for the general public.

Chapter Forty-One

As Williams and Everson continued their visit, catching up on everything from the latest terrorist attacks to which team would make it to the Super Bowl and the Stanley Cup, Karen and Tom were relaxing in the rear of a Lincoln town car being chauffeured to Whistler. Knowing Karen's penchant for quality white wine, Tom arranged for a chilled bottle of Noble Ridge's Chardonnay 2009 and an appie plate to greet them upon sliding into the luxury of soft black leather molded seats with surrounding high gloss wood trim and privacy glass behind the driver. Once nestled and enveloped by the leather, Tom slid a flash drive of personally developed eclectic collection of Jazz, touched the intercom and the surround sounds of bassist John Clayton, trumpeter Chris Botti, saxophonist Denis Solee and pianist Diana Krall embraced them with a romantic mood enhanced by the aurora of Vancouver's nightscape.... the town car crossing the Lion's Gate Bridge, heading for affluent West Vancouver, past Horseshoe Bay and onto Whistler.

As Scott saddled up before heading down the mountain, Rebecca received a text while shopping. Jessica was advising the sale of the Yellowstone weed and the $200,000 + waiting for her to persuade the Idaho contacts to deal her regarding the merchandise transportation. Jessica had returned to the Ranch and was meeting with Jasmin, welcoming her to her new job, albeit temporary, making sure she was settled, then advising her that her job description included bringing a family of new kittens and their mother into the Ranch House to, as Jessica joyfully stated, "Bring unconditional love and caring into their lives," but what she was really doing was fulfilling a promise to herself when she left her Washington flat to have another heartbeat in her life.

While the town car glided through the curves and elevation changes of the Sea to Sky Highway, enhanced for the 2010 Winter Olympics, they passed the vast murkiness of Howe
Sound to their left and the iconic Stawamus Chief rising eerily and foreboding on their right.

Slowing down through Squamish, they glanced at several après restaurants where skiers were choosing the pristine, solitude of the Sea to

Sky Gondola society to refuel and recharge with climbers and sharing the day's adventures, the latter bragging of their accomplishing the Chief's 700 meter/2,300 feet, in record time while avoiding the nesting and endangered Peregrine Falcon.

Chapter Forty-Two

Bruce had given Jasmin a tour of the Ranch and its various facilities as much as her limited security clearance would permit, and the last building was the horse barn. He did not mention the kittens or her additional task to be assigned by Jessica. Bruce always came across as a total hard-ass but that was for the troops, not kittens, so he stifled a smile when he…just happened…to come across the litter in one of the unused stalls, the little ones just gaining their mousing legs. Jasmin was duly impressed, immediately sitting in the hay while the litter crawled all over her. Bruce made an excuse that he had to get back and for Jasmin to rejoin him whenever.

Bruce had just sat down at his desk when Jessica popped her head through his open door, "Hi Bruce. Everything squared away here?"

"Squared and ready for the feline invasion. I just gave Jasmin a tour and left her with the kittens. How do you think she will take to this additional task?"

"I know she will have no problem. It is straight forward. She puts them in one of the spare bedrooms on this floor with a comfy box and mom, food, water and a litter box and it will be a go from there. She is not a horsey person so I needed something to distract her between caring for our detainee. I think it will be fun."

"I do too. Seems like a nice kid. I can not believe I just said that. I am getting old." "Don't feel bad, I thought the same thing when I first met her, but changed my mind when I heard she took over the president's hospital wing, controlled the scene and saved our suspect.

"And speaking of Mr. Thiessen, I best be getting' and see what bullshit story he has to offer. When was the last time Jasmin checked him?"

Bruce glanced up on the wall to his series of atomic clocks showing the precise time in various world centers. Unaware that the very clocks he was consulting were generated by Cesium, a chemical that was about to change his life in an agonizing and frightening way. "About an hour ago. She said he was okay to be interrogated, adding that he is healing quickly and would not need medical supervision much longer. She has all of her test records on a tablet left with security."

“Great. I am off. If you hear screaming, just crank the tunes,” she quipped as she did her 180-toe spin and bounced out of his office.

The brig was the closest building to the Ranch House and situated at the end of the barracks. Jessica chatted with Marc briefly, filled a large white ceramic mug with black, tucked her laptop under her arm, then headed out and around the paddocks, stopping to chat with several of the sociable mares.

As she ran her hand down the neck of a Sorrel, she said, “You know Abby, this is kinda of a big deal into which I am headed. This colleague of mine, David with CSIS. That’s Canada’s spy agency just in case you didn’t know. Anyway, he has heard rumblings of subversives planning a huge attack on one of the political conventions and/or those attending. CSIS and the CIA are picking up internet chatter regarding either Al Qaeda or ISIS smuggling refined uranium out of Iran from their facility at Natanz, south west of Tehran. It’s all preliminary right now and we are hoping Chapman’s new system will enable fast tracking of all information.

“So far, we have confirmation of Al Qaeda sleepers operating on several south-western reservations, teaching several insurgents bomb production. The FBI has investigated numerous explosions without finding a suspect. That is what Rebecca was doing before she joined the ‘J’ Team. Anyway, if this uranium makes its way to the states and is combined with a compound already here, they have a dirty bomb. So now I must go and interrogate this asshole and see what I can discover and if there is a connection between what we are finding here and what CSIS discovered. Wish me luck,” she concluded, giving Abby a nose kiss and shaking her head, not believing this Berkley girl was confiding in a horse.

The only door to the military jailhouse led into the barracks where the Military Police (MP) slept. Ultimate security. Guards stood on either side of the steel door, snapped to attention and saluted as Jessica approached. She managed a quick wrist snap, then waited for one of the MPs to unlock the door as she mused about their need to salute her even though her position didn’t require it. Commander in Chief’s residence she speculated.

Thiessen was already seated at the bare metal table with one wrist handcuffed to a large steel ring in the center. Behind him was Army Ranger

Staff Sergeant Curtis Leithead, a specialist in detention, interrogation and, what he like to call, persuasion. Leithead nodded to Fukishura as she took a seat across from Thiessen. Jessica could see immediately that Leithead's presence was influencing the detainee. The Staff Sgt. was about six feet and around two hundred pounds of solid. His shoulders and arms would be impressive at a weight lifting event, but here he could very well make the difference in what vital information she could glean. She was positive Leithead's close cropped hair, his square jaw and somewhat round-face and cold stare were having a collective effect.

"Good morning Mr. Thiessen. I am Special Agent Fukishura with the Secret Service, I trust you have been treated as well as one would expect. You have met the Staff Sergeant, I am hoping you two do not have to become better acquainted.," she concluded with a smirk. Thiessen raised his head and stared, eyes unblinking, possibly attempting to come off as a tough guy, but failing miserably. He was unshaven and although Jasmin had given him a sponge bath, his appearance was somewhat repulsive with his hair uncombed and the wrinkled hospital gown barely covering his body.

"Before we chat about why you are here, we are going to share a video," she said, pulling the metal chair out opposite the detainee, placing the laptop on the table. Opened. Turned on. Jessica sat back, crossed her legs, revealing the expensive pattern of the factory distressed jeans and her low top, cocoa Kelsi Dagger Jenson Booties, with lace-up from toe to ankle and 3 ½ inch heels.

The opening scene was of the inside of Bam Bam's cockpit with the following conversation between Captain Michelle "Bam-Bam" Nicholodian, her co-pilot Lieutenant Keely O'Reilly and shooter Second Lieutenant Billy Rae Boyanton, "Okay gang, this stupid mother fucker wants to play with Bam-Bam, let's give it to him. Billy Rae, we are fuel short and have no time to screw around here. Keely and I will make one more pass at him and you take out the pick-up. Show this piss ant why I'm called Bam-Bam."

The screen then split into two, one scene of the cockpit and the other from the Cougar's nose camera. The latter showed the chopper almost on top of a pick-up. She hit pause. "Bring back any memories Mr. Thiessen?"

The detainee just stared at the screen, in shock.

"Mr. Thiessen, this is the point here where you say something."

He rubbed his face with his one free hand, then through his hair and leaned forward staring more intently at the screen, with an expression of disbelief.

"Let me help you here Mr. Thiessen. From what I can tell, you are a decent guy. You have worked for Mr. Bakus for many years, done an excellent job for which you were paid higher than the going wages for wranglers. Checking your background, you had some run-ins with the law as a teen, problems which you obviously outgrew. Reasonable success on the rodeo circuit until, I presume, age and injuries caught up with you.

"So, a reasonably likeable guy. Honest worker. No religious or radical political issues. What prompts you to become a terrorist?"

Thiessen's head snapped up, jarring him back to reality, just as Jessica closed the lap top.

"Terrorist? Who said I was a terrorist? What the fuck are you talking about lady? I'm a fuckin' ranch hand, I'm no terrorist," he said, his voice gaining volume with each fearful word.

"Yeah, you are Len. Think about it for a moment. You are a bright guy, naive maybe, but bright. That conversation to which you just listened was from the cockpit of a United States Air Force Attack Helicopter that the Secret Service sent after you when you left the Ranch, reputedly to pick up colt supplies. That, is you in the pick-up. We have your cell with the last call received from a burner…your handler thinking we couldn't trace it. You fled right after that call, so why not start there?

"Harold Richards. Why don't you begin by telling me how you met and what he asked you to do for him?"

Thiessen ran his free hand around his face a few times and seemed to relax, possibly resigning himself to the reality of his situation.

"I met Richards in a bar's restroom. I was minding my own business when this guy comes up to the urinal beside me and starts telling me about myself; where I was born, my high school. Shit, he even knew about my run in with the law as a kid. Then he offered me a job for more money in six months than I earn in a year."

"Didn't it seem a little weird to you, maybe a little off, that a guy would start a conversation in the men's room? Guys usually don't socialize there…or do they?"

"No. yeah. I mean, no, guys don't usually talk when they are taking a leak. And yes, I did think it weird, but he moved so quickly into telling me stuff about me, then the job offer, I didn't think."

"Maybe that is the key here Len. You didn't think.

"When and where else did you two meet?

"That was it the first time. Actually, he didn't mention money then, just that he had a job for me, gave me a prepaid burner and said he would be in touch.

"A week or so later, I was moving cows in the upper pasture and he calls, says he wants to meet at a coffee shop on my next day off. That is Sunday. My only days off are Sundays. I sometimes go to church if I get up in time, but usually I just hang out at the bunk-house."

"Back on topic Len. So, you met him on a Sunday. Where"

"My Place, it's a small restaurant right on the main drag. We sat in the back and he chatted, saying he had seen me at the Evangelical Church sometimes. He asked me about whether I was a Democrat or Republican. I told him I didn't know. I had never voted and didn't follow politics."

"Did he ask you why you worked for the president if you were not interested in politics?"

"No. He never mentioned the president by name at all. When I got the job, it was to work for a man and woman who ran the ranch. They never said anything about who the ranch belonged to, or nothin' like that.

"We ordered lunch and he was very kind, telling me to order anything I wanted. Even asked me if I wanted a beer, but I don't drink on Sundays. Then after lunch, he paid the bill and we left. In the parking lot, he came real close and said that he would pay me a thousand dollars a month, in cash, left in a storage locker in Sheridan for texting him anything new that happened at the ranch. I asked him what he meant, like if a calf was born or somthin' like that.

"I think he musta' thought I was kinda dumb, 'cause he smiled weird like, then said, no, he wanted to know when new people came to the ranch, or if I overheard anything about Mr.
Bakus comin' for a visit."

"You didn't think that was a lot of money for just gossiping?"

"I suppose. But no, I didn't think anything like that. I make twelve hundred bucks a month plus room and board but the government says I gotta pay taxes on the room and board, so they take a big bunch out each month. I just figured twelve thousand dollars for the year, cash, no taxes, was good as long as I didn't have to steal nothin."

"You understand now that you were spying on the president of the United States?"

"Aw, geez, lady, when you say it like that, you make me out to be some kinda asshole. All I was doin' was givin' this guy some information that he could probably have found out eventually in town by just listenin' to people talk."

"Agreed Len, but you see, you were giving him first-hand information, something he could act on immediately. Richards is not a good person Len. In fact, he is a very bad man who we are going to catch and put in prison for a very long time."

Of the many interrogation techniques Jessica had learned at the academy and over the years, bravado and threats were ineffective and the information gleaned was historically either false or flawed. She is proving it…again.

"The corrupt are treacherous and deceitful, proud of themselves, flaunting their abilities, indulging in cravings, grabbing profit, totally heedless."

Zen Lessons
Master Huili Fang

Jessica was tiring of this banter and wished she could cut to the chase and get the information immediately, but her experience told her patience was a virtue here.

Thiessen started to appear more relaxed than when she first came in to the interrogation room and she thought that odd, considering the magnitude of his crime, so she continued with, "Len, do you understand what is transpiring here? You have been charged with a federal crime and will do a long stretch in a federal penitentiary, probably in isolation because of the terrorism label. You might even be sentenced to *Guantanamo of the North*. Any idea where that is?"

"Are you sayin' you are going to send me to that place where they keep those rag heads from Iraq and places like that?"

"What I am saying Len, is that you are in deep trouble here. But no, not Cuba, that prison is being closed. I am referring to the place where those remaining terrorists who can't be tried or released are now living in solitary confinement in a Super Max prison in upper state New York, with only one way in and out...by plane. You remember those guys who escaped from the New York prison and tried to make it to Quebec? Well, this place is so remote, there is no way to escape and no place to go if you did."

"Aren't I supposed to have a lawyer here or something? I'm not dumb and I know I have some rights."

"Actually, no you don't Len. You remember the tragedy of the Twin Towers in New York. Right after that, Congress passed the Patriot Act, which defines money laundering to include making a financial transaction in America to commit a violent crime. Spying on the president is construed as just that, a violent crime. This gives me tremendous latitude over what happens to you because of national security. Depending on how you co-operate and the information I get, I can guarantee your jail time will be served here in Wyoming and the official charges, as they appear on the prison documents, will not mention terrorism or national security.

"So, let's get back on track here and see what we can do to make your next few years as comfortable as possible. You just may come out of this thing with a decent future."

"I think the most useful technique would be to act in a manner that is inconsistent with their expectations. Doing this give you immediate leverage because the other person is taken off guard. You didn't act as they thought you would, so now they have to adjust their reaction. It takes the wind out of their sails, so to speak.

"I used this technique as a gang detective. They expected me to be authoritative, judgmental and abrasive. Instead, I was friendly and conversational."

Stephanie Conn
Registered Clinical Counselor
Blue Line Magazine

She spent the next two hours digging, explaining, cajoling, baiting and otherwise moving Thiessen forward to where he felt comfortable making a formal statement implicating Richards, Sarkowski, both Joe and Martha, several church elders as well as those living on the farm. Much of what he offered regarding the church was hearsay and would never be allowed in court. Thiessen would never testify, but his statement would be used to intimidate and force a confession out of some, if not all, of those implicated.

Jessica was further ahead after the lengthy interview than before. She didn't know Richards' whereabouts, but presumed he was on the run. Joe Sarkowski thought he was in the clear because of the federal charges against the others being dropped, but he was wrong. Bruce had the interview statement transcribed, sent a copy to Sorento who obtained a federal warrant. Bruce then put a tap on Joe's land line, his cell and office numbers. If Richards didn't try and reach him, there was a good chance Martha would and Bruce had all her phones tapped as well.

Sheriff Jones had used Fukishura's influence and tapped the compound on Huckleberry Mountain, the Nez Pearce offices and several of the band leaders and was starting to reap benefits.

Jessica had texted Rebecca about the sale of the outfitter's weed by Chief Braket, and that she had heard from Chuck and his arrangement with Everson, so now she was just waiting for Rebecca to get back to move the money and chemicals to Huckleberry Mountain.

Chapter Forty-Three

Spencer had been participating in the chemical formula development and was fascinated by the numerous tests performed by the grad students in a massive grassy meadow within walking distance of the main lodge. He accompanied them under the pretense of being responsible for their safety, carrying the scoped .308 and clearing the trail by making lots of noise thirty minutes before their arrival, then following them into the meadow to set up their experiment.

Some of the research was performed in fifty-gallon barrels using a variety of chemicals and fertilizer, seeking the right composition with the greatest impact. Many were conducted with old tires Jenewein had flown in. They would stack the tires using rebar for reinforcement, then place the chemicals inside the center tire. As they improved on the detonation velocity, they constructed numerous cement containers, also reinforced with rebar. The enclosed space expanded the velocity exponentially, their theory being, if they can maximize a detonation in a reinforced space, that formula would maximize itself in a Suburban.

Jason had been busy trying to skirt Sandra's advances, sometimes successfully, and other times finding himself trapped and alone with her. It was the latter where he didn't ignore the quiet door knock at midnight, Sandra slipping into his room, dropping her robe as she closed and locked the door. During the numerous post-coital discussions, he learned a great deal about her dad and his political convictions. Often, when she had a little too much of the exceptional Falcon Winery's Cabernet Sauvignon Jenewein had flown in, she implied the democratic national convention would not occur, that her dad and his group were intent on stopping it.

Although Jason had been vetted to participate in the research, he was not part of the inner circle and therefore not read in on the big picture. He had to tread lightly for fear of creating suspicion, so he always cloaked his queries around the chemical experiments themselves and was successful in learning that there were to be a series of interruptions across the country using, among other delivery devices, black Suburbans with forged government license plates. He had gotten in the habit of playing back the video from the outdoor cameras over a cup of coffee each morning before the others made it into the kitchen. Each night the infrared cameras picked up someone walking around the exterior of the lodge. The person never got close enough to the cameras to distinguish features and Jason thought of placing more cameras further out but the distance was too great for the wireless system.

When he shared his observations with Jenewein, he didn't refer to the visitor Big Foot or Sasquatch but Jenewein did. He was convinced the intruder was the mythological creature which had created an entire sub-culture of believers. Jenewein reiterated his observation of the destroyed door on one of his supply trips, the cabinets doors torn off and the food thrown around the kitchen, in what he felt was a fit of rage, since nothing was locked and whomever it was could have helped themselves. There was also the reality of the hair stuck on the top of the door jam.

Spencer wasn't convinced. First, he was not a believer in lore and secondly, he had seen the videos of the intruder walking quite upright, wearing a jacket and baggy pants. It had long hair and a full beard, but you could tell it was not the hairy face seen on the YouTube videos showing an ape-like creature.

Chapter Forty-Four

Rebecca and Pen arrived back at the Four Seasons ladened with the spoils of Nordstrom's exceptional quality and pricing. They had called ahead to the concierge to have two bottles of California Napa Valley Chardonnay, glasses chilled and another plate of the delicious appies they enjoyed the previous night waiting for them by the pool.

They rummaged through their bags tossing their new purchases on the bed until they found the bathing suits and immediately undressed, both ending up naked in front of each other. Rebecca was first to stop, turn and leer at Pen, running her eyes up and down the taut body in front of her, stopping to run her tongue over Pen's breasts, around her nipples, then descending to her pubes, drinking in the aroma of another woman.

Pen responded by brushing her hands through Rebecca's hair, around her neck, glancing her thumb across her lips, then stepping in to softly kiss her lips as she caressed her derriere. Rebecca returned the kiss…aggressively, then pushed her away saying, "We may never make it to the pool if we keep this up. Let's go and we can come back to this after dinner." Penelope's reluctant agreement was emphasized with a gentle hand slid across Rebecca's stomach, then turning and bending over in front of her.

They pulled their suits on, tying each other's bra, grabbed towels from the bathroom, their small satchels containing their identification, money and credit cards, headed out the door and to the elevator and headed up.

The rooftop luxury was mind blowing when the door opened to the expansive presentation. The pool terrace was a landscaped oasis, a natural bliss one might expect in California's Beverly Glen or La Jolla, with geraniums and lobelia in hanging pots mingling with Juniper and Aspen trees. The pool was constructed with deep blue mosaic tile, and surrounded by Colorado buff sandstone. There were about twenty or thirty people milling around the massive heated pool. Most guests were couples, either by themselves, enjoying the peace and beauty or in small social groups. Rebecca's radar quickly spotted several single guys milling about the diving board acting aggressively toward each other. She couldn't tell if they were drunk, morons or both. She quickly slotted their presence in her field of vision and returned her attention to Penelope.

Finding two empty loungers with a side table, they quickly deposited their towels and satchels while Pen caught the attention of the server. Seeing Pen waving, the young male server beamed with delight and ran around the pool, jumping over a couple sunbathing, then slid to attention in front of Pen. "Yes Ma'am. What can I get for you?"

"Well aren't you an eager lad," she remarked glancing at his name tag.

"Darren, we are in room 601 and called in an order for wine and appies. Would you be a sweetheart and fetch them for us?" she asked, smiling coquettishly.

"Certainly Ma'am. I will be back in a flash."

"Pen you should be ashamed of yourself," Rebecca said, leaning over and laughing.

"Why, whatever do you mean Rebecca?" Pen retorted with a huge grin.

While waiting for Darren, they walked over to the diving board, purposely ignoring the leering fools with their junior high behavior and walked the board, Rebecca leading the way. They tip-toed to the end and maneuvered themselves so they stood side-by-side, then jumped. Swimming the breast-stroke to the pool's end they switched to their backs and did the back-stroke back to the deep end, treaded water for a while, then headed for the ladder, back to their table and toweled off...Rebecca keeping her peripheral on the clowns.

Darren arrived momentarily with their order, uncorked one bottle, poured an inch in a plastic wine glass and handed it to Pen. She nosed, sipped, sucked air through the mouthful, then handed the glass to Rebecca who did likewise.

Nodding to Darren that it passed their test, he smiled broadly while keeping his eyes glued to Pen's chest and tried to fill her glass and pour one for Rebecca. Pen encouraged him by giving him her sexy eye contact while using her upper arms to push her breasts together, allowing them to almost pop out of her swim-top.

Rebecca thought she was going to explode in laughter, but was able to maintain her composure until the poor lad had exited, probably with the biggest boner he had achieved in weeks.

Pen watched Darren leave then grabbed her glass and held it for Rebecca to clink for a toast. "To us!"

"To us and what lies ahead," replied Rebecca.

They were busy chatting, munching on their goat cheese and fuchsia bread appies and on their second glass when Rebecca caught the clowns approaching. Ignoring them wasn't an option, she placed her glass on the table, stood and walked toward them smiling broadly. "What can I do for you fellows? she asked, placing her right hand on her hip and turning her body slightly.

"Hi blondie. What brings you girls to Denver?" said one of the clowns, having difficulty enunciating girls and Denver.

"Just passing through boys and sorry, we are not interested in socializing today."

"Now that isn't very sociable to not be sociable," offered another degenerate as he took a long swig of his oversized beer.

"Really. Not interested boys. But thank you for your interest."

"Boys? What are you chicks, a couple of lesbos? You don't recognize men when you seem them? Oh, maybe you don't know what to do with men, it that it? Come on guys. This lesbo thinks we are boys, we need to encourage her and her homo friend over there to come party with us in our room. How about it blondie, can we show you we are men and not boys?"

"Boys," she emphasized the word, "I tried to be polite but now you are pissing me off, so just fuck off and go find someone else to harass."

"Son-of-a-fucking bitch, did you hear what this lesbo bitch just called us?" the first shouted, now getting the attention of several couples sitting near Penelope.

"Come here bitch" he yelled, grabbing Rebecca by her left wrist.

As he pulled her to him, she used her forward momentum, pivoted on her left foot and propelled her body into him, smashing his jaw with her right palm snapping his head backwards. She then quickly brought her right knee to his groin, causing him to double over. Once his head was down, she put both palms on the top of his head and blasted her right knee into his face breaking both cheek bones, his jaw and nose.

This all occurred in seconds, catching the other two by surprise. Once they realized their buddy was down and out, one attacked Rebecca, attempting to execute a bear hug, coming at her with his arms spread. Rebecca balanced on her left foot, curing the toes on her right foot backwards, exposing the four metatarsal heads, snapped a front kick to his face, broke his nose, spattering blood across the pool deck. The attacker grabbed his nose, looked at the blood and passed out, just as the third guy made his move. Rebecca had landed on her right foot and immediately spun in the direction of the next attack, balanced and performed the identical kick to the third attacker, using her left foot, catching him under the chin, snapping his head back so fiercely that it propelled him into a glass table and chairs, scattering the set against shocked observers and knocking him out.

Rebecca was in her zone and bounced a few times standing in the middle of the three unconscious idiots when a spontaneous applause erupted from the other guests, all of them standing, some pushing their fists in the air, showing their support, while others looked at the blood, broken bodies and destroyed patio set shaking their heads in astonishment.

Penelope continued to sip her white wine and nibble her goat cheese fuchsia throughout the fiasco. Having seen Rebecca fight previously, she was totally unfazed by the violence. She did however stand as Rebecca approached, gave her a hug and handed her a glass of white. Rebecca's breathing had not increased, nor had her heart rate. As she sipped her white, women began to gather, the men choosing to stay in the background.

The first woman, a striking brunette of about thirty wearing a lemon-yellow bikini which barely covered her thirty-six-inch boobs, said, "Holy fuck girl, I have never seen anything like that. I need to give you a hug." And she did.

Immediately the other women gathered tighter, creating a cacophony of interest. The questions were non-stop; "Where did you learn that?" You did it in bare feet." "How can I learn to do that?" "I love your bikini, where did you get it?"

The chatter was interrupted by two Denver Police officers accompanied by the concierge attempting to push through the crowd.

As the women parted a lane for the officer, the senior cop said, "Excuse me ladies, might we have a word?" directing his attention to the obvious points of interest.

"What happened here?"

Before Rebecca or Penelope could respond, the crowd began telling the officers of the incident.

"Whoa, whoa, ladies, please, one at a time." And they did, starting with the hugger who detailed the entire incident, pointing out that the drunken clown had grabbed Rebecca. A tall blonde in a black bikini chimed in, emphasizing that Rebecca dropped him, then finished off the other two who attacked her next.

The three clowns were just coming around as officers were cuffing them, officers commenting on the suspects' obvious inebriation.

"Ms. Rebecca, may we see some identification?"

This was a moment of truth Rebecca always feared but to date had never had to address during her career. Now she had to respond the best she could...which she did by retrieving just her Wyoming driver's license, not her Secret Service badge and ID. Pen anticipating she would be asked as well, pulled her license from her satchel and the officer took both simultaneously.

"Well, Penelope and Rebecca, may I call you by your first names? I would ask what prompted these suspects to target you two but, and I mean no disrespect, the answer is obvious," commented the lead officer.

Before either Rebecca or Penelope could respond, advising the officer it was okay to call them by their first names, the crowd acknowledged the officer's comment with, "Hey, what the hell kind of sexist comment is that," came a question from the crowd.

"My apologies, ladies. I'm sorry," he replied, his face turning red and realizing that his attempt at friendliness just backfired big time. "Please, I am sorry. Let me start again and I will leave motivation out of the equation. On second thought, will you ladies give your witness statements to the other officers and I think we are done here," he said wisely.

He motioned for one of his colleagues to step in and complete the interview, the first officer's sheepish, scarlet face telling his partner the entire story.

The second officer began with, "When do you head back to Wyoming?"

Pen was quick to answer, feeling overwhelmed by all the attention, "Monday morning officer."

"Rather than have you come to the station tomorrow, how about I check with my superiors and see if you can give your statement to StoneHead police when you get back?"

"That would be great officer. We appreciate the latitude. We just want to get on with our mini-holiday and get home," responded Rebecca.

He stepped away from the group, pulled his cell and made the call. Speaking briefly, he walked back to the group and handed the phone to Rebecca saying, "My sergeant wants to speak with you. She says you know each other."

Surprised and somewhat concerned, Rebecca took the phone, "Hello."

"Is this *The* Rebecca Simpson with the Secret Service? Before you answer, I need to know if you are working openly or covert. Say yes, for the latter."

"Yes"

"Well, I will be damned Rebecca. I will not keep you long but I wanted to speak with you personally because we trained briefly in Washington back in the day. You were kicking ass all over the gym and making quite a name for yourself. I think every female federal officer at that training session left with a new outlook on their job and an enlightened appreciation of women in law enforcement. We know all three of these suspects as they have been charged with sexual assault previously. I know you can't testify so we will work around that. Thanks for making my day. You do not have to say anything, just give the phone back to the officer…and kudos Rebecca. Enjoy the Four Seasons."

Rebecca gave the phone back to the officer trying, with great difficulty, to hide her smile. The officer walked away with the phone to his year, listening. Momentarily, he returned and said, "I don't know what just went down between you and my supervisor Ma'am. She has a reputation for not giving quarter to anyone, but that is none of my business. You are free to leave and thanks for cooperating. We will be in touch with StoneHead PD."

The officers left with their suspects in tow while Rebecca and Pen's supporters maintained their presence, seemingly not willing to leave. A woman who appeared to be in her mid-forties, and dressed in an Elan Cobalt Blue beach cover-up dress stepped forward and said, "Girls, I propose that we honor this occasion with a couple of bottles of chilled Dom Perignon Brut 2005?"

Pen was embarrassed but quick to respond, "That is a very kind offer but totally unnecessary."

"Penelope, I am a business woman who has seen the harassment of females for decades and observed zero changes, zero effort by society to change and I believe it is time for that change. Please allow us to give a small toast to the two of you, pioneers of change."

Pen turned to Rebecca who shrugged and said somewhat embarrassingly, "Well okay. Sure. Thank you very much."

"Terrific," replied Cobalt Blue as she hailed their server and ordered the Dom. Rebecca glanced out at the group of men behind their partners and noticed one broadcasting a huge smile, figuring their benefactor must be his partner...and proud of it.

After an hour or so, the women began drifting off to rejoin their social groups, leaving Pen and Rebecca to commiserate on the excitement, spending the remainder of their afternoon chatting about the strange turn of events with their entourage and how a potentially distasteful situation could result in new friendships.

Shortly after the group disbursed, Pen's curiosity got the better of her and she asked, "Do you mind if I ask who that was on the phone? It seems very weird that the cop questioning us was preparing for a trip to the cop shop with us, then his entire demeaner changed after the call."

Rebecca was tiring of having to lie to Penelope and made a mental note to speak with Jessica about ending the entire charade, but in the meantime her quick thinking responded with, "That was the strangest thing, the sergeant and I went to the University of Montana together, she graduated in criminology. We rodeoed together and she remembers the harassment we both endured being the only female bronc riders and the two of us beating most of the men." Penelope had a gut feeling there was more going on here than Rebecca was revealing, but she didn't want to spoil their weekend, so she said, "Okay. I was just curious. I have never been around women like these at the pool, have you?"

"Never! But you know the experiences I have had, like that at Cassandras' parking lot, women often appreciate that someone stands up to assholes.

The reply seemed to mollify Penelope, but Rebecca was sure Pen was mulling over the incident and that the topic would appear again.

They remained at the pool until 4:30, getting in and out of the water, diving frequently and enduring the admiring looks and smiles from every woman, and a few men as they walked by the various social groups. Once when Rebecca climbed out of the pool, a group of her new fans started chanting, "Becca, Becca, Becca and clapping their hands to Rebecca and Penelope's mortification.

Rebecca, astonished with the attention and quite embarrassed, couldn't think of anything else to do but perform a little bow and curtsy, then drift off to their table to dry off and finish the last bottle of white.

Chardonnay empty, they gathered their belongings and headed for the elevators. As they waited for the down signal the concierge came over and said, "Ladies, I have worked for the Four Seasons for ten years and have never seen anything as spectacular as this. I bow to your incredible talent to tame the beasts and the skillful interaction with the officers." As he left, he turned once and formally bowed, swinging his right arm under his chest.

Pen and Rebecca smiled, nodded and quickly entered the waiting elevator. Once in their room they saw they had less than forty-five minutes to get ready. Pen showered first, stripping and walking into the bathroom, all pretense of modesty forgotten. Rebecca laid out her new Ted Baker outfit of his Whimsical Forget Me Not Print pants, black double-breasted cotton/poly blend jacket, black camisole and Urmi lace back t-shirt, then stripped and leaned against the wall, her arms behind her back accentuating her sexuality.

Penelope was quick to shower and in ten minutes exited the bathroom naked with a towel around her wet hair. She spotted Rebecca, grinned and slowly, very slowly, sashayed toward Rebecca, her eyes never leaving Rebecca's face. As Pen got closer, Rebecca spread her legs ever so slightly, revealing more of her pubic cleavage. Pen's gaze didn't falter and as she reached Rebecca, her right hand reached down and caressed Rebecca's labia, drawing a deep moan as Rebecca tossed her head back against the wall. Pen continued caressing with her right hand while bending slightly and taking a nipple in her mouth. Rebecca moaned several more times as she felt a mini orgasm ripple through her body. As it subsided, she quickly gained her composure, kissed Pen and ran into the bathroom, stopping briefly to turn and blow Pen a kiss.

Penelope shuttered as she felt her anticipated orgasm fade. She leaned against the wall to regain her composure, assured they would continue later. She pulled herself out of her arousal to think of her outfit. She had planned on wearing her Mikado Osaka pants, persimmon scoop neck tank, orange mesh pullover sweater and new wedge sandals but changed directions, slipped into the hotel's fluffy robe and was putting on a light blush and pale lipstick when Rebecca came out of the shower, her hair dried and hand set with gel. As she passed Pen, she ran her palms gently over Pen's derriere, cupped her cheeks and pulled Pen's pelvis tight against hers, the sexual tension exquisite with their combined female aroma salivating deliciously.

Rebecca untied the robe exposing Pen's breasts…then moved ever so slowly forward and kissed Pen, running her tongue over her lips, gently grasping her head, caressing her neck and moving the robe off her shoulders, allowing it to fall around her now slightly spread legs. Without hesitation, Rebecca began kissing and licking Pen from her neck across each breast and nipple and down to the V below her navel.

Penelope separated her legs an iota, then pushed Rebecca's head down feeling her tongue extend itself to create a magical sensation that circled her body through her nipples and back to her groin. Rebecca began with a gentle caressing/kissing of her lips, running her tongue in a circle, first going in one direction then the other while pulling Pen's labia into her face. Moments seemed like forever as the glow increased with intensity, causing involuntary moans and guttural groans and her head to swing from side to side until Rebecca's tongue glanced over her clitoris...then Pen's body began to shake with such magnitude that she let go of Rebecca's head and grasped the wall behind her to maintain her balance.

As Penelope's body vibrations subsided and her head cleared of ecstasy, she pushed herself from the wall, took Rebecca's hand and led her to the bed and gently seated her, then pushed her back, lifted her legs up, then climbed between her legs and slowly repeated the joy she had experienced.

Moments into her intoxication, Penelope swung her legs over Rebecca's head and continued her delicious exploration of her labia and clitoris. As they climaxed simultaneously, they rolled back and forth on the bed shaking violently, each moaning between the other's legs. Sweaty and satiated with sexual pleasure, Penelope swung her legs around and nestled beside Rebecca. She had read many claims of women exhorting the ecstasy of a woman's touch. As an immediate convert, she said, "Did you know that Cosmo recommends we engage in orgasmic meditation? I stroke your clitoris for fifteen minutes then you do me," she stated with a deadpan expression.

Rebecca was a regular Cosmo reader but hadn't heard about OM so she replied, "I will go down on you anytime Pen, anytime, anywhere," she replied into Penelope's neck, then pull her into an embrace while reaching for the covers, pulling them over their bodies and snuggling, wondering if she would have enough strength in the morning for a try at OM.

"You give but little when you give of your possessions. It is when you give of yourself that you truly give."

Kahlil Gibran
American/Lebanese Poet
1883-1931

As Rebecca relished in the comfort of Penelope, she reflected on how she was more relaxed than ever before in her life. She wasn't thinking about tomorrow's agenda, who had wronged her that day, even the little pricks trying to flex their muscles for each other didn't bother her, albeit recuperating in the hospital…she smiled to herself.

Maybe her anger at boys and then men had nothing to do with their seemingly odd behavior or sexist attitude toward her, maybe it was her all along, not knowing who she was and striking out at everyone and everything. Her mind wandered back to her high school and college days when she thought at the time that she was too busy studying and rodeoing to date. Is it conceivable that she didn't want to date boys and didn't know the underlying reason? How could she have known she was gay? How could any teen know, other than raging hormones? But if a teen kept so busy as to not discover either boys or girls, she thought it was possible to end up in one's mid-thirties and discover true sexual identity.

She reflected on the hundreds of training sessions where her goal wasn't to achieve the instructor's approval but to punish her male colleagues for what she felt at the time was disrespect for women and general sexism. She smiled to herself and felt somewhat guilty, knowing now that her behavior had absolutely nothing to do with men, but her inner struggle with sexual identity. What had it been, fifteen, eighteen years striking out at society when what she really was struggling for was the real Rebecca to emerge and to fulfill her sexual identity.

I'm gay. Could that have been the problem all these years? Anger towards men, pissed off at society, at my jobs? Mm, she heard herself utter the comfort tone as she snuggled further under the duvet, taking in Penelope's jasmine fragrance.

30,000

Early morning and Sandra had just left for her own room. Jason retrieved his encrypted cell and sent a text to Jessica detailing Sandra's revealing conversation about her father and the CFBA objectives and their timeline.

Chapter Forty-Five

Karen and Tom's town car slid gracefully under the Chateau's elegant portico, stopped, and before Tom could open a door the driver had one and the Chateau's doormen had the other. Once exited, the driver and doorman retrieved their bags from the town car, placing them by the massive front doors. Tom thanked both men, shook the driver's hand and said he would see him Sunday afternoon per schedule. Their bags were taken to Reception where a junior clerk had the necessary paperwork ready, Tom having advised the hotel of their somewhat late arrival and the staff doing its due diligence.

A bellhop appeared immediately, took their bags and the key cards from the clerk, welcomed them to the Fairmont Chateau and guided them to the bank of elevators. Stopping at the eighth floor, they were quickly ushered into the Junior Valley room with a view of Rainbow Mountain. It was an extremely luxurious bedroom with a private den, French Doors opening to a small balcony and a huge jetted tub with separate toilet area in the bathroom.

Karen tipped the bellhop twenty dollars, carried her bag to the bedside and collapsed into one of the two chocolate microfiber occasional chairs, kicked off her shoes and wiggled her feet with a sigh of relief. Tom took her que and did likewise, not bothering to undo his shoe laces.

They were mentally and physically exhausted. Momentarily Karen said, "If I don't move now I will sleep in this position," then pulled herself from the chair and headed for the bathroom.

While Karen showered, and wrapped herself in one of the hotel's massive white terrycloth robes, Tom ordered room service from the Chateau's Wildflower. For Karen, he chose the Dungeness Crab Linguini with chili, lime, arugula and gem tomatoes tossed in white wine and garlic butter while he selected the New York Steak Frites Black Apron beef with drizzled spicy peppercorn sauce, grilled asparagus and hand cut truffle fries and of course a bottle of chilled Chardonnay. Perusing the wine list, the Fairmont had a world-wide selection but with Canada and particularly British Columbia wining various awards in excellence he wanted to support local, so he chose a bottle from the Gray Monk Winery in British Columbia's Okanagan Valley.

The meal arrived just as Karen made her entrance from the bathroom. She quickly moved out of view of the server while Tom got the meal placed, signed then poured two glasses. Karen jumped from the bedroom and ran to the offered wine glass. They toasted and after Tom took a sip, he said, "Give me five to take a shower."

Before Karen could object, figuring the meal would get cold, he was gone. He was indeed back in five minutes with wet hair and wrapped in the matching robe.

They enjoyed their meal and the delicious Gray Monk in relative silence, stopping periodically to comment on the seminar's presenters. They were equally impressed with Chapman and wondered how their joint task will be influenced by her comments.

An hour later they brushed their teeth, crawled into bed, kissed, snuggled and were out within moments.

30,000

Her encrypted cell blasted them awake at six. David Kopas. Karen answered on the third ring.

"Good morning David. What's up?"

"Hi Karen," he began quickly, obviously in a hurry to impart his information. "Cesium has been stolen from the Manitoba mine. The RCMP believe it is on its way west but they have not been able to determine its exact destination. I need you two to co-ordinate with the Alberta Mounties and find this stuff before it leaves the country."

"What makes you sure it is destined for outside of Canada?"

"It may not be, but we do know it is heading west from traffic cams. Although every major law enforcement agency has a BOLO on the van, the RCMP are leading the search. Traffic cams picked up the van as it left the road leading from Babine Mine and turned onto Highway One east of Winnipeg. Originally the Mounties thought they would be headed for the airport but surveillance cameras showed nothing. Then a few hours later cameras west of Winnipeg showed a succession of photos of the van

maintaining a clear westerly destination with three occupants. "The report and any forensics will be available soon from the Members investigating the robbery. Apparently, there are three armed suspects who hijacked the van a few kilometers from the mine. It took several hours before the delivery was noted as missing when the crew failed to check in at the designated time. I have advised Fukishura so her team is in the loop.
"This may all be academic within hours if the Mounties or city police pick them up. The Force has the lead on this and Edmonton detachment commander and her team are expecting you Monday. I told them not to look for you until late. You guys need to take this weekend to refuel and regenerate."

"Okay. Got it. Thanks, David. Will let you know when we arrive."

She put the phone down on the night-stand, turned to Tom, swinging her leg over his chest, letting her pubic hair brush his stomach, gazed down at his tasseled hair, stubble and waited for him to ask, "So, what was that all about. I can kinda guess by your side of the conversation."

Karen recapped the situation culminating in a huge grin and added, "We still have the weekend. We can catch an early morning flight to Edmonton Monday and be at the detachment in the late afternoon."

"Sounds good to me. What are we going to do with two full days to ourselves?" he grinned.

Without saying a word, Karen kissed him, then nibbled his ear, knowing that was all it took to get Tom a full erection. She could feel it start to rub between her butt cheeks and momentarily reached behind her, grabbed it with her left hand and gently guided it into her saying, "Oh, one of us will come up with some ideas," as she started to move up and down, enjoying the exquisite sensation his erection had on her G-Spot. She had found the exact angle needed to stimulate the G when they were on the mini-vacation in Santa Monica and had managed to work it into their love making at least three times a week.

It didn't take too many thrusts and hip gyrations and Tom licking her nipples for her to begin a massive orgasm, with Tom climaxing along with her. Tom knew once she started to rotate her hips and tell him how deep he was; it was only a matter of seconds before he exploded. Karen continued to ride Tom until he became flaccid, then rolled off him and grabbed the sheet end to wipe the sweat off her face and chest. "So, that was my idea, what do you have in mind?" she quipped as Tom took the other end of the sheet and wiped down his body, grinning sheepishly.

"Well, now that we have worked up an appetite, I say we head down for breakfast at the Wildflower, but first, how about some coffee? Do you want to shower first while I check my messages and order coffee?"

"Deal," she replied, sliding out of the Queen and heading to the shower, giving her butt a little shimmy and shake looking over her shoulder running her tongue over her lips.

Tom smiled, shook his head and worked to keep his heart from racing and get his head back on track. He knew that since he was sequestered to CSIS, all communication would be through David but he checked anyway. Nothing. He made a quick call for coffee then headed into the bathroom to use the toilet and shave. He had a clean face when the door knock arrived. He grabbed his robe and did a two-step hop to door, accepted the coffee, signed and had a cup poured for Karen when she waltzed out of the bathroom naked.

She was running a towel through her hair as she slowly made her way around the bed heading for the balcony. Tom stood almost mesmerized and thought back to when she had called him out of the blue in Toronto. He had met Karen and Jessica at the Police Academy and they renewed their friendship. He had kicked himself in university for not following his heart and asking her out. Not having heard from her in years, he had moved on. Their first date resulted in Karen taking out a knife wielding thief in the restaurant's parking lot then incredible sex at her place and him spending the night, something he had not done with a woman since the University of Ottawa and a drunken coed had slept in his bed with him on the floor.

Karen's opening of the French Doors awakened Tom from his reverie. As she stepped out naked, he poured a coffee for himself and joined her, albeit robed.

It was early enough on a Saturday that the area below their seventh story room was deserted, so Karen was confident her exhibitionism would bring neither the concierge or male gawkers. Besides, it would appear by

Tom's erection returning that he was enjoying the view, which made the cool breeze worth the slight chill.

As Tom joined her, they clinked coffee mugs and she reached inside Tom's robe and stroked his phallus, then said with a leer, "We better get to breakfast or I will be the only one eating."

Tom almost choked on his coffee, spitting some out through his nose as he absorbed Karen's candidness. He regained his composure and replied, "I think we could both dine in this morning, but I get your point," he said as his palm glanced across her left butt cheek, turned and headed for the shower. Karen stayed on the balcony a while longer, enjoying her strong Black and taking in the spectacular view of the sun rising over Wedge Mountain. Black gone, she heaved a pleasurable sigh, turned and went back into their room to dress for the day.

The Wildflower breakfast was as spectacular as they had heard. Their view was of the base of one of the lifts, with the short distance between their window seat and the base covered in a deep summer green, dotted with hundreds of wildflowers. Being early risers, they were alone and quickly served. Karen chose the Whistler Mountain, a combination of two scrambled eggs topped with salsa with six sausage links, potato hash, roasted tomato, asparagus, and more Black. Tom enjoyed their Corned Beef Hash of shredded potato sautéed with corned beef, bell peppers, scallions topped with two poached eggs, tomato fondue, toast with Rootham Preserves from Guelph, Ontario and more Black.

Chapter Forty-Six

The morning after the cesium robbery, two hunters stumbled, literally, upon the white van with the drivers barely conscious and cognizant. The hunters called 9-1-1 which summoned the Mounties and paramedics. It took some time for both to arrive given the truck's seclusion. One hunter left his rifle with his buddy and walked out to the main road to guide first responders. The second hunter untied the victims and encouraged them to drink a little warm tomato soup he had made for his lunch. Once he had gotten them to consume liquids, he left the van, picked up both rifles, checked to ensure they were empty then took them into the bush, out of sight of the Mounties. He knew they would be required to produce their firearms and licenses, that wasn't the problem. He knew the law enforcers would arrive pumped and in a state of Orange in the Color Code of Awareness he had learned in the military police and he didn't want to start their relationship flat on the ground, cuffed and under suspicion.

Unknown to the hunters, the RCMP had become involved shortly before their 9-1-1 call when the recipient of the shipment called the mine asking its whereabouts. So, when the 9-1-1 call occurred, several Members were in route and were indeed in code Orange. When the man on look-out on the main road heard the sirens, he immediately stood with one arm out to his side and the other pointing up the side-road. Both cruisers slid to a stop with the ambulance and paramedics immediately behind them. All four officers quickly surrounded the hunter, one asked for identification and another for specifics of the call. Satisfied that the spotter was not involved, he was placed into the cruiser uncuffed so he could guide them the short distance up the side road.

Once at the location of the stolen van, one officer had the first hunter join his buddy and give their statements while the other three Members ran to the van with the paramedics. The victims were stabilized and transported to the nearest hospital with one officer accompanying them, while the others secured the scene, had the van towed to Winnipeg RCMP Crime Scene facility, then notified their superiors that the cesium was in the wind.

Chapter Forty-Seven

Karen and Tom spent the morning playing eighteen holes at the Fairmont Chateau Golf Course. Neither had ever played before…but it was something different and they were up to the challenge. Saturdays being the course's busiest day, they created a foursome with another couple who had been playing for years. The experts had some reservations about having to lag, but then thought it might be a nice change of pace not having to play as though they were training for the next PGA.

Tom was surprised how amiable the couple was, particularly the guy. Tom had always believed golfers were like fishers, neither liking to deviate from their sole purpose, but this guy was very friendly, so much so that after they stopped keeping score, they suggested the four have lunch together.

Noon hour dining came in the form of the Longhorn Saloon at the base of Whistler Mountain. The pub had opened in 1981 and had become an instant legion. The two couples were surprised with how crowded it was for a summer Saturday. They were seated close to the front and fortunately away from any of the massive stereo speakers. The service was quick for it being so busy. Megan and Karen ordered the Thai Wrap of roasted chicken, Amarillo rice, peppers, spring onion, and shredded carrot in a flour tortilla with a Thai peanut sauce. Tom and Samson had the Beef Burrito with spicy ground beef, Amarillo rice, pinto beans, jalapenos, cheddar cheese in a flour tortilla, with a side of fresh salsa, sour cream and guacamole.

Conversation was light but informative. The couple were from northern Ontario and owned a motel in the Collingwood ski area on the south end of Georgian Bay. They laughed at their desire to see what a real mountain was like, but in fact Blue Mountain was owned by Intrawest, the same company which operates Whistler/Blackcomb, so there was probably a little marketing research going on. Neither shared more than that, which was fair since Tom and Karen didn't tell them they were with CSIS, which worked out well when the conversation turned to the attack on the Parliament Buildings. Megan and Samson commended the RCMP and particularly Sergeant at Arms, Kevin Vickers who took out the shooter.

Samson was so taken by Vickers' movements of diving around the pillar, landing on his side and shooting that he stood up and demonstrated Vickers' tactic.

Since the subject was broached, Karen asked what they knew about the Canadian Spy agency and whether it should have had the shooter under surveillance. To the agent's delight, the couple were well informed and knew that there were so many domestic insurgents, that law enforcement couldn't track all of them.

Socializing on the issue continued through the meal, extrapolating into other country's participation in fighting terrorism and all four agreed that Canada and America had to do more to coordinate their efforts.

After lunch, the couples went their separate ways, wishing each a great time in one of the world's leading ski resort.

They spent the rest of the afternoon store hopping in Whistler Village, back to the Chateau for a nap then readied for their six o'clock dinner reservation at Araxi in the village.

Tom figured he was probably not much company after their nap as he couldn't keep his mind off Monday's assignment and wondering where the cesium was destined and praying the Mounties had intercepted the shipment. He managed to throw off the cloak of anticipation and changed his outlook when he dressed in taupe slacks, a yellow open collar button down dress shirt, a sport coat with muted blues and greens and brown tassel loafers. He felt particularly good when Karen emerged from the bathroom in her Gucci striped caban buckle and brown halter top with wide leg, off-white, cuffed riding pants. Hiding her shoulder holster was a belted sand safari jacket.

Tom made the appropriate admiration of how lovely she looked and to his surprise she reciprocated. Although Tom's six feet of compact muscle, dark blond short wavy hair and square jaw drew constant female glances, Karen was the first woman he had dated who commented on his looks frequently and he was relishing in the attention.

At five-thirty they headed out to meander their way to Araxi. They walked down Blackcomb Way and immediately noticed the social mix had changed remarkably since their time at the Longhorn. Gone were the families and couples. In their place were large groups of young males, wandering aimlessly heading to the Village for bar-hopping. An awfully early start thought Tom as he took Karen's hand and swung around several groups shouting obscenities to each other.

Karen looked at Tom with raised eyebrows and said, "Are you wondering why the Members are allowing these guys to gather like this?"

"My thoughts exactly. The Mounties must be deployed within the Village itself if they are anticipating trouble. I wasn't aware that Whistler took on such a sinister outlook on the weekend."

Just as Tom swerved around another group, one of the guys he passed reached out and grabbed Karen by her left upper arm. Karen allowed herself pulled toward her attacker then she twisted her arm inward and around her attacker's own upper arm, thereby trapping it tight against her left side. All in one motion she struck him in the eyes with two fingers then drove her knee into his groin. As he hit the ground, she kicked him in the ribs twice.

Instinctively Tom turned his back to Karen just as the second attacker rushed him. Tom stepped to his left and delivered a crimpling kick to the guy's right knee, cracking it and dropping him instantly. Karen was prepared to strike the third guy when he looked at his buddies, turned and ran.

Tom straightened his jacket, brushed off his pants and said with an infectious smile, "There is something about dating you that brings out the assholes."

Karen retorted with, "And I thought it was you attracting all the attention," she quipped with a huge grin then continued, "Shall we dine?" taking Tom's arm and continuing their stroll down Blackcomb Way and into the Village.

They arrived shortly before six, not losing much time from the interaction enroute. The maître d' seated them immediately, pulling a chair out for Karen at a window table. The sommelier was right behind the maître d' with a welcome to Araxi offering a complimentary glass of Noble Ridge's The One 2009 Sparkling wine to each, choosing Tom to do the first taste.

"Not a bad start to the evening," noted Tom as he nosed the glass, swirled, sipped, sucked a little wine, then offered Karen a toast.

Just as she was clinking, Karen glanced out at the Village Common to see four Mounties on bikes heading toward the Chateau and said, “This might turn out to be an exceptionally exciting evening; kicking ass, dinner with a very hot detective and outrageous sex afterwards,” raising her eyebrows slightly and winking at Tom.

Tom laughed so hard and loudly that he snorted his wine up his nose. He bowed his head, grabbed a napkin, wiped his face, revealing a huge grin, then raised his glass to toast Karen again saying, “You are impossible…gorgeous, outrageous and impossible.

Casually scrutinizing his environment had become a force of habit, practiced by many, if not most law enforcers. Tom was often unware that a casual observer might think his covertness was intrusive. As he glanced around, his attention was drawn to Araxi’s ambiance, which was dominated by glass. He caught bartender Rene Wuethrich in his peripheral immediately and noted the entire ceiling was beveled glass creating a distorted reflection of the bartender and seated customers waiting for their table.

The bar itself was white marble with the leg area a chromatism of marble squares, their brilliance reflecting off the overhead mirrors creating a multi-colored spinning wheel effect which caught the eye as patrons entered the restaurant. The marble squares were repeated on the numerous structural columns dispersed throughout the dining room.

The room was divided into numerous private dining areas separated by contemporary styled partitions adorned with numerous Italian Renaissance art replicas.

Tom’s attention returned to Karen as their server walked to their table and said, “Welcome to Araxi. My name is Robert and I will be your server for the evening. Are you enjoying The One? It is new on the menu this month.”

Karen raised her glass to note its emptiness and said, “Delicious Robert and thank you for the introduction to Noble Ridge.”

Robert didn’t miss a beat and immediately filled her glass and did likewise for Tom, then added, “Our Executive Chef James Walt has prepared his special Oysters for your enjoyment.” Robert stepped aside as another server arrived with two square smoked grey plates, Robert continued, "This array of Beach Angel oysters is from Cortes Island off our British Columbia coast. They are considered deep cup, offering a briny, tangy, clean kiwi like finish. Please enjoy and I will return with your menus," he finished as he slowly backed away from their table, turned and headed into the kitchen.

Karen looked at Tom and said, "What is going on Tom? This service can't be the norm."

"Probably not. I called yesterday afternoon, made the arrangements and just happened to mention that it was a special occasion, neither of us having been to Whistler or Araxi before."

"You continue to amaze me Tom Hortonn," she said beaming with delight. "Please do not change," she added, leaning over, placing her hand behind his cheek, then glancing her lips gently and seductively across his.

Karen leaned back just as Robert arrived with the menus, almost having a heart attack seeing the butt of her 9-mm pistol. Neither Tom nor Karen noticed the change in Robert's demeanor as they turned to welcome him back to their table. Robert cleared his throat and politely introduced the menu and the day's Dungeness Crab special, bowed, backed up and returned to the bar area nodding at the general manager to follow him into the kitchen.

Karen and Tom mused over their choices and with much angst of having to pick just one, Karen decided on the BC Dungeness Crab and Matane Shrimp Roll wrapped with wild smoked sockeye salmon, avocado and egg crepe yuzu mayonnaise and avocado salsa verde, while Tom settled on the Canadian six-ounce Beef Tenderloin Steak, baked potato and aged cheddar gratin with buttered baby carrots, grilled chimichurri and red wine jus.

Robert returned to take their order with his normal comportment. He listened to their choices but wrote nothing down, then recommended a somewhat tart Mission Hills Chardonnay for Karen's seafood and a very dry 2008 Three Sister's Bench Red from British Columbia's Naramata Bench for Tom's protein choice. Robert refilled each of their glasses and noted their meal would be prepared personally by Executive Chef, James Walt.

While the law enforcers were enjoying the wine, the ambiance and each other's company, six Mounties and two ambulances had converged on Blackcomb Way where the paramedics were attempting to revive two of the assailants. Supervising the containment of the crime scene was a sergeant conversing on his cell phone with the detachment commander, a woman not too pleased with being disturbed on one of the few days off she enjoyed. "Alright sergeant, let me recap my understanding. You have several intoxicated men, some unconscious, one with a broken knee and another with a broken arm and no witnesses. Do I have that correct?"

"Yes Inspector. Exactly."

"Well, let me throw a wrinkle into your evening. I just got off the phone with dispatch who advised me there is a woman dining at Araxi who is carrying a firearm. I am almost to the village now and will deal with this, you wrap that scene up as soon as you can and get that area back to normal. I do not want calls from the mayor telling me we are screwing up their tourist trade."

"Yes ma'am. But hold on a moment. One of the constables is waving me over. I think he has somewhat of a statement from the least injured victim."

There was dead air as the Inspector waited for the sergeant to return, giving her an opportunity to park her Suburban and start walking toward the village.

"Okay Inspector, here is what we have so far," said the sergeant as he ran through what occurred, that there were two attackers, a man and a woman, both in their mid-thirties.

"I am almost at Araxi. Get all the suspects identified and I want them cuffed to their respective gurney and a Member assigned to each at the hospital until you get that sorted out. I may need back-up at Araxi so send a Member here but have him out of sight until I signal," she concluded, hanging up on her colleague and opened the door to the iconic Whistler establishment.

Tom and Karen were seated at an angle to the window with each slightly back, creating a street view of an empty table. Each had a direct angle to the front door and their instincts activated simultaneously as a forty-something woman entered alone. With shoulder length, black wavy hair, an angular face with a round jaw, she presented a five foot, ten-inch stature and spoke briefly with general manager Neil Henderson, then stepped momentarily into an alcove, exiting quickly with a Ted Baker peony print lightweight silk scarf over her hands and walked directly to their table.

As she approached, Karen noted the outfit the visitor was wearing was one she and Jessica had considered buying at Holt in Toronto on their first shopping spree. It was a Veronica Beard jacket with a single-button closure, peak lapels with long sleeves and button cuffs over a white-on-white poplin blouse with a three-inch white bow tie. The outfit was casually set off by a pair of tight leg distressed jeans and a pair of Vince Camuto angular cut-out booties in khaki suede.

Stopping abruptly in front of Tom and Karen, she said, "Hi. Good evening folks. I am Bryn Matter. May I have a moment of your time. I do not wish to intrude and it will only take a moment."

Karen's experience knew there was something here out of the normal so she didn't hesitate and waved a hand gracefully to an empty seat as Tom pushed his chair back and placed one leg over the other with both hands on his lap.

Matter kept her right hand covered by the scarf while she withdrew a small wallet from her inside pocket and presented it to Karen saying, "I am Inspector Matter with the RCMP. I am the Whistler detachment commander and I have a little problem with which I am hoping you good folks can help."

"Sure," said Karen. "What is the problem and how might we help?"

"Before I begin I need you to know that I have a 9-mm Smith & Wesson pistol on my lap," she said expecting a reaction that was not forthcoming. Neither Tom nor Karen responded other than giving her stern blank stares.

"Well this is an interesting response to my telling you I have a weapon trained on you ma'am. Irrelevant I guess. We were called because you were seen with a gun under your jacket ma'am and although I do not know yet if you are locals or visiting, but here in Canada it is unlawful to carry a concealed firearm. Might you care to share?"

Karen was first to respond with, "We completely understand Inspector Matter. Might I offer you my identification?"

"Slowly. If I see anything but paper, I will blow your boyfriend's nuts off."

Karen stifled a grin, immediately liking this kick-ass Mountie. She methodically withdrew her identification and handed it to the inspector, who quickly held it up so she could observe the two diners while perusing the document, then smiled and said, "Son-of-a-bitch! I assume you sir, have similar identification?"

Tom simply nodded and retrieved his ID and handed it to Matter.

"Are you armed as well Mr. Hortonn?"

"Yes."

She shook her head, removed the scarf from her hand and furtively slipped her weapon into its holster and said, "I have been with the Force for quite a while now and this is a first for me. Might I ask, without breaking confidentiality, what brings you to Whistler? Not business I hope."

Tom replied with a smile while taking his identification back from Matter, "No ma'am, not business. We were attending a Vancouver conference and thought we would take advantage of the weekend and enjoy your hospitality before flying out Monday for Edmonton. Our sincere apologies for causing a problem. We hope we have not caused you, the other Members or Araxi staff an inconvenience."

"Not an inconvenience Mr. Hortonn. Robert and Neill are the only two who are aware of the situation and I will allay their concerns when I leave. But I do have a question that is possibly related. My staff are attending to three assault victims just up the way a bit on Blackcomb Way. All three are being transported to the hospital as we speak. One has a broken, another a shattered knee and the third a possible concussion. Their description of the attackers is a man and a woman in their mid-thirties. Might you know anything about the incident?"

Karen smiled and offered an explanation. Once her brief delivery was complete, Matter said smiling, "I am not surprised by their behavior nor am I bewildered by yours. I mean, how unfortunate can these clowns be taking on two CISS agents. We have been inundated with the lower mainland goons coming to Whistler and causing trouble. Usually it is drunk and disorderly. We arrest, stuff them in the tank overnight, present them to a justice of the peace the next morning and they are released on their own recognizance, but this is new. I suspect my staff have processed the three and they will undoubtedly have a record. The boozers do not usually go in for physical assaults, so their motivation will be interesting to discover. Either way, might you two stop by the detachment tomorrow and provide a statement? I promise, you will not be called to testify once their attorneys hear who their potential victims were. Just out of curiosity though," she added with a smirk, "Who broke the knee and who the arm?"

Tom raised his arm and said, "Knee", then Karen said, "Arm...by default."

"Bryn. Do you mind me calling you by your first name, now that we are not under arrest?" asked Karen.

The inspector laughed and said, "Well, considering you are not under arrest, at least not yet, sure."

Karen joined the mirth and invited Bryn to join them for a drink.

Tom was still squirming over the near loss of his genitals at the hands of this Mountie, had she shot him from under the table, but he recouped well enough to chime in with, "Yes, please, join us and tell us something about Whistler others may not know and maybe about yourself; how did you become an inspector of such a huge detachment at a young age."

"Thank you very much for the invitation. I accept. Just let me call the Members and provide an update. I'll be back in a flash," she said, getting up slowly and buttoning her Veronica Beard.

"Love the scarf by the way," added Karen as Bryn headed to the entry alcove.

After she left, Tom turned to Karen and mouthed, *Wow*! but said nothing more.

Matter returned quickly commenting that being in charge had its advantages; filling staff in without complex explanations. She was followed by Robert carrying three drinks. After he pulled Bryn's chair out, saying, "Inspector," he tabled the drinks and departed.

Bryn raided her glass and offered, “A toast to your skills, grace and for removing some of Whistler’s trash.”

Karen and Tom clinked with hers and Karen replied, “Glad to accommodate. Now. What about the Whistler dirt?”

They spent the next twenty minutes chatting primarily about the 2010 Olympics and the vast preparation the detachment experienced, the numerous CISS agents who were assigned to the area as well as various military units. “Most folks do not know that JTF2, Canada’s Counter Terrorism Unit, was deployed here from the games here in Whistler, south to Squamish…all in the mountains. The unit had snipers covering every game, every event and presentation from the forests and no one knew. I kinda liked that covertness of the security. Let’s see, what else? Oh, yes, the Force combined operations with the Canadian and American Coast Guards and we had the coast covered from Bellingham to Prince Rupert. Nothing could have gotten through our floating sonar detection and rotating patrols.”

The commiseration continued until Bryn noticed Robert hovering. She gracefully rose from her chair and offered her hand and said, “It has been a pleasure, even under the weird circumstances.”

The agents responded in kind just as Robert arrived with their meals followed by Sommelier Samantha Rahn and their wine. As he placed their meals, he commented, “We are delighted you had an opportunity to meet our detachment commander and we are terribly sorry for the confusion.”

Rahn was pouring their wine as Tom replied, “Think nothing of it Robert. We are happy it all worked out,” not adding that he had thought for a nanosecond they were going to have a major incident, which would be difficult to explain to David.

The rest of their evening was enjoyable and uneventful. Karen delighted in the Dungeness’ presentation; shell top removed with the body and legs resting on a bed of purple kale surrounded by halved cherry tomatoes. The oblong plate hosted the shrimp rolls wrapped in salmon drizzled with the avocado yuzu mayonnaise at the opposite end. The presentation was so inviting, Karen was tempted to photograph the plate, but thought the move would be a tad tacky for the Araxi.

Tom's cuisine was a more traditional appearance with the sixteen-inch diameter white plate hosting the massive piece of Canadian beef with the jumbo Prince Edward Island baked potato split, topped with sour cream and chives, with a half on each side of the steak, while the buttered carrots surrounded the rest of the meat. A side dish of chimichurri, a blend of cilantro, parsley, oregano and red wine vinegar accompanied the steak to be spooned by the diner over the meat as desired.

The village excitement died as quickly as it began. Their window view was of couples strolling, enjoying the ambiance of Whistler's enchanted evenings. Most of the women were attired in either boots with heels, tight jeans and a long sweater or in a frumpier style of Patagonia jackets, baggy jeans and hiking boots. Gone were the inebriated and the agents remarked to one another that Matter must have had the Members do a sweep, using portable breathalyzers and arresting violators for public intoxication. Couples and families undoubtedly had no idea what transpired and how their evening could have turned out quite differently had it not been for the efficiency of the RCMP.

Dessert was a Chocolate Ganache Tart, a semi sweet chocolate ganache in sweet pastry with hazelnut meringue and chantilly cream which they inhaled, each commenting on the richness of the chocolate and creaminess of the meringue cream. As they were tempted to lick their plates, Sommelier Samantha Rahn appeared with two beautiful long stem wine glasses. As she tabled them she introduced the Summerhill Ice wine as, "This is a delightful grape from Kelowna's Summerhill Winery. A 2013 chardonnay ice wine with Neill's compliments. It boasts a citrus, apple and peach fruity allure each rounded out with hints of toasty butterscotch on your nose while your palate will experience rich flavors of gooseberry and apricot. Enjoy."

Tom raised his eyebrows and asked, "This has turned out to be more of an exciting evening than either of us planned, wouldn't you say?"

"That it has. Almost as much as our first date at the Calgary in Toronto. Remember the parking lot?"

"I do. You kicked ass then too. But I must say I remember the rest of the evening with far greater clarity, joy and thrill than team work in the parking lot," Tom added as he raised his glass and offered it to Karen.

Winthrop, not often at a loss for words, blushed visibly, extended her glass to clink with Tom's, then said with a flirtatious grin, "I agree," kissed her glass, blew it to Tom and sipped her Chardonnay ice.

Now it was Tom's turn to blush, acknowledging her coquettish smile and knowing the sexual experience ahead would probably blow his mind.

Chapter Forty-Eight

The stolen cesium had made good time heading west from Winnipeg and was on Alberta Highway 3 just outside of Blairmore, heading to the British Columbia border when RCMP Constable Rick Drought's cruiser picked up the license plate of the stolen van. Drought's police car, PC, was equipped with Automated License Plate Recognition, ALPR, software which interfaced with two roof mounted cameras, enabling the on-board computer to scan over four thousand plates an hour. Plate numbers are automatically linked to uploaded data from the Canadian Police Information Centre of stolen vehicles. The system was used successfully in a British Columbia abduction when a Sparwood boy was taken from his home. Police used ALPR throughout B.C. and Alberta to block all the kidnapper's escape routes.

Drought always drove in a state of Orange, of the Color Code of Awareness, meaning he was primed to act immediately, rather than come out of comatose White, the state one would be in taking a shower, to move slowly up the reaction chain. He was heading East from Crowsnest Pass, one of sixteen communities policed by the Blairmore detachment, when the ALPR system sounded an alarm and flashed a photo of the stolen van he just passed heading west. He watched his rear-view mirror until the van was out of site, then slowed slightly and performed a perfect 180-turn and hit the after burners on his Jaguar 3.0-litre, V6, supercharged, 380 as he called for back-up from any available units. The Jag was first introduced to Western Canada's Mounties in North Vancouver with impressive results in vehicle pursuits with several Alberta detachments adopting the rapidly accelerating vehicle.

Dispatch responded immediately with the reality of rural policing; the closest unit was in Lundbreck Falls, a good forty minutes east. Drought acknowledged the transmission as his unit closed the distance on the stolen van. The ALPR software was also equipped with a GPS monitoring component. Once the system locked onto a plate number, Drought didn't have to keep the vehicle in sight.

His plan was to follow at a distance until back-up arrived. That didn't work out as planned, as his computer screen showed the van turning

South on an old forestry road. Moments later, Drought did likewise, then stopped. He knew this expanse well, having patrolled the three hundred and seventy-three square kilometer enforcement area for a number of years. The road dead-ended about five kilometers in.

Drought radioed his position and received an update on the occupants and van with the information they were suspected in the theft of cesium. Drought didn't need to know the cesium's particulars to understand the gravity of the situation in which he found himself. Determined to end the thieves escape attempt, he moved cautiously ahead, not sure whether the van was heading to the road's end or somewhere in between. He knew there were no off roads, so he could presume they were heading all the way in, but officers had died presuming and Drought was not a fan of his own death so he proceeded with extreme caution until he saw a bend in the road, three hundred meters ahead. He stopped, turned his PC at an angle blocking the road entirely, hit the overhead emergency lights, radioed his position again, exited his vehicle, retrieved his C8 Military Assault Carbine from the trunk, injected a thirty-round magazine, chambered a round and set up position using the engine block as cover.

The Colt C8 Carbine is a semi-automatic version of the fully automatic used successfully for years by Canadian Special Forces. Made in Canada, it weighs three kilograms with a thirty-round magazine. Drought had two additional magazines in his duty pants pockets. The law enforcement semi-automatic version fires its 5.56 x 45 mm NATO rounds at 900 meters per second with a velocity of 2,940 fps as quickly as the shooter can pull the trigger. The black, aggressive looking rifle is incredibly accurate at four-five hundred meters, a shooter placing thirty rounds within a two-inch circle. Drought was very precise and proficient with the Colt having used it extensively in his military career.

Drought didn't have long to wait before he heard the van speeding toward him, having dropped the cesium off at the road's end. As the van turned the curve, the passengers immediately keyed into the reality that after the theft and several day's journey, their extremely profitable heist was being terminated by a rural cop. The suspects were from Minnesota and made the mistake that Alberta's rural policing was like that in America, often patrolled by inexperienced officers with limited training.

That mistake cost them their lives. Alberta was policed by Mounties, Canada's federal police force of highly trained and effective officers.

Once the driver spotted the PC, he rapidly increased speed intending to ram Drought off the road. One shooter positioned himself stretched out the passenger window and opened with a fully automatic weapon, which Drought figured had to be an M-16 style. The rounds were tearing up the Jaguar's front end, most of them either hit the engine block or ricocheted off.

Thirty rounds on fully automatic are dispensed quickly and as the shooter handed his empty rifle to a second gunman, leaving the space between them and the PC bullet free, Drought opened up on the van. His shots didn't ricochet…all hit the windshield. Drought aimed for the driver, leveling two rapid shots, killing him instantly. Drought swung the Colt slightly to his left and squeezed the trigger quickly twice as the van swung a hard left and crashed into the bush.

Drought waited a moment to see if the third gunman exited. When he didn't, he quickly got back into the cruiser, radioed in again, waited for confirmation for a supervisor and an ambulance, then put the vehicle in gear and raced to the van, blocking it in. Taking his Colt, he approached the van from the driver's side, knowing the threat level from that angle was less. He called out numerous times of police presence, and not hearing a response or movement in the van, he quickly and covertly approached the vehicle. At the rear doors, he yanked one open as he dropped to his butt, leveling the rifle into the back of the van. Nothing. No one.

Slowly he rose to his knees, then to his feet and observed what had occurred as the van went out of commission. The driver was slumped over the steering wheel with the back of his head missing. The shooter's upper body was hanging out of the window with his weapon dropped in his lap. The third shooter had the empty rifle in his hands but appeared to have struck his head on the dashboard as the vehicle crashed into the bushes.

Drought slipped into the back of the van and approached the driver and first shooter, checked the two for a sign of life. None. Checked the third shooter, found him to be alive, breathing and no visible signs of injury. He removed all weapons, checked each suspect for additional guns, knives etc. then hauled the third shooter out of the back of the van, laid him on the side of the road next to the van and cuffed his right hand to the rear bumper. Having secured the crime scene, he immediately called in the incident from his shoulder mic and waited for back-up.

"When you see a rattlesnake poised to strike, you do not wait until it has struck before you crush it." Franklin D. Roosevelt (1882-1945)

Chapter Forty-Nine

Neither wanted to leave, but the lights were dimming and Robert was hovering. Tom made the first move. Pushing himself from the table, he smoothly skirted the table and assisted Karen to rise, kissing her on the neck as she attempted to drain the last of her Chardonnay Ice, damp her lips and rose from the chair, trying to be graceful while goosebumps controlled her movements.

Karen admired the numerous paintings adorning the vestibule while Tom paid the tab. Her fingers graced the frame of the oil painting of The Last Supper by Leonardo da Vinci, thinking how appropriate for Araxi. She glanced over at Tom as she continued her tactile joy and a warmth enveloped her as would the glow of a welcoming fireplace on a snowy day. She knew the feeling wasn't an appreciation for his physical abilities or his lovemaking, although they were equally attractive and certainly encompassed his charm. No, it was more than that. She hated to think in clichés, but Soul Mate came to mind. As quickly as she tried to dismiss the triviality, it remained. Glancing once again, she noticed Tom returning his personal credit card into his wallet, noting on her Keeper List, his ethics of not putting the dinner on CISS.

Tom joined her momentarily, held the door for her and once outside, took her arm as they reversed their stroll to the Chateau Whistler, allowing the white twinkled tree lights to whisk them through the Village's magic land. Neither spoke, words seemingly the breaker of moods as they bathed in each other's presence.

The Chateau's doorman greeted them by name, bowed and opened the massive double doors for their entry and wished them a good evening. They walked casually, arm in arm through the massive reception lounge adorned with thick taupe carpet and highly polished heavy tile, which reflected the outdoor aqua center through an end wall of floor to ceiling peak glass. The elevator ride continued the silence but still arm in arm. Tom carded the door lock and held it open for Karen, then double locked it and turned to Karen and said, "So, what do you think?"

Winthrop smiled, shaking her head and replied, "I agree. But first, let's finish off this Okanagan delight on the balcony, then we can call for an early cab."

Undress. Fluffy white robe. Sashay to the balcony, stopping to pick up two fresh wine glasses and the chilled bottle of White from the electronic wine chiller, Karen joined Tom as he sat with his right butt cheek on the railing, soaking in the resort's black beauty.

Karen poured three fingers of the chardonnay into the choice stemware, sat the bottle on the deck table and joined Tom with her butt on the railing and offered a toast, "Tom, I am not going to embarrass you with compliments about how terrific you are and how you have taken my breath away this weekend, but I must say that I have never felt this happy and yet professionally committed. Your personality and character have joined the two and for that I toast you, Mr. Thomas Hortonn!"

"Well, thank you for not embarrassing me even though I can feel my hot flash extending to my neck. I feel the same about you Karen. I have been thinking frequently these last few days, how well we work together, can switch from professional persona to personal and back again without hesitation or reflection. You are good for me Karen and I hope we can move our relationship forward."

"Wow, Mr. Hortonn, you certainly know how to, mmm, how do I say this?" Karen added as she offered her glass for a toast. "To us!"

She placed on hand on his leg and attempted to extend herself to kiss him and felt her body falter and quickly dropped off the railing laughing, turned and grabbed him off the railing and kissed him passionately with one hand behind his thick wavy hair and her wine in the other. "I kind of fascinated about hiring a chopper to take us back to the airport but at $3,300 one way I think we need to call for an early cab," your thoughts?

Tom sipped his wine and said, "I think we would have a very difficult time billing that to David, so yes, I agree. I will call the concierge. It will take about three hours early in the morning, say leave here at three? I will ask him to arrange the first flight out, which if my memory serves me correctly, is seven-thirty getting us into Edmonton around ten. Does that work for you?"

"It does but it leaves little sleep time, so how about you make the call, I will get under the sheets and we can get as many hours as possible. How about a one-thirty wake-up call with bagels, cream cheese, fruit and coffee?"

Tom smiled, reached down to run his hand through her hair, placed a passionate kiss, refilled her glass, then his and headed into the den to make the call.

A three am taxi request was not exceptional given Whistler's international clientele but it still took Tom a while to ensure the instructions were accepted and the wake-up call, breakfast and taxi were guaranteed. The process took about ten minutes. He hung up the phone and headed back to the bedroom to find the lights out. Thinking nothing of the darkness, he checked to make sure the balcony door was shut and locked, then slipped under the covers. As he pulled the sheets and duvet up to his chin, he turned to Karen, paused to collect his thoughts and heard a soft snoring.

Smiling to himself, he snuggled into the bed's comfort and quickly fell asleep.

Chapter Fifty

Intrepid was not totally forthright with Harold. Money was tight. The party had spent millions over budget and with the on-going controversy regarding the declared candidate some of the wealthy donors were backing off. Christians for a Better America had its own financial support from far-right wing party members and supporters but the group had spent a fortune getting Shepherd and Marrington and their team out of FBI lock-up, leaving the coffers near empty. He felt the time was ripe to kick in their contingency revenue generators.

Orange County, outside of Los Angeles, California was a bastion of conservatism where Shepherd and Marrington had a vast support base. Shepherd's daughter was equally well known and the community supported her participation with the research team working on the chemical combination at the university's research facility North-West of Denver, Colorado. Orange County was a strong Christian community sustaining one of their own.

The movement for financial support began in this county and those areas west and south of Los Angeles. Rancho Palos Verdes, Laguna Beach and particularly Marina Del Rey near the Los Angeles Airport, LAX, conducted perpetual fund-raising dinners; at least one of these communities held a dinner monthly. This process was repeated in hundreds of other cities and towns across America with dinner running as little as twenty dollars a plate in less affluent areas, to upwards of five thousand in parts of Chicago, New York State, Maine and Washington, DC. The only person who knew the true destination of the raised funds was the CFBA organizer. Attendees were led to believe their generous tax-deductible donation was advancing the conservative cause to regain control of the White House, Senate and maintain dominating the House.

With success hanging in the balance with every primary won or lost, some over-zealous, extremist CFBA leaders across the country had taken the fund-raising movement to another level…extortion. In most instances, those on the receiving end of the threats were wealthy but were not totally committed to the movement. They were often prominent citizens who refused to contact law enforcement for fear of too close an examination of their financial position. It was cheaper and safer to pay.

In the Marina Del Rey, there was a segment of the CFBA which fell back on the age-old extortion system of threatening store owners. The take was much smaller but when multiplied by several hundred with weekly *donations*, the bottom line was considerable.

Today's target was a well-known and profitable drinking hole. The Firewalker Pub was located on Admiralty Way, right on the water where patrons often arrived in their sailboats, skidoos or dinghies they unloaded from their yachts. On a Wednesday afternoon, shortly after the noon lunch crowd had thinned and staff were gearing up for a busy evening with their Pot Roast special and half priced margaritas, three well-dressed CFBA agents entered the pub and asked for the owner, then took a seat in the back. In hindsight, they should have noticed the Navy memorabilia, the SEAL Bell on the bar with the names of beer and mixed drinks named after those lost in battle. But they didn't. This was just another stop on their list of businesses to encourage participation. The three had developed a pitch which, to date, had been flawless.

Tobias Armishaw joined them with a welcome handshake and a tray of coffees, assuming the three were there on business and not able to enjoy a Firewalker Special.

The men accepted Armishaw's hospitality, bypassing small talk and moving right into their pitch. It was a short presentation with the request for two hundred dollars a week contribution to the conservative movement.

There was something amiss in the three's evaluation of their current situation, or maybe they were tired from so many pitches that day, but either way, they missed the signals which might have prevented the unfortunate incident.

Armishaw was a profiler's dream. He was in his mid-fifties, close to six feet, about two hundred pounds, a barrel chest, piercing green eyes, square jaw and sporting close cropped grey hair. He didn't display the typical belly of other men his age...his slim waist and fifteen-inch biceps reflected hours in the gym.

A little research would have signaled to the CFBA agents that this was one business to avoid, but they didn't Google. Had they put that little bit of effort forth they would have found that Armishaw was a retired, thirty-year veteran of the Navy SEALs, having been on active duty around the world for twenty years, then an instructor for another ten, retiring as a Commander with a reputation as having a no bullshit personality and an attitude of kicking ass first and introducing himself second.

What their research would not have revealed was the fact that Armishaw carried a .45 custom Kimber in a small-of-the-back holster. Armishaw practiced daily...after his morning workout on Venice Beach and before he came to the Firewalker. It is also doubtful that any patron or local would have revealed the pub's nom de plume, so to speak. Customers were all encompassing; you were or you were not. Although the SEAL moto of, *The Only Easy Day was Yesterday,* was etched in brass with a polished mahogany background over the bar, Armishaw wanted the pub's name to reflect what he and hundreds of other warriors had endured, *Walking on Fire* for America. The orthodox drinkers knew the history, knew that Armishaw loved the Navy, still does. He had a romance with the lifestyle, the bravado camaraderie, living on base unfettered by civilians or their live style. He was entirely unprepared when mandatory retirement stuck its ugly head into his life. But he received a reprieve, at least momentarily, of a year to find something to do in retirement. The Navy honored his devotion to duty, his heroism, numerous Purple Hearts, battle ribbons and allowed him to be duty free, maintain his housing and all that encompassed his lifestyle for the year.

He had amassed a small fortune after thirty years of limited expenses and investing his salary; ninety thousand a year at retirement. He did his due diligence and after about seven months found the Marina Del Rey pub which had been allowed to fall into disarray with limited clientele. With the help of a retired Marine, now a prosperous realtor, he made the retiring owner an offer which was immediately scooped up. The next five months he drew upon his many contacts, both current and retired, to completely renovate the building and recreate a combination of an enlisted mess hall and officers' club. It was a renovator's dream and the Navy's designated watering hole once it opened.

It didn't take much of an explanation to a San Diego interior designer for the plan to come together. The interior was massive with seating for one hundred and fifty comfortably. The finished product was a bar which stretched from just inside the door to the end of the room with the ubiquitous brass stools topped with dark brown leather seats. The bar was three recycled bars professionally joined, sanded, dark stained, shellacked and adorned with various polished brass ships fittings. The entire wall behind the massive bar was beveled mirror with various chandeliers spread the length twinkling in its reflection. The back wall of the Firewalker itself was polished mahogany with brass plaques honoring the fallen Frogmen from World War Two and every Navy SEAL since the Warrior unit's inception. Each honoree was highlighted with an individual subdued ceiling light so subtle that you had to peer into the ceiling to see the light source. The Wall was a spectacular memory of the hundreds who gave the ultimate for their country and there was never a patron who did not spend many quiet moments reflecting on their presence.

There were the usual Sports Bar high definition television screens dispersed throughout the Firewalker and one in each of the upstairs restrooms, or Heads, accessed via a curved staircase. The establishment was unique in many ways, principally in that there was no sound coming from any television. The best way to describe the audio ambiance was to call it respectful. Firewalker played a little country, a little old-time rock and roll, jazz and considered itself eclectic, which blended with the atmosphere. Neither music, nor television was the center of a patron's thoughts. Diners could sit and chat, reflect on their individual experiences, honor those they knew had died and enjoy a quiet, meaningful dining adventure.

The Firewalker didn't need a formal announcement, place ads in the local papers or on television. The Coronado Naval Base's commanding officer took the liberty of announcing the grand opening with a caveat; each day was devoted to a base command and with over five thousand personnel, Opening Day, took several weeks.

Firewalker reached the hearts of every Naval man and woman, regardless of their command, as well as thousands of locals who overwhelmingly were Navy supporters. Armishaw was a survivor and knew it was with the grace of God that he was not killed many times over. He knew it was his duty to give back, to provide for those families who gave the ultimate for their country, for the Navy and for the SEALs.

Shortly after the overwhelming success of Firewalker, he met with two SEALs, one an accountant and the other a tax attorney. These men designed a charitable foundation with fifty thousand of Armishaw's seed money and invested another five hundred thousand in the foundation. The foundation's board was comprised of current and retired SEALs, widows of SEALs as well as several siblings of those lost in action. The board met once a month to approve requests for financial assistance, not only to Navy personnel and their families but to hundreds of children and others in need of a leg up. They paid for many university scholarships, fulfilled the dreams of children suffering from debilitating and terminal diseases and enriched the lives of thousands yearly.

Armishaw was the reason the Firewalker didn't know a slow day. With ten percent of the daily receipts going to the foundation, patrons were constantly overpaying their bill, some by as much as a hundred dollars, giving the server instructions, "Give it to the kids."

So, when the CFBA received no reaction from their pitch and cranked the pressure, Armishaw was taken aback…considerably. The pub owner and philanthropist was a very easy-going guy, albeit strong willed, and even though he would categorize himself as a conservative, he was apolitical, not having faith in either party. So, when the agents implied that the Firewalker might be the recipient of a destructive fire if there wasn't a two hundred-dollar a week contribution to the conservative party, Tobias asked for clarification. That enlightenment came as one agent pointed to a bottle of Jamieson's Irish Whiskey and said, "That empty bottle filled with gasoline and a wick could be an encouragement to participate Mr. Armishaw." The explosion was instantaneous.

Armishaw jumped up from the table, pulled his Kimber and yelled, "You disrespectful mother fuckers. You have the fuckin' gall to come into a Navy SEAL pub and threaten me? Fuck you. Stand up. All of you fuckers, stand the fuck up, *Now*."

All three CFBA rose rather arrogantly, not sure what to make of this idiot with a gun, but chose to appease him while someone in the Firewalker called 9-1-1.

Armishaw yelled over his shoulder to one of his staff, also a SEAL, working his off days to contribute to the foundation, "Jerry, these three just threatened the Firewalker with destruction if we didn't pay them a weekly fee. Call the base commander and tell him we want the Secret Service and FBI here immediately. These boys are going with me into the back. Text me when they get here," he added as he waved the .45 to indicate the three should move down the back hallway.

It was that moment of truth of which the agents were unfamiliar, the shit hitting the fan.

When Armishaw asked for a favor, no questions were ever asked. The government agents arrived within fifteen minutes to find all three-plastic cuffed to chairs and gagged in a storage room with Armishaw sitting on his desk, feet up, Kimber laying across his lap.

"It was like a party on the Titanic, we knew the iceberg was out there, looming in the darkness."

Chris Kyle (1974-2015) Navy SEAL
American Sniper

Joe Sarkowski wasted no time in complying with Intrepid's directions. He had packed his few belongings, sterilized his office as best he could, destroyed any evidence of CFBA activities and headed to Southern California. Paying cash for all his travel needs, he stayed in cheap motels and ate fast food attempting to avert the curious and avoid cameras. He was just south of Barstow, California when his colleagues were being questioned by the FBI and Secret Service agents, while Armishaw enjoyed a cold Ricker's Red, feeling satisfied he had not dismissed his three detainees as derailed politicos.

Chapter Fifty-One

Brian Sawyer had acted immediately after receiving the cesium, loading it in his Quad trailer, moving swiftly to the Canadian Pacific holding area Southwest of his massive marijuana operation. The rail cars were already in place waiting for track clearance to head into Idaho. Pulling alongside the pre-chosen rail car, he quickly backed the trailer up to the lead-lined steel container his boss Stan instructed him to build and install weeks previously. The trailer coupled evenly with the box suspended under the rail car, allowing Sawyer to smoothly glide the cesium container into the box, seal and lock the door with an official CP band, the bands and locking device having been stolen previously.

Sawyer left as covertly as he had arrived and sprinted back to his compound to dismantle the operation and prepare to disappear forever. The process had been planned well in advance from the inception of the operation with numerous fail-safe systems incorporated into the vastly successful grow-op. He had few personal possessions except for the ancient fifteen-foot trailer and beater pick-up. After the last crop was shipped to Idaho, he hadn't replanted so the underground cavern was empty except for the grow lights, air filter and hydroponic systems. They would remain, as would the diesel generator hidden in the adjacent cave, the entrance concealed by years of brush growth. Disabling the generator and padlocking the steel door to the grow-op, he hitched his trailer to the pick-up and headed out, not the way the delivery had left but via a brush road he had cut, extending from his compound, skirting the end of the forestry road and connecting with highway three several kilometers east.

Once on the main highway, he headed for the border, stopping momentarily at the first rest stop to wipe down the trailer of his prints, puncture a tire and abandon it. The rig would sit there for several days before a curious local or Mountie enquired. By then he would be lapping margaritas in his Costa Rica home established year previously…complete with a safe, holding millions in American currency.

The last leg of his departure, once he crossed the border unfettered, was to gas his Piper Seminole, grab a coffee from the small airport's self-serve dispensary and take off for Limon, Costa Rica, a trip he had made dozens of times with four fuel stops.

Brian had spent many of his Alberta winters in Costa Rica. Originally his objective was a secure location to lay low. It took some time to find a community with zero expat Canadians, Americans or Brits but once he found the best for him, he rented a cheap room and spent months mingling with the locals, learning the language fluently and otherwise becoming a resident. The step to purchase a house was quite easy given his success at slipping into the economic and social sphere of the community. He knew buying a house with cash would draw far too much attention, so over the years he had deposited a substantial amount in a local bank, creating a substantial down payment over time.

30,000

Cst. Drought didn't have long to wait for his back-up. Several PCs, including a supervisor, arrived within fifteen minutes along with a forensics team, paramedics and two ambulances. His suspect had regained consciousness and been checked for any sign of injury.
Drought had helped him sit upright against the van so he was completely cognitive when the supervisor arrived.

Forensics started with the location of Drought's shooting, taped off the area, photographed and diagramed the scene while others of the team worked similarly on the van plus one hundred meters south of the final scene and surrounding area, collecting spent shells, photographing/videotaping and documenting the crime scene.

Law enforcers are familiar with supervisors second guessing the work of those on the front line and in many cases, act like the proverbial Monday morning quarter-back in hind-sight evaluation. It was often this scrutinizing and second guessing that created doubt with some officers, creating unnecessary stress.

Drought and other street cops no longer must attempt to justify their actions since all their activities are recorded on their uniform mounted video cameras. Drought allowed a forensics Member to remove the camera and replace it with a new one. Drought signed for both, documenting the chain of evidence. The supervisor counter-signed, then asked Drought for a capsulated version of what went down.

Drought pointed out that time was of the essence since the Cesium was not in the van, encouraging the supervisor to allow Drought and another Member to head south and investigate its whereabouts. Granted.

Drought found there wasn't any evidence of the suspects stopping anywhere between the shoot-out and the road's end. Stopping in the cul-de-sac, they radioed their position and retrieved their Colt C8s from the vehicle trunk. The trail split left and right at the end of the road. Quad tracks were evident in both directions…the Members took the trail most used…to the right. A few hundred meters in, not knowing how far the trail went, they decided to return to their PC and opt for a far more high-tech system to scrutinize the area.

30,000

Night had fallen as Jack Johntree and Billy Sam were unloading the Cesium from the Canadian Pacific car staged in a rail-yard just north of the Clearwater River and the northern border of the Nez Perce Reservation. Once onto their Quad trailer it would be taken into the reservation, secured into a high-end coffin which they would seal and attach a Lewiston, Idaho mortician's certification for transportation. The cargo would then be loaded into a five-ton cargo van emblazoned with Boise Mortuary on both sides and rear panel.

Chapter Fifty-Two

Rebecca woke early the next morning feeling a glow throughout her body that was entirely new to her. It was as though her skin tingled and her vulva had a movement all its own; as she lay in bed gazing at Penelope, she felt a tingle there and was positive her labia were moving. She slid her hand under the covers out of curiosity and discovered she was wet and her clitoris was enlarged. Not wanting to wake Pen just yet, she smoothly rubbed her index finger over the swollen gland and felt an immediate climax resulting in an uncontrollable shaking she was sure would waken Penelope. It didn't and Rebecca felt her body relax, then the climax afterglow splashed over like a warm wave almost taking her breath away for the second time in seconds.

Once she felt her legs stop shaking, she flipped the covers off quietly and tip-toed to the bathroom, gathering her encrypted smartphone from her suitcase. Closing the door behind her, she quickly checked for voice or text messages. There was a text from Jessica advising that three FBI agents with horse and bush experience had the chemicals loaded in pack boxes ready for the mules. She told Rebecca to enjoy her Sunday but be at the Yellowstone Outfitters first thing Monday morning.

Rebecca entered her code, acknowledging receipt of the message and replied, *Will do.* Must talk soonest re personal. Penelope and I are a couple!

After using the toilet, she retraced her steps, turned the smartphone off and hid it in her luggage and slipped back under the covers, noticing Penelope was quietly sleeping.

Chapter Fifty-Three

Sheriff Joe had very little difficulty investigating the Nez Perce Tribal Police Chief Jorge George's murder once Jessica had cleared the red tape with the FBI. His first task had been to examine all the video feed from the reservation cameras, particularly those located in and around the northern section near the rail cars. George's body was found off the reservation in a ditch. Regrettably forensics didn't examination the body at the time due entirely because of the FBI's low priority of First Nations crime, and George was buried. Not wanting to exhume his body the Sheriff had George's clothes, which were still in evidence at the police station, sent to the FBI Crime Lab at the Marine Base in Quantico, Virginia, an action he took with considerable trepidation given the federal agency's obsession with rejecting local police requests or cooperation with them.

Fukishura must have tremendous juice with the FBI, Joe thought, when the results and clothes were returned within a week. After examining all the video feed and reading the forensics results, he called Jessica to arranged the paper work for a federal search warrant. The FBI insisted on serving the warrant with their special weapons and tactical team, SWAT, but Jessica refused, insisting Sheriff Joe and the Tribal Police had to maintain their honor and investigative flow.

Once Jack Johntree and Billy Sam were arrested, they searched the rambled shack the two called home. Examination of Sam's jacket hanging on the back of the entrance door revealed what appeared to be traces of blood. Washington State Highway Patrol forensics lab in Spokane later identified the stains as George's blood. The Smith and Wesson Model 41 was under Sam's mattress along with banded twenty-dollar bills in stacks of one thousand, totaling ten thousand and change. Sheriff Joe had the firearm examined by the WSHP and found traces of plastic on the barrel from the blow-back of the close-range murder using a plastic coke bottle as a silencer.

Neither suspect offered any explanation for the money or why they had such a huge stash and yet continued to live deplorably.

Sheriff Joe spoke with Jessica and reiterated that valuable time had been lost by having to play bureaucratic games with the FBI. Advising her that he would personally interrogate the suspects and call her back, he arranged a Restorative Justice, RJ, circle created with the suspects, a facilitator, victims and Tribal Elders.

RJ is a system requiring suspects to face their victims, in this case the entire community, since Jorge George was both an elder and chief of police. The elders have years of experience handling small petty crimes, turning potential prison inmates into honest members of the reservation by shaming and requiring the suspects to explain their actions, apologize to the victims and to perform penance. Often, and these two men were examples, suspects were so ashamed of their behavior, so embarrassed to have to sit in front of their aunts, uncles, siblings and neighbors and explain why they took a life, that any information Sheriff Joe wanted was quickly forthcoming…because of the pressure from the elders.

Within a couple of days of the arrests, Sheriff Joe was on the encrypted phone again to Jessica explaining how a murder investigation had morphed into the suspects confessing to the movement of the Cesium to Minneapolis. The suspects didn't know the van's license plate number but they were forthcoming with the mortuary's name on the vehicle. This last piece of information was extracted from Sam by his aunt who stared him down until Sam started to cry and apologize to the woman in whose home he had spent so much time, enjoyed her hospitality and food and now had killed a tribal member, the respected and honorable police chief.

Chapter Fifty-Four

Communications were flying fast and furiously at the StoneHead tech office with emails and texts coming from across North America. Everything had to be collated and categorized for Fukishura. Marc had set up a food and drink table in the middle of the large office allowing agents the ability to swivel from their monitors, eat, drink and move back without having to take food from the table. Most of the traffic was coming from various jurisdictions through Chapman's system as well as other cities' law enforcement agencies. On-going or new investigations were being highlighted on CHAP with key words and phrases regarding explosives, religious groups and a minor few which had been prematurely labeled terrorism or domestic terrorism.

Jessica had been overwhelmed by the volume of material Cheryl's system was producing and was delighted Bruce's team could filter the data and provide her just that which pertained to their investigation.

Currently she was taking a break with Jasmin in the living room, sitting on the elongated couch each with a tall glass of Cabernet Sauvignon and enjoying a plate of Marc's goat cheese and cucumber appetizers. All the kittens were either on the couch or the ten-foot coffee table, trying to get to the goat cheese. Some were crawling on Jasmin and Jessica.

Jasmin asked, "Jessica, I really appreciate the opportunity to work for you, short as it is, and I hope I am doing a good job but why the kittens? Bruce told me you wanted me to bring them in from the barn and domestic them."

"That one is easy Jasmin. I have been a Secret Service agent for some time, always travelling, never having a duty that lasted more than thirty days. This posting is the longest I have stayed in one place for as long as I can remember. I have an apartment in Washington, DC and when I left for this assignment, I realized I didn't have anyone for my landlady to care for during my absence and that bothered me. There is no other heart beat in my life other than my own. I make a direct connection to my life in general and other than my parents, there isn't anyone. Sure, I have dated and the first dates are often quite nice until the guy learns what I do for a living and boom, that's it, no call. I have often called them only to receive the brush off. I need these kittens to be part of my life and I asked you to bring them inside because I didn't have time and I wanted you to have a fun activity during your downtime with Thiessen."

"Well, that kinda puts a different perspective on these kittens, doesn't it?" she said with a huge smile while scratching under the chin of a male ginger. "Will you have Dr. Penelope do the spaying?"

Jessica raised her glass as a toast to Jasmin and replied, "For sure. Once she and Rebecca get back from their Denver shopping holiday, I will book a time, so probably next week," she said as she reached across to the coffee table to push a black tortoise shell kitten away from the appetizers.

They enjoyed each other's company for a while, playing with the kittens and Jasmin sharing some of her limited work history and childhood experiences, then Jessica excused herself and headed back to her office.

Once inside the secure facility, she began to peruse Bruce's filtered communications. The expansion of the investigation, thanks to Chapman, was extensive. She no longer felt the need to be a facilitator or moderator country-wide since so many agencies and competent law enforcement officers were joining the criminal analysis. Participating agencies were logging into Chapman's system, observing the scope of the investigation and assuring themselves that they were moving forward and not duplicating Fukishura's efforts.

Los Angeles FBT and Secret Service agents had uploaded their interrogation of the three CFBA suspects with the information they had gleaned through intimidation and threats of prison life for three white guys convicted of terrorism if they refused to cooperate. While the three suspects were in federal custody, Joe Sarkowski called one of their cells to arrange a meeting and update. The FBI agents didn't answer the phone as they hadn't progressed to the point of coercing the CFBA suspects to cooperate. Elisabeth had monitored the call, so while the agents mused their options, she sent the data to Bruce, allowing Jessica to obtain a confirmation of Joe's involvement. It was a quick interface communication via CHAP for the FBI to be included.

30,000

Joe was very familiar with the Marina Del Rey area having attended high school and junior college in the west end of Los Angeles County. He passed the CFBA contact house several times and noted the house was dark. Considering Harold and Denver's instructions, he rejected the physical contact, suspecting a law enforcement trap and headed for the Harbor Bay Inn. Using his Canadian passport, he checked in as Damian Dawidowski. Being late at night and the off season, he had somewhat of a choice of rooms and chose one on the top third floor at the end of the hall with an emergency exit right beside his door. His knowledge of the area was proving invaluable; he had a clear view of the Marina Del Rey Convention Center.

Chapter Fifty-Five

FBI agents were convinced the three extortionists were a separate CFBA cell being controlled by Denver but hadn't any further information about their contact. The suspects' end of the operation consisted of collecting the so-called contributions from fifty successful Marina Del Rey businesses, then depositing the weekly ten thousand into a bank account using a debit card restricted to deposits only. The FBI agents were quick studies and sent the data to Chapman, who obtained a federal warrant for the balance of sixty million, asking the bank to continue to accept deposits but seizing the ongoing balance and for the bank to electronically note on the account, *Activity Unavailable Now.* Chapman's further investigation revealed there were fifty plus deposits spread across the country, weekly, of over ten thousand each.

When Jessica logged onto Chapman's system and read the interrogation report, she couldn't help but smile at the poor ignorant schmucks who hadn't a clue that Joe's call attempt with them had been accessed by Elisabeth.

The Los Angeles FBI agents had Chapman's link to Elisabeth's recording of the conversation between Denver and Harold, contacted their Denver office which put a trace on the number from which Denver called.

30,000

Jackson and Elisabeth had met with the school district's superintendent separately, thanking him for his cooperation with the federal investigation and for allowing them to work undercover in StoneHead district. The superintendent had lost all pretense of propriety and exuberantly thanked Elisabeth and Jackson for the year of exceptional excitement. Neither agent understood how he could be excited as he didn't have any connection with them at all at school and no one else in the district knew their identity, but they kept quiet and allowed him his crime prevention fantasy.

Jackson was the last to express his appreciation for himself and the Secret Service, then went back to his rented rural house, packed his meager belongings, drove to Elisabeth's, helped
pack her equipment in the back of his pick-up, save her laptop, and the two headed to Minneapolis.

Chapter Fifty-Six

Harold had arrived in Minneapolis after stopping off in Sioux City, South Dakota to swap license plates with an identical vehicle in an equipment rental lot. He followed Intrepid's advice and did not call Martha, but circled the safe house numerous times around 9pm and spotting her surveillance, parked several blocks away, then hopped several fences and came into her backyard covertly.

Martha had been living in the house with no internet, phone, television, cell or other way to communicate with the outside world. The safe house had a massive book and video library which helped her pass the hours and days. The freezer contained enough frozen food to last several residents months, so sustenance was not an issue…her sanity was.

When the tapping sounded at her back door, she felt her heart squeeze in her chest, assuming it was the FBI. Her mind raced for an answer, for a plan, for something to give her direction. She felt herself begin to shake and sweat wondering if this was the culmination of her years of dedicated nursing and one dumb ass mistake. The tapping continued unabated, not increasing in crescendo, but incessantly, maintaining the presence of something, someone at the door.

The back door led right into the kitchen so Martha could sneak into the room and peek out the one window that looked out onto the yard. Harold!

She breathed a tremendous sigh of relief and caught herself quickly, realizing his presence didn't bode well for her well-being, so she left the light off, unlocked the door, stepped aside to allow him in with his duffle, then closed and locked the door behind him.

Leading her into the living room, Harold noted with pleasure that she had the black-out curtains pulled and only limited lighting. He began the conversation by saying, "You have a surveillance team a half a block away. I hope you haven't left here."

"No, Harold," she said angrily. "I haven't been out of this house in weeks. I am scared shitless, not stupid. How do you know I am being watched?"

"That part was easy. Two men, dressed in suits, sitting in what is obviously a government car with the numerous antennae sprouting from the trunk, facing the house. What I am surprised is that some resident didn't call it in as a suspicious vehicle, given this being an upscale neighborhood."

"Okay, okay. Sorry. Just checking. I am pretty freaked, but we must continue with the operation and not allow anything to divert our attention or our cause," she stammered, running a hand through her rumpled hair.

"As you may recall, I was never in for this in any big way, just supporting Joe. I see and hear where the CFBA is heading and the great possibility of our success in getting control of Congress and the White House. I see these objectives but the process to those ends seems evil somehow."

"Martha, you had plenty of time to leave months ago. Yes, it would have meant you and Joe splitting since he is in one hundred percent, but you have no choice now. If you step outside this house, you will be arrested."

"So, what you are saying is I am trapped."

"That is putting it negatively. I mean we are all in this together. The CFBA made a commitment after Obama got elected the first time, that the election system is so crooked we wouldn't see a Republican president in our lifetime. We couldn't take a chance of allowing another Democrat in the White House and we needed to solidify the Republican hold on Congress and take the Senate. That is not going to happen if we allow the present Electoral College system, the super pacs and media moguls to control another election. Look at what happened when Obama was elected for the second term. Look what happened to Romney and how the media manipulated reality."

"Look, I get it, I do. I guess I am just really scared. I do not want to spend the rest of my life in jail. If I am caught, there is no way I am an innocent bystander after killing the Secret
Service's suspect in the hospital."

"Yeah, that. Well, I hate to the bearer of bad news but he didn't die. The recently hired nurse, Jasmin, found him near death and revived him.

He is currently in custody in the Secret Service compound at StoneHead Ranch."

"Oh, fuck. That is just great," she spouted, throwing her hands in the air and walking in circles. "What are we supposed to do now? Is the shit hitting the fan as we speak?" she asked, stopping her pacing, wrapping her arms around her chest, seeking comfort.

"No! Relax," he replied, trying to bring calm to an otherwise explosive situation. Martha was never part of the movement and was only involved because of her husband. She could be the proverbial loose cannon. Considering the pressure Denver was imposing on him, he had reason to be worried Martha could unravel years of work, so he continued, "The feds can't prove you had anything to do with the guy's relapse and he knows very little anyway. If you recall, he was recruited to provide us information about the who, what and where of the Ranch. He knew me and that was it. He had no idea why I wanted the information. The money we provided was more than enough to stifle any curiosity. He isn't too swift and probably figured I was seeking information about when Bakus would be in residence so local businesses could capitalize on the president being there, at least that is what I implied.

"I have confirmation that the cesium is on its way from Idaho. I will receive a text when it arrives. Our job is to ensure it is loaded onto the specific flight carrying the Democratic delegates to the convention in Los Angeles. In the meantime, we lay low here."

"Okay I guess. My options are pretty limited anyway," she sighed. "I was just getting ready to go to bed. I will show you around and you can make yourself at home, so to speak. There is wine and some leftovers in the fridge. You can drop your duffle in the bedroom and then I will give you a tour.

Chapter Fifty-Seven

Jason knew the star of the compound's night videos was not some kind of Sasquatch or Big Foot as believed by Jenewein and the urban researchers. Under normal circumstances he would have left the issue alone but his involvement in the treacherous explosion formula was wearing on his conscience and he needed a diversion.

One evening after dinner, he begged off the usual post meal board games or television and took a walk behind the compound. Starting at Camera One, he paced off the distance to the spot their visitor chose every evening. After meandering through the various trails for thirty minutes, he returned to the compound and locked himself in the video room and drew up the last digital feed, then using his high school trigonometry and the distance he paced off, he calculated that their Mystery Man was around six-foot six and with boots his height could account for the human hair in the kitchen door frame. He sat back in the office chair, put his feet on the desk and watched the rest of the feed, determined to meet this person soon.

30,000

Jessica had become overrun with the amount of data she was required to analyze and was losing her perspective. The data that overwhelmed her was Jason's intel regarding the Suburbans and Sandra's family connections. Jessica had sent Elisabeth and Jackson to Minneapolis to take over surveillance of Martha and Harold, but now knew that was a mistake. She texted a message to them in transit, advising the change of tactics, to get to Los Angeles immediately and to log into Chapman once they were settled. The next communication was from Rebecca and she smiled, saving it for later.

Exhausted, experience told her this was the time to get help. She made a quick walk to Bruce's communication center and called Sorento. After bringing him up to speed he quickly approved her request. Once back in her secure unit she placed the conference call and gave her request...which took only a matter of minutes. She asked them to pack a bag.

Knowing relief was on its way, she leaned back, breathed a sigh of satisfaction; seemingly having overcome much of her pent-up anger, with the bonus of being more clearheaded and focused. She returned to the volume of communications and waited for the troops to arrive.

Chapter Fifty-Eight

Rebecca had fallen back asleep after texting Jessica and now, several hours later, she was being woken by Penelope caressing her nipples and gliding her fingers over her vulva. It didn't take long for her to be the first to engage in orgasmic meditation by gracing Pen's clitoris with her tongue for fifteen minutes. Fifteen turned to forty-five before they were both sweaty, surfeited and ready for a shower...which they took together after ordering room service breakfast of Belgian waffles, whipped cream, peaches and coffee.

Over their breakfast, they shared their reaction to the last two days and brain stormed what and where their future was headed. Rebecca was tempted on numerous occasions to tell Penelope the truth, knew this was neither the time nor the place, but made a personal commitment to reveal her true-identity and prayed it would not damage their promising future. On a practical and realistic scale, she acknowledged, with considerable self-chastisement, that she could be prosecuted for violating her federal security clearance conditions.

Dressed in one of their new outfits, they spent the day exploring various local attractions and events. The morning was a shuttle bus to Pike's Peak, two-hours south-west of Colorado Springs, then lunch in Colorado Springs, then back to Denver for an outdoor concert featuring classical guitarist Christopher Hernandez. They finished off the day with an hour in the hotel pool, dinner pool side and in bed, asleep by 9pm, getting a 3am walk-up call.

Their wake-up call arrived so blaringly that they both jumped out of bed in the dark, adrenaline on over-drive and Rebecca reaching for her weapon. Penelope was the first to grasp the reality of the moment and turned on the light only to see Rebecca had rolled off the floor and was in a crouch with the semi-automatic in her hand, the barrel pointing slightly down.

"Holy shit Rebecca, what the fuck?" screamed Penelope as she pulled the pillow over her abdomen to protect herself.

Rebecca lowered the pistol and returned it to her holster, then jumped on the bed to give Penelope a hug through the pillow and said, "I am really sorry Pen. It is a reaction I developed years ago, and I am very sorry. I will try and wean myself of the habit of reacting like that to loud sounds. I am really sorry," said, taking Pen's face in her hands and kissing her gently, hoping to hell that her sincerity was believed in the face of overwhelming bullshit behavior. *This has to stop,* she thought.

Penelope took a deep breath and hugged Rebecca back saying, "That's okay, I was just really startled too and to see you with a gun I thought someone broke into our room and you were going to shoot him over my head," she laughed, pulling the pillow closer to herself thinking somehow the goose feathers would stop a bullet.

Rebecca joined the laughter, the two rolling around on the bed, enjoying the lightened mood. After a couple of minutes, Penelope jumped up and walked naked into the bathroom saying, "We had better motor or we are going to miss our early flight.

They quickly showered, did their minimum make-up, packed and were out the door within an hour, having called for a cab from their room and heading for the airport.

The entire flying process was uneventful and they arrived back in StoneHead delighted with their new relationship and ecstatic with their new wardrobes.

They embraced at their vehicles and Penelope headed for her clinic while Rebecca drove straight to the Yellowstone Outfitters to meet up with the agents and start their journey into the National Forest, thinking all during the drive that, *I'm getting too old for this covert shit.*

Chapter Fifty-Nine

Karen and Tom's wake-up call was a classical piece from Giacomo Puccini's La Boheme, which entered their bedroom gently through the Chateau's hidden speakers, waking them slowly, Karen being the first to fully rouse. As Tom stirred, she slipped back under the covers, lightly caressing his body beginning with his stomach and moving intently downwards. Tom was slowing awakening as was evident by his erection. Karen took advantage of the moment, taking it in her mouth, maximizing his endowment. Once he was rigid, she tossed the covers, straddled him and guided his erection between her legs and bottomed out immediately. She leaned forward slightly allowing the now fully cognizant Tom to caress her breasts and nipples. Her success at finding her "G Spot" immediately brought her orgasm within seconds. As she gyrated on Tom, she leaned down and lightly bit his ear sending him into an immediate sexual spasm allowing them the joy simultaneously.

After what seemed like an eternity to Karen, she slipped off Tom and rolled into a cuddle position, wrapping her arm around his middle and squeezing. He responded by swinging his arm under her head and embraced her.

Tom was the first to break the mood, slid out of bed and headed for the bathroom. Karen stayed under the covers until she heard the shower running, then flipped the covers and bounded off the queen size and ran to the bathroom to use the commode while Tom was in the shower.

She had just finished and was putting on the guest robe when room service arrived with their breakfast and coffee. Signing for the meal, she left a twenty-five percent tip, thanked the staffer profusely for such an early offering, closed and locked the door, then poured two cups of black, sipping hers while laying out her outfit for the day.

Momentarily, Tom exited the bathroom wearing his robe, drying his hair while approaching Karen at the end of the queen. He put the towel down, embraced her passionately and kissed her while trying not to spill her coffee. Karen backed away slightly, kissed his nose and said, "Let's enjoy breakfast while it's hot, then I will hit the shower," heading to the circular table with adjoining bar stools.

They toasted by clinking white mugs. As they began eating Karen said, "This has been one of the most memorable weekends I can ever recall. Thank you, Mr. Hortonn for a terrific time, albeit, sans the little skirmish with the imported drunks."

"Thank you, Ms. Winthrop for I too had a terrific time. I presume we must don our super sleuth hats and get to gettin' to Edmonton. Is there anything I can do to assist in your getting ready?" he mistakenly asked a woman not really knowing where the dumb-ass comment came from.

"No, smart-ass," she quipped. "I am quite capable of moving my butt quickly. Maybe not as fast as you, but still fast enough so you are not waiting for a woman."

"Whoops. Sorry about that," he replied then took his foot out of his mouth and forked a piece of egg into his embarrassed mouth.

Their banter continued throughout their meal, until Karen wiped her mouth, drained the last of her black, pecked Tom on the lips and danced to the bathroom, commenting over her shoulder as she gyrated, "I may just beat your time in the shower."

Tom had dressed, packed and was sitting on the balcony finishing his coffee when Karen came out of the bathroom dressed, hauling her suitcase and heading for the door saying, "Okay slowpoke, let's go."

The door had closed before Tom realized what had just occurred. He set down his coffee mug, rushed into the room, grabbed his suitcase, exited the room and ran down the hallway to catch up with Karen before she got into the elevator alone.

As he met her at the bank of elevators, she turned and smiled just as the down ding sounded, the door opened and she rushed in, turned and said, "Well, are you joining me agent
Hortonn or staying for another day?"

Tom couldn't think of a cute retort and had learned just moments ago that trying to match wits with Karen Winthrop was a losing proposition, so he simply smiled, caught the elevator door as it was closing and maneuvered his suitcase alongside hers, turned, kissed her gently as he reached for the lobby button.

Tom had expressed checked them out the previous night so they bypassed the empty reservation kiosk and walked out the front door directly to the waiting taxi, placed their suitcases into the trunk and settled in for the drive to YVR, Vancouver International Airport.

Their cab drove the entire distance in darkness, arriving at YVR at 6am. They made a quick cab exit, badged their way to the Air Canada VIP window, paid for their tickets, then circumvented security with their status, asking the agent to advise the flight crew of their armed status and boarded with ten minutes before their 7am flight departed. They asked for two seats in the back of the plane for privacy. Given the last four rows were empty, the flight attendant granted their request quickly.

Knowing the ninety-minute flight would be quick, they used the time from the gate and onto the tarmac to make calls. Tom reserved a car at the Edmonton airport while Karen called Superintendent Elise Laina at the Edmonton detachment. Speaking quietly, Karen received an update on the cesium and was delighted to hear the Members had stopped the thieves and had one in custody. The unknown whereabouts of the cesium was disturbing, but a light shone on the investigation with Staff Sergeant McDonald's discovery. Time being of the essence, she explained Chapman's system, that the RCMP and CSIS were in the process of being tied into it, gave her the access link and code and asked her to contact McDonald so he could be updated on the ongoing investigation in the US.

She had just clicked off when Air Canada began its decent into Edmonton, so she quickly filled Tom in on her conversation with Laina as the plane hit the tarmac.

Chapter Sixty

After returning to their PC, the RCMP officers radioed their sergeant who had them secure the location while he communicated with the detachment. It took only a couple of minutes before he was back on the radio telling Drought the staff sergeant had deployed the detachment's Aeryon Skyranger drone and to watch for its arrival. Although the detachment was small, it covered a vast enforcement area and were often involved search and rescue. The rugged terrain of the Rocky Mountains made it impossible to cover the area on foot and often inclement weather prevented aircraft involvement, hence the drone, which had proven to be all the Ontario manufacturer had boasted.

Drought's geographical coordinates were uploaded to the drone and travelling as the crow flies, was overhead in an astonishingly short time frame. Drought didn't hear it and only saw the Skyranger when it dropped down in front of the PC startling both officers. Drought was positive his staff sergeant was having a great time operating the controls and getting a chuckle out of scaring them.

The drone took off immediately once seeing the Members acknowledge its presence. The drone fed its video back to the detachment which recorded and redirected the feed to Drought's PC allowing the officers to monitor the airborne investigation.

The trail was not long but it was overgrown which would have prevented any conventional vehicle, save another quad, from wending its way to the objective. Skyranger zoomed through the trail, stopping periodically to peruse a possible break in the bush, but as Drought noted, each stop proved to be the entry into a game trail, not human traversed.

What seemed like only moments, but was in fact fifteen minutes, the drone hovered over what appeared to be a flat, matted grass area, possibly the location of a trailer, since removed. Skyranger moved very slowly only inches from the ground, seeking clues to what, or who, had been here and what happened to the cesium.

Rotating clockwise, the drone increased its distance from the flattened grass. Finding nothing unusual it increased its search field, zigzagging around boulders and brush, stopping in front of a rock face. It looked left then right, then backed up and scanned the rock face upwards attempting to glimpse at the height. It appeared to be somewhat short in elevation blending with the general topography of bush and impassible solid rock. Dropping down to ground level, it zoomed in on the roots of several bushes and waited for Drought to see that the bushes had been pulled out of the ground and replaced, just sitting on the surface.

Moving up slightly, Skyranger zoomed again and lighted the area with its high intensity lamination revealing the entrance to a cave. Observation was the extent of the drone's capabilities, venturing too close to the brush would incapacitate its propellers, so it backed away and continued to examine the rest of the area.

While Skyranger continued its reconnaissance, Drought radioed his observations to his supervisor, suggesting further investigation to determine if the cesium was being hidden in the cave, if the cave was a storage area for subversive materials, living quarters or what.

Returning his attention back to the police car's monitor, Drought noted the drone had completed its cursory investigation and had increased its elevation to three-hundred meters, just above the tree tops and was proceeding east, zigzagging noting another quad trail almost obliterated by the massive forested area. About thirty-minutes into its flight, it viewed train tracks. Increasing its speed, it was over the area in seconds, then hovered above what appeared to be a staging area with long sections of track and an automatic switching station. Dropping down to almost ground level, it began scanning the area around the tracks stopping quickly only moments later and hovered again. Quad tracks.

Skyranger did about five 360 twirls in celebration, then headed back to Drought's location, landing in front of the PC. The staff sergeant was on the radio immediately relating his suspicions of the cesium's location. He advised Drought and his partner to remain in position and join the rest of the search crew when they arrived with the RCMP's Quad Squad while Staff contacted Canadian Pacific to confirm his theory and determine the destination of the cesium, presumably concealed on a rail car. He also contacted Alberta "K" Division headquarters in Edmonton with an update and was blown away when he was immediately connected to Laina.

She had already sent him the secure link and took the time now to explain Chapman, now coined just CHAP by President Bakus…not an acronym but a simple identification after its developer.

McDonald moved quickly getting to CHAP, logging on and reading the status update on the investigation. He saw that his officers' investigation of the cesium was too late to contribute but he added his analysis anyway noting his officers would continue their investigation into the compound to where the cesium was delivered.

Having completed his contribution to the investigation, McDonald was experiencing an adrenaline rush he hadn't enjoyed in a long time, so much so that he radioed his sergeant to advise that he was in route to join the Quad Squad in the compound investigation.

While an ambulance transported the deceased suspects to the closest morgue, the surviving shooter was escorted back to the detachment and transferred to the custody of the Alberta Sheriff's department which moved the suspect to the Edmonton detachment for interrogation.

Chapter Sixty-One

Law enforcers Jones, Braket and Williams arrived with a collective excitement none had experienced in some time. It was unprecedented for any federal agency to collaborate, let alone invite local law enforcement to participate in an investigation.

The men had met at Williams' office and caravanned to StoneHead Ranch, choosing to drive separately in case any had to leave unexpectedly. Once at the main gate, their identifications were checked as well as each vehicle, but otherwise they were sprinted to the Ranch House by the military escort, allowed to park, then escorted into the building by an Army Ranger Lieutenant.

Jessica, dressed in a pair of distressed denim pants, tan, Italian Lost Valley's Booties with slender straps crisscrossing the instep, a one-inch heel and back zipper closure along with a cordovan, roll-tab sleeve tunic, extending to mid-thigh, met them just inside the door, proffered a casual, professional presence, shook hands, had them drop their bags in the living room, introduced the group to Bruce who gave them a cursory tour of the communication center, then provided an introduction to Chef Marc who, having been privy to their arrival, had coffee and cinnamon buns with sour cream drizzle ready.

All four thanked Marc profusely, grabbed a mug of black and arranged themselves in a semi-circle in front of the empty fireplace. While enjoying the pastry and coffee, Jessica extended her appreciation for the three responding so quickly and provided an overview of her initial analysis.

Once finished with their buns, Jessica invited her colleagues to the secure office where they settled in and she began her lengthy, detailed observation utilizing an overhead, several monitors and intercom with Bruce. Each man had brought his encrypted laptop, so once Jessica gave them the Wi-Fi access code, they each began their own analysis.

Chapter Sixty-Two

Rebecca drove directly to the guide outfitter's compound where her colleagues had the pack train ready and a horse saddled for her. They headed into the mountains moments after her arrival.

Williams had texted Troy advising him of Rebecca's departure time so Everson had time to set up his listening equipment prior to her arrival at the rendezvous site.

As laborious as a pack-train can be with the animals lumbering along, they can make impressive speed given the terrain's complexity and rising elevation.

This being her first trip through these mountains she was pretty much travelling on instincts, drawing on her tracking experience in Arizona. She also had no idea where the exchange would take place and hoped the team would have a little advance notice rather than Marrington and Shepherd popping out of the bush somewhere.

She didn't have long to wait and her anxieties were ill founded. Three hours into the trip and a gain of about four-thousand feet, they had just leveled out on a short plain when they spotted two riders sitting in the clearing, their horses tethered to nearby trees. StoneHead being at five-thousand feet elevation, Rebecca's team's horses needed time to adjust to the change, which was probably why the CFBA leaders chose this location knowing they would need a break and would have the advantage over Rebecca having to adjust to the elevation change.

Rebecca and each of the agents gave a little wave to acknowledge the waiting pair and slowly approached. Rebecca and her colleagues wore western style holsters carrying American made Dan Wesson .357 revolvers with three-inch barrels, the holster strapped to their thigh. The agents would have preferred their duty nine-millimeter Sig Sauer fifteen round magazine weapon, but that would have raised questions. The agents knew Marrington would recognize American made and that would give them just a slight edge.

Rebecca was leading and was the first to rein up, turning her horse's head to the left, leaving Marrington and Shepherd side by side and her a clear shot if they tried to take her team down.

"Who the fuck are you?" said Marrington with a somewhat snarly expression.

"Simpson. I took over from James. He got himself arrested and I scooped in and took charge of this shipment before the feds could confiscate it," she replied, tossing the pack-train lead rope to Marrington.

"That's it? You expect us to accept you as the delivery person with your boys in tow? No questions asked?" retorted Shepherd.

"Not at all," countered Rebecca. "Here is from the stored weed. I took it too and here are the proceeds. I am taking it out of my saddle bag slowly so don't shoot my ass as it will be the worst financial decision you ever make," she added reaching for the plastic bag containing the two-hundred thousand dollars, then tossing it to Shepherd.

He grabbed it out of the air and while Marrington continued to stare at the cowboys and Rebecca, Shepherd opened the bag. "Two hundred thousand you say?"

"That's it. If you like the money, I can buy the guide outfitters place for a song, dummy-up on runnin' a business with these guys," she flipped her hand backwards indicting the cowboys, "and bring your chemicals each time, sell your weed. Win/win for you guys."

"And what do you get out of this?"

"How about ten percent of what I sell the blue sage for? You know I did you right with this shipment. You know exactly what the going price is and you have it in that bag. I have nothing to gain by screwing you out of a few bucks."

"What about the product stored at the church farm, what happened to that?" asked Marrington, knowing full well that Denver had notified them that it had been abandoned to distance themselves from the congregation who were misguided and of little help in the achieving the ultimate goal.

"I have no idea. I am a horse trainer and saw an opportunity and took it. Where is the exchange pack-train? I can't sell what I don't have. Do we have a deal or not?"

"Let us think about it. Give me a number and we will text you our answer and if we are a go, we will meet again with our exchange product."

Rebecca pulled a piece of paper from her saddle bag, a pen and wrote down her personal cell number and handed it across to Marrington who snatched it from her hand, maintaining the dominant sneer.

As the two men turned to leave, Shepherd looked over his shoulder and said, "You better not be fuckin' with us girly, because if you are, you won't live to regret it." He turned back to the trail and with the pack-team in tow and headed back to the compound.

Rebecca stifled a smile as she nodded to her colleagues, turned their horses and slowly headed back to Yellowstone Outfitters, not knowing what Jessica's operation entailed but confident these two would be in custody shortly.

Once back at the facility she unsaddled the horses, wiped the sweat off, giving each a good rub-down then turned them loose in the paddock with three flacks of grass hay and a coffee can of sweet grain for their recuperation. The other agents were settled into the bunk house and would guard the facility for the remainder of the operation while Rebecca headed to her house and called Pen, inviting Pen to dinner. Driving back to town, she turned on Katharine McPhee singing Sinatra and thought of how her life had changed so dramatically and how, unconsciously, she had jettisoned her cowgirl persona.

Chapter Sixty-Three

Everson had paralleled Simpson after the first hour, maintaining a whisper of a presence about one hundred meters away, advancing with the team, stopping briefly as they did, then moving on simultaneously. During the exchange, he had Marrington's chest in his Winchester's sites, prepared to eliminate him if he drew on Rebecca. The loop lever action gave him the huge advantage over a bolt action with the element of speed to move the weapon slightly from a fallen Marrington to Shepherd so quickly the second terrorist would be hit before he could acknowledge he had lost his partner.

As the train moved toward the Idaho compound, Troy was recording their entire conversation, as limited as it was. He knew a technician would have to filter out the mule sounds, the wind and the incredibly loud Black-Billed Magpie with its incessant nasal-sounding *mag! mag!*

The distance to the compound was short and he anticipated, hoped really, that the two would engage in a conversation while unloading the chemicals.

They did.

Shepherd took the lid off the first pannier, which was a substantial size at two feet by two feet by eighteen inches deep, and handed it to Marrington. Neither man noticed the tiny transmitter tucked in the corner under the lid. Marrington placed the rather light weight can on a pallet. Neither were experiencing déjà vu of Jackson's previous encounter here, an experience Marrington did not share with Shepherd and wished to forget being attacked, knocked out and subdued just before the FBI SWAT team descended months previously.

"What do you think of the blonde broad?" asked Marrington. "She looks like she could take care of herself. With Harold and Joe gone from StoneHead, we haven't a contact there and I certainly wouldn't trust Mr. Holiness himself, the reverend."

"I don't think we have anything to lose," replied Shepherd. "We have the two hundred thousand which we will quickly funnel into the

CFBA account and these chemicals will bring cash when we transfer them south."

"Which brings up another factor. We need to get this shipment to our guys in Marina Del Rey in the next couple of days. I suspect they are in the process of filling the barrels and we can't take a chance of them running out and having to postpone the surprise we have for the Democratic Convention."

"Okay, I will get on the phone and get some guys up here tomorrow and we can have it on the road by noon."

"Good. Now back to the blonde broad. Spring through fall, our Alberta supplier can add a huge balance to nationally so I say we give her a try. It is certainly worth it financially. What do you say?"

"I agree. If she double crosses us we can eliminate her."

Hearing this conversation delighted Troy as any observer could tell, as his face broke out in an Alice in Wonderland Cheshire grin. He was done. He backed away and headed to his mountain retreat to send this information to Williams, who would email to his Secret Service agent at StoneHead.

Everson was feeling particularly fond of himself, no, that wasn't it, proud maybe, that he was contributing to society again without the bullshit of which he had grown terribly tired. He whistled all the way home, something he thought his lips had forgotten to perform.

Chapter Sixty-Four

The Colorado research group had finalized their experiments and were just starting the process of evaluating the data in conjunction with Jenewein's explosive experts he had flown in from the university. The graduate students had no idea that Abida Chahine, Qalat Ghazi, Zaranj Beydown and Meymaneh Rahmani were Al Qaeda operatives who, until just recently, had been instructing south-western aboriginals in the science of bomb making.

The four were there to provide their expertise in choosing the final formula for both the Suburbans and decoy vans. As the operatives were wakening and making their way to the dining room, Jason, who had been up for several hours, made coffee and prepared a tray for two of sticky buns, butter, jam and two mugs of strong black coffee, was sitting on a log about one kilometer from the lodge, sipping his Black…waiting.

The first operative in the kitchen prepared coffee using a special Arabic product Jenewein had picked up in Denver to ensure hospitality and to make his guests feel as much at home as possible. The coffee was 3 tablespoons of ground Arabic coffee beans, three cups of water, one tablespoon of crushed cardamom, six whole cloves and a pinch of saffron. He sat the blend aside to brew while he prepared a platter of jam, bread, cheese and a dip called, za'atar a spice mix made with thyme, sumac, sesame seeds, and salt, fresh fruit, vegetables, olives, pickles and hard-boiled eggs. When his colleagues joined him, they drank their coffee first and chatted about what they had observed the first day, coming to a consensus that the young Americans were motivated by politics, not ideology, their preferred incentive. They agreed that although problematic, they would work through the issue to guarantee their success and that of their organization. That settled, they poured more coffee and enjoyed their breakfast.

Although the four had met Jason the previous day and were somewhat drawn to him, given how he was different from the younger researchers both in physical appearance, maturity and life experiences, they had no idea he was back in the bush, had poured a second coffee and had it and the sticky bun in his hands, walking around in circles, positive that his midnight visitor was watching.

And he was.

Kian O'Brien had been watching the lodge since well before dawn, as he did every day. Months would pass when the lodge was empty and so he took advantage of the human contact, albeit at a distance, to people watch. He enjoyed the solitude of months without any human contact, much to his preference, otherwise he wouldn't be living a hermit's life, but sometimes he needed an emotional connection, something, someone to remind his psyche that he was in fact still connected to the human race.

O'Brien had been living in the bush for what seemed to him to be eons. He had vague relationships with the folks in Kent, a small town a half day's walk from his home-made cabin, but locals found it difficult to get close to him given his lifestyle and emotional distance. The small-town citizens knew him well, but as helpful and supportive as they tried to be, they had no idea what he had gone through in combat or at the hands of the government.

Sometimes he wanted to disengage himself from civilization completely, no time more so than some time previously when he watched the lodge's pilot drag a man's body from the float plane, haul him back in the bush and burn his possessions, leaving the body for the wolves and coyotes.

He had been an explosive expert with Delta Force in Iraq with the mission to destroy everything that could be used against the Coalition Forces. That meant blowing bridges, stone structures housing enemy leaders and similar facilities. He was a walking arsenal of explosive technology and had observed the numerous experiments conducted by the youngsters at the research lodge, wondering if they would come up with a solution to whatever problem they were trying to solve. Their ignorance became an obsession since he had experimented in training with many of the same chemicals they were using, the difference being, he had learned from trial and error in the field and narrowed his choice of explosives to a few. *Blowing up tires is a great contrast to a house of Taliban soldiers or a bridge over a chasm connecting two Taliban territories,* he mused.

Watching Spencer from the dense bush, he was considering their possible objective, when he made the snap decision to meet the dude with the dreads. He had situated himself with the rising sun to his back, forcing this potential adversary to shield his eyes as O'Brien approached.

There was a wide-open space between the edge of the forest and Spencer's location on the fallen tree as O'Brien approached, arms extended straight out from his body and wearing a huge smile, albeit somewhat obliterated by a full black beard.

As he was within ten feet of Spencer, he extended his right hand and said, "Delta Force Operative Kian O'Brien, and you are?"

Jason stood, walked towards O'Brien and replied, "Jason Spencer, LAPD."

"Son-of-a-bitch. For real huh? So, what have you got to eat LEO Spencer?"

"Sticky buns and strong black coffee," he offered, handing the two to O'Brien adding,

"Have a seat."

The sticky buns, coffee and the obvious law enforcement connection seemed to break the ice between the warriors and a conversation began immediately. O'Brien shared what brought him to the Colorado forests and the tale brought immediate sadness to Spencer because Kian was another victim of untreated Post Traumatic Stress Syndrome, PTSD. Thousands of American soldiers were mustered out of the various services suffering from seeing too much evil, too many dead bodies and what he learned from Kian, too many explosions.

Spencer offered an explanation to his presence at the mountain retreat, of his former law enforcement service and wanting to make changes in his life, hence, environmental studies.

After about two hours Spencer thought he had better head back in case his absence brought unanswerable questions. He thanked O'Brien for meeting him and they scheduled a time for the next morning with Kian asking, "And more sticky buns and coffee please!" proffered with his masked smile.

Jason slipped into the kitchen, put his dirty dishes into the dishwasher and headed to the lab where the experts were explaining the pros and cons of each of the researchers' experiments. Jason took a seat at the back of the room, realizing no one had missed him and that his rendezvous with Delta Force was unknown at this point.

The rest of the day was a continuation of the previous with each experiment being repeated for the Al Qaeda visitors. Jason chose to keep a low profile, staying in the back of the group so he wouldn't be engaged. He was successful for the most part, but as is often the case when groups of strangers mingle, those with similar physical or professional backgrounds tend to gravitate to one another. Spencer's dark complexion and dreads were the light to which the moths were drawn. Rather than engage in a conversation supporting his cover, he chose to leave rather covertly and returned to his room without communicating with a soul.

The next morning, he left an hour earlier carrying the pot of coffee and four sticky buns. It was still dark and as his flashlight negotiated the trail, he found O'Brien already sitting on the meeting log with his arms spread, indicating he was waiting for the buns.

Although Spencer had considerable knowledge of PTSD, he avoided the subject, not wanting to ignite the unspeakable. Kian shared his numerous experiences as a Delta munitions expert. Some of his stories depicted bravery and others regrettable sadness, the latter often the result of young lives lost. Spencer suspected it was the latter which haunted him.

O'Brien explained that he had done three tours in Iraq and Afghanistan with just a couple of weeks rest between. America ran out of regular troops early in the war and relied upon National Guard personnel and reservists, both of which were never intended for regular duty but were trained for emergencies. Washington took men and women from their homes, jobs and families, many of whom never returned.

Drone strikes often created considerable collateral damage, which the military was desperately trying to reduce…unsuccessfully. Kian said that drones would obtain a target, then he would parachute solo into the area, carrying his C-4 and PETN, lay a charge on the target, then have to escape on his own, unprotected. If he had been captured, the military would disavow him. Often it would be weeks hiding in the mountains from insurgents before he crossed into friendly territory and the stress from the experience was overwhelming.

When he was discharged, the mandatory psych exam clearly revealed signs of emotional and mental stress but the Army offered zero counseling. Basically, they wished him well, a handshake and he was gone. He quickly found there were no support groups, Veterans Affairs offices or other institutions with which he could make emotional contact. Nobody wanted an explosives expert with covert experience, so after six dead-end jobs in six months, he packed it in and headed to the mountains.

He expounded on his cabin making skills and how the first attempt resulted in a leaky roof and drafty walls, the heat drying out the moss and the cold slipping through the cracks. He endured the first winter in that disaster, then enlisted assistance from the building supply guys in Kent who air lifted a prefabricated house to his cleared landing…complete with written instructions. He smiled broadly while sharing this experience, saying it was the first supportive connection he had with another human being. The community had raised the cost of the airlift, the kindness bringing him to tears on numerous occasions.

Now when he went to Kent, a half-day walk east, he hit the ATM for some of his retirement money, then headed to the spectacular White River Guest Ranch where he luxuriated in their spa-like showers, fine bed linens and exquisite meals. He had purchased slacks, shoes and several dress shirts which White River kept for him during his absence. Three to four days was his maximum and he would bid his adieu and head back home.

Spencer was unaware of Sheriff Williams' association with Troy Everson, for had he been, the similarities would be profound, leaving Spencer to wonder how many thousands of vets were living similar lives either in the bush or homeless on America's streets.

Their time together seemed to float by with neither seeming to care about any obligation. Kian knew he had none. Spencer felt he could explain his absence, but right now he seemed to be connecting with this vet who had found solace in the mountains when his government had abandoned him after risking his life for their cause.

As the men sat sipping their Black, O'Brien wondered how to broach the subject of the munitions experiments but finally just forced the comments, "Spencer, your researchers don't know shit."

Jason looked surprised and stiffled a mock snorting laugh at the bluntness of his new friend, that Kian felt comfortable being so frank.

"Why is that Kian?"

"Their outdoor experiments have been my source of entertainment since your arrival. I thought the entire group must be wannabe subversives, watching these kids play with explosives and I wonder if they are trying to kill themselves or someone else."

Jason knew he could not take Kian into his confidence, so he replied, "These kids are university graduate students who were chosen by the defense department to experiment with various explosives they think might be used by terrorists against America. They seem to be near completion and will file their findings with Washington. What exactly is your concern?" he said trying to show a genuine interest knowing full well what Delta had seen.

"Thanks for the explanation, but my feelings are the same," he replied, walking in circles, gathering his thoughts. "What they have been working on, Delta rejected years ago, having invested considerable expertise, mine for one, in determining what the multitude of terrorist groups might use, then coming up with a defense mechanism. What the kids produced is nothing like what Al Qaeda will deploy. Their choice will be PETN, pentaerythritol tetranitrate, a plastic explosive, either by itself or to create Semtex. C-4 is also very popular and all three are very hard to detect. The kids have made it here and are aware of its unique destruction properties. The white powder is almost undetectable. I suspect America's terrorists will use it in luggage or mechanical equipment. They can create a hundred pieces of unclaimed luggage. All they need is one lazy airport security flunky to be paid to allow its passage or be busy doing something else, and it goes by unnoticed. There are scores of American airports where security is lacking. An altitude activated detonator is all the PETN needs to take a plane out of the air. Do you remember Carlos the Jackal? I read about his bomb designs with Delta. He used PETN in 1983 to attack the Maison de France, the French Cultural Centre in Berlin.

My bottom line would be to scrap all the other formulas and have them present PETN in detail, coming up with a way to detect it at airport security screening terminals. Currently there isn't a reliable detection system because it doesn't vaporize sufficiently for the odor to be picked up by dogs."

Spencer acknowledged his friend's input and said that he would share with the research supervisor. He suppressed the fact that he had just been handed exceptional intel and that he needed to relay it to Jessica immediately.

The sun was well on its way to total light when he decided to head back to the lodge and decided to lighten the mood and leave Kain with a bit of humor that would make his day. He told him about the decision to install the exterior cameras and what the lodge residents thought they had captured on film. O'Brien put down the rest of his coffee and roared with laughter, acknowledging that he could see their being drawn into the enigma, so he said, "The beard and my height, I see how they made the connection but come on LAPD, isn't Sasquatch supposed to have body hair?" which drew another round of laughter as he rose to leave, giving Jason a high five with a comment that he hoped to see him again the next day.

Jason hustled back to the lodge and found their guests were ruminating the previous day's lessons, so he repeated yesterday's return and blended into the back row and listened. What he was hearing was so shocking, he began to extrapolate their dialog, knowing that America's intel was disastrously short on what Al Qaeda and other terrorist groups had in mind to bring the country to its knees.

Spencer didn't know which guest was which, but he had been successful in retrieving their individual finger prints by retrieving their morning coffee mugs and had a digital recording of each of their faces as they meandered behind the lodge. He had uploaded that data to Jessica, who was in the process of sorting Jason's intel along with scores of other materials, with the assistance of her colleagues. Spencer prided himself on his covert skills honed-in Northern Africa. He planted micro GPS trackers in each of the guests' luggage. Unless they jettisoned them along the way, Elisabeth would know their whereabouts when it came time for the mass arrests.

Jenewein had taken over addressing the group, advising that their guests were flying out later in the day and that if anyone had questions, now was the time to take advantage of their expertise. Several had pertinent queries, all pertaining to the experts rejecting PETN and similar plastic explosives. The guests held the opinion that these choices had been used in the Middle East to such an extent that the West had developed detection systems making them ineffective and basically useless. They encouraged the CFBA researchers to choose one of the liquid options such as kettle bombs using propane tanks.

Spencer knew such a recommendation was bogus and as such he was beginning to think these experts were actually planning subterfuge against CFBA. Why, he had no idea.

He knew that PETN mixed with a plasticizer created a powerful explosive device, which was used against the USS Cole which killed seventeen American sailors on October 12, 2000 while refuelling in Yemen's Aden Harbor. But if CFBA planned as extensive an attack as he was gleaning from the overall conversations, they couldn't produce the necessary quantity for the attack. He mused the complexity facing him all night, finally falling asleep in the early morning.

Later that morning, after Jenewein had taken off with Al Qaeda, Spencer made his case for using PETN over liquid explosives but failed to win over the researchers. His methodology was to convince the group to use the PETN thereby maximizing the magnitude of the attack. But he couldn't justify his opinion by revealing his relationship with O'Brien and with his lack of a chemistry background, his argument was weak. Even if he chose that dangerous route, he doubted the grad students would consider Kian's opinion worthy of their consideration given their judgemental approach to those who harness views different than theirs.

A compromise was reached to use Timothy McVeigh's formula in four utility vans using fertilizer, the ammonia nitrate along with diesel fuel, both of which were stockpiled in a Los Angeles warehouse waiting for the go ahead.

But they needed the chemicals in Los Angeles, which is where Jenewein came in. He had made the round trip to Denver, quickly dropping off the Al Qaeda operatives and now the chemicals were being loaded into the float plane while it sat in the water with the engine idling.

Once loaded, he headed back to Denver to transfer the cargo to a five-ton moving van which sped to Southern California in fifteen hours, using two drivers. The cargo arrived at the warehouse on West Jefferson near Loyola Marymount University the next day where the Suburbans' rear seat facades were ready to install the explosives.

Chapter Sixty-Five

Elisabeth and Jackson made good time to Los Angeles by sharing the driving. Elisabeth had never driven a modified vehicle before, let alone a truck and enjoyed the acceleration and maneuverability. She thought the suspension could use a little loosening and the huge tires made it almost impossible to enter gracefully, *but then she was never one to be considered graceful*, she thought, grinning to herself.

Their first task was to interview the pub owner, hoping to obtain additional information regarding the extortioners, so they checked into the Ramada in Marina del Rey, which was modest accommodations for the Marina at two-hundred and forty dollars a night...each. Arriving in the middle of the night, they hauled Elisabeth's equipment to her second story room with an adjoining door to Jackson's, then they both hit the sack agreeing to meet for the hotel's complimentary breakfast at eight. The plan was to activate the equipment immediately so they could begin monitoring and log into CHAP and begin their surveillance, but after the long drive they knew neither had the cognitive skills to do so until the morning, or what was left of it.

30,000

Not far from the Ramada, Joe had just completed a conversation with the CFBA agents who had converted the four black Suburbans with three rows each of hollowed back seats. The cavities were filled with fifty pounds each of PETN, newly arrived plastic explosives from Denver, for a total of one-hundred and fifty pounds per vehicle. The research team had experimented on small amounts and their calculations indicated 100 grams would destroy a vehicle. Jenewein shared Spencer's suspicions of the Al Qaeda operatives and made an executive decision to go with the PETN knowing that it was foolish to try and follow in McVey's footsteps. One pound was equivalent to four-hundred and fifty grams. The Suburbans were identical to those used exclusively by federal agents and with the counterfeit license plates they would navigate Los Angeles' streets completely undetected.

Chapter Sixty-Six

Stephan Odermatt was a fifty-four-year old Swiss-German American who had been a commercial pilot for over twenty years. Starting as a bush pilot in Northern Manitoba, he gradually increased plane size and responsibility as his hours and training expanded. In 2009, he was captain of a Mahalo Airline flight returning to Seattle from a round-trip to Oahu when Chesley Sullenberger safely landed his U.S. Airways Flight 1549 Air Bus A320-214 on the Hudson River off Manhattan in New York City. Stephan remembers vividly the report he received while taking a break from the controls. He instinctively looked out the window, not expecting to see anything but blue sky and the occasional cloud but knowing that if he had a similar incident, he would be landing in a vast ocean, not a river where rescue was imminent.

His safe landing in Seattle was routine, which is to say he had become complacent, taking for granted the hundreds of lives for which he was responsible. His cavalier attitude bothered him during his brief layover, so much so that he spent his rest time to search for and enroll in a fully hands-on water landing course where he would learn what was euphemistically coined, *The Sully Landing.*

After completing the course, his confidence sored and the ache in the pit of his stomach subsided. He felt good about his abilities to safely land in the ocean...albeit not so much in a stormy sea.

He was sitting in the crew lounge waiting for maintenance to indicate they were ready for his inspection of the Boeing 737 Mahalo flight from Minneapolis to LAX then on to Maui. Watching Ben Affleck in *Argo* with the scene of the Boeing 747, a huge aircraft not unlike the one in which he was about to navigate above a vast expanse of water, and he began musing about Sully, his flight, courage and his own training, wondering if he would be able to pull it off…landing in water.

He sipped his black Starbuck's, peered out the lounge window at his waiting ride and mulled over his Swiss-German heritage connection with Sullenberger, felt confident he was made of the same core character as Sully and could handle the big 747 nicely as a seaplane. Then he chuckled to himself and his wry sense of humor.

Chapter Sixty-Seven

Following a late rise and quick workout in the hotel gym, Elisabeth had her equipment installed and operational within fifteen minutes and began downloading data from CHAP and Jessica. Elisabeth transferred the information to Jackson's monitor sitting beside her so he was working at the same speed and time frame.

An hour into their reading the data and on-line and cell chatter, it became clear that Joe was in Marina Del Rey. Their law enforcement instinct, call it gut feeling, was that the CFBA operation was eminent. They decided that Elisabeth would continue to monitor information from StoneHead, CHAP, the local cell communications and relay any pertinent data to Jackson on his encrypted cell while he interviewed Armishaw at the Firewalker and see if he could add anything to his previous conversation with the FBI.

Jackson researched the pub before leaving the hotel and was impressed with the establishment itself and particularly the SEAL who ran it. He looked forward to the chat as he drove the short distance, parked in the rear of the pub and entered through the staff door. Once inside he was immediately confronted by Armishaw filling the short hallway, legs spread, his huge arms across his chest.

"We're not open yet sir, unless you have business with me and that I doubt very much."

"You must be the infamous Armishaw my FBI colleagues told me about. I am Jackson Pennington with the Secret Service," he replied, taking out his identification and extending it to the pub owner.

Armishaw took the identification, lifting it to eye level so he could read the data while keeping an eye on Pennington. Satisfied that his early visitor wasn't a threat but wary none-the- less, he said, "I am not sure what more I can add to what I told the FBI Mr. Pennington. The three pricks tried to extort money, it pissed me off and I hauled them at gun point into the back while my guy called the FBI."

"May I come in and chat. It will only take a moment."

"Sure," he said and stepped aside, allowing Jackson to turn sideways and make his way into the kitchen and into the pub dining room while handing back Pennington's credentials.

"Have a seat anywhere. I'll get us a coffee. Black?"

"Yes, black would be nice. Thank you," he said, as he sat in the nearest booth.

Tobias brought the two coffees in white mugs, sat them down then shook hands with Jackson apologizing for his abrupt behavior saying, "So, what can I add agent Jackson?"

"It has been a while since that event and the three remain in federal custody. From my research, you must know a lot of people and I know this is a long shot, but might you or one of your employees have seen these guys around? The addresses and identification they gave the FBI are phoney but they must have been operating from a near-by base. Any thoughts?"

"No, I have racked my brain trying, asking myself the same question, but then we got slammed several days in a row and I forgot about it. Let me call my manager and see what she has to say," he offered, then pulled his cell out and punched in a number from memory then put the phone to his ear. Momentarily he said, "Rose. Hi, yeah. I have a Secret Service agent here asking me if any of us remember seeing the three dick-heads who tried to extort us, you know around town or where ever. I can't recall, do you or maybe one of the guys?" he waited for her to reply then added, "Okay, would you give them a call and get back to me right away? Great. Thanks."

"Rose is going to call the staff and get back to us in a few. Let me get the pot and give us a refill.

While they were waiting for the call back, Jackson got up, walked around the pub carrying his coffee and commented about the various plaques and the significance of each.

Tobias was more than pleased to educate and took his time to explain who was who. Pennington shared his personal background and received a broad smile from the SEAL, the only recognition he would receive, but one that spoke a thousand words.

The return call came moments after the brief exchange and Tobias answered, "Whatdayahave?" He waited a moment for the reply then went to the bar and grabbed a pad and paper and began writing. When he was done, he said, "This is terrific Rose. I am sorry we dropped the ball too. This should make up for it though. Right. See you in a bit, and thanks."

"Here you go Delta," he said with the same huge grin. "Rose made some calls to our guys who did likewise. You know all my employees are either SEALs or Marines, right? Anyway, they narrowed these guys down and Rick, an active SEAL who was volunteering on the day these assholes came in, he says one of his friends saw the short one with a white five-ton van gassing up at the Shell on Lincoln just up from Jefferson."

Jackson almost had to grab something to steady himself from anticipation. He thanked Tobias, pulled out his cell, stepped away, called Elisabeth and relayed the information. Jackson told her he was on his way there and would call back. As he turned around, Tobias was primed with a question but Pennington spoke so quickly, he beat Tobias out.

"This is terrific news Tobias. We are deeply appreciative of your help. I will leave you to your business."

"Just a comment agent Pennington if you will. I don't know whom or what you are investigating but this area is inundate with Marines and SEALs. We have our own private social media page and everyone has a smartphone. If you will allow us, we can get the physical description of the prick Rick's friend saw and the five ton and have all these guys on the lookout. What do you say?"

"Give me a minute Tobias and I will get back to you," he offered and stepped away again and called Jessica. She needed all the information and although she was hesitant to involve civilians, she justified her approval by commenting that these men were not civilians.

Jackson closed his phone then turned to Tobias and said, "You got it Tobias. If you can hand me that pad, I will give you my cell which you can post along with the information and have your guys call if they spot the suspect or van. And I don't have to tell you that this is highly confidential."

"Got it agent," as he handed the pad to Jackson. "But remember sir, we are SEALs and Marines and our honor is above reproach," he added with a broad smile.

Jackson thanked him profusely as he ran out the back door and yelled over his shoulder, “Thanks for the coffee,” and headed to the gas station. Jackson wanted to shout, “Oorah” but neither he nor Tobias were Marines, so it would have been inappropriate…cool, but inappropriate.

30,000

Jessica no sooner had hung up from Jackson when she called Elisabeth, relaying the update. Elisabeth told her she had checked every hotel, motel and B&B registration in the area for Sarkowski and he wasn’t on any guest list. Jessica acknowledged the information and said she would have LAPD patrol officers check the Marina and surrounding area for Sarkowski from his driver’s license photo.

Jessica made the call to LAPD senior administration and was told they would have Sarkowski’s photo on every squad car’s computer screen within the hour. Elisabeth logged into CHAP and filed the current information from Jackson and Jessica, the information which would allow LAPD quick access and uploading to their officers.

Having completed these simple data tasks, she returned to monitoring the data coming in via CHAP from across North America on the investigation. Taking a sip of her black, she mused about how effective CHAP was proving to be in avoiding duplicate investigations and getting thousands of law enforcement officers and agencies to co-operate. She made a mental note to take a few days off and do dinner and drinks with Cheryl to show her gratitude and just maybe find out a little more about the enigma that is the female SEAL software designer of CHAP.

Chapter Sixty-Eight

Harold Richards and Martha were sitting in the safe house watching reruns of Friends and eating last night's leftovers when Richards received the long-awaited text, *Here*.

"Okay. That's it. We are out of here. The van just arrived in the area. I want you to get in your car, exit the garage slowly and nonchalantly, turn south. Drive to the nearest mall, park and go in as though you are shopping without a care in the world. I will be on the front walk as you do that, waving to you like a couple having a relaxing evening."

"I get it. Am I the decoy, or are you? Wait, it doesn't matter. Are you staying here or what?"

"I will go back into the house, put on my hat and coat and leave again, walking away in the opposite direction in which you drove. Last check, there was only one surveillance team on us, so I will walk by them without making recognition, walk over to my car and drive in the same direction I was walking, go to a gas station and take my time filling up, go to the restroom, by something in the store. That kinda stuff. This should confuse the one surveillance team and they won't have time to get back-up. The van is cleared to drop off their cargo at the Mahalo Airline freight center. The paper work is beyond questioning so the casket will be processed without incident. The two in the van will exit the airport and ditch the van in the most crowded parking lot, wipe down the entire vehicle, leave the keys in the ignition and vanish."

"Sounds good. Keep them trying to second guess our movements. Do we come back here or do we meet up again?"

"Do you remember the second safe house on your list in case this one was compromised? Go there and do exactly the same thing as you did when you arrived here."

"Got it. I'm on my way," she said as she headed to the attached garage.

30,000

Stephan Odermatt was doing his pre-flight inspection which, as the captain, involved a cursory walk around the plane's exterior looking for any abnormalities of the giant aircraft. Once on board he and his first officer would do a comprehensive check of the entire system prior to passenger loading.

As Odermatt was doing his walk-about, the cargo was being loaded and he stopped to watch a casket strapped to a pallet being raised into the hold. The sight brought him back to his morbid thoughts in the crew lounge, then caught himself, shook his head to clear the pessimism, continued with his inspection, then entered the plane and proceeded with the detailed analysis.

30,000

Marcus Jones died the previous week in Lewiston, Idaho. His will stipulated cremation and the ninety-two-year old gentleman passed in his sleep believing his wishes would be respected.

They weren't.

The mortician was a member of the CFBA and unknown to Marcus, had become part of the Democratic National Convention operation in the development of a unique casket. Marcus was a slight man. His passing weight was about ninety-pounds and he stood five feet, five inches, therefore he didn't take up much room in the casket, allowing for the installation of two layers of lead, shaped to fit the interior with a six-inch space between. At each end of his body were hollow square blocks of lead, one housed the cesium, the other electronics having been developed by the university grad research students with undergraduate degrees in electrical engineering. Between the layers of lead under his body, contained a small ampule, half filled with mercury. At each top end were electronic leads connecting to an altitude control device. In the same lead cavity was a timer wired to the cesium container's screw on top.

Chapter Sixty-Nine

Jessica and her colleagues were busy coordinating the massive information, logging it into CHAP and commiserating about each lead. At one-point Williams jumped up from his monitor and yelled, "We got them Jessica. Son-of-a-bitch, we got them. Marrington and Shepherd, right here on Everson's recording. We are going to get these bastards, all of them. The others quickly gathered around and listened to the recording and gave each other a high five, a few yelps and a couple of positive profanities, then returned to work.

Williams logged the data into CHAP, saved it into Barry's system and made a copy on a flash drive.

Everyone was getting tired so Jessica suggested they grab some food Marc had prepared and get a few hours sleep. Chef Stucki presented large white platters overflowing with his own recipe of saffron fettuccine with clams and bacon and a spicy tomato sauce. Knowing the officers would not consume alcohol during this crucial stage of the investigation, he had managed to locate a local brewery which produced an outstanding malt beer with zero alcohol. Chef, with his refined palate immediately purchased several cases in preparation for the law enforcers. His selection along with the fettuccine and strong black Kicking Horse coffee made a hit with everyone working on consolidating the massive data.

Sheriff Joe was the first to leave. He took a plate of food and a glass of beer to his room, quickly ate and laid down in his clothes and was asleep in minutes. He had just left when CHAP sounded a warning that new information had just been logged into the investigation.

Jessica quickly accessed the data and read that not only did Martha just leave the safe house but Harold was walking away in the opposite direction. *Well,* she ruminated, *this unveils the mystery as to what happened to him. What were they up to?*

The agents conducting the surveillance had followed Martha and asked for a second team to follow Richards. It would take a little time to roll out the second vehicle but Richards didn't appear to be in any hurry, whereas Martha was mobile and needed to be followed.

Jessica interrupted her team, shared the information and suggested they brainstorm for a consensus on the two CFBA terrorists' agenda and how to find the shipment from Idaho.

Braket was the first with an idea and said, "That area must have a massive CCTV coverage. Can we get the Minneapolis and airport police to send their feed to CHAP and have her scan for a white van? If we narrow the field to a few hours, calculating how long it would take two drivers to get to the airport there, an operator may be able to zero in on the one we want, particularly if we isolate the request to all highways leading to the airport."

"Excellent idea," Jessica exclaimed, rolling her chair back to her monitor. "I think it can work. Give me a few minutes as I get on the phone to both departments. It shouldn't take too long for them to upload the data."

30,000

Jackson's interviewing the gas station staff was a bust. It was evident that without a better description of the driver, given the business volume, remembering a white five-ton van was impossible.

He had just returned to his car when his cell went off. It was Tobias with news that a Marine had just spotted another five-ton van heading down Jefferson, possibly toward the same gas station with the same driver. Different van, but same driver. What the hell is going on, thought Jackson. He thanked the SEAL, punched off, then motored across the street and parked in a fast food lot, facing the gas station.

Chapter Seventy

Karen and Tom had moved quickly to gain access to the suspect Cst. Drought had arrested. The detachment commander was in the dark regarding the entire investigation, the Alberta RCMP Division "K" not having followed up on the CSIS data on CHAP. While Karen was briefing her, David Kopas arrived and began the interrogation, which turned out to provide limited information given the scope of the operation. Fingerprints of the deceased and the surviving suspect showed they were two small time hoods from the Denver area. The survivor swore they received their instructions through a friend of a friend. "Just like buying a gun," said the suspect. "We was sittin' in a bar and some guy comes in. We've known him for a long time. He sits down and asks us if we want an easy job moving a crate out of Manitoba. Guns, van, ski masks, everything provided. Good money. We don't have no passports so we get plane tickets to Fargo, North Dakota and some suit meets us. We hop in a pick-up and he drives us to the border and through some farmer's field and then we are in Winnipeg. There is the van, instructions and a wad of cash. We were to get the balance after we delivered the package in Alberta. Who the fuck would think some country cop would be sittin' in the middle of the fuckin' road blastin' the shit out of us. That mother-fucker killed my friends you know," he said, shaking his head acknowledging the futility of his predicament.

Karen, Tom and the commander were watching the interrogation from the adjoining observation room through a one-way mirror and the last comment drew a smile from all three. The American thought Alberta's law enforcement was conducted like many states, with officers having little training and no national emphasis. "I wonder if he has heard of CHAP," quipped Karen, drawing a snicker from the other two officers.

"It's obvious he has never heard of us," quipped the commander, referring to the iconic Royal Canadian Mounted Police.

David grilled the suspect for quite some time before calling it quits for the day, coming away from the interrogation with the name of the bar and the contact but not much else. He gave that to the commander who said she would get into CHAP immediately for the contact info of the

Denver PD and have them work that angle to find out who put out the contract for the cesium theft.

Chapter Seventy-One

Constable Drought, his partner and detachment commander McDonald with his Quad Squad, found the cave and the adjoining underground operation with little difficulty. They breached the reinforced steel door with munitions set by a member of the Quad Squad who acquired his skill as a member of Canada's Joint Task Force 2 during two Afghanistan tours. The enforcement team was excited about gaining entry. They knew that if the operation had been a weed production, all traces of the product would be gone, but they were hoping the cesium had been stored underground with some evidence at to its presence.

Right and wrong.

The only evidence of an illicit operation was the row upon row of grow shelves, each previously illuminated with high-power grow lights which hung dark, on limp cords waiting for their next assignment. Still intact was the professional electrical and exhaust system, the latter being vented to the cave.

The forensics Member processed the entire facility with a GAC, Global Avenue Consulting, digital scanner, then sent the data to the Canadian Criminal Real Time Identification Services, CCRTIS, of the Forensic Science and Identification Services of the RCMP for identification. McDonald added his personal caveat to the transmission asking the CCRTIS to first check their system then to log into CHAPS.

In the depths of the cave, they found a massive diesel generator, the type used to operate a hospital during a power-outage. Alongside were ten, two-hundred-liter barrels of fuel with automatic pumps connected in series, so when one tank emptied, the next one began filling the generator automatically. The team calculated the system could operate 24/7 for a month and by the tracks up to the tanks, the operator was transporting the fuel with a three-quarter ton pick-up, as was evident by the tire tread pattern.

There wasn't any sign of the cesium, drawing the investigators to conclude it was relayed almost immediately after delivery. McDonald's aerial surveillance of the trail leading to the rail side-tracks coupled with its absence on the grow-op grounds, he deduced the material was now in

Idaho. He uploaded the team's conclusions and supporting video to CHAP, then strung crime scene tape around the entire operation and across the mouth of the cave, placed an official *Under RCMP Investigation, KEEP OUT sign* on the now destroyed steel door. He assigned a Member to remain at the scene until the Sheriff's department could arrange 24/7 guard detail until the scene was officially released by the Edmonton forensics team.

Heading back to the detachment with the Quad Squad with Cst. Drought and his partner returning by vehicle, McDonald smiled and thought to himself, *today had to count as one of the best of his career.*

Chapter Seventy-Two

Jessica had obtained a warrant to tap the mortician's phone, the guy Sam's mother identified, but the surveillance hadn't revealed anything of significance. She mused over the sheriff's previous comment on how he could investigate the police chief's murder once access to the reservation was granted. Applying for the warrant, Sorento showed the federal judge CHAP's extensive file on the investigation and she granted access almost immediately.

She mused that Chapman's integrated intelligence system was going to be a significant factor in keeping America safe when all agencies will be working together without dealing with jurisdiction issues.

30,000

The Minneapolis federal agents had kept a tail on Harold, observing that his actions were purely evasive. Using several surveillance vehicles, they allowed him to feel success in evading observation as he seemingly wandered the streets, into malls and stores, then picked up his vehicle, travelled aimlessly, then parked several blocks away and snuck in the back door of the original safe house. Once confirmed that Martha was not with him, agents covertly sealed him in.

Another team followed Martha to another safe house where she entered the garage, closed it automatically and basically disappeared. This team closed ranks around the house, sealing her in until an arrest warrant was issued.

30,000

It was but a few hours from the time the request was acknowledged by the Minneapolis and airport police forces to when Barry advised that both agencies had used identification software to segregate all white vans entering the city and the airport. They narrowed the suspect vehicles to just those which passed from out of town then into the airport. One stood out. One with South Dakota plates. Barry sent the video to all the officers' monitors allowing each to make their individual assessment, then collaborate.

Gathering around Jessica's monitor they acknowledged an even though a more extensive sweep for white vans would be wise, but since Joe was in Marina Del Rey, time was of the essence. Jessica zoomed in on the windshield and noted two white males, late twenties or early thirties, faces partially covered by ball caps. There wasn't a business name on the side panel and the license plate, if this was the target vehicle, had been switched in South Dakota.

They followed the vehicle through a series of captured video clips eventually noting it backing up to a Mahalo Airline's Boeing 737.

"There it is," said Jessica pointing at the screen and touching the vehicle. "We need to see what was unloaded. Bruce can you try and get that feed from the airport? The time stamp is two hours ago so we are in a time crunch here."

"Will do Jessica. Give me a few and I will be back," he noted as he wheeled his chair back to his monitor and began hitting keys.

Chapter Seventy-Three

Jenewein made the second return trip in one day with plenty of daylight left to fly the students back to Denver. He would return in the next few days to fly all their personal gear out. The grads ate all perishables the last day, then cleaned the refrigerators, turning them off, leaving the doors open. The walk-in freezers were about half full of food that would be edible months ahead so they left that system as is.

During the flight to Denver, Sandra did everything possible to extend the brief intimacy she shared with Jason. She was disappointed to learn he was taking his term break in Boston to visit his brother, but held hope that they could see each other when he returned and during the next study session.

Jason didn't want to cut off the relationship since he had no idea how long the operation would last. She was a wealth of information which he was finding invaluable.

Once on the ground, he grabbed his one duffle and took the school van back to campus where he quickly ditched the others, found an alcove by the Engineering building and called Jessica.

She brought him current on the investigation, the law enforcers' team and gave instructions on how to access CHAP. Jason told her about the PETN in route to Los Angeles, the time frame, the Al Qaeda guests and their attempt to sway the students' recommendations towards liquid explosives because America had developed detection systems for plastic. He didn't have to tell her that such a statement was a lie but why the diversion?

"Leave that to us for now Jason. I need you at the Marina yesterday, so take the first direct flight. I will advise Jackson and Elisabeth. You text your ETA," she said quickly, then hung up.

Jason walked off campus quickly, looking anxiously for any sign of Sandra or the other grads as he wanted to avoid chatting or explaining his plans for the break. Once off grounds, he hailed a cab, headed to the airport and was able to get a last-minute ticket for a non-stop flight to LAX.

Chapter Seventy-Four

Detective Sergeant Paul Francescutto of the Denver Police Department had just signed in for his shift and turned on his computer when his lieutenant yelled at him, motioning for a one-on-one in his office.

"Paul, we have a situation with the Secret Service which needs your immediate attention." The lieutenant filled him in on CHAP, gave him the phone number of the suspected CFBA leader and told him to call Fukishura immediately with any information, then log the data into
CHAP.

"Sounds good Lou," replied Francescutto as he accepted the paperwork from his boss. As he turned and left the office, his brain kicked into overdrive thinking, *what, or who is a CHAP?* He discovered the answer once he was seated and scanned the documents. First to jump out at him was, *Possible Terrorist Cell.*

As he read on, he noted the cell number on the local approved warrant, that it had been authorized in the middle of the night and the attached sheets documented activity on the identified cell number; a throwaway, available at many convenience stores with a bank of minutes, a phone number…cash sale.

The phone tap was on a local business so the department didn't have to sift through hours and possibly days of red tape with the National Security Agency and their mammoth Utah electronic gathering facility. Their collection was done electronically, locally and every call or text, sent or received, was recorded, then downloaded.

The business in question was a restaurant in the Afghanistan cultural community catering to recent immigrants, refugees and locals who enjoy cultural differences.

Most law enforcement officers do not believe in coincidences in relationship to crime and criminals but the guy who had recruited the Cesium thieves shared Paul's taste for fine cuisine.

Food for the Soul, was one of the many ethnic restaurants Francescutto frequented when he was out of the office at lunch time. Interestingly, he knew the owner who was always trying to give Francescutto his meal without charge saying, "Sergeant sir, I am a very grateful Muslim who is happy to be living in America. America saved me and my family from certain death and now I am making money, people are happy here. Please, let me share my happiness with you."

Francescutto would always extend his appreciation and explain that enjoying his cuisine, particularly the Kabuli Pulao with chicken, which he ordered every time, was a compliment to Food for the Soul and to him personally and that it was against department regulations to accept complimentary meals. The owner always accepted the rejection of his generosity with grace, a bow, a smile but was prepared to try the next time the police officer dined with him.

The detective thought he might have an opportunity to contribute to the investigation monumentally so he quickly finished reading the documents, made a few notes, then spent the next hour researching local groups known to support radicalism or dissidents. He made a quick call to the department's Special Investigation Unit (SIS), then locked the paperwork in his desk, removed his handgun from the locked drawer and slipped it into his belted holster, grabbed his suitcoat and headed to lunch.

Food for the Soul was always packed at lunch with a line-up at the door, running down the street, so Francescutto arrived around 11:30 and could meet with Mr. Shahnawaz as he was giving directions in Pushto to his staff. "Mr. Detective Sergeant, you are here for your favorite lunch early. Please, let my staff get your table ready before the rush," he gushed as he guided Paul to the back corner and pulled out a chair.

"Please Mr. Shahnawaz, join me for a moment please sir. I need some help on official business, then I will let you get back to your delightful presentations."

The sergeant explained his problem, asking if the owner or his staff knew a customer by the name of Yousafzai. "But of course. Mr. Yousafzai is a regular here and at my mosque as well. Very good customer and a very nice man. How can I help you with Mr. Yousafzai?"

Paul's heart skipped a beat with the information as he felt the adrenaline rush and replied, "I need to speak with him regarding a matter of great concern to my department. Not involving him mind you," he lied, "but someone he may know with whom we need to speak."

"That will be easy. Please, let me bring your lunch and when Mr. Yousafzai comes in for lunch, I will introduce you," he said with a huge smile, as he got up from the table and signaled a server to provide their guest with sweet tea, an Afghani hospitality favorite, served in a small porcelain cup.

The detective was in the middle of his meal, enjoying the mouth tingling flavor of the variety of spices and chicken, served with focaccia bread and more tea, when Mr. Shahnawaz caught his attention that the man to whom he wished to speak had just entered. The owner quickly guided Yousafzai to the sergeant's table.

The guest was of average build, five-foot ten inches in height with medium to dark complexion, black hair brushed back from his forehead and over his ears stopping at his shirt collar. He was wearing off the rack baggy black pants and a pale blue long sleeve shirt buttoned tight at the collar. He appeared to be in his late twenties or early thirties with a smoothly shaven, slim face.

Paul rose as they approached, extended his hand and pulled out the other chair, signaling his guest to sit while introducing himself only as Paul Francescutto, without the career designation.

A server quickly arrived with more tea, which the man accepted with an obvious trepidation. Looking at Paul nervously he said, "Who are you and why are you here in an Afghani restaurant wanting to speak with me?"

Francescutto moved slightly to adjust his seating which would enable him to sprint out of the chair if it became necessary…which he hoped would not as he didn't want to embarrass his host. He noted that his guest had a strong American accent, giving no hint to his Pashtun heritage.

"Mr. Yousafzai, this is my favorite restaurant where I eat lunch several times a week. Please do not become annoyed but I am with the Denver Police Department," he quietly offered, but almost too late as his guest started to rise from his chair to leave.

Paul put a hand on his guest's and pressed firmly and said, "Leaving is not an option sir as there are several police officers in back and out front to prevent you. I just want to speak, then you are free to leave. Mr. Shahnawaz is only aware that I wished to discuss a matter of great concern. I knew you ate here because your cell phone was traced to this address. Now, please sit down and let's chat. Either that or we can leave together in a police car. Your choice."

His guest glared at Paul with disdain, pulled his hand from under Paul's pressure and sat down, yanking the chair out so forcefully and slamming it down that several patrons looked at him with concern.

The detective began immediately without preamble, "You hired three men to steal a van from a Manitoba mine. We have the three men in custody," he lied. "I know you didn't hire them for yourself, so who? Before you think to lie to me, let me explain how this is going to work. I need that name and his location now, before you leave the restaurant. If you choose not to tell me, I will finish my delicious meal, then I will place handcuffs on you in front of all these people whom you obviously know, and we will travel to the police station where I will turn you over to the FBI. They are not very tolerant people and just may decide you are a risk to national security and lock you up for an extended period."

Yousafzai took a moment to consider his answer. The world knew of the FBI tactics, Guantanamo and similar black detention centers and he had no desire to become entangled within their web of questionable interrogation tactics as had many of his friends so he said, "If I give you the name of the person who hired me to find these men, I can leave and you will not bother me again?"

"That is right. I am a detective sergeant and you have my word that you are free to leave and no one will bother you again," he lied…again.

The man took a quick sip of his tea, ran his hand over his face, put the tea down, then said, "Okay. I have no choice, do I? He likes to go by Intrepid, no last name, but he is Khawaja Aadhean. You should know him because he is a senator for your conservative government in Washington," he said with a smirk.

Paul almost gagged on the last of his meal as he listened to what his guest was revealing. The mastermind, the brains behind the theft of the cesium, is an American congressman.? *Unfuckin' unbelievable* he thought, *unfuckin' believable.* It took him a few seconds to regain his composure before saying, "You can't expect me to believe that a congressman hired thieves?"

"You asked me who hired me and I told you. Now may I go?" he said impatiently, starting to rise.

"Just a minute. Where did you meet this man? How do you know him?"

"He is a member of my mosque and I suppose he asked around for the name of someone who could do special jobs and people gave him my name. Now may I leave or what?"

Paul thought of the ramifications of this discovery, this incredible information and wondered if this guy was bullshiting him or if there was any validity here. But he had a surveillance team outside and his guest would be followed 24/7 until Paul released the tail, so he wasn't worried about losing this guy so he said, "Sure. You are free to leave and thank you for your information. You are a loyal American."

As the guest got up to leave, he bent over and said, "Fuck you! Fuck America and all your American friends," and walked out.

30,000

Captain Odermatt had just leveled off at thirty-thousand feet when Marcus Jones' remains muffled the slight "Click" from the timer atop of the cesium container as it began its crucial task to count three hours exactly.

Chapter Seventy-Five

Francescutto was finishing the last of his tea and reaching for his wallet to pay the tab when the owner approached. "Mr. Detective Sergeant, I trust your lunch and meeting went well. We do not want anything bad to happen here at our lovely Food for the Soul. Please tell me you and Mr. Yousafzai are friends. We go to the same mosque and I would be shunned if I brought embarrassment upon a respected member."

"We had a lovely visit Mr. Shahnawaz. I can assure you that our relationship took on a most favorable turn. In fact, I expect you will see us together enjoying another of your delicious dishes very soon," he lied for the third time.

The owner gushed with pride and relief, put his hands together in prayer and bowed saying, "I am so very happy to hear the good news Mr. Sergeant sir. Thank you for choosing Food for the Soul for your meeting place. Now, please, may I pay for your meal?"

"You are most welcome sir, but thank you, no. My bosses would be very upset with me as I would be accused of misusing your exceptional hospitality."

"I understand. I do not want to cause you any trouble for you are one of my favorite customers," he said, bowing slightly and returning to his duties.

Paul checked on the surveillance team once back in his vehicle, then called Jessica and relayed the essence of his meeting and advised her that he would log the information into CHAP once back in the office. Jessica expressed her appreciation and support, clicked off, then called Elisabeth immediately. Once the tap was in place she gathered her team and shared the update.

Williams was the first to express his dismay by saying, "You know, every since 9-11, I have had a fear in the pit of my stomach that there were sleepers here who were waiting to be woken and spread their terror, but a US senator? That blows my mind, really blows my mind."

"I agree," replied Jones, who had more than his run-ins with federal law enforcement which refused to believe aboriginals could be involved in domestic terrorism. He continued, "Jessica, may I volunteer to dig into this senator and find out who, what, where and heaven forbid, when?"

"Sure, go ahead Sheriff. We will continue working on the other data while waiting to see if this Intrepid suspect will make a call." She didn't wait long.

Elisabeth had just made the connection and began the automatic recording when Yousafzai made his call…as suspected, to Denver. It was precise, advising Denver of his interview with the police and how he had refused to cooperate, bragging how he had walked out of the restaurant and gave the cop the finger.

Intrepid thanked Yousafzai for his dedication and allegiance to Allah, then clicked off and immediately called Joe in Marina Del Rey. Finished with the short communication, he punched in another number from memory, gave instructions and clicked off.

Chapter Seventy-Six

Rebecca got home too late to have dinner with Pen but called her to set something up for the next day. Penelope was tired too so they chatted for a while reliving their shopping trip, then said they would call each other the next day, whoever got a free moment first. Clicking off, Rebecca quickly returned to her pick-up and headed to the Ranch through the back-forest road, showed her credentials to the guards, drove the few kilometers and parked in front of the ranch house, scanned her eye, hand print and today's code and entered as Barry said, "Welcome back agent Simpson," over the hidden speaker.

Entering the situation room, Jessica welcomed her briefly without turning from her monitor, waved a hand over her head, introduced Rebecca to the investigative team then brought her up to speed. Rebecca was to coordinate with Elisabeth after logging into CHAP to understand the sequence of events.

Jessica returned to her monitor and read the latest developments from Denver PD and their uncovering Khawaja Aadhean as Intrepid. She had never heard of him and hadn't any knowledge of his politics, but her ignorance was not an issue. She immediately instructed Paul to set up surveillance on the senator 24/7 and to log their actions into CHAP. She then arranged for a tap on all Aadhean's communications: cell, office and home phones, all personal and business emails with the results to be monitored by Elisabeth. Right now, they had no evidence against the politician, the accusations of an admitted criminal middleman were useless in court. Barry had scanned the data provided by the airport police to locate a closer view of the white van and transferred it to the teams' monitors, then slid behind Jessica as she manipulated the image for clarity, stopping as the view of the casket became clear.

"What do you think gentlemen, is that where the cesium is hiding?" Braket said, "No doubt about it Jessica."

"I agree," added Williams.

"You too Jones?"

“Yeah, me too. I just can not believe the criminal element sometimes. Using a casket, to which airport security would give a pass, given the presumed contents.”

“Give me a sec here,” she offered as she brought up another screen image, this one of departures from Minneapolis Airport. Scanning the data for Mahalo Airlines, she stopped scrolling and tapped the monitor screen.

“There, right there, is the flight heading to LAX. Barry, will you text the information to Jason, have him connect with Jackson once he is on the ground and co-ordinate with LAX security to isolate that flight once it lands and have the FBI and our LA agents meet it on the tarmac?”

“Got it Jessica,” replied Barry as he wheeled his chair back to his monitor and began hitting the keys.

Jason received Barry’s text and immediately forwarded it to Jackson giving him his ETA and asking him to pick him up at LAX arrivals.

Rebecca continued the conversation with, “I read Elisabeth’s comments on CHAP regarding this suspect’s phone call to Sarkowski which in itself is not legally incriminating. How far will this blanket federal court order allow us to go? Do we have enough to access his data files? We need a list of the CFBA members, otherwise this will be just one operation gone array to them and they will remain in operation?”

“Therein lies the problem Rebecca. Suggestions anyone?”

Braket was the first to respond, “These cesium suspects, there is one left, right? The Edmonton RCMP interrogated him. He hasn’t much of a defense given Cst. Drought took him down. Just the shoot-out alone with a fully automatic weapon is enough for at least ten years, but, other than that, possession of the stolen van is all we have on him. No one at the cesium crime scene saw the van load the cesium or that the cesium was in the van at all. Even tracing the cesium was just a guess. The guys on the receiving end in Lewiston said they had no idea what they were transferring, but the mortician knew if it is in fact in the casket. I don’t think we can make a case until we see the casket. Once that is in place, we can backtrack, get the mortician to flip on Intrepid. What do you think?”

“That makes sense,” noted Jones. My guys grilled the suspects from the reservation. They were as dumb as door knobs and were trying to make a deal for the police chief's murder, so there was no reason for them to withhold information. I agree with Braket, let's wait and get the casket. When Mahalo Airlines lands it isn't going anywhere so we will have plenty of time to have LAPD, the FBI and the Secret Service examine the casket."

"Williams, Simpson, you guys agree?"

Both nodded their heads in agreement.

"Alright, so now we have the senator under surveillance, Harold and Martha controlled in Minneapolis and Joe, what about your guys taking down Shepperd and Marrington?"

"My guys don't know about CHAP but I told them to call me as soon as they have them in custody along with the chemicals. Let me give them a call right now."

Joe slid away from the others and pulled out his cell and punched in a number from memory, let it ring a few times, put the phone on speaker, then said, "You guys have them in custody yet?"

"Not yet Sheriff. We have them in sight and are waiting until we get outside of Boise so we are not drawing a crowd and making sure the community is safe. We have contacted the Boise PD and they are on board. They are tracking the suspects on a parallel road and have the fire department on stand-by in case these guys flee and we have a spill."

"Sounds good. Let me know immediately and guys, have the Boise PD set up a roadblock well ahead with spike belts across the highway and the ditches," he concluded and clicked off.

"We can put those guys on the list of controlled. There is no way they are getting away from my guys," he said proudly.

30,000

Jason received a reply from Jackson almost immediately advising he was unable to comply and that Jason was to rent a car and meet him at the address on Manchester where Jackson had staked out the warehouse holding, which he was pretty sure held the vans and Suburbans. Jason send a short, *Ten-Four,* then sat as his anxiety levels rose to an almost uncontrollable level. He knew Jackson would have only his service weapon and not an extra to give him, so he excused himself from his seatmate and made his way to the galley identifying himself to the steward and asking if he could make a call in private. The steward congenially complied, leading him to the staff lavatory where Jason shut himself in and made the call to Los Angeles.

3,000 Feet

Chapter Seventy-Seven

Jackson sat in his rental across the street from the gas station at which the previous van had fueled. He was impatient, tapping his fingers on the steering wheel, his head darting back and forth, taking in vehicles passing in both directions of busy Lincoln Blvd. He anxiously wanted to call Jessica or Elisabeth but knew that would be a waste of time; he hadn't any news to contribute and his being on the phone may tie up a line and take either or both agents from monitoring the operation.

Time seemed to grind to a halt, his impatience slowing reality, positive the traffic had decreased to twenty miles per hour…when he spotted a five ton, white van as it pulled into the station. The driver exited, swiped a credit card and began fueling. He cursed himself for not having a pair of binoculars, but quickly used his phone to zoom in on the license plate number, then take several photos of the driver. He needed back-up so he could get the credit card details while the other officer followed the van.

On a hunch, he hit Elisabeth's speed dial number. She answered immediately, "Can you hack into a gas station's computer system to get details of the transaction?"

"Surely you jest Jackson," she quipped, "Details quickly."

He gave her the information, then clicked off just as the van pulled into traffic and headed south on Lincoln, with Jackson following a few cars behind, several vehicles in between. Jackson was unware that the van he was following was an empty decoy, the active vans being spread around LAX in residential neighborhoods sometime previously; Beethoven Street, Hager Street, Yale and on the south side of the airport, Eucalyptus Drive. They were parked innocuously and unobtrusively, anyone walking or driving by wouldn't have a clue as the magnitude of destruction which lay in wait, like an Oklahoma explosion, times four. The four Suburbans had likewise left the warehouse and were heading east to the 405 freeway, then north to the 90, getting off at Admiralty Way and slowly proceeding to the front of the convention center, parking nose to back. All eight CFBA suspects were dressed in dark suits, white shirts and black laced shoes. Each man had short cropped hair and were wearing ear buds connected to Sarkowski, who was observing their success from his hotel room.

They exited and split off in groups of two giving any observer the impression they were situating themselves for security posts when the Democratic nominee arrived. Every few minutes they would move further away from the Suburbans until they were safe from the impending explosions.

Sarkowski sat on the balcony of his Harbor Bay Inn room with binoculars glassing the Pacific Sands Convention Center, confirming the lack of security in the area where the Suburbans would enter. Had he adjusted the glasses slightly to the west, he would have seen a grey Corolla slide out of a parking area, let two vehicles get behind a large white van, then pull into the lane heading south on Jefferson. As it was, Jackson's behavior went completely unnoticed.

He laid the glasses on the cocktail table and made small adjustments to the matte-white, commercial Mirage Drone that sat on the deck at his feet. The small, twelve-inch diameter device operating sound was undetectable to the human ear, emitting a slight buzzing as it passed above a person as close as fifteen-feet. Once deployed, the Mirage would descend to its target at forty-five miles per hour, moving its three pounds over the target in seconds. The matte finish made it near impossible to see in the mid-afternoon Los Angeles sun's glare.

Sarkowski used the remote control to start the propellers, raising it up and down slightly, ensuring it was ready to be deployed with the small remote sensor bolted to the nose.

Satisfied that he was ready, he sat back and sipped his sweet black tea, gazed at the ocean in the near distance and wondered how the day would end; would he live to see another sunrise or would this be his last contribution to the conservative movement?

2,600 Feet

Chapter Seventy-Eight

LAPD detectives were scouring the Marina Del Rey hotels with a photo of Joe Sarkowski. Jessica's request to their Counter-Terrorism and Special Operations Bureau, CTSOB, which is comprised of Major Crimes and Emergency Services divisions, was supervised by Captain Julio Jerrera. After listening to Jessica's plan, he issued orders for an immediate blanket intelligence assault on the marina, then did a quick analysis of CHAP. After logging into Chapman's software system, he realized the overwhelming extent of the investigation and the threat to Los Angeles. LAPD Pacific Division had to seal off the marina, immediately, but covertly, with squad cars, so he overrode senior management and made the call.

Such a tactical maneuver was very difficult to execute, but the street warriors were in place within thirty minutes. They couldn't physically block the arteries to LAX and other vital economic areas at this point so they idled by the side of each intersection, not allowing any black Suburbans or five-ton white vans to leave the area.

While scores of marked police cars sat with their engines idling at every intersection encircling the marina and convention center, the entire Pacific Division roamed the streets searching.

During this operation, two LAPD detectives entered the Harbor Bay Inn, introduced themselves and asked to speak with the manager. The hotel was on the high end of the five-star classification with rooms running in the mid five-hundred dollar per night range. The manager was somewhat nervous having the police at his establishment and invited the officers into his office to save the embarrassment to staff and clients.

"Okay Mr., what's your name again?"

"Driediger, sir. Neil Driediger. And I can assure you the Bay Inn is a very well-respected establishment with never a blot on our reputation. I can assure you that we do not have any guest who would draw your attention."

"Be that as it may Mr. Driediger, we have reason to believe this gentleman is registered here and we need to know to which room he was assigned," offered Detective Foster showing the manager the photo of Sarkowski.

"I don't recognize him but then I am not always on duty out front. Just give me a moment and I will ask our front desk clerk to join us," he said as he punched an intercom giving his instructions.

Momentarily a twenty something female entered, saw the detectives and almost passed out, grasping the wall to steady herself. She appeared frazzled, her persona drained from working too long without a break. Her shoulder length hair needed a brushing and make-up a touch up. The officers assured her there wasn't a problem and asked her if she had seen their suspect, showing her the photo.

"Sure, I have seen him. I recall him quite well because he checked in with a Canadian passport but didn't have an accent."

"What do you mean, an accent? Canadians speak exactly like us."

"No disrespect officer," she added, regaining her composure, "but they do have a slightly different way of speaking when enunciating some letters and of course they say, Eh, whereas we say Huh and this guy is not Canadian."

"Okay. Whatever. Which room is he in?"

They followed her to the front counter where she accessed the main computer system, drew up the list of occupied rooms and said, "He is in our corner suite facing the convention center on the top floor."

Foster turned to his partner and whispered, "Bingo."

"Thank you very much for the help. We will be staying here for a little while. We promise to be inconspicuous."

The manager and clerk looked at each other, the clerk raising her eyebrows, the body language asking what she is supposed to do. The manager waved a hand dismissing her, directing her back to her duties while he walked quickly back to his office, no doubt calling the hotel's general manager for instructions.

The detectives walked to a deserted corner of the massive foyer, Foster turning his back to the wall while his partner placed a call to Jessica, taking a few moments to provide the crucial details, the implication of which they were not privy.

Chapter Seventy-Nine

Jessica called Sergeant Paul Francescutto with the Denver PD and asked him to arrest Yousafzai as a material witness and to keep him in total isolation, requesting that Francescutto choose the corrections staff to guard him 24/7, and obtain a statement implicating Denver reminding the Denver detective that Yousafzai was their only link to the senator.

She uploaded her comments and the conversation into CHAP and read Elisabeth's contribution regarding Jackson and Jason.

Jason had showed his credentials to the Mahalo Airline crew, asked them to call ahead for a car rental and was the first off the plane. A Mahalo staffer greeted him immediately, gave him the keys to a four-door plain Toyota and told him to settle-up latter, Mahalo would cover the charges etc. during the interim. Jason ran through LAX drawing considerable attention from passengers, but fortunately none were from security who had been advised of his status. Their description was impossible to miss, *Tall black guy with long dreads*.

It took him less than an minute to run the distance to the Toyota waiting at the curb with an LAPD escort. The two vehicles made excellent time as was expected, with the squad car pulling over just east of Sepulveda allowing Jason to join Jackson at the warehouse on Manchester.

Jason pulled up behind Jackson's Toyota of the same color and model, cut the engine, then the two began texting. Jackson advised Jason that SWAT was moments out, then told him to look up. As Jason did, he saw Jackson shedding a huge grin, holding up a 9mm pistol and three spare magazines. Jason smiled broadly and nodded his acknowledgement, planning to get the weapon when SWAT arrived.

Jason remembered his many operations with the LAPD SWAT teams when he worked undercover as an arms dealer and would set up the buyers with the automatic weapons, then advise command and SWAT would take down the buyers.

He was hoping to relive that experience as he saw the SWAT van pull up behind him, disgorging the team of twenty officers. He and Jackson jumped out of their cars, Jackson handed the 9 and magazines to Jason and they followed the team up Manchester a short distance and into the warehouse parking lot, then rushed the door with a battering ram and were inside within seconds to find…

Nothing. Absolutely nothing. The warehouse was entirely empty, not a scrap of garbage, waste paper or a sign that anyone or any vehicles had been there.

The SWAT commander looked at Jackson with raised eyebrows, then stepped aside to call it in while telling his men to give the place a thorough search. Jackson called Jessica with the update, then clicked off, grabbed Jason by the upper arm and said, "Plan B," and the two headed out the door and back to their vehicles to head to the marina.

The SWAT commander and the team were right behind them, having received orders to rush to the Harbor Bay Inn and connect with two LAPD detectives in the lobby.

1,800 Feet

Chapter Eighty

Stephan Odermatt and his crew had just passed the three-hour cruise time and received the approval from air traffic controllers at LAX to begin their decent, when the cesium capsule top was activated by the timer created by the Christian Fundamentalist University graduate students in Jason's research group and installed by the mortician who prepared the casket. The top slowly unscrewed itself, creating a two-inch circular gap. Within seconds the cesium elements began to spread throughout the cargo area permeating the electronic control area. Odermatt was concentrating on his landing instructions from the traffic controllers while his co-pilot engaged the auto-throttle to decrease their speed to about 200 KIAS, knots indicated airspeed, but it would not respond. She couldn't proceed with the landing process without reducing the plane's momentum. She quickly got the captain's attention and explained the problem as she worked her way through a recovery program and prepared to move to manual. Her next step would be to dial the plane's ILS, instrument landing system, frequency to Nav 1 and set the ommibearing selector to the assigned runway. She was then to decrease her speed to 160 KIAS and apply flaps to full, according to the maximum flap placard speeds. Once flaps were at 10, she was to lower the landing gear, but these procedures were moot given the plane was maintaining the maximum speed.

Odermatt listened to the details and his body went into action, attempting to reduce speed manually. All his effort failed as LAX came into view just a few miles ahead. ATC, Air Traffic Control, was directing him to reduce his speed immediately or to return to fifteen thousand feet and circle until he could comply. Odermatt responded, advising ATC that he had lost control of the plane, that manual override was blocked electronically and that time had run out to resolve the problem in-flight. The controls were allowing him to drop the plane's nose but not bring it up. The landing gear manual control was not responding and he requested a gear-up landing if he could get the speed reduced quickly.

ATC acknowledged the emergency while the co-pilot spoke on the intercom to the passengers, the majority of whom were Democratic Party super-delegates from most of the blue states, advising them to brace for impact. The delegates had gathered in Minneapolis, either driving or flying so they could arrive at LAX in mass for an arranged press conference showing their solidarity at a time of national disunity and derisiveness. Little did the delegates know they were about to have an experience of a lifetime.

Odermatt knew by now that he was about to draw upon his water landing training and prayed that he was sufficiently accurate to land them safely. He advised ATC that he could not make a gear-up landing at LAX, would overshoot the runway and land in the Pacific. ATC responded quietly and in a very controlled voice that the Coast Guard had been notified. They would deploy air rescue from Point Mugu on the Pacific Coast Highway just north of Malibu and the Coast Guard Cutter Williamsburg from Long Beach.

The captain knew that even if they could deploy the landing gear manually, it was too late to land on the tarmac. As he controlled the yoke, his co-pilot rebooted the electronics, attempting a restart of the entire system.

As she was entering various codes, the small quantity of Cesium was depleting its energy, resulting in the plane regaining its GPS system first and then the auto-throttle. Seeing this, she immediately engaged the electronics to reduce the speed to 160 KIAS to which the plane responded instantly giving Odermatt the confidence he needed, knowing he could bring her in on the calm ocean.

Flap control returned next and she could set them at ten and could feel the plane respond again, reducing speed. Although the landing gear operation light blinked on, she ignored the function return, knowing that to lower the gear would create a drag against the water preventing a smooth landing of the plane's undercarriage against the water surface.

As the three-hundred-ton mammoth passed over LAX the captain slowly reduced speed to just above stall-out, then dropped the altitude to five-hundred feet, disengaged the auto-throttle and prepared for landing. As they approached the Pacific he could see the Coast Guard Cutter Williamsburg heading for his intended landing area. Odermatt just prayed they would not be so close as to create another hazard. *Landing in the ocean was enough of a challenge, he didn't need to add avoiding a ship to the mix,* he reflected.

1,400 Feet

Chapter Eighty-One

Marina Del Rey is situated right on the Pacific Ocean between LAX and Venice, offering several hundred boat slips for dwellers at a cost per foot. A seventy-foot sailboat runs thirty-one hundred dollars a month with a one bedroom twelve-hundred-foot apartment averaging thirty-five hundred a month. Residents were used to having the best of everything and having it all protected by someone else. They paid little, if any, attention to the behavior of staff at their complex or those working at any of the nearby hotels, convention center or spectacular restaurants, so seeing eight men leave in four sparkling black Suburbans didn't appear on their social radar.

Each CFBA agent walked purposely into a hotel and made their way to the public restroom on the main floor where they changed into shorts, short-sleeve shirts, ball caps and sandals, stuffed their suits and brogues into garbage cans, exited the hotel and disappeared.

They were aware that Sarkowski could see their movement and was checking their exit on his timetable, knowing they had but a few minutes to maximize their distance from the convention center to survive.

Within a short time, they had dispersed onto the boardwalk in Venice, Loyola Marymount University campus and a nearby warehouse discount store, blending in with the crowds.

Foster was receiving instructions through his ear bud from Captain Julio Jerrera of CTSOB advising him that many uniformed units were converging on the hotel's back entrance and Foster was to lead them in evacuating the hotel immediately.

Foster was still listening to his supervisor as he approached the manager. "Mr. Driediger, where is the young woman I spoke with earlier?"

"Working in the back. Why?"

"Just get her immediately please," he barked with such force, Driediger hadn't time to object and responded by turning and rushing into the back room, returning with the woman. "Ma'am I need you to evacuate the building immediately. I can not give you details at the moment but uniformed officers are entering your back door as we speak and need master key-cards to enter each room to ensure compliance. Can you do that at once?"

"Wait just a moment here officer. I am in charge and I need more information before I inconvenience our guests."

Without answering the manager, Foster turned, spotted a uniformed officer and waved him over.

"Officer, please take Mr. Driediger into custody, place him in a squad car and make sure he stays there until I authorize his release."

Driediger was flabbergasted, pissed and shouting that he would sue the department for this breach of protocol and treating him like a common criminal, as the officer grabbed him by the upper arm and guided him through the narrow hallway to the back of the hotel.

"Now, ma'am, those key-cards please. And quickly."

She ran around the counter and proceeded to process the masters as they came out of what looked like a debit card reader, gave them to the detective who handed them off to the sergeant in charge of the search. Once each officer had a master, they spread out to cover each of the six floors, leaving the seventh for Foster, his partner and two uniforms.

The evacuation process went smoothly with only a few questions the officers were not authorized to answer. The first five floors were vacant, with the sixth and seventh nearing completion when Driediger decided that his job, maybe his future in the hotel business, was in jeopardy because he failed to take command of the evacuation.

He was not in handcuffs as he sat with his behind on the seat in the back of the police car and feet sitting on the pavement through the open door. The officer was walking around nervously, listening to communications through his shoulder mic when the manager made his decision and acted immediately. He sprung from his backseat detention and ran in the opposite direction from the officer who was totally unaware of his charge escaping.

Driediger used his key-card to enter another back entrance and ran the short hallway into the lobby, turned slightly, grabbed the wall mounted fire alarm, then walked to the registration counter and waited.

Foster, his partner and the two uniforms were in the middle of the evacuation of the seventh floor when the alarm was sounded and all hell broke lose. Every door, save the one at the end of the hall, opened spewing guests in a variety of dress and shoe attire. Foster had the officers take control of the pandemonium while he and his partner ran the hall's length, drawing their service pistols as they approached the last door.

1000 Feet

Chapter Eighty-Two

Sarkowski was nervously checking his watch against the time table when the alarm shattered his concentration. Jumping up from his operation crow's nest, he leaned over the balcony expecting to see a deluge of guests complying with the fire drill, only to see a score of people craning their necks, scanning the hotel for signs of smoke or the reason for the fire alarm. Whatever the alarm's cause, he knew it was only a matter of minutes before emergency crews would be knocking on his door demanding his evacuation. That couldn't happen. The delegates were supposed to have crashed and the west coast delegates should have been at the convention center by now. The vans spread around various residential communities were scheduled to detonate ten minutes before he launched the drone and he couldn't do that until the west coast delegates were inside the convention center. The entire operation was disintegrating around him.

"Where the fuck ARE you?" he shouted to the wind, pounding his fist on the small cocktail table.

"Fuck, fuck, fuck," he continued, as he tried to concentrate on how best to regroup. Okay, the thought, the plane crashed, there was no doubt there, but why aren't there any people milling around the convention center? The operation had obviously been breached, how and by whom was immaterial right now. He had to make the best of the years of preparation, so he bent down, picked up the drone, sat it on the cocktail table, grabbed the control and manipulated the controls to launch it toward the Suburbans.

As the Mirage approached the black targets, Sarkowski punched and held the detonation button sending the vehicle twenty feet in the air, taking out a small section of the convention center. Seconds later the next SUV exploded in the same manner, as did the third and fourth, raining plumes of fire, debris and smoke hundreds of feet in the air, destroying every building and vehicle within a radius of several hundred yards.

Smiling to himself, Sarkowski was satisfied he was able to salvage part of the operation after it had been breached. As he looked to the short distance to see the result of his expertise, he heard shouting from behind him and knew his participation in returning Washington's control to conservative leadership was over. He prayed those who would follow his sacrifice would be as honorable a man as he, then stood on the cocktail table and jumped.

600 Feet

30,000

Jackson and Jason were speeding toward the marina when they saw the plumes of smoke rising hundreds of feet over the area between the marina and LAX and knew they were too late. They continued their frantic trek, each wondering how they would be able to contribute to stopping further carnage.

Chapter Eighty-Three

Captain Odermatt blanked all thoughts out of his mind of post landing procedures or what caused the system failure and concentrated on the landing of a lifetime. His speed was minimized to just above stalling, flaps were completely engaged and her nose was up. Off to the north he saw both the Coast Guard Cutter and Coast Guard helicopters quickly closing the distance between them and the 737.

Wind is always heading toward land so that helped keep her airborne as Odermatt laid her down gently on the glassy ocean with such finesse that the passengers were cheering before the plane had stopped its forward movement.

Engines were immediately shut down and flight attendants busied themselves organizing passengers to exit over the wings even before the Coast Guard was along side. The staff were amazed by the calmness of most passengers given the possibility the plane could have broken apart upon impact.

There wasn't an impact, which, in the weeks to follow, would astound aviation experts and the plane's manufacturer. The 737 landed on her belly, wheels up, locked, and due to the strength of the plane's structure, the engines weren't torn off by the landing.

It wasn't five minutes before the Coast Guard Cutter appeared along side with the MH-65 Dolphin helicopter crew from Coast Guard Forward Operating Base Point Mugu rescue divers jumping into the water, swimming to the wings, climbing aboard, ready to assist passengers into the Cutter's launch boats. Once the divers and boats were in place the flight attendant opened the wing emergency door and assisted passengers onto the wings, aided by the Coast Guard Rescue Team. Members of the Rescue Team later commented as well, that they were surprised at calmness of the passengers and crew.

The plane maintained its buoyancy during the entire rescue mission as the rescue boats ferried the two hundred passengers to the Cutter.

The California Marine Salvage crew were dispatched when the Coast Guard received the SOS from the Mahalo Airline's 737 and were on sight shortly after all passengers, except the captain, were safely aboard the Cutter. The CMS supervisor boarded the 737 and formally took possession of the plane for Mahalo, allowing Odermatt to join his crew and passengers aboard the Coast Guard Cutter.

On board the CMS barge were agents from the Secret Service, FBI and ATF to supervise the plane's loading and transporting to a secure Long Beach facility. On board as well, to take charge of the cesium, ensure it was no longer threatening, were members of the FBI Bomb Technician Squad.

Time would tell whether any of the passengers felt so upset by the experience as to ignore the incredible skill of the pilots and crew and file a lawsuit. It happens. Federal law prohibits the filing of any suit during the first forty-five days after an accident.

Speculation was running rampant as every media outlet in North America was on the scene within the hour via helicopter, so many in fact, the Coast Guard Cutter Commander called for their immediate removal so as not to impede the rescue mission, particularly the Dolphin and its crew.

Chapter Eighty-Four

LAPD was advised of the Coast Guard's success, that there weren't any casualties or traumas and that all would be transported to the Guard's Long Beach facility where medical teams would evaluate each passenger before releasing them. Mahalo Airlines sent several representative to meet the passengers and to ensure them they were doing everything possible to discover the cause of the emergency landing. The FBI had agents connecting survivors to the manifest, obtaining identification and contact information to aid in their investigation. Captain Julio Jerrera received the rescue news, confirmed that the salvage barge was in place and prepared to remove the 737 from the water before any further damage or fluid leaks occurred, then logged into CHAP and noted their progress.

As he logged off CHAP, he reflected on the last few hours and how training, organization and dedication saved hundreds of lives. His team had never deployed the blankets in an actual terrorist threat, having honed their skills through bomb disposal drills for months. When his uniforms spotted two white vans in the same proximity, they checked the plates. Stolen. They called for support and the other two vans were identified quickly as ten LAPD squad cars descended on the residential area.

The bomb squads arrived without any knowledge of a detonation time or if the vans were being observed to be detonated remotely. With little time to evaluate the situation, and being fathers themselves, they didn't ask permission or call for directions, they manipulated their blankets and, risking their lives, four officers draped the massive Armor Shield impact blankets over each van, fastening them to the chassis with heavy gauge Stainless Steel Flex Wire. The ballistic resistant blankets were constructed of inner-layers cased in outer layers to capture high velocity explosions and shrapnel, limiting the blast's range. They would not contain the blast but reduce the intended carnage.

The technicians had no idea when the vans would blow; it could be within seconds or minutes but there was no time to debate the issue. The entire area for several blocks had been evacuated by the discovering officers, some going into apartment buildings with airhorns telling people to get out while others drove up and down the streets warning residents, using their vehicles PA system. There wasn't time to knock on the doors of thousands so the officers were hoping…and many praying…they were one-hundred percent successful.

Draping took fifteen minutes, an eternity in the lives of sixteen LAPD Bomb Squad members, then they ran one hundred yards back to their armored vehicles and deployed a robot to each van hoping to defuse each before their explosion. Their experience said the vans would be linked to detonate simultaneously or within seconds of each other, if they were timed and not being activated remotely. But such was the conundrum of their occupation.

The robots were preparing to activate a drill system using an arm similar to the NASA's Canada Arm when the first van blew. The technicians had seen many vehicles of similar size and what they presumed to be thousands of pounds of explosives, detonate with the blast wave destroying everything within hundreds of feet. This device, being contained with the blasting blankets, developed maximumly. The supersonic outward expansion of the energy was reduced such that none of the buildings were affected. The vehicles were a different result; all within the blast range were destroyed, many being blown several feet vertically, then landing on the roof of another. The blast wave wasn't followed by negative wind pressure, which usually sucks the debris back in towards the ignition site.

The loss in vehicles, the robot and twenty-year old Evergreen Ash trees which had lined each side of the road, was considerable, but there wasn't a loss of human life or injury.

Chapter Eighty-Five

Jessica and her investigative team were feeling more and more confident that they would be able to arrest most of the CFBA leadership, but were realistic that thousands of supporters would be in the wind, only to surface again under new funding and direction. But for now, for this election, they had stopped the planned manslaughter.

They were gathered around the fireplace in the living room where Chef Marc had prepared several appetizer plates of his own buffalo wings recipe, strong black Kicking Horse coffee and plenty of napkins.

Marc had been incredibly efficient during the entire operation, seeming to know when they needed a break and/or sustenance. Bracken commented that he did not feel any guilt enjoying the White House chef's contribution, a comment for which he received a round of applause.

"Let's quickly recap where we are. Joe?"

"I just received word that Shepherd and Marrington are in custody with the chemicals secure. My guys got a kick out of these two as they flapped their gums about their civil rights and that their attorneys would be all over the federal government. Of course, my guys said zip, just smiled as they cuffed and stuffed.

They are being held in isolation in Boise PD custody until the feds decide where they will be tried. If we have any input here Jessica, I suggest they all be tried in a Denver federal court.

"Good suggestion Joe. About our mountain boys, they are going to have a rude awakening when the federal prosecutor releases the tape during discovery and their attorneys must explain the implications. Anyway, that is down the road a little bit. So far, we have," nodding to Sheriff Joe, "our mountain men and the surviving cesium suspect with Edmonton RCMP. Thanks to Denver PD we have Intrepid's phone tap recording and Yousafzai in custody. Sergeant Paul Francescutto has obtained a statement from him and I am sure the FBI will make him an offer he can't refuse. So far, we might convict on conspiracy of murder for hire under federal statutes but that may be a stretch given he probably wasn't aware the three thugs would try and kill Cst. Drought, but we can get him on hiring the cesium thieves, since they crossed state lines. That will be a shoe-in. I think we can offer him maybe a year, three months with good behavior if he flips on the senator.

Once we have that wrapped up we can get a warrant for Khawaja Aadhean's home and office computers. We will try and expand the warrant to search his house, garage, vehicles and office for any connections to a known foreign terrorist organization, but my gut tells me these guys are our own creation, perverted, but our own."

Braket offered, "Detective Foster and the uniforms were blindsided by the hotel manager's ego and quest to make sure he got his fifteen minutes of fame by being involved with whatever police activity he perceived. He set off the fire alarm just as Foster had most of the top floor cleared of guests. Foster immediately stormed Sarkowski's room but arrived on to the balcony just as Sarkowski detonated the Suburbans, then jumped. They have forensics sweeping the hotel room but it is doubtful they will come up with anything incriminating. The only items other than his personals was the control system for the drone, which Foster suspects will reveal zip. The drone itself is going to be difficult, if not impossible to retrieve given it kept flying after the last explosion. Presumably Sarkowski had no use for it where he was going. Without the controlling device, anyone locating it will find it useless. They may be able to configure some use for the body itself, but they can not convert the remote detonator to anything useful."

Chapter Eighty-Six

Jackson and Jason pulled up beside a street barricade guarded by two LAPD officers, exited their Toyota and presented their creds. One officer read the documents while the other took several steps back and placed her hand on her nine, her eyes darting back and forth from Jackson to Jason.

"Creds or not, Mr. Pennington and Mr. Spencer, our orders are, nobody but nobody gets into the crime scene."

"Hey, come on guys, this is obviously an act of terrorism which involves us. We can leave our vehicle here if you feel it will compromise the investigation. But we need to get in there," offered Jason.

"No can-do guys. Now, if you will excuse us, we need you to move your vehicle." Jackson wanted to tell these two goons to go fuck themselves but knew that decorum had to be maintained otherwise the officers' body cams would be the end of his career.

Jackson said, "May we just step aside here for a moment and contact our supervisor? Only a minute and we will be on our way."

"Sure. Go ahead. But make it quick," said the spokesperson, now resting his hand on his pistol.

The agents walked briskly to the sidewalk with Jason pulling his phone out and clicking a digit from memory.

"Yeah, what have you got?"

"Jessica. We are just on the perimeter of the blast that looks as though it took out part if not all the convention center. The locals will not allow us in to join the investigation. Where would you like us?"

"Hang on and give me a moment," she said, covering the mouth-piece and chatting with her team. She came back and continued, "Go around the crime scene and back to the hotel and see if LAPD needs any assistance. I doubt they will. They have the entire building taped off as a crime scene and the hotel staff is relocating guests, all of whom are pissed not being able to get their personals. But hey, that's their problem, not ours. If you are not needed, join up with
Elisabeth and help her put the evidence together to encrypt and get to me immediately."

"Got it," replied Jason and used his hand to make a twirling motion to Jackson standing by their rental. He clicked off, made his way to the Toyota and filled Jackson in on their orders. They made their way back out of the grid lock and maneuvered in a wide circle back to the hotel parking lot several blocks away and attempted to enter this crime scene, hoping to have more success with these crime scene attendants.

No.

Jason tried another approach thinking he could use his LAPD history with the gate keepers by first showing his creds, then providing them with his history with LAPD. Nothing. He had to give these guys credit, he thought. They are definitely following orders.

He asked to speak with Detective Foster, and the mention of a specific name brought him more results than his trip down memory lane. One officer raised Foster on his hand-held then handed it to Jason, "Detective, Special Agent Spencer here, Secret Service. I am here at the edge of your crime scene with Agent Pennington. We have been involved in this investigation from the beginning. Might we be of assistance?" He listened to a brief reply then said, "Thank you sir. We are on our way," and handed the talkie to the officer who listened, then lifted the crime scene tape allowing Jackson and Spencer to enter, nodded his acceptance of their being approved, then turned back to his duties.

As the agents approached the smoldering ruins of what was once an elegant convention center, they were immediately met with the pungent odor of cordite, burned plastic and debris dust. As they got closer there were a number of golden labs with their handlers sniffing the ruins for further explosives. What was left of the four Suburbans was barely identifiable, but as they advanced, they saw one of the crime techs dusting a white government license plate for prints. "That answers a huge question right there," Jackson noted, pointing to the plate. "Given our prime suspect is a federal senator, we may be able to track this back to whomever is the traitor with the Secret Service."

Jason took out his smartphone, meandered slightly to his right and snapped a perfect shot of the plate number held by the tech, without her being aware of his, what she would consider, intrusive behavior, then uploaded it to Jessica with a short, encrypted explanation.

Chapter Eighty-Seven

Khawaja Aadhean sat in his unassuming Denver office located in a quiet business district among local and state officials. The building was of modest construction with two rectangular banks of windows on each side of the main door leading to the government departments and within walking distance to the nearest mosque. Khawaja made the short trip once daily to give his morning prayers then performed the other four in his office where he had a prayer rug and could lock his door for privacy.

The senator had seven offices throughout the state in high density areas, excluding his primary office in Washington. He didn't maintain a specific daily schedule, choosing to decide the night before if he intended to visit a specific constituency.

Peltowski had been tracking his movements and all communications since directed by Fukishura. She not only knew his current work choice for the day, but what he had ordered from Story's Bar and Grill, within walking distance from his office. He could have walked there himself or had it delivered, but he chose to have one of his new female staff members perform the monotonous task so she would know her place in the office hierarchy, the majority of which was male. He wouldn't have any females in his employ had he a choice, but state and federal laws mandated a given percentage of women be employed by all government departments. One of the drawing factors that brought him to Abdallah Azzam Brigades years ago, was their dedication to strict Islamic social codes, namely Sharia Law. The AAB began in Pakistan and considered itself to be the supreme Islamist militant group for global jihad. They were aligned with Al Qaeda and currently fighting in Syria, and in Lebanon under the name of Ziyad al Jarrah Battalion, the latter taking its name from the 9/11 terrorist responsible for the hijacking and crash of United Airlines flight 93.

His day was about to start, but as was his daily practice, he took a few moments to reflect on yesterday and put his emotions in play for the day's activities. Sitting on the black leather couch, his feet on the contemporary thick plastic coffee table adorned with several collector books on his state, he thought of the progress of the operation. He couldn't know how it had been compromised, maybe Yousafzai talked, but he knew nothing other than Aadhean's cover name of Intrepid. If that was the only breach, and at this moment that was the extent of his knowledge, the process was still unwinding and he should hear soon of their success. He sipped his strong Arabian black, imported from Dubai monthly and smiled, content that the years of preparation were coming to fruition.

The Russians expended considerable energy to influence the upcoming election with their propaganda, contentious support for the Syrian regime and their constant hacking of Democrats' emails, attempting to cast aspersions on various candidates with no substantial proof of any wrong doing, but generating sufficient turmoil to question the candidates' honesty and integrity. He thought also of the surly, bombastic Republican designate and knew that CFBA and his organization had done more in the short few months than any others vying to prevent the Democrats access to the White House.

He thought back to the day he met, what he thought were Colorado constituents, wanting to finance his next campaign but in fact were the money behind CFBA. Two Americans who represented a committee of ten, whose wealth matched that of Forbes top twenty billionaires. His later research showed that these men worked in the shadows of Washington politics, making the necessary finances available to obtain the right candidates and manipulate elections. He remembered how they broached the subject of his involvement, playing on his ego and bitterness of his fight to the top, of the years of scorn and ridicule of his skin color, his religion and his parents' immigrant status. He thought he had buried the anger, thought he had moved beyond the hurt, until the visionary entrepreneurs convinced him that he would control more of America than he ever thought possible and that success would bury those who opposed him. And the money, the money was more than his parents had ever dreamed possible for him, the immigrants' kid. It was beyond his imagination, the initial deposit confirmed in an off-shore account. Not only were they making him an instant multimillionaire, but they offered to finance the entire CFBA operation. He smiled at the memory, lunch in the Ernest Petinaud Congressional Dining Room, named after another immigrant, a busboy for dining legislators and of Intrepid's reply, *I'm in. Life was good and about to get much better*, he thought. *Quite possibly a cabinet position or the very least an ambassadorship.*

"If your actions inspire others to dream more, learn more, do more and become more, you are a leader." John Quincy Adams

30,000

Sergeant Paul Francescutto had consulted with the FBI and several Secret Service agents early in the morning as they prepared for their assault on the senator's office. Separate warrants were going to be served simultaneously in each of his Colorado and Washington offices as well as his home and Aspen condo. The team had created a covert perimeter around the senator's Denver office building with agents observing from unmarked vehicles, waiting. Francescutto had the DPD Bomb Squad cruising two streets over so as not to draw attention.

The Denver PD sergeant sat with three other detectives and on the agreed upon time, he received an encrypted text from Peltowski advising that their subject had just used the intercom to advise his staff that he was ready to start the business day. She also disclosed that she had blocked all communications in and out of the entire building, including cell phones, texts and land lines.

Francescutto hit the *Go* button on his two-way and all agents converged on the building.

Chapter Eighty-Eight

Happy with the start of the day, Khawaja Aadhean buzzed his staff to signal that he was ready and for his assistant to provide a briefing of the day's activities. His male assistant was usually exceptionally prompt so when he didn't appear momentarily, Aadhean rose from the couch and walked to the main door leading to the waiting area. Hearing what sounded like commotion from the next room, he stopped to listen, wondering if his ears were picking up the sounds of a faulty heating system. The sounds of Pakistani music from two high intensity speakers behind the couch, filtered outside noises, particularly the tones of the flute like sarangi and the tabla, a percussion instrument.

Shaking his head in confusion he figured his assistant was held up with an office issue, delaying him for the morning briefing. He opened the door and immediately backed up as a wave of blue jacketed FBI agents rushed into his office, one grabbing his shoulders forcefully, spinning him around, handcuffing, then stuffing a warrant into his jacket pocket and handing him off to a uniformed Denver Police officer to transport.

He resisted, twisting and spinning, shouting his outrage in Urdu, the language of his beloved Pakistan, was out of his mouth before he realized the magnitude of his outburst. He quickly back-tracked and said, "What is happening here? What are you doing in my office? I am a United States Senator and I demand to know what is your purpose and authority for invading my office," but it was too late. As he struggled with his restraints, attempting to remove himself from the officer's hold of the handcuffs, he noticed the raised eyebrows on the lead agent, which told him all he would never want to know. He had allowed complacency, one of the first…and often the last element of the ideology which he had lived all his adult life, to short circuit his years of devotion and accomplishments.

Hanging his head in defeat, he complied when the officer kicked his feet out to each side and frisked him, removing everything in his pockets. The officer stood to the side with one hand on the handcuffs while the suspect watched his life being destroyed. Aadhean felt nauseous and lightheaded, wishing he could create an immediate end to the humiliation, yet he took solace in the knowledge that Allah would provide and that Allah would have his vengeance.

As he complied, he thought of a philosophy which had guided him on many a journey, "*There are risks and costs to a program of action. But they are far less than the long-range risks and costs of comfortable inaction.*" He was unaware of the irony; the philosophy was that of John F. Kennedy.

He watched complacently as the other agents disconnected his computer/hard drive and handed them to others who spirited them out of the office, while others packed out boxes of files. Agents cleared every piece of paper and all electronic devices from the entry office with Sergeant Francescutto supervising the process from the office's front door. No one spoke and Aadhean knew better than to protest, that would come later during a national press conference. He was slowly regaining his composure with his smug inner demeanor resting on his belief that the encrypted files would reveal nothing to his adversaries.

He had not meet Peltowski.

Once the process was complete, the FBI agents retreated to their respective vehicles and sped off for the Denver FBI field office on East thirty-sixth street where the confiscated material would be cataloged, the electronics scanned, data downloaded and everything analysed for the suspected connections. Their suspect was hustled to the top floor lock-up where he would be detained until a federal prosecutor's arrival later in the day.

FBI forensics agents would find a cornucopia of incriminating evidence, so much so that the agency would indict hundreds of CFBA participants over the next few months. Other federal investigators would view hundreds of hours of recorded CCTV digital recordings of every person who visited the senator back to his first day in office as well as all the material of the various committees on which he served, his neighbors, friends and where and with whom he dined. A monumental and daunting task that would consume thousands of agency hours, but which would prove to be worth the investment.

Back in his office, Detective Francescutto placed a call to Fukishura with an update. She was ecstatic with the operation's success, asked him to log his operation into CHAP and to begin an investigation into Sandra Shepherd, William Shepherd's daughter, explaining her involvement in the research and development of the explosives. Jason's belief that Sandra was ignorant of her vital role in the operation aside, Jessica had to know the extent of her involvement and Paul was the person for that job.

She had just clicked off from Francescutto when her phone rang, or more precisely, a siren, which she had always thought very cool. She had already received high fives from the investigators and smiled as she punched the green button, "Agent Fukishura," she said, feeling much better about this greeting over, "Yo." which is what she had used for years. It was Sorento.

"Jessica, I just received the information regarding the Suburbans and the government plates. It took a while and I had NCIS, National Criminal Intelligence Service, do the tracing which enabled full transparency. Agents found four of our Suburbans with Postal Service license plates."

"Oh my God sir, I know you are not shitting me but that sounds too bizarre to comprehend. Any idea who was involved?"

Sorento laughed at her freedom of speech to her supervisor, then said, "I too was blown away. Kind of ingenious really. Processing goods back and forth across the country seems to be all in-house with this group. As you know, they have refined the person-to-person covert information exchange, so I suspect that is how the plates got to Los Angeles. NCIS is combing the weeks of garage surveillance footage and so far, the suspect list is huge. Not only the garage supervisor but all mechanics and every agent who has been in there for the last six months. It will be a while for anything concrete to surface. In the meantime, we have confirmation that what brought the Mahalo flight down was cesium hidden in a coffin. Some poor schmuck from Idaho who died without relatives was schedule for cremation, but became a decoy layered in the coffin between sheets of lead with the cesium at one end and a time capsule at the other. When the plane hit thirty-thousand feet, the timer began. At mark three hours, which put the flight on a descending path to LAX, the cesium capsule exposed the molecules which in turn cut out the plane's electronics."

Jessica took all this in, applying it to what they already had and replied, “Have you heard how badly the convention center was damaged, how many fatals and injured?”

“The convention center is gone. It will have to be demolished and rebuilt.

“When your guys from LAPD surprised Sarkowski, he set the attack in motion much too early. The time line has been confirmed by Jason and Jackson that the plane was to take out all the eastern Democratic delegates and the Suburbans all those arriving from west coast states. The latter hadn’t begun to arrive when LAPD kick-started the process. There are about fifty injured and seven killed. Those who died were staff, either out front having a smoke break or were putting the finishing touches on the landscape. President Bakus is contacting the injured in hospitals directly and the families of the deceased.”

“What about the cesium sir, Manitoba for sure but how was it stolen and what transpired?” she asked, knowing the answers were in CHAP but trying to see if there was anything the data processors missed.

“You have the info on the actual heist. After that, the stolen van headed west on the TransCanada Highway and made it all the way to the southwestern part of the province before a Mountie’s electronics picked up on the stolen plate. The rest you know. What I need from you Jessica is for your Idaho sheriff to find and arrest the mortician and anyone else involved in the concealment of the cesium. Minneapolis Police are checking video surveillance trying to ID the mortician van but we are not holding out much hope. Let me know ASAP when you have something new.” Knowing Jessica was about to mention CHAP he quickly said, “Yes, I know CHAP and it is fantastic. It will revolutionize our entire national security paradigm but humor this old cop will you and call?”

Jessica snickered at her boss referring to himself as old. He was all of forty-five and exceptionally fit for a desk cop, but she stiffled her humor and said, “Certainly sir. I will ask Sheriff Joe to get on the mortician immediately and get back to you.”

“Sounds good Jessica, and please extend my personal appreciation to your team for obtaining the evidence against the Idaho Mountain Boys and capturing them with the chemicals. And Jessica,” he paused for effect,

"I am really proud of your superb talent in creating the working group of investigators. That is the way we are doing things from now on. It may take a while to convert the old guard but it will be done. I believe CHAP will be the key to their conversion. Raise a glass of Marc's vino in your honor from me."

Somewhat embarrassed to be called out on the transformation, the magnitude of which she was not completely aware herself, she responded, "Thank you sir. It has been a long process and I believe I have control of my male issues. I will get back to you shortly." Click.

She gripped the phone tightly, putting it against the side of her head, then put her head on her lap and moaned to herself, *I do not believe I just said that to Sorento. He is going to think I have completely lost my perspective to comment on my personal life during an investigation. Well, what is done, is done. Hopefully he is shaking his head and smiling, not filling out transfer papers.*

She rose from her desk and left the communication room to find Sheriff Joe.

Chapter Eighty-Nine

Rebecca hadn`t been home since she joined the investigation at the Ranch after her Denver trip and she was anxious to move on with her decision…she had to speak with Penelope first. It had only been a matter of a few days, although it seemed ages ago, that she was lavishing in Denver, enjoying the company of another soul for the first time in years, maybe forever. She had talked with Pen several times on the phone since their return, always bowing out of meeting for coffee, lunch or Cassandras and she suspected Pen was wondering if Rebecca was having second thoughts about their Denver time. Rebecca knew she had to move quickly on this relationship before any negativity smoldered and blew into a full-scale catastrophe.

She was sitting in The Ranch's living room staring at the massive fireplace as the flames danced and swirled, performing their shimmying ritual as old as time. She wanted to get this ordeal over with and join Pen to move on with their lives, but simultaneously she feared rejection. Not from Jessica being upset with her leaving the service, but with Penelope for lying to her all this time.

She sipped the herbal tea Marc had left for her, leaned back into the folds of the rich leather and planned her conversation. As she tried to relax and formulate a plan, two of the kittens came bounding across the highly polished tongue and grove hardwood floor landing, skidding to a stop and bouncing up on her lap. She smiled and spoke softly to each, stroking under their chins. Within a few moments both had curled up on her lap and were asleep.

She allowed herself to gravitate back to how she was going to convince Pen that their initial meeting had nothing to do with the service, that their relationship was theirs alone and totally unrelated to work. She hoped that Pen wouldn`t connect the dots regarding the collapsed arrangement with the guide outfitting business. That was the proverbial can of worms she did not want to open, but if it did, she would remind Penelope that it was her offer to put money into the project, not Rebecca`s. *No*, she thought, *that would be the worst approach, taking an offensive tactic against someone you love. Wait a minute* she thought, *did I just acknowledge my love for Pen?*

She was startled out of her romantic musing by Jessica's exaggerated fall into the couch's folds sighing, "I am so tired my bones are screaming for a hot tub," as she turned to face Rebecca. Seeing her wide-eyed look, she continued, "Sorry, I didn't mean to spook you from your dozing. How are you feeling? Wait, we need something stronger than herbal tea," adding as she rose from the couch, pushed herself up with both hands and headed for the wine cooler nestled into a corner of the living room, grabbed a bottle of Road Thirteen Vineyard's Chardonnay, two stem glasses and a corkscrew, walked back to the inviting fire, popped the cork, poured two glasses, handed one to Rebecca, clinked and returned to her seat and took a long sip, swirling it around in her mouth, allowing her palate to enjoy the beauty of the British Columbian elegance, turned to Rebecca, then said, "I am sure you are as exhausted as I am and ready for some down time."

Rebecca's pensive look prompted Jessica to add, "The operation is over and yet I see you are still concerned. Something of which you can't let go?"

"No, its not that Jessica. I just have something personal on my mind that I need to talk to you about and I am not sure how you are going to take it."

"Aw, geez," she exhorted, not really knowing what to say or what was coming. "What is wrong Rebecca? Anything I can help with?"

"Thanks Jessica. I appreciate your offer. I really do. It is a personal problem that I have been wrestling with for some time and have decided. The bottom line is I must leave the Service. Now before you react, let me give you the background," she offered and proceeded to explain her relationship with Penelope, how they met, the social life they developed, the great times at Casandra's and of course Denver. When she was through, she took a deep breath and was waiting for the expected tirade from Jessica but was unprepared for what she received.

She continued, "I'm in love Jessica. I didn't think I'd ever find it. Maybe I don't know what love is. Maybe I'm making a huge mistake, but I have to go with these feelings. The time we had in Denver was incredible, magical even and I am sure Penelope feels the same about me. What has been driving me nuts since we got back and I've been working the case, is she has no idea why I am not seeing her and I can't lie any more. It is tearing me up inside to think I am starting a relationship on lies and I don't know how to tell her."

Jessica's face broadened into a warm grin, slid over on the couch and wrapped her arms around Rebecca and held her. She could feel Rebecca start to shake and knew the tears were there, dammed by her friend's years of stoic demeanor. Then they came. Jessica rubbed her back, quietly hummed and held her tightly, pressing their bodies together, offering her comfort. Jessica had no idea where this caring was coming from, she had never behaved this way with anyone, not even her parents. The last time she cried was after one of the nightmares when her mom had told her the details of the Montreal Massacre, the shooting of twenty-eight women, the killing of fourteen, the killer separating the women and men before opening fire, the men not helping, but slithering away cowardly. She had no idea she could comfort another human being like this, but she stopped thinking and just held on tight until Rebecca was spent.

After a few moments, Rebecca pulled back, wiped the tears away with her sleeve and Jessica offered, "How about this? We are done here, just mop up category now. Invite Penelope here for dinner tomorrow night. Marc will make something spectacular and the three of us will have a delicious time and let me break the ice with her. Let me take it on, explaining the secrecy of the job. If she is the woman you believe she is, you will have no problem with her understanding. What do you say?"

"It will be okay to have a civilian here? Sorento okay with it?"

"Not a problem. When it is time, I will share your plans with him, but not now and I know Marc will prepare something that will have all our taste buds dancing.

Now, tell me all about this fabulous Denver trip, the clothes and most importantly and I want to know more about Penelope. This is incredible news."

30,000

While Rebecca and Jessica chatted, the rest of the investigative team collected their personal belongings from their rooms, checked out with Bruce and almost tip-toed out the hall and past the living room, not wanting to intrude in what was obviously a personal discussion. Sheriff Joe had called his officers earlier in the day and the mortician had been arrested, with the standing federal warrant through CHAP, was in custody and deputies and a forensics team were scouring the facility where the fake casket had been produced. Minneapolis Airport Police and the municipal police department had worked together in collecting evidence from the casket transporting van and had come up with a match for the driver and passenger, initiating an arrest order for both. Updating CHAP with the data, both agencies knew there was little chance the terrorists who transported the cesium would be free for long.

Chapter Ninety

Elisabeth, Jackson and Jason were packing their gear while waiting to hear from Jessica. They hadn't a clue as to their next assignment but they had agreed to squeeze out some down time while at the Marina…the bonus being, Uncle Sam was footing the bill for the lavish accommodations while they waited for reassignment.

Gear boxed and locked in the walk-in closet, they set out for a meal together. Jackson had shared his experience regarding Tobias Armishaw and the Firewalker and they all agreed that their celebratory meal would be with him. Elisabeth suggested they get somewhat dressed up for the occasion and chose a floral pink and cream print, button down blouse from Tory Burch and a pair of light pink trousers by Maison Margiela with a pair of taupe ankle suede booties by Vince Camuto with a two and a half-inch heel.

The guys were wearing cargo shorts; Jason a pair of black Helly Hansen shorts with an open collar Calvin Klein long sleeve white shirt, untucked. Jackson chose Levi chocolate brown shorts with a Ralph Lauren cotton pull over sweater in Safari Heather, mock neck and half zip collar. Both men wore Sperry boat shoes without socks; Jason's in black and Jackson's sahara. They jumped in Jason's brown paper loaner with Jackson driving, Elisabeth riding shotgun and Jason offering a running commentary on the bomb site clean-up. They made one stop before the Firewalker, and were early enough to find the parking lot relatively empty. Walking through the main doors which resembled ship's portals, they found the staff gearing up for the dinner customers.

Tobias saw them enter and immediately stopped fussing with table arrangements and exuberantly jogged over to greet them, extending a hand first to Elisabeth, then Jason and finally Jackson saying, "Welcome to the Firewalker! Please, let me show you to a table and get menus. Jackson, I presume these fine people are your Secret Service colleagues?" he said, then dropped his head slightly and lowered his voice, "You aren't undercover or anything are you? We can be open as to who you are?"

Jackson put his hand on Tobias' shoulder and said, "Not undercover sir. You know about the explosion. We weren't able to stop that but it could have been worse except for the help you and your friends gave us. Finding the vehicles loaded with explosives was paramount and the LAPD Bomb Squad were able to minimize the damage."

"That is good to hear. I will make sure the guys hear of your gratitude. Maybe I can get some of them here tonight for, you know, a little party. And, please, I'm not a sir, just Tobias," he added as he pulled a chair out for Elisabeth, and as she sat, he extended his hand again and added, "Ma'am, I extend the appreciation of the community and the United States Navy SEALs for what you guys did," then backed away leaving the three somewhat speechless. They had never been thanked by a civilian for their work, ever.

Tobias returned quickly with a tray holding three tall glasses of beer, menus and said, "I know you didn't order this but I want you to try a new entry to our craft brew, it's called Jack Wrap from a local brewer in Santa Monica. I know you can't accept comps, so we can settle-up later. Let me know what you think and if you truly don't like it, I won't be offended."

The trio picked up their glasses simultaneously, clinked and took a large swallow. Elisabeth nodded her approval to Tobias and took another sip while Jason lifted his hand and gave the waffle sign of maybe and Jackson chugged most of the glass, slamming the glass down on the table and said, "Whose driving?"

Tobias left shaking his head acknowledging that these guys were no different than SEALs or Marines.

They each took a few minutes to peruse the menu and were surprised with the details of each item. One that caught Elisabeth's eye as a burger by Jamie Oliver with a list of the ingredients. Her thoughts went no further and decided on the Firewalker which boasted a signature BBQ sauce, bacon, Canadian Cheddar and avocado with a side-salad and raspberry vinaigrette dressing. Jason and Jackson both chose the Flaming Mexicans which were a trio of tacos filled with spicy beef and jalapenos. Jason commented on the short bio of the chef at the bottom of the one-page menu, "Have you guys ever been to Restaurant Row on La Cienega in Beverly Hills? This chef, Scotty Ballantine, apparently rotated through about five of the top eateries there over the past twenty years. Tobias must have made him an offer he couldn't refuse to leave La Cienega, but maybe it was time for Scotty to live a slower pace. Or, maybe he is Navy," he added with a huge grin knowing he was probably correct.

While Jackson took a moment to read the bio himself, he and Jason chatted about Ballantine and Elisabeth excused herself to attend the restroom. Jason continued his comments about the legendary restaurant strip by adding, "While I was at UCLA I used to park cars there on the weekends. Made incredible money and drove some of the wildest rides imaginable."

Jackson was about to reply when Elisabeth's return caught his eye. He decided to wait for her to rejoin the trio before rejuvenating the conversation. He was sipping his brew when he saw Elisabeth stop beside a table of four twenty-something men. What happened next excited him so much he wanted to cheer, but he restrained himself to enjoy the interaction.

Elisabeth was wending her way through the scores of occupied tables heading back to her party when she felt a hand on her rear-end. She stopped and looked down at the man holding her right butt cheek. He smiled up at her, proud of his accomplishment. Pleased with his intuition that this hot chick would respond to his aggressive invitation to a physical interaction, he was too engrossed in his narcistic behavior to see the anger from the woman whose buttock he held with his left hand. He would later try to explain to the Military Police that, what he claimed was an unprovoked attack, coming so fast and furiously, he had zero time to react.

Reality was, he couldn't have done anything to protect himself had he been sober, or had more experience interacting with assertive women.

Elisabeth froze while her aggressor began to move his hand in a circular motion, laughing and looking to his buddies for approval…encouraging them to get in on the action. The moment the butt grabber's head turned back to look at Elisabeth, she moved into him, fast and furiously, wrapping her right arm over and around his left bicep, locking it against her upper body as she jumped on top of him, throwing her weight against him and the chair, forcing both backwards onto the floor while screaming, "Kiai", but what sounded like an animal screech, as she drove her index and middle fingers into his eyes, grabbed his throat and squeezed until he gasped for air, choking, trying to gain air through his nose. Elisabeth maintained the arm lock with her left knee jammed into his right bicep, locking his body to the floor as she used the heel of her right hand to pound his face, breaking his nose, jaw and one eye socket.

Tobias was helping out at the cash register when he heard the scream and came scrambling around the tables with two bouncers behind him. As he passed Pennington, Jackson put a hand out and touched Tobias lightly, catching Armishaw's attention and smiled saying,
"Give her a moment, will you Tobias?"

Somewhat confused, Tobias nodded and motioned the bouncers to sit for a moment while the action two tables away played out.

Elisabeth had her groper pinned to the floor, her heart rate never rising above sixty-five. She turned to the other four at the table and said, very quietly, "The next time I'll break every fuckin' bone in his body, then start on you four."

With that comment, she rose from the floor, adjusted her Tory Burch and Miason Margiela, touched her hat to insure its placement and sauntered back to her table, pulled out her chair and sat, while Tobias and his bouncers continued to stare, dumbfounded at what they had just witnessed.

Pulling himself out of the stupor, the Firewalker owner turned to the bouncers and whispered instructions, then stepped over to Elisabeth and extended his hand. She took it with a smile which Tobias returned with a nod then gently backed away.

Neither Jackson, nor Jason spoke as their actions were clearly loud enough…they raised their glasses and toasted their colleague.

The bouncers grabbed the groper by the armpits and lifted him off his feet and gently guided him to the front door. Once outside they checked his wallet for a name, then placed a business card which stated simply, *You are 86ed from the Firewalker…For Life.*

They placed a call to a cab company, with which they had a standing contract, told the dispatcher they had a ride for the base and then waited for the two minutes, holding the groper upright not allowing him to relief the pain in his eyes or throat.

When the taxi arrived, they placed him gently into the backseat and advised the driver to deposit him at the main gate, closed the door, then placed a call to the Marine Military Police asking the duty sergeant to place a note in groper's file of his status with the Firewalker. The duty MP sergeant didn't hesitate to grant the Firewalker's request given Tobias' reputation. The compliance would follow the chain of command all the way to the base commander…if the incident ever moved past the base police report.

The bouncers returned to the pub to see their boss bending over talking with the remaining party, seeing all four men moving their heads up and down in resignation. Tobias had just turned from the foursome as the Jackson party's meal arrived. The unperturbed owner shuffled quickly to intercept and served his guest personally. He bowed graciously, backing away, returning to the bar while the agents began their journey through taste-town, un-phased by the short skirmish with the uncouth.

There wasn't much chat as the trio attacked their meal, coming up for air periodically for a beer swallow. By now the Firewalker was almost packed with just a few bar stools empty, creating a huge one hundred and fifty pro Navy, pro military crowd. Jason was just finishing the last of his Flaming Mexican when he asked, "Should we do it now while the mood is somewhat tame?"

Jackson and Elisabeth nodded their agreement, both pushing their chairs back and joining Jason as he led them over to Tobias at the bar.

Elisabeth took the lead, offering, "Tobias we sincerely appreciate the fabulous meal and beer and although we are nowhere near ready to call it an evening we want to make a contribution. Jackson, would you do the honors?"

Pennington took the cue and casually walked over to a thirty gallon, stainless steel bucket emblazoned with, *Swabby Bucket-For the Kids.* He reached into his cargo pocket and withdrew a batch of bills; fifty, twenties, expanded the wad and gently placed them in the bucket, already half full of currency. He stepped to the side allowing Elisabeth to repeat the offering, followed by Jason, all putting the identical amount into the coffer.

The agents were unaware that their presence had been noted by every patron who knew who they were, for what agency they worked and how they were involved in thwarting the terror plot to destroy so many of their lives.

Tobias and the bar crew were looking on, not completely understanding what they were seeing. Then it became obvious to the Firewalker owner that he was witnessing a tremendous charitable contribution by three heroes who should be the recipients, not the givers. Tobias lost no time in grabbing the moment and jumped up on the bar and rang the SEAL bell three times, stopping all conversation and pausing the mellow music.

"Ladies and gentlemen, and for you SEALs, I use that word loosely, these three before you are the agents whose names have been buzzing around the Firewalker all night. Please, let me introduce you to Secret Service agent, Elisabeth Peltowski, she is the one who just kicked the ass of the jerk who groped her." He was about to continue when an raucous applause resounded from one hundred and fifty patrons giving her a standing ovation.

Tobias waited out the minute-long recognition then continued, "Secret Service agent Jackson Pennington who coordinated his effort with us here at the Firewalker and scores of you here tonight to locate and take down the bombers. Please give a round of applause to Jackson and to yourselves for your contribution to America's values." What followed was another standing ovation, creating embarrassment for the agents.

Tobias continued, "You may or may not have heard that the attack came on several fronts with the Mahalo Airline flight from Minneapolis landing in the Pacific. Secret Service agent Jason Spencer, this handsome dude in front of me with the dreads, was instrumental in preventing that incident from becoming a disaster. How about another round of applause for Jason, who by the way is an Angelino."

Once again, the crowd erupted in deafening applause and gratitude with Tobias adding a final comment when the applause died down, "And these three are not just our heroes for their bravery, they just made a huge contribution to the Bucket. The kids and their families will be forever grateful Elisabeth, Jackson and Jason. God bless you."

With his last comment, the crowd knew it was okay to mill around the agents and offer their personal appreciation, buy them a drink and chat. The single women gravitated to Jason and Jackson, thinking the men looked particularly hot and sexy in their shorts with Jason in his red Bailey

Fedora with a three-inch brim and Jackson fashionable in his natural straw Fedora with a two-inch brim. Elisabeth drew both genders, many women commenting on her pink outfit with the stunning Ralph Lauren Cream Cloche hat and half inch black band.

Everyone was either military or related to a service person. Many of the women were enthralled with Elisabeth's performance, with one saying the groper must be related to Joe Biden, which drew a huge round of applause of agreement until another woman added, "Or Donald Trump," and that got the entire crowd going again.

As the evening wore on, the crowd didn't thin as per usual, everyone seemingly wanting to stay and enjoy rubbing shoulders with their heroes. But by midnight, Elisabeth said she was ready to leave and get some sleep. The guys agreed, so they made their way to Tobias to settle their bill. They had to wend their way through the crowd to get to the bar since the entire place was on its feet, milling around chatting. As the trio walked by, they received back pats, several women jumped up and gave Jason or Jackson a cheek kiss, the latter creating a natural reaction with both men placing one hand on their firearm as they accepted the accolades and honors. The threesome arrived at the bar and waved Tobias over to pay. He walked over slowly and a shit-eating grin on his face and nodded, as to say, *Whats up*?

Elisabeth had to yell to be heard, asking for their bill. Instead of complying, Tobias maintained his grin and jumped up on the bar and yelled, *Oorah! Oorah*!, and everyone quieted down. He spoke quietly, saying, "These agents are asking for their bill. What should I tell them?" That brought another roar of applause with a chorus of, *Oorah, Oorah*, the Marine chant. Letting it gain momentum for a few seconds, Tobias finally raised his hands for quiet and said to the crowd, "Elisabeth, Jason and Jackson, there isn't a bill. We know you can not accept anything from the public, which is fine with us. Do you see that guy at the back, about 6' 4", two fifty? He is a Marine stationed at Pendleton and passed a hat, actually many hats and your bill was paid for by all these folks standing in front of you." Another round of *Oorahs* followed with Tobias raising his arms again continuing, "There was a little more collected than your bill's total so the folks put it in the Swabby Bucket. Twenties and tens add up quickly with this crowd and the donation is around fifteen hundred dollars."

It was impossible to be heard once again as the crowd erupted in cheers, this time with *Hoorah* a derivative of *Oorah* specifically for the Navy Special Weapons Teams, but just as loud. They didn't try. They simply stood side-by-side, place their right hand over their heart, bowed at the waist and slowly made their way to the front door, overwhelmed by the support and enthusiasm from the military families.

On the drive back to the hotel Jason asked, "So, what do you figure we have, about one day before Jessica gives us our new assignment?"

Elisabeth said, "Not more than that is what I figure too. I wonder if we will ever settle in one place and stop living out of a suitcase. What about you Jackson?"

"I have been bouncing all over the place since leaving school, I don't know if I could adjust to settling down in my own place. But, hey, that is for some time down the road. What are you guys going to do with your one day tomorrow?"

Jason offered, "I am heading to LA and give my Mom a day. I haven't seen her in a very long time, although we keep in touch with texting and I talk to her every couple of weeks. She never knows where I am since I have to be secretive about what I'm doing and my location. This time I can honestly tell her I have no idea what I am going to be doing or where I am going. It was particularly rough on her when I was in North Africa and didn't communicate for over three years. So this will be nice. I will give her a heads-up call tomorrow morning though so she doesn't have a heart attack. What are you guys going to do?"

"I am staying right here at the Marina and laying on the beach all day. Jackson?"

"I am heading to Point Mugu Naval Station outside of Malibu and check it out. I have heard a lot about the base and never had a chance to see it first-hand. You want to meet back at the hotel around six for dinner?"

Elisabeth and Jason resounded with a positive, "Yes" as they entered the hotel's parking lot.

As they headed to their rooms, they hadn't a clue as to the conversation taking place at The Ranch between Rebecca and Jessica.

Chapter Ninety

Rebecca and Jessica chatted at length, totally oblivious of the time. The investigators had left and the staff had retired for the night. Marc had slipped in quietly with another bottle of Road Thirteen Vineyard's Chardonnay and a few more appetizers, his compassion helping through the difficult discussion.

In the end, Jessica convinced Rebecca she should follow her heart and allow a natural course of events to develop without excessive planning. Money was not an issue, nor were future job prospects or a home and Rebecca began formulating a tentative plan to present to Penelope.

Around nine o'clock Rebecca called Pen, invited her to dinner for the next night, that she would pick her up and that the evening was a surprise. Penelope offered to meet Rebecca wherever but Rebecca insisted she needed to drive for the surprise to be, well, a surprise. Pen relinquished quickly and then asked rather furtively about a dress code. Rebecca almost laughed thinking Cassandras didn't have one, which is probably where Pen had in mind. Penelope couldn't be further from the truth.

Once the call was made with Pen being so receptive and not critical of her few days of isolation, Rebecca felt better. Actually, better than better, much like a new person with her entire life opening before her. She thanked Jessica profusely and headed home to get about fifteen hours of sleep.

Saying good-bye to Rebecca at the front door with a hug and a small back rub, Jessica meandered back to the living room, poured herself another glass of Chardonnay, plopped herself back into the leather folds, allowing the kittens to make their way onto her lap.

She wasn't worried about Rebecca leaving the Service or any possible backlash from Sorento about tomorrow's dinner. There would be nothing negative from him other than sorrow that he was losing a good agent but, she thought, *maybe I can put something together after a while that will mitigate the circumstances.*

She allowed her thoughts to coagulate into a formidable plan, set it aside in her memory to do list and gravitated back to the discussion with Rebecca and the unusual feelings of support for her she was able to draw from her inner being. She had no idea the location of the empathy, whether it generated from her own experiences or lack there of, or from deeper, maybe to her soul itself, but it felt good to connect with another human being, particularly one with whom she associated on such a spiritual level as Rebecca. *Really good*, she thought as she bent slightly forward, grabbed the bottle of white, poured the last into her glass, ate the remaining morsels, scooped both kittens in one arm and with her glass in the other and headed to bed, more at ease with her self, more comfortable within her own skin than she had ever been.

She made a short detour to the kitchen and left Marc a note about their special dinner guest tomorrow, asked if he could make a memorable meal, then headed to bed carrying the kittens and white slowly down the hall.

30,000

Chef Marc saw the note immediately upon entering his kitchen the next morning. The information drew a huge smile of anticipation since he hadn't had an opportunity to dazzle the agents with his culinary skill since their arrival. He knew immediately what he was going to serve, wrote it out to confirm a shopping list, then called down to the market for delivery of the ingredients to the main gate where one of the guards would transport it the rest of the way.

The Market was new to StoneHead. During the past year Syrian refugees settled in StoneHead and with the help of local ranchers, opened an ethnic market specializing in various delicacies previously not offered in the community. What made the new resident success sweeter was that the various herbs and vegetables were grown by their sponsors. Locals were hesitant at first but when the cattle ranchers held a complimentary BBQ with truffles, chanterelles and strong pungent cheeses from Denver, folks were convinced, or rather their palates were.

Chef Stucki decided to start the dining experience with an appetizer of truffled gnocchi: hard seared gnocchi, small egg & potato dumplings, morel and chanterelle mushrooms in a black truffled fricassee sauce, topped with grana Padano cheese and shaved truffles.

For the entrée, he chose a pork tenderloin for which he would use a cooking system called sous vide, precision cooking. The process uses a thermal immersion circulator tubular electronic device to create a water bath in which he immersed cryovaced prosciutto wrapped pork tenderloin at fifty-eight degrees Celsius. Once cooked, Marc would remove the pork from the wrap, pan seared it for two minutes and plate it with gorgonzola pomme purée, Italian blue cheese and pureed apple, black kale and sautéed oyster mushroom, preserved plums, and grainy Dijon for a pork reduction.

Dessert was going to be equally memorable with his personal Chocolate Mousse recipe of white and dark chocolate, pretzel crust, salted caramel and roasted peanut crumble.

Chapter Ninety-One

Jessica busied herself for most of the day reading CHAP on the process of rounding up the tremendous number of CFBA conspirators, as the FBI worked its way through the plethora of seized electronic documents. The federal government's technical squad had discovered the connecting links between the isolated terrorist cells through the confiscated computers. One suspect led to twenty others and the significance of the find extrapolated significantly with participants hiding in plain sight under the guise of state and local bureaucracies.

At five, she closed the office and dropped by the kitchen to see how Marc was progressing. As she passed through the dining room she spotted his table setting for three. Marc had slid the massive dining table to the far end, undoubtedly with staff help, and had brought in a matching Balustrade round table. It was gorgeous in its fourteen or fifteen-foot diameter pedestal designed cherry wood that matched its big brother tucked away at the end of the dining room. Marc had added three chairs, not evenly spaced around but close, with just enough elbow room to be intimate but not confined. He had left the table almost bare with a starched white table cloth that covered just the table's middle, allowing the square poppy toned place setting and silverware to stand out against the cherry wood's sheen. Jessica stopped to get a closer look at the flatware, and smiled at Chef's dedication to detail; Spanish Lace Sterling Silver, sparkling, with each handle enhanced with an intricate lace design.

She moved on to the kitchen and quietly stuck her head through the portal doors and was overtaken by the aroma of Marc's preparation. She caught his eye but didn't interrupt. He just smiled and she knew that the evening was going to be a memorable dining experience. She poured herself a glass of Red from an open bottle of Weston Winery's 307 Blend of Cabernet Sauvignon, Syrah and Zinfandel then headed to her room to shower and dress for the evening. With little fuss over her hair, save a little mousse, and two minutes for eye liner and lipstick, she was quickly in and out of the bathroom. She chose a pair of drab olive pants with a winter floral pattern of blacks and browns by Spanner, then added a cowl neck bone cashmere sweater and a deep mossy olive green over-sweater having an embroidered, deep back. She tied it all together with a pair of wine ankle boots.

Chapter Ninety-Two

Rebecca woke around ten rested, and excited for her evening with Penelope and Jessica. She spent the day washing and vacuuming her truck, grocery shopping; letting the positive vibrations of her new lease on life control her actions.

She chose one of her new Nordstrom outfits; the pair of Galla Ted Baker cropped pants with the floral print, the black double-breasted jacket, black camisole, lace back T-shirt and booties. She knew her look would draw Penelope to their time in Denver. How could it not?

Rebecca picked Penelope up at six, shocked to see her standing outside her house waiting. She looked stunning in her dark orange Mikado Osaka pants with the muted yellow and orange pattern. Rebecca smiled when she noticed Pen had paired it with her new persimmon scoop neck tank and orange mesh pullover sweater and knew, even though she couldn't see her feet, that Penelope would be wearing the Blondo ankle boots.

Rebecca's sound system was playing Andrea Bocelli's Love in Portofino, which she was counting on to set the mood for what she prayed was going to be a memorable evening. "You look absolutely stunning Penelope, absolutely gorgeous," she offered as she undid her seatbelt and slid across the bench seat, guided her right hand across Pen's shoulder and gently brushed her lips, not wanting to smudge.

Pen responded immediately giving Rebecca assurances that although the entire day from last night's call, was odd, she was trusting her and responded with, "Thank you! And you as well. I love that jacket. Very stunning. Oh, and you are wearing Baker's pants too. Mm, what do you have planned tonight? Are you going to get me drunk and seduce me?" she said with a hint of seduction in her own voice.

"Quite possibly Pen, quite possibly," she said with a provocative grin. "But for now, you must agree not to ask any questions until we get to our destination. Agreed?"

"Agreed," replied Penelope with a little hop in her seat as she adjusted herself for the seatbelt and stifled her excitement.

Rebecca pulled away and joined up immediately with highway fourteen heading west. The short twenty-minute drive passed quickly with neither speaking, but both stealing flirtive glances. Rebecca slowed ahead of The Ranch driveway, glancing quickly at Penelope to see the expected confused look as Pen bent at the waist to see where they were headed. "Remember, no questions," Rebecca said as she put on her right blinker and turned into the wide driveway and slowly made her way to the main gate. Stopping under the bright lights, she reached inside her jacket, retrieved her ID, rolled down the window and had it ready for the guard.

"Good evening Agent Simpson," the Sgt. said, as he accepted the identification. He knew Rebecca on sight and therefore could forgo the iris scan.

Penelope's eyes revealed that her current situation was far from what she had anticipated as she dropped her head slightly again to see the other guards... automatic weapons trained on the truck.

Before he could comment on Penelope, Rebecca offered an explanation, "Sgt. this is Dr. Penelope Barker. She is on your list with Agent Fukishura's approval. Dr. Barker can provide identification if required."

"Not necessary Agent Simpson, but we will proceed with the vehicle protocol," as he nodded to one of his colleagues who approached and scanned the truck's undercarriage with the stick mirror, looked in the bed, scanned the interior with his flashlight, then nodded to the Sgt. who indicated to Rebecca that she was to drive forward slightly and stop over the X-Ray panel. Once she was cleared, the forward gate opened and a jeep with four armed troopers appeared from her left, stopped and indicated she was to follow them.

Rebecca followed the jeep and as they pulled off to circle the ranch house and head back to the main gate, she pulled in front of the main door, parked and indicated to Penelope with a wave of her hand that she was to follow.

They were stepping towards the massive oak door when it opened and Jessica appeared, extended her hand saying, "Hi Dr. Barker, I am Jessica Fukishura. Please come in and I will explain the mystery."

Penelope looked at Rebecca, who smiled conspiratorially while extending her arm in a sweeping motion, indicating Pen should proceed her into the foyer.

Jessica led the way, bypassing the security center and on to the living room. She invited Rebecca and Pen to join her on the couch just as Chef Marc, dressed in black slacks, a starched chef's jacket with the White House seal and his name blazoned across the breast and a tall chef's hat, arrived with a plate of appetizers and two bottles of wine.

"Agents Fukishura, Simpson and Dr. Barker, to start your evening, I have prepared truffled gnocchi with morel and chanterelle mushrooms and grana Padano cheese and I have paired it with Wyoming's Weston Winery's Chris LeDoux, a blend of reds named after the famed poet who died in 2005." he offered as he sat the plate, wine and stem glasses on the coffee table. "Please, relax and enjoy, while I prepare your entrée," he grinned, as he turned and headed to his kitchen.

Jessica poured, handed each a glass, a small china white plate, cocktail forks and napkins, then passed the plate of gnocchi. She purposely wanted to wait until Penelope had savored Marc's cuisine and at least one goblet of the LeDoux before broaching the subject.

Jessica smoothed the tension by beginning the conversation about how stunning The Ranch is, almost overpowering to some visitors, then highlighted the western décor and how the late Ms. Bakus love the country and ranch background trivia, its history and how Chef Marc came to work for President Bakus. Segueing to the subject was easy given the moans of contentment as they luxuriated in the flavors of Marc's cuisine. Twenty minutes into their enjoyment, Jessica began.

"Penelope, I have struggled with the many ways to share Rebecca's information. It was my suggestion we meet here tonight, not only as an explanation but that I might get to know you better while explaining, from my perspective, then Rebecca will give you the particulars. "I am a supervising Secret Service Agent, and as you know, we are tasked with protecting the president. Mr. Bakus had not planed on using The Ranch during his presidency, but world circumstances dictated he have a somewhat remote meeting location other than Camp David for a summit. Since The Ranch didn't have security, my job was to effect an analysis and have the ranch sealed. I chose a team of colleagues to join me. Part of their task was to determine if there were any covert threats locally against Mr. Bakus, and Rebecca's part was in the role in which you met. She is, in fact, a horse trainer, but I will let her tell you all about that at a later point.

"Through Rebecca's efforts we found several threats against the president, many of which stretched across the nation, but had their origin in StoneHead. You will be reading about it in the media in the days to come but for now, it is important for you to know that Rebecca has been working undercover for the Secret Service shortly after university. To bring anyone into her confidence would not only violate that secrecy, but jeopardize a number of operations, many terrorist related.

"I am sure this entire evening is confusing for you but when Rebecca shared her concern for you and your relationship, wanting full disclosure, I offered to share my thoughts. None of us ever expect to have a serious relationship while working undercover and some of us never do even when working at the White House. But I am digressing. Should I leave now so you guys can continue?" she asked, watching Penelope's face for any sign of bolting. Seeing a strange, rather resigned, calm expression, she finished with, "Rebecca, do you want to continue?"

Jessica made a move to extricate herself from the deep folds of the leather couch when Penelope said, "That's okay Jessica, please stay," as she turned to Rebecca with an infectious smirk and nod.

Rebecca felt herself becoming uncomfortable. She thought she had her delivery memorized, so she could get it out and then clarify any specifics, but Pen's demeanor was disrupting her flow and her mind was stammering, but she managed to begin, "I have been undercover with the Secret Service, as Jessica mentioned, almost since the day I graduated from the academy. The assignment prior to this one was in Arizona working with the FBI. I was the only female on the team and the only agent with any country experience. The men treated me like a rookie cop, even though I was the only one producing. Then Jessica asked me to join her in this assignment and I jumped at the chance to get away from Arizona.

My cover here, as you know, was as a horse trainer, which I did as a kid in Montana for fun and spending money. I participated in rodeos, I graduated from the University of Montana, taught elementary school and was a deputy Sherriff in Montana before joining the service. When we met, I was working for Tom. We had such good times together that I was conflicted between my duty with the service and my growing affection for you."

The last comment drew a bit of a wide-eye expression from Jessica and an honest smile from Penelope, neither of which Rebecca wanted to read, so she continued, "I knew we had something in Denver, then when we got home I immediately went back on assignment with several colleagues into Yellowstone with a pack-train. All during that trip I mulled my options; I love my job but I love you more and I knew I couldn't maintain the two. After that trip, I came here to help complete the job for which we were assigned. That finished yesterday, and yesterday, I quit the service," she paused to catch her breath and didn't realize that she had been speaking by rote, neither to Jessica or Penelope, just from her heart. Penelope took her pause as an indication she could speak, but Rebecca carried on, casually glancing between Pen, Jessica and the aura of the dancing flames.

"I have a ranch outside of Santa Barbara. It isn't much but it is paid for and a neighbor takes care of the place for me. He doesn't know what I do, did, for a living. I would like you and I to move there, start our own investigative firm, you could open a practice or do something else. Whatever we do, I want us to do it together. That's all I have in the way of an explanation. I am sorry I had to deceive you, but I was between a rock and a hard place, so to speak. There were some very bad people here in StoneHead and if they found out who I was, that knowledge could have destroyed the entire operation and as it turns out, my secrecy helped to bring hundreds of terrorists down." She felt she was rambling, so she leaned back into the couch, pulled her legs up to her chest and looked at Penelope who was smiling, a reaction totally unexpected by Rebecca. "Rebecca, sweetheart," she began as she scooted across the couch and put her arm around Rebecca, "I am not surprised at any of this."

"Really? And you're not mad?"

Penelope laughed slightly and said, "Mad? How could I be mad at you? I kinda figured you were more than what appeared on the surface, but the person I have come to know and love is right here beside me. I find it refreshing and very sweet that you and Jessica wanted me here for dinner. Actually I feel very special to be in the President's house, with you two regardless of the reason, but especially that you had the desire to do all this for me, for us.

Do you remember when we were in the Bread Basket and the deputy asked you if you had a weapon on your person?"

Rebecca nodded.

"Well, I knew then that there was something going on. I mean, how many times do you meet anyone who is a horse trainer who carries a firearm? I mean, from whom or what could you be protecting yourself? Even before that, do you remember that guy Jake or Jack, in Cassandras parking lot? When you stood up in the restaurant, I was sure you were going to kick his ass there, and you did in the parking lot. It all started to come together. Then, come on, I mean, when you undressed in Denver and had the pistol strapped across your stomach? But the moment I knew for sure there was more of you than I could detect was when we were at the pool and those drunks grabbed you. Holy shit Rebecca, you kicked, chopped and broke arms, all without breaking a sweat. Then, I was dumbfounded when the officer handed you his cell, you chatted with someone for a couple of moments, then the officer wished us a good day and left with the drunks cuffed. Whomever you spoke with, cleared the way of any issues.

"I knew, but it didn't bother me, not in the least, because I was sure you would tell me when you could, or wanted to and besides, as I said, you are more than your job. And yes, let's go to Santa Barbara."

Rebecca was facing Penelope, almost at the exclusion of Jessica, and said, "Oh Penelope, I am so relieved that you are okay with all of this. I truly apologize and promise, there will be no further subterfuge," then instigated a passionate kiss which Pen returned, followed by a hug.

Jessica felt the time was right to move on so she offered, "Group hug coming, then let's enjoy Marc's incredible masterpiece," as she rose from the couch and extended her arms for a hug. Rebecca and Penelope jumped up and embraced Jessica, talking over each other, expressing their gratitude for orchestrating the explanation and a smooth separation from the Service.

Jessica was first to break the embrace and guided them to the round table, pulled a chair out for Penelope first, Rebecca next, then stuck her head into the kitchen to let Marc know they were ready, at his convenience. Marc smiled again, nodded and returned to work. Jessica grabbed another bottle of wine as she passed the rack, uncorked it while walking and with a flourish of hands and body, she refilled all three glasses, took her seat and offered a toast, "To you two, may you settle in Santa Barbara, enjoy the beach, the mountains, the ranch and most importantly, each other, and have a wonderful new adventure together. Oh, and a spare bedroom because I will be visiting a lot."

Rebecca and Penelope clinked glasses with Jessica and commented that their door would always be open for her and the "J" Team. They chatted about Santa Barbara, California and its seemingly liberal politics, marijuana and Jessica teased that within a year the two would be the Weed Queens of Santa Barbara with a huge grow-op at their ranch.

Their conversation stopped abruptly as Marc entered the dining room pushing a serving cart accented with the same wood as their table. He stopped in front of Jessica and with a flamboyant swing of his arms, took each dish, plated on a smaller version of the square diner plate, and placed it in front of each woman. Once served, he bowed graciously and returned to his kitchen.

Penelope was the first to exclaim her pleasure about the presentation saying, "This is gorgeous. I can see why the presentation of cuisine is the origin of a dining experience."

Jessica didn't reply as her face was hovering her plate, savoring the tenderloin's aroma, but Rebecca looked up from her plate and replied, "Perfect dinner setting for a beautiful occasion," then leaned into Penelope with a kiss.

As they began their meal, Marc appeared again and offered, "The tenderloin is wrapped in prosciutto with gorgonzola pomme purée, Italian blue cheese and pureed apple. The side is black kale and sautéed oyster mushroom while the drizzle is preserved plums and grainy Dijon for a pork reduction. It is a pleasure to share my expertise with such charming and beautiful ladies. I will be back shortly with dessert," then he bowed again, turned and left for his kitchen.

The trio chatted lightly during their meal, so engrossed were they in the delicate nature of the flavors they wanted to concentrate on that experience alone.

Marc's timing was so impeccable, Jessica wondered if they were on camera. They had just finished their entrée and were enjoying the last of the wine, when he appeared with the cart to clear the table. Each woman exclaimed how much she enjoyed his tenderloin, the blend of flavors and that the tenderness was mouth watering. Marc thanked his guests, returned to the kitchen with the table clearings and almost instantly came out again with dessert.

"Dessert is my personal Chocolate Mousse recipe of white and dark chocolate, pretzel crust, salted caramel and roasted peanut crumble, paired with Inniskillin Riesling ice wine from British Columbia. With the ice wine, you will taste a hint of apricot, peach and tropical fruit with a crisp acidity. You may pour it over your Mousse or I have ice wine glasses here for your pleasure. Enjoy." And he was off again.

"This is absolutely divine," exclaimed Penelope, "I wonder if we could persuade Marc to relocate in Santa Barbara?" she asked while adding the ice wine to three tall, tubular glasses.

"You know that isn't a bad idea Pen. I have an obscene amount of money saved over almost twenty years. There is enough for us to get started in Santa Barbara and finance him in his own restaurant. I mean, if President Bakus doesn't win a second term, he will be returning here and he won't have a need for an executive chef full time with just himself.

What do you think Jessica? An idea worth pursuing?"

"I don't see why not. I've never talked to him about his future. I mean, the guy is only in his early thirties and is a presidential chef! He can write his own ticket and that just may mean wanting to do his own thing."

"Well, since I am not investing in a guide outfitter business," Penelope said gracing Rebecca's shoulder, "I have money to invest too," she quipped as she raised her ice wine for a salute.

Rebecca replied, with a huge smile, "How about we get ourselves settled in Santa Barbara first and by then the election will be over and he will either have a job or not and if the latter, we can invite him to our place and pitch him our offer."

"Sounds terrific," replied Penelope, as she continued to devour the chocolate mousse, while occasionally sipping the ice wine.

Their evening wound down shortly after dessert with Rebecca and Penelope offering their appreciation to Marc and Jessica for an exceptional evening, gave each a hug, then left arm in arm for the front door, Jessica chose not to show them out, allowing them to enjoy their new relationship unhindered.

Jessica offered to help Marc with the clean-up but he wouldn't hear of it. He thanked her for the great opportunity to highlight their evening and that he would see her the next day. She accepted his offer with grace, poured the rest of the ice wine into her glass and headed off to bed, thinking she just might take Rebecca and Penelope up on their offer sooner than they think.

Acknowledgements

This work was the suggestion and encouragement of writer, educator and friend Les Wiseman, who shaped my writing style through many classes, The Province newspaper experience, successive column years and contribution to periodicals.

Thank you Les for encouraging my eclectic writing/interviewing style and comparing it to that of famed journalist Jack Webster. I appreciate the compliment.

The inspiration for Jessica Fukishura is my former student Jessica Fukushima who epitomizes the "J" Team's will, determination and superior martial arts skills.

Tracy Moore of Cityline's Fashion Friday provided many of the styles and fashion sense. Interpreting the fashions goes to Elise Laina, who shared which fashions would catch your eye and in which shoes/boots the women could fight. Elise deserves special recognition and appreciation for her incredible Italian cuisine expertise and her continuous flow of support, information, suggestions and encouragement.

My martial arts expertise must be credited to my Jen Do Tao tenth degree Black Belt instructor and the many law enforcers, both civilian and military, with whom I've trained and taught combat martial arts, a style in which I hold a 6th Degree Black Belt.

Appreciation goes to Cst. Rick Drought who portrays himself as an RCMP officer in an Alberta detachment and to retired Cst. Roy Davidson for details of the cesium theft.

Retired Assistant Police Chief Jack Ross offered his expertise on the assembly of pack trains; the choice of animals, tack and mountain terrain.

Medical expertise is heaped upon Kasteen Beltowski with her many years in emergency room trauma centers for sharing her anatomy knowledge.

The intricacies of the international railroad system couldn't have been successful without the assistance of Shawna Phillips at CP Rail. Thanks for all the guidance.

Dr. Barrie Bennett's teaching methods are highlighted in several chapters with the same success as I have experienced while implementing them in classrooms. The advantage children experience with Barry's approach takes them to new levels of learning.

Lt. Col. Dave Grossman, U.S. Army (Ret) has been a huge impact on my life, so a loud "Oorah" to Dave for his contributions and for the use of his motivational quotes.

Taser International for suspect control tactics, Jim Gregg, master shooter and his "Hole in One" concept and shooting advice and Sgt. Curtis Leithead with the British Columbia Corrections for lending his name.

The “J” Team Series would not be the same without famed Marc Stucki, who portrays himself as President Bakus’ personal chef. Marc’s flair for unique and delicious cuisine creates a personal drawing to the plot and characters.

And through the months of writing and listening to me sort plot details, my spouse Judy whose support I am forever grateful.

My sincere appreciation to all. The Series’ success is the result of your incredible contributions.

Watch for *Santa Barbara Secrets* in 2018

“Prefer knowledge to wealth, for the one is transitory, the other perpetual.”

Socrates. Greek philosopher 470 BC - 399 BC

Prologue

It was a murky, moonless night one-hundred, and fifty nautical miles off the Costa Rican coast, with waves churning to three meters, as an easterly storm gained velocity to batter the Central American coast. Fishing and tourist vessels had sought protection hours previously when the weather warning systems sounded alarms. Not all boats wanted shelter, or wished to navigate the tropical eastern Pacific before the storm hit, some were maneuvering with total disregard of the surface turmoil.

Lurking one-thousand meters below the choppy surface was a two-person, Germanischer Lloyd classification Mini Submarine, identical to those seen on various television documentaries, with fixed pontoon tanks on each side and a raised glass bubble conning tower, currently unlighted save for the few control switches and buttons providing an eerie perspective of the stealth, low-profile vessel.

The unnamed device was neither detectable from the surface by the naked eye, nor by sonar from coast guard cutters, neither of which were currently relevant since all personnel had sought storm protection along with every other ship from Mexico to Columbia, leaving visual sighting impossible and sonar inconsequential.

The use of sonar was disallowed by International Marine Law within two-hundred nautical miles from any coast line, to protect marine life; primarily dolphins and whales. With the protection of the raging surface storm and the absence of visual or sonar contact from law enforcement, the Mini maintained a steady, undetected, northerly course at thirty nautical miles an hour, with its multi-million-dollar cargo three hundred meters to the rear, propelling between Cocos Island and the mainland.

Cocos Island National Park, owned by the Eastern Tropical Pacific Marine Corridor, a marine conservation network, is known locally as Isla del Coco as well as, Isla del Tesoro or Treasure Island. It is a world-class diving destination, home to numerous endangered species such as the

Scalloped Hammerhead shark, Silky Shark and the Galapagos Shark, drawing enthusiasts to a unique marine ecosystem.

The mini-sub's captain had to ensure his course didn't vary from the coastal protection or veer into the Isla del Coco's coral reefs as he maintained a northerly route emitting a GPS signal.

Following semi-blindly behind the mini was a Columbian drug cartel's latest transportation vehicle carrying an impressive pay-load of two-hundred tonnes of cocaine. The thirty-meter/one hundred-foot submarine was the proud development of Adrian Achterberg, the son of a WW Two German Boatwright who gained fame within the Nazi regime for his U Boat designs. Adrian had learned the trade quickly under his father's tutelage, acquiring his own notoriety within the boat industry for his steel fabrication brilliance.

Never considering himself a Columbian, regardless of Medellin being his birthplace, Achterberg harbored considerable resentment against western powers for what he felt was an unfair treatment of his father, who fled Nazi Germany on the tail of the Nuremberg Trials, fearing reprisal for his role in the development of the deadly submarines which killed hundreds of allied sailors and destroyed millions in cargo and a wealth in lost vessels.

When the cartel approached Achterberg at his shipyard with the request to design and build a thirty-meter submarine capable of carrying a two-hundred tonne payload and four crew members, capable of thirty-knots submerged and an air supply for ten days, he asked few questions, taking delight in the opportunity to retaliate against the Canadians and Americans whom he blamed for his father's decades of anguish, while reaping several-millions dollars for his efforts.

His creation was pure marine brilliance and so eclectic in appearance few would have made a connection between the sub and its use in any nefarious activities. It didn't have a coning tower of a traditional submarine, nor did it have any of the outer fittings usually associated with subs. The surface was smooth, almost glass-like to the eye and touch. The exterior was coated with phononic crystal, an acoustically tuned material off which sonar waves bounce, or more accurately, bend off the hull to loop back around to the vessel's surface again and again, never returning to the source of the sonic pulse, thereby creating the impression the ping did not meet a solid object, as in contacting a submarine. The cargo space was generously spread throughout to provide adequate balance, particularly during submersion and surfacing. Propulsion was created with lithium batteries, designed by a British Columbia firm, which were less than half the size of conventional power supplies and rechargeable from a diesel engine, so quiet that it was undetectable with coast guard hydrophones. The hybrid system was designed jointly by Ontario and Nova Scotia firms designed for commercial, law-abiding vessels.

Achterberg borrowed NASA and International Space Station technology to design a system to recycle urine, crew sweat and breath to create a water source and the electrolysis of water to generate oxygen, the power for the process provided by the lithium batteries. In the case of an air supply failure the sub would rise just below the surface and extend a tubular air intake, just long enough to absorb a twelve-hour air supply. The sub lacked radar to detect patrolling ships and planes so their reconnaissance was strictly visual, necessitating as short a surface time as possible and relying completely on the mini-sub. A back-up emergency air supply with autonomous breathing devices was available for each crew member, along with a vessel escape hatch from which they could surface while scuttling the vessel and cargo in case of a total system failure.

Finding competent seamen willing to stay submerged for ten days wasn't as complicated as the cartel had anticipated. As politician Michael Myers of the Philadelphia House of Representatives was noted as saying in 1943, "Money talks and bullshit walks," and the drug kings had little difficulty finding unscrupulous retired U.S. Navy submariners willing to take the job for a few million each, half deposited in a Caribbean bank before they sailed and the other half when they deposited their cargo in California. Considering one shipment from this vessel would bring a street value of five-hundred and sixty billion, a few million-crew costs was irrelevant.

Loading and launching the Chica de oro, Golden Girl, was as unobtrusive as one could imagine amidst the turmoil surrounding the Columbia peace accord which ended one of the world's longest-running armed conflicts. The half-century war which killed two-hundred and twenty thousand people, disrupted six million lives and consumed ten billion dollars of American involvement, saw ten thousand guerrillas demobilize, come in from the jungle and transition to civilian life, created a party atmosphere throughout the country with friends and family of the freedom fighters jubilant with celebration, creating a cloak under which Achterberg supervised the loading and launching of Chica de oro.

Night and day were obscured as the mini-sub led the way north with its billion-dollar cargo trailing behind, destined to capture the souls and minds of substance abusers in North America.

Chapter ONE

Rebecca woke leisurely, without a start, without her usual trepidation, something she hadn't experience during most of her adult life. She turned her head slightly and noticed Penelope almost completely enveloped by the light cream duvet with spring birds and flowers, which thwarted the fifty-five-degree mountain night temperature which slipped quietly into their bedroom through a slightly open security window.

Rebecca inhaled deeply, propped her head up with one hand as she gazed at Pen. She was almost overcome by Penelope's scent as she sighed and gently, with a slight whisper of motion, swung her legs out of the queen size and traipsed lightly across the master bedroom's avocado Italian tile to the bathroom, oblivious to her nakedness. Gently closing the door, she used the facilities, then donned one of her full length, cobalt blue bathrobes she had acquired from Nordstrom at the Grove in Los Angeles years ago. She had purchased two, only because she loved the style and color, never thinking she would be sharing the second one with the person who had changed her life so drastically.

She shuffled over to the ten-foot fuchsia and cream patterned Italian marble counter in her matching cobalt blue fuzzy slippers and looked at herself under the bank of six bone tear-drop lights above the mirror, fluffed her short 'do, then drawing closer to the mirror, she thought, *I think I look about five years younger. No, wait, make that ten years,* she corrected herself, allowing her face to break into a huge grin. Noticing the uncontrolled expression of happiness, she laughed outload, something she had never done, ever…then did a little self-expression dance of pure joy.

She reopened the bathroom door, saw that Penelope was still asleep, gently closed the door partially, then exited the bathroom by the opposite entry and made her way to the kitchen.

Her walk down the short hallway was just a murmur as her slippers graced the oak hardwood floor into the open concept kitchen, past the Miele Stainless Steel, Double Door, Built-in Fridge, stopping in front of the double-wide country sink and white framed bay window. Stretching over the sink, she extended her upper body to see if there was any morning frost in the garden. None. *Good,* she thought, as she glanced upward toward Big Pine Mountain just as the morning sun's sliver made its way over the sixty-eight-hundred foot/two-thousand-meter peak.

Rebecca had owned the house for many years, having obtained it on the advice of Alan Auberée of Birdcage Investments, her financial advisor for the past decade. Auberée put her into Warren Bates' Berkshire Hathaway Investments immediately upon taking her as a client, investing her entire monthly salary in Hathaway. He invested six thousand dollars for six shares on the date of Berkshire's IPO, initial public offering and that amount every month since. The current value of one share was two-hundred and sixty-thousand. Auberée knew Rebecca worked for the federal government, but not that she was undercover and had zero expenses not covered by the secret service. Her portfolio grew over the years, to which she liked to refer, an obscene fortune.

When the California housing market collapsed, Auberée took a loan out on Rebecca's portfolio, which produced an interest a fraction of what she was earning on her investments. His astute planning allowed her to avoid qualifying for a mortgage, a move that would have revealed too much of her covert activities. The spectacular Mediterranean estate with a dual gated entrance and four car-garage was previously owned by a hedge fund manager who found himself heavily in debt with two mortgages on the estate when the market disaster hit. The two banks foreclosed and with zero buyer initiative it sat empty for several years. Auberée purchased the property in Rebecca's name and she signed the documents in StoneHead while working undercover against the Citizens for a Better America. Jessica, although unable to practice law in any state, having never taken a bar exam, could act as a notary and certified Rebecca's signature.

Early in her career, Rebecca knew she didn't want a White House or protection detail and acknowledged that working out of embassies would force her to leave the service out of boredom, which was why she jumped at the opportunity for permanent undercover.

It didn't take much effort on her part to become a minimalist, renting furnished apartments for several months, then leaving without a trace. But she did miss horses, the aroma of fresh droppings, the essence of their bodies as she groomed, curried and saddled for a few hour's ride into the back hills…somewhere. She couldn't return to Montana for her R

& R since every sheriff deputy within the state's boundaries, and a few outside of them, knew her on site which would invite too many questions.

It was while sequestered to the FBI in Flagstaff, Arizona, beating the desert for Al Qaeda trainers, that she stumbled on an infomercial while doing a surveillance gig at the Hacienda de Cerveza in Winslow, Arizona. Having tailed two suspects from the Hopi Reservation into Winslow, she followed them into the bar, ordered a Bud Longneck and surreptitiously watched the two males meet up with two others, who were obviously First Nations but only slightly in contrast to the Al Qaeda with their long-braided hair, sun weathered complexions, sinuous, gnarly hands and arms.

She had feigned interest in a broadcast of the Northern Arizona University Women's Lacrosse Lumberjacks and took a slight joy in watching the University of Berkeley (Jessica's alma mater) sweep the Flagstaff team embarrassingly while mentally recording the suspects behavior and body language. It was during a game commercial that she was drawn to a tourist ad for Santa Barbara with its breathtaking beaches, green mountain trails and clean air that she decided to give it a visit during her next R & R.

Her initial holiday grabbed at her heart and soul and it was shortly thereafter that she met Auberée and began a profitable relationship.

"The secret of success is learning how to use pain and pleasure instead of having pain and pleasure use you. If you do that, you're in control of your life. If you don't, life controls you."

Anthony Robbins *Awaken the Giant Within*

47162311R00195

Made in the USA
Middletown, DE
18 August 2017